© Andrew Crowley

Rachel Abbott began her career as an independent author in 2011 with *Only the Innocent*, which became a number one e-book bestseller, topping the chart for four weeks. She has now published fifteen psychological thrillers plus a novella, which together have sold over 5 million copies. She is one of the top-selling digital authors of all time in the UK (published and self-published), and her novels have been translated into 21 languages.

Praise for *And So It Begins*:

'What a storyteller Rachel Abbott is . . . I was hooked from the start'
Cara Hunter, author of *Close to Home*

'Really gripping and menacing – compulsive reading'
Harriet Tyce, author of *Blood Orange*

'I raced through this compelling, twisty novel. Loved it'
Laura Marshall, author of *Friend Request*

'A truly compelling, twisty, enthralling and satisfying read . . . Absolutely AMAZING'
Angela Marsons, author of *Evil Games*

'The Queen of psychological thrillers does not disappoint with this dark and tense tale' *Fabulous*

'Abbott's first traditionally published novel is a powerhouse combination of psychological thriller and intense courtroom drama – and the twists just don't stop coming' **Lisa Howells, author of** *Heat*

'Abbott debuts in print with an explosive thriller. It's a minefield of surprises . . . It twists and turns like a snake in an oil slick' *Peterborough Telegraph*

'*And So It Begins* is a dark, extremely readable, well-plotted psychological thriller culminating in a courtroom drama . . . It's obvious why Abbott has attracted her huge audience' *The Times*

'If you're a fan of *Gone Girl* and *The Girl on the Train*, Rachel Abbott's *And So It Begins* won't disappoint . . . Abbott leaves you guessing until the final few pages' *Herald*

'It's easy to see from this gripping story's frequent twists and bluffs, in a narrative that's rooted in psychology, how word-of-mouth recommendation from one reader to another allowed Abbott to stand out in a crowded market' *Morning Star*

Praise for *The Murder Game*:

'A brilliant read, full of suspense' *Closer*

'Abbott is a gifted storyteller and this book is a total delight' *Daily Mail*

'A twisty-turny plot that had my head reeling, and my mind full of intrigue. Superb plotting from the mistress of suspense'
Mel Sherratt, bestselling author of *Hush Hush*

'A grand re-imagining of the best kind of crime caper, filled with underlying tensions, fancy rooms and a detective hungry for answers'
Magic Radio: April Book Club Pick

'Fantastic and gripping – I loved the intriguing concept and the brilliantly atmospheric Cornish setting'
Karen Hamilton, bestselling author of *The Perfect Girlfriend*

'This gallops along at a cracking pace, and manages to keep the twists and surprises coming thick and fast'   *Crime Monthly*

'*The Murder Game* plunges you slap-bang in the middle of a very dangerous game, and Abbott adds to a list of tales to take your breath away'   *Sun*

Praise for *Don't Look Away:*

'As ever I was entranced with the perfectly formed characters, grippingly tense storyline. OUTSTANDING'
Angela Marsons, bestselling author of the DI Kim Stone series

'The master of suspense, Abbott has weaved a twisted and engaging plot which will keep you guessing until the very end'
Caroline Mitchell, bestselling author of *The Village*

'A gripping read with intriguing characters. A real masterclass in simmering tension that builds until the shocking end. I loved it!'
K. L. Slater, bestselling author of *The Girlfriend*

'Packed with suspense, *Don't Look Away* is a dark and compelling read. Powerful storytelling by the talented Rachel Abbott, making it one of my top reads of 2023. The tension kept me gripped until the final page'
D. S. Butler, bestselling author of the Detective Karen Hart series

'A masterclass in writing the gripping psychological thriller. There's just no let up in the tension, the twists, the turns, the brilliance of the plot, as Nancy searches for her sister'
Caro Ramsay, author of the Anderson and Costello series

'*Don't Look Away* is a brilliant, compulsive story, full of believable characters. Rachel Abbott has proved again that she's one of the brightest stars in the crime writing firmament. Be warned, the end of this book will take your breath away!'
Kate Rhodes, author of the Isles of Scilly mysteries

'A wonderful blend of a well-created Cornish backdrop, with highly relatable characters and a terrific twisty plot, as well as a very clever conclusion' *Daily Mail*

'"Queen of the page turner" Rachel Abbott doesn't disappoint with her latest thriller' *Hello!*

'Pulse-pounding' *Crime Monthly*

'Rachel Abbott moves the story along at a cracking pace and keeps the twists and turns coming' *WI Life*

Also by Rachel Abbott

DI Tom Douglas Series
Only the Innocent
The Back Road
Sleep Tight
Stranger Child
Kill Me Again
The Sixth Window
Come a Little Closer
The Shape of Lies
Right Behind You
Close Your Eyes
No More Lies

Sergeant Stephanie King Series
And So It Begins
The Murder Game
Don't Look Away

Novellas
Nowhere Child

THE LAST TIME
I SAW HIM

Rachel Abbott

WILDFIRE

The right of Rachel Abbott to be identified as the Author of
the Work has been asserted by her in accordance with the
Copyright, Designs and Patents Act 1988.

First published in paperback in 2024 by
WILDFIRE
an imprint of HEADLINE PUBLISHING GROUP

1

Cataloguing in Publication Data is available from the British Library

ISBN 978 1 0354 0341 7

Typeset in Dante MT by CC Book Production

Printed and bound in Great Britain by Clays Ltd, Elcograf S.p.A.

Headline's policy is to use papers that are natural, renewable and recyclable products
and made from wood grown in well-managed forests and other controlled sources.
The logging and manufacturing processes are expected to conform to
the environmental regulations of the country of origin.

HEADLINE PUBLISHING GROUP
an Hachette UK Company
Carmelite House
50 Victoria Embankment
London
EC4Y 0DZ

www.headline.co.uk
www.hachette.co.uk

Saturday

1

Tonight, the clocks go back. Not far enough, sadly. For a moment I fantasise that I might wake up tomorrow to find time has rewound not just by a single hour, but by four thousand, three hundred and eighty hours. Six whole months.

Perhaps then I would be able to breathe.

My fantasy is interrupted by the sound of splashing water. Russell is taking a shower, but he isn't whistling. He always whistles as he soaps his body, and much as the relentless chirpiness of the sound has been known to irritate me, right now I would give anything to hear it again. But why would he whistle? He's as miserable as I am. The only difference is that he doesn't know why. I hope he never has to.

An ice bucket sits on the table, glistening with a cold, metallic sheen, beads of condensation forming on its surface, converging into tiny droplets that trickle down its sides like tears. I stare at myself in the mirror and try out a smile. It's not convincing.

The weight of my mistakes sits heavily on my shoulders. Sometimes it's an effort to move, to perform the simplest of tasks. The desire to unburden myself is overpowering, but while I might feel some relief, it would only pass the load to my husband – a good man who doesn't deserve what I've done to him. What I'm still doing to him. He knows there is a barrier between us, one he has no idea how to break down, and I'm certain he's hoping that a week away in this lovely hotel is going to solve our problems.

It won't, but the least I can do is make an effort and allow him to believe that everything is okay.

As the bathroom door opens I blink away the tears which, despite my best efforts, are pooling in my eyes, and pick up a blusher brush to make some pretence at getting ready for dinner.

'Champagne, darling?' Russell says, advancing towards me with a towel wrapped around his waist.

Watching him in the mirror, I can see two lines of confusion between his brows. I've been out of the shower for half an hour, but I'm still in a bathrobe, sitting at the dressing table, nowhere near ready. He checks his watch and the frown deepens. He hates to be late, although our table at the hotel's restaurant is reserved for the whole evening and I don't think ten minutes either way will make any difference.

He resists the urge to ask why I'm taking so long to get dressed and lifts the champagne from the bucket. As he pops the cork it flies into the air and the wine cascades down the sides of the bottle.

'Oops,' he says with a failed attempt at a chuckle. 'I've never perfected the knack, have I? Never mind – it feels more of a celebration.' He looks into my eyes in the mirror. 'And it *is* a celebration, Juliette. I know you've found the last few months difficult, but we're okay, you and me. We're a good team.'

He hands me a glass with one hand, gently stroking my hair with the other. With a breath, I turn from the mirror towards him.

'We are,' I tell him, raising my glass to his. 'And I love you.'

That's true, and never more so than now. I love his

predictability, his desire to make me happy, his perpetual good humour. But there's a void between us. Where we used to knit together, there is now emptiness, and I don't know how to fix it. Anything I do, anything I try, will inevitably make matters so much worse.

Russell casts another surreptitious glance at his watch.

'Why don't you get dressed, Russ, and go and have a drink in the bar while I finish getting ready? Ask them to let the restaurant know that your wife is being slow to get her act together.'

He nods, looking relieved, and finds a teaspoon from the tea tray to pop upside down in the neck of the champagne bottle. 'This will keep it fizzy. We can finish it later.'

With that, he heads to the wardrobe. He will already know what he's going to wear. He may have even hung his clothes in order of days and evenings. He is methodical, organised and believes I can do no wrong.

Sadly, he's mistaken.

2

'Stephanie, are you listening to me?'

Noticing a hint of exasperation in her mum's voice, Stephanie drew her gaze away from the activity in the bar.

'Sorry, Mum,' she said with an apologetic grin. 'You know I'm hopeless. I can't help people-watching. It's my job, after all.'

Amanda King gave a theatrical sigh. 'Yes, darling, but I asked you to come away for the weekend with me because I never get to spend time with you. Maybe you should sit with your back to the room so you won't be distracted.'

With a pang of guilt, Stephanie reached out to touch her mum's hand.

'I'm all yours, and I want to apologise for not being around much lately. What with the house, trips to Norfolk and work, I never seem to have time to breathe.'

Stephanie was thrilled that she and Gus had finally bought a house together. It was a few miles further away from her work, but it reduced Gus's commute to a manageable forty minutes. There were still times when Gus had to travel further afield, though, and on the nights he couldn't get home she felt his absence like a silent echo in every room.

Although the stone farmhouse they had fallen in love with was in need of some renovation, it felt like a perfect family home. Any time they could spare was spent stripping old wall-paper and painstakingly removing black gloss paint from the original oak beams. And of course, whenever they could get more than two days off at the same time, they headed to Norfolk to visit Gus's daughter, Daisy.

'How are things going with the little girl?' Amanda asked.

'Pretty well. At least, I *think* so. She's adorable, Mum, and we're going to decorate a bedroom for her so it's ready if ever the time is right for her to come and stay with us. We're desperate for her to feel that we're her family too. Her mum, Paula, has been great, but it's been a bit harder for her husband.'

'I can only imagine,' Amanda said.

The two women were silent for a moment, thinking of all that had happened in the last few months. Gus had only discovered he had a daughter – the result of a one-night stand when he and Stephanie weren't together – when the child became seriously ill and needed Gus's help in the form of a stem cell transplant. But it had been hard on Philip, the man who had been Daisy's dad since birth. He had always known there was a possibility that Daisy might not be his, but had never expected Gus to become part of the little girl's life.

'So what's the plan? Is Daisy going to continue to think you two are just friends of her mum and dad?'

'We don't know. We're playing it by ear. She's still quite weak after the treatment, and she's not quite three years old, so how can she understand who we are?'

Amanda shook her head. 'I don't know. The only thing I would say is that if it's kept a secret it will get harder and harder to tell her the truth. She won't understand it now, but if she's told Gus is her father and Philip is her dad she'll get used to the idea and she'll ask questions when she's ready.'

'I know, Mum. That's what I think too, but I'm the least important person in all of this.'

Amanda's eyebrows shot up. 'No, you're not! Don't even think like that. You might have the least emotional investment right now – although that will change over time – but you have the opportunity to be the voice of reason. So use it.'

Stephanie chuckled. 'We both know that keeping thoughts to myself isn't a speciality of mine.'

Glancing over her mum's shoulder towards the bar, Stephanie noticed a bald man with an open, friendly face who she'd spotted earlier, sitting alone, anxiously watching the door, checking his watch every couple of minutes. Suddenly he sat up straight, and Stephanie followed his gaze. Another man had arrived, pausing at the top of the short flight of steps that led down into the bar, glancing around the room like a celebrity making an entrance. There was something of a swagger to his walk as he headed to the bar, and the first man stared, hovering at the edge of his seat, as if not quite sure what to do. He clearly recognised the newcomer, and after a few hesitant moments and another glance at his watch he jumped to his feet and sidled over to the bar to stand next to the man, trying – and failing – to look nonchalant.

What was that about?

With a sense of suppressed eagerness, the first man thrust out his hand in greeting to the other, who looked rather taken aback, as if he had no idea why this person was speaking to him. Somehow his surprise looked fake to Stephanie. She watched as the two men shook hands, the first seemingly overjoyed at the encounter, the second wearing a rather condescending smile.

'Stephanie!' Amanda hissed. 'You're doing it again.'

'I know, but there are two men behaving a bit oddly.'

'And is that any of your business?'

'No, it isn't. You're quite right. Especially as there's so much else to look at in this place. It's hard to take it all in.'

Her eyes roamed the room, admiring the décor of the newly refurbished hotel, an old manor house by the coast. The walls of the bar and restaurant were painted a muted dark blue and adorned with vivid modern art, the chairs covered in crimson velvet. Stephanie would never have thought it could work as a scheme, but it did.

'It's a fabulous place, Mum. Thanks for bringing me here.'

According to the brochure, the hotel had just ten rooms in the main building with six deluxe suites, converted from outbuildings, bordering a cobbled courtyard in the grounds. Amanda had booked a refurbished stable with two bedrooms and a sitting room, saying she was paying for it with a recent Premium Bonds win.

'I know people don't seem to go for them so much these days,' she'd said when she told Stephanie about her good fortune, 'but I've had mine for years. When I was married to your dad I used to save any money left over at the end of the month and buy more. I never told him. He'd have found something or someone else to spend it on.'

Amanda was unable to hide the sour tone in her voice. She had never quite recovered from her husband leaving her for her best friend, and after nearly twenty years her lips still tightened when she spoke his name. Stephanie had resented her father for a long time and blamed him for her distrust of men, but she wasn't prepared to let her mum dive down that particular rabbit hole tonight.

'Shall we have a look at the menu? What do you fancy?'

'Everything,' she answered, scrutinising the short list of delicious-sounding options.

While Amanda was making her choices, Stephanie surreptitiously scoured the rest of the room. The restaurant tables were placed around the outer edge on a raised level, four steps up from the bar area, offering a perfect view of the whole room. The two men she had noticed earlier were still down in the bar, but had moved to stand by a magnificent old olive tree in the centre of the space, its gnarled branches reaching up towards a giant skylight.

As she watched, both men turned towards the door. A slim woman with long blonde hair was poised in the doorway, scanning the room in search of someone. She looked the picture of understated elegance and confidence in tapered cream trousers and a loose-fitting apricot linen shirt over a silk camisole.

Her face, however, told a different story.

3

After Russell left to head to the bar, it took me forever to get dressed. The last thing I wanted was to go to a busy restaurant, smile, make conversation and force myself to eat. I have an uncomfortable feeling that as soon as I step into the room all eyes will be on me, seeing right through me to the secrets hiding just below the surface of my skin.

Our suite in the old tack room is a haven, and I'd far rather have curled up on the comfy sofa watching mindless television programmes than go to the restaurant, but I have to think of Russell. He has such an open face, one that can't hide his thoughts. He no longer has any hair on top, and his wide deep brow makes him appear vulnerable. I'm desperate to see him light up with laughter again, as he always used to.

I was relieved when he suggested getting away for a week. I thought I could leave my worries behind in Bristol, but they've followed me every step of the way, and being with him for twenty-four hours a day makes it so much harder to keep a smile on my face. At least he will be working for part of the time and I can escape to walk the cliffs alone.

As a lawyer at a talent agency, Russell has been asked by the director to negotiate a contract with a singer who lives in the local village. She performs here in the hotel a couple of times a week, so we had a perfect excuse for the trip.

'Raoul discovered her,' Russell told me. 'Someone had posted a video on Instagram of her singing here, so he decided to check her out. He says she's a perfect addition to our list.'

Apparently she's singing tonight, and I know my husband wants to finish eating before she begins her performance. He'll want to concentrate one hundred per cent on her, so I've finally managed to pull myself together, put on a minimal amount of make-up and get dressed. It's the least I can do for him. With a last look in the mirror and a shake of my arms to try to ease the tension in my shoulders, I'm as ready as I'll ever be.

The walk from our suite to the restaurant is short but quite lovely. The old stone outbuildings sit either side of a cobbled yard lit by soft lanterns which light the way without intruding on the atmosphere. The night is still, the sky clear, and there's an autumnal chill in the air. It's so quiet I can just make out the sound of the waves gently lapping the beach.

As I step into the hotel, I hear a buzz of conversation and take a deep breath as I head towards its source. Pausing at the top of the four wide steps at the entrance to the bar area, I look down, scanning the room for Russell.

The bar is busy, the hotel full despite it being the end of October. A few people are already seated at dining tables, and I expect Russell to be waiting there, ready to order. But there's no sign of him. I cast my eyes around, trying to spot him among those by the bar.

Then I see him in the centre of the room, chatting to someone standing on the other side of the fat trunk of an old olive tree. Russell raises his hand, smiling, happy to see I have finally arrived. He says something to whoever he is talking to, and a man steps out from behind the tree and looks towards me with a smile.

I freeze. Every centimetre of my body prickles as if a thousand tiny fingers are tickling the surface of my skin.

This can't be happening.

4

'Do you know what tuna tataki is?' Amanda asked.

'Pardon?'

Stephanie was only half listening. The woman who had stood frozen to the spot in the doorway seemed to have composed herself and was walking towards the two men. The bald man – the one who had been glancing between his watch and the door – smiled a welcome with what appeared to be a tinge of relief in his expression. The other, the one with the swagger, was a tall man with wide shoulders and a full head of grey hair that flopped either side of his sharp-featured face. Despite its apparent casual styling, Stephanie had the sense that every strand of hair was meticulously placed.

'Have you actually looked at the menu yet, Stephanie?'

She dragged her attention back to her mum. 'Yes, and I'm definitely going for the tuna. It's Japanese and delicious. I'll have fillet steak and spinach salad for my main. How about you?'

'No idea. Still enjoying studying the options.'

Stephanie had barely glanced at the menu but was quite happy with her choices. She was far more interested in what was going on in the room.

She watched as Bald Smiley Man introduced the woman to Floppy Hair, who held out his hand to shake hers. Even from where she was sitting, Stephanie could read the tension in her shoulders. The woman didn't need an introduction. Clearly, this man was no stranger to her.

The husband – if that's who Bald Smiley Man was – was animated, chattering away as if this was a particularly thrilling moment. He had totally missed the woman's unease. Floppy Hair was playing along, but there was no doubt that he was enjoying her discomfort.

'Okay. I've decided.' Amanda closed the menu and put it down on the table. 'While we wait, tell me about the changes you're planning for the house.'

Despite being fascinated by the behaviour of the three people in the bar, Stephanie owed it to her mum to be good company.

'It's just what we need, Mum, but the previous owners lived there for over forty years, and there's no sign they'd decorated at all in that time.' Stephanie pulled her phone from her bag to show Amanda some photos of the interior. 'As soon as it's habitable, you'll have to come and stay. At the moment we're managing in one room with a microwave and a camping-gas stove for cooking. Gus is speaking to some builders while I'm away – there's only so much we can do ourselves.'

A quick expression of concern flashed across Amanda's face.

'What's up?' Stephanie asked.

'I've just realised I've left my phone in the room.' She started to push her seat back. 'I'll go and get it.'

'What do you need it for? I've got my phone.'

'No, I need mine. Sorry, Steph. I'll just be a moment.'

'Mum, sit down. If you need it, I'll get it. But what's so urgent?'

Amanda's lips twisted to one side as if she was reluctant to explain. Then she shrugged. 'It's Luke. He might call, and he'll

15

be upset if I don't answer. I'm a bit worried about him being on his own.'

Stephanie's brother, Luke, had suffered from depression for years and still lived at home with his mum, a situation which didn't seem to benefit either of them. Stephanie had huge sympathy but was incapable of coming up with a solution that would give them both what they needed. She worried about Amanda, who had had a busy social life until her husband left. It had taken years for her to get some confidence back, and now she hid behind her commitment to Luke.

'I can text him, Mum, let him know he can call my phone if he needs to speak to you.'

Amanda shook her head. 'I think he'd be uncomfortable. I'll just go and get mine.'

Stephanie held up her hand. 'No, I'll go. You stay here. Study the menu.'

Pushing back her chair, she picked up the keys from the table. 'I'll be back in a moment.'

As Stephanie headed towards the door she noticed Bald Smiley Man was back at the bar, ordering a round of drinks. She glanced over to where the woman stood, ramrod straight. Floppy Hair was standing close to her, talking quietly. The woman wasn't looking at him, but Stephanie saw her flinch. He was touching her, running a finger down her spine.

The woman closed her eyes as if she wanted to scream.

5

Celia Cobain looked at her watch for the third time in five minutes. She wasn't sure what to do for the best. Ellis had refused to wait for her while she called home to say good-night to the children, saying that as usual she was making an unnecessary fuss. The kids were perfectly happy with Jeanette, their nanny, and Celia would irritate them as much as she was irritating him.

He didn't understand that she *wanted* to speak to them. She hadn't wanted to come away – it was half term, and she'd thought of all kinds of activities they could share. But it was never a good idea to go against Ellis's wishes so, as always, she had said nothing.

She'd dithered about whether to stay in the room and call them, or go to the restaurant with Ellis.

'For Christ's sake, woman, why do you have to make life so difficult? I'm going to the bar and you can come or not. I really don't care. But if you do come, don't make a show of yourself, and keep your mouth shut. No one wants to listen to your inane chatter. And try to look the part.'

Celia's chest had tightened, a bead of sweat forming on her top lip as he stalked out, slamming the door.

She'd taken several deep breaths and decided it would be

better if she stayed where she was, spoke to the children and ordered room service. That way, there was no chance of her embarrassing him in public. She would feign sleep when Ellis returned and hope he didn't wake her to berate her for her behaviour. She had no idea what particular form of punishment he would mete out, if he was angry enough. She sometimes wished he would hit her, because it would be over quickly. But Ellis preferred more subtle forms of torture.

Putting to the back of her mind thoughts of what might, or might not, happen later, Celia picked up the phone.

It was a relief to be able to speak to the children, to listen without interruption as each child shared the highs and lows of their day, but by the time she'd finished the call Ellis had been gone an hour and she worried whether she had made the right decision. He was bound to be angry, and maybe he was right. She needed to make more of an effort. She no longer knew what the right thing to do was.

Their suite – a double-height barn at the far end of the court-yard – felt eerie and echoey with just her there. Perhaps she should join him. Ellis wouldn't have eaten yet. He had it in his head that someone of his standing should eat supper, as he had recently started to call it, no earlier than 9 p.m. Anything before that was too suburban. She strongly suspected that the hotel wouldn't view its sophisticated restaurant as serving supper, given the term's connotations of informality, but she never contradicted her husband.

She didn't like eating late – particularly in a restaurant – and was uncomfortable waiting until the last possible minute to order food. It felt inconsiderate, knowing that restaurant staff worked long hours and the kitchen might be staying open just for them. But there was no point trying to make Ellis see her point of view. He'd just say they're staff. It's what they're paid for.

Celia pushed her hand into the pocket of her cardigan, an item of clothing that Ellis hated but the first thing she put on when he wasn't around. It was warm and cosy, and she could wrap it tightly round her, like a cocoon. And she could hide her amethyst spirit quartz crystal – said to dissolve self-imposed limitations and boost confidence – in its pocket. She didn't know if it worked or not, but she grasped it tightly, more in hope than in expectation.

She looked at her watch again. Would Ellis be angry if she didn't turn up? Or would he be more angry if she did?

With a deep breath and another stroke of the crystal she pushed herself to her feet, slid off the cardigan and hid it in the bottom of the wardrobe. She looked at the array of satin shirts which, according to Ellis, 'looked the part', whatever that meant. Each one was a variation of the shade 'dull' so it didn't much matter which she chose, and she randomly pulled one from its hanger.

'Oh good,' she sighed. 'Sludge green.'

Before she could stop to think, she quickly got dressed, picked up the old-fashioned heavy metal room key from the coffee table and made her way out into the night.

As Stephanie walked towards the suite she was sharing with her mum, she pondered what she had just seen in the bar. The woman with the long blonde hair and the man standing next to her had pretended they didn't know each other when they were introduced, and it seemed the husband – if that's who the bald man was – hadn't noticed anything. But even if they *had* only just met, it was difficult to see why the unwanted attention and the very intimate way Floppy Hair ran his finger down her back hadn't resulted in at the very least some words of polite discouragement, if not a full-on bash on the nose.

Smiling to herself as she thought what Gus would say about her unrelenting nosiness and constant desire to read people, Stephanie decided to give him a quick call.

'Hey, Steph, I wasn't expecting to hear from you yet,' Gus said.

'I know. I've just popped out of the restaurant to get Mum's phone, so I thought I'd take the opportunity.'

'Glad you did. I've just got home, and I have to tell you, Stephie, the house feels very empty without you.'

Stephanie laughed. 'The house feels empty because it *is* empty! No carpets, curtains and not even much furniture.'

'You are *such* a romantic.'

She didn't bother admitting to Gus that she felt the same when he wasn't there.

'Are you having a good time?' he asked.

'We are, yes. I've neglected Mum a bit recently and I'm glad we came. I'll tell you all about the places we've visited later – especially the sculpture gardens. Given me loads of ideas.'

Gus chuckled. 'I think it will be a while before we can get creative with any landscaping.'

'I know. Listen, I only wanted to say hello, and to warn you it might be late when I call. There's a jazz singer performing, and she's supposed to be good.'

'Doesn't matter. Call any time.'

Stephanie said goodbye and ended the call just as she arrived outside their room. She was about to open the old stable door when a woman stepped into the courtyard ahead of her. She must have come from the end property – a barn with a full-height glass wall at one end and views across a strip of field to the shore below. It looked stunning, and Stephanie could imagine waking up to gaze out at the sea, whatever its mood.

The woman was walking towards her, head down, her dark shoulder-length hair hiding her face. But when she heard Stephanie's metal key rattle in its lock, she looked up with a start.

Stephanie smiled at her. 'Good evening.'

The woman seemed slightly shocked that someone had spoken to her and stopped for a moment before hurrying forward.

'Excuse me. I'm sorry, but have you just come from the restaurant?' she asked, her voice slightly breathless as if she had jogged from the end of the yard rather than walked a few metres.

Stephanie had no idea what she was sorry about, but smiled again. 'Yes. It's lovely, and there are some tantalising smells coming from the kitchen.'

'Has everyone started eating?' The woman bit her bottom lip.

'No, not yet. My mum's ordering for us now, so I'm sure you're not too late, if that's what's worrying you.'

'No, but are there still some people who aren't at their tables yet? Or people sitting on their own?'

The woman was clearly troubled about something. 'Are you looking for someone in particular? Do you want me to go and find someone for you? I need to get something from my room, but I'll only be a moment.'

'No, no. I don't want to be any trouble. I think my husband's there, but if he's already started eating he won't be happy if I turn up in the middle of his meal.' She glanced at her watch. 'You know, it will just cause confusion for everyone.'

Stephanie felt an unfamiliar urge to put her arm round the

woman. She was clearly anxious, and judging by her pinched brow, this was an almost permanent state.

'Okay, why don't you wait while I pop in, then we'll go together. If you're looking for your husband, I'll help you find him. I'm sure he'll be delighted to see you.' The woman frowned slightly, and Stephanie touched her arm. 'I'll just be a sec.'

She made her way into the suite and less than a minute later she had the phone and was at the door.

The courtyard was empty. She glanced to her left to see a figure disappearing back towards the entrance to the barn. The woman had gone.

6

Nadia Shariq closed the door of the storeroom she'd been allocated as her dressing room and looked around. Along one side stainless-steel shelving units were groaning under the weight of all forms of crockery, from huge platters to the smallest side plate. The back wall was furnished with more shelves, this time piled high with tablecloths and napkins, and Nadia remembered Oscar, the restaurant manager, saying this was the storeroom for weddings and events. Along the top were centrepiece vases and candelabra.

When the hotel wasn't full she was given one of the bedrooms to change in, but tonight every room was occupied. Great news for the hotel, but Nadia would have preferred to have a full-length mirror to check her appearance and a bit of space to move around. She liked to pace backwards and forwards before singing, taking deep breaths to relax her shoulders, not to mention running through her warm-up exercises: yawning and sighing, humming, lip buzzing and vocal slides. If she tried that here, she would be heard in the kitchen and maybe even in the restaurant.

To be fair, Oscar had done his best to make the room welcoming, pushing a small table and chair against one rack with a mirror resting on a shelf, and he'd brought in a hairdryer, should she need it. She didn't. She just needed to get changed.

Nadia pulled off the clothes she'd arrived in and slipped into black silk trousers and a camisole top. Her thick ebony hair fell below her shoulders in a slightly untamed way, just as she liked it. She took a wide-toothed comb and ran it through from root to tip just once, then shook her head to restore its bounce, ruffling it lightly with her fingers. She didn't wear heavy make-up. Her dark eyes, strong brows and clear olive skin needed little help, but when she was performing she emphasised her eyes with plum eyeshadow and a darker shade of eyeliner, and applied a lip ink that gave her matte colour without the sticky lipstick feeling she hated.

There was a knock on the door.

'You decent, Nadia?' Oscar called softly.

'Yes, you can come in.'

He popped his head round the door. 'There's a full restaurant tonight, but they've mainly finished eating. Just a couple of stragglers, so not much cutlery noise for you to compete with. You okay to go on in ten minutes?'

'Yeah, that's fine. With any luck, they'll like what they hear and not talk all the way through. If they do, I'll shoot daggers at the buggers.'

Oscar chuckled, mistakenly thinking she was joking. 'The first set's always the most difficult, but the great thing is they love listening to you, so they hang around in the bar for your second set. Just what we want.'

Rubbing his hands together, he gave her a beaming smile. He had told Nadia that he often wanted to leap on the bar and tell everyone to be quiet while she sang, but people usually fell silent once she had started, and the staff moved softly round the room, taking plates, filling wine glasses, with the minimum of fuss. It was rare that anyone was rude enough to talk loudly during her performance, although she had once – in her days of singing in Bristol – burst into the opening lines of 'Shut Up' by the Black Eyed Peas. She smiled at the memory.

Oscar turned to where she had hung the last item of her outfit and raised both hands to his mouth. 'Oh my word! Nadia, is that what you're wearing?'

Nadia looked at the long pleated-silk kimono that she would slip on at the last minute, leaving it open to hang loose and flow behind her as she moved towards the piano. First impressions were everything.

'It's so vibrant!' said Oscar, himself a lover of the flamboyant, as he walked across the room to peer more closely. He held out his hand, just an inch from the fabric, and looked over his shoulder. 'I won't touch – promise.'

Nadia knew the jacket was an extravagance she could ill afford. But when she had seen it and read the description of the colours – black tulip and purple chrysanthemum – she had to have it. It was her, or at least the person she fully intended to become.

'You're not trying to dazzle someone special, are you?' Oscar said, wiggling his eyebrows suggestively.

'Just trying to look the part,' she responded, not quite ready to share the fact that she was hoping there would be someone in the audience she needed to impress.

'Well, you'll certainly do that! Anyway, it's nearly time. Do you still get nervous?'

Nadia shrugged. 'I need an edge of adrenaline to give my best performance. The minute I get bored, that's when I'll know it's time to give up.'

This wasn't entirely true, but she wasn't about to admit to the jitters in her stomach, even to Oscar.

'I'll leave you to psych yourself up. When you're ready, you know what to do.'

With a last encouraging smile and a lingering look at her kimono, he left the room and shut the door.

Nadia closed her eyes and focused on slow, deep breaths. She was hoping, praying, that tonight was the night. She had waited a long time, but this might finally be her chance. It had to be.

She tensed and relaxed each of the muscle groups in her body, releasing any remaining tension, then pulled the silk jacket from its hanger and slipped it on.

'I deserve this,' she said quietly.

7

'You're quiet, Juliette,' Russell says softly as Ellis turns away from the table to order an extravagant bottle of Côte-Rôtie from the wine waiter. 'You didn't mind me asking Ellis to join us for dinner, did you, darling? With his wife not feeling too well, it seemed a shame to leave him to sit on his own, and I've been wanting to meet him for a while. What a coincidence that he's here!'

Coincidence indeed.

I try to give Russell a reassuring smile. 'I was hoping for some time alone, that's all.'

I feel a stab of guilt at Russell's remorseful expression. He thinks he's done something wrong when his only intention was to be kind.

'It's fine,' I say, touching his hand where it rests on the table.

Ellis turns back. 'I think you'll both enjoy my wine selection.' He raises his eyebrows, as if to say *See how generous and clever I am*. At least, that's how it looks to me, and it's all I can do not to glare at him. 'An excellent vineyard – one of my favourites.'

'It's very kind of you,' my husband says, although I can see he's a little uncomfortable at the eye-watering cost.

'It's hard to believe we've never met before, Russell. I've heard of you, of course, through my philanthropic work in

27

the performing arts, and you have some first-rate singers and musicians on your list. Bumping into you here is something of a bonus.'

'It's an honour to meet someone who gives as much to support the Bristol music scene as you do.'

I want to cringe as Russell speaks. I know it's from the heart, but Ellis Cobain doesn't deserve the compliment.

'I don't get to events too often,' Russell continues. 'I tend to keep to the office, really. It's not my job to identify new talent, only to negotiate their contracts.'

Ellis turns to me, as I knew he would. 'And you, Juliette? So good to meet you too. What do you do?'

I try hard not to scowl. 'I'm an interior designer.'

Russell gives me an encouraging nod, expecting me to expand, but I'm struggling to speak. My tongue seems to have swollen in my mouth as if I'm about to be sick.

'Do you do private houses or offices? Maybe restaurants?'

'Both.'

As you very well know.

Russell can't understand why I am being so monosyllabic, but Ellis knows and he's enjoying himself.

'Anyone famous?'

'Nope. No one very interesting at all, to be honest.'

I can't look at Russell, but I can imagine the look of shock on his face. He shuffles in his seat, clearly trying to think of something to say that will take the charge out of the atmosphere.

'Actually, Ellis, the reason we're here tonight is that I have to meet the young woman who's performing later.' He looks at his watch. 'Soon, I think. We're eating a bit later than I'd intended, but I can give her my full attention during her second set.'

The reason we're eating late is, of course, because Ellis made some comment about how provincial the British had become, eating supper so early. I had felt an overpowering urge to throw my drink in his face and resisted only for Russell's sake. Now, because of Ellis's ill-mannered intervention, Russell will have to try to focus on the singer while simultaneously eating his dinner. For a man who lives by routine, it's a hell of a concession. And Ellis has chosen the seat facing the piano, so Russell will have to turn his chair to watch. I'm sure he's done that on purpose so my husband will have his back to me.

Just as our starters arrive, a door opens and a young woman heads towards the piano. Russell twists round to look to where she is taking her seat, and I glance at Ellis, expecting him to be watching her too. But he isn't looking her way; he's looking at me. And with Russell turned away he reaches out with his left hand and strokes the side of my right breast with the back of his fingers.

Under cover of a light smattering of applause from the diners and those in the bar, I scrunch up my napkin, throw it on the table and push my chair back.

'Fuck you,' I whisper to Ellis.

Russell can't have heard what I said, but he turns back to the table as I stand up.

'You okay, darling?' he asks, concern etched into his features.

I shake my head. 'You stay here and listen, Russ. I'm fine. Something's made me feel a bit queasy. I'll be back.'

As I walk towards the door the woman starts to sing, her voice rich and velvety with a husky, soulful tone. She's starting with a slow, jazz version of 'I'm Not In Love', and my eyes flood with hot tears as I push my way through the people standing in the bar.

8

Stephanie and Amanda had just been served their desserts when a hush fell over the room as a woman in a dramatic flowing kimono strode into the restaurant and took her seat at the piano.

'Mum, you need to squidge your chair round,' Stephanie said. 'The singer's starting, and the restaurant manager told me earlier that she has a wonderful voice.'

'Maybe she's his girlfriend,' Amanda said, somewhat cynically.

Stephanie grinned. 'I don't think so. I would hazard a guess that she's not his type.'

With the help of a passing waiter, they rearranged their chairs as the first notes sounded on the piano.

'That jacket is stunning,' Amanda whispered. 'Those colours just shimmer in this light.'

She was right, but nothing was quite as mesmerising as the woman's voice. She started with an old song, but Stephanie had never heard it sung like this before, as if the singer was feeling every word. The room fell silent. Even those still eating paused, caught in the spell of her performance.

As she listened, Stephanie thought back to her encounter with the woman in the courtyard. Looking around the room, there was no sign of her. It was a shame she was missing this. She had seemed so unsure whether she should join her husband for dinner, and it was sad to think someone could be so conflicted about what should be such an easy decision.

Wondering who the husband might be, Stephanie scanned the bar area and couldn't see any men on their own. No one appeared to be watching the door as if waiting for someone. There were a couple of restaurant tables with an unbalanced number of men and women, and she immediately spotted the two men she'd noticed earlier – Bald Man and Floppy Hair. They were seated at a restaurant table together, although the woman she had presumed to be Bald Man's wife had gone. Neither man was watching the door, both had their gaze firmly fixed on the performer.

Stephanie's ruminations were interrupted as the song came to an end. There was a moment of silence, then the diners began to clap or bang lightly on their tables.

'She's amazing,' Amanda said. 'What a voice.'

'I know. I love jazz-style versions of old songs. I think I must be getting past it, Mum, because that 10cc song from the 70s sounded better to me than any current music. Definitely getting old!' She pulled a rueful face and Amanda laughed.

They were quiet for the rest of the set, soaking up the atmosphere the singer was creating. Stephanie wished Gus was here with them. He would love this. Perhaps, with luck, they could manage a night here some time, even if not a whole weekend. Money was tight with the renovations and the trips to Norfolk, but she would find a way.

Finally, the singer stood and turned towards the audience, many of whom were on their feet. She took a slight bow and scanned the room as if looking for someone.

Her face changed. Her lips parted and her eyes widened. Most in the audience would no doubt think it was a reaction to the applause, but Stephanie knew better. The woman was beyond surprised. Her sudden triumphant smile suggested she was elated.

Nadia could feel her heart pumping as she made her way back to the storeroom.

He's here!

She had to keep calm. She couldn't let her eagerness show, but she was so glad she had worn her new jacket and gone to so much trouble with her appearance. She had performed well, too. It couldn't have gone better.

There was a knock on the door and she nearly jumped out of her skin. She took a deep breath. She mustn't appear too excited. She had to play it cool.

'Come in,' she said, swallowing hard.

A face appeared round the door, and she breathed out. *Oscar.*

'You, my lovely, were *amazing*! I know I always say this, but that was the best ever. We'll have people coming from all over the county and beyond to see you before long. I'm going to talk to the boss about advertising more widely, focusing not just on the hotel, glorious as it is, but on what we offer over and above – in other words, you! I can just imagine special events for lovers, weddings, anniversaries. You really tug the heartstrings, you know. Maybe we could get a drummer, or a bass player or something. What do you think?'

This was good to hear, but Nadia wanted him to leave her alone so she could think. She didn't know how to feel. Was this a moment of triumph, or should she be terrified of what was to come?

'Are you going to sing "The Look of Love" in your next set? It's my favourite – so slow, so sexy.'

'Probably, but Oscar, lovely as it is to know it went well, I really need some time for the adrenaline to drain away and to build myself up for the next set. I've got an hour to recover, so if you don't mind . . .'

Oscar looked horrified. 'Oh, darling, I'm so very sorry. I was just so excited. You sit, rest, and I'll get someone to bring you something – food, wine, anything you like.'

'I'm fine for now. I've got water, and I'll come and find you if I need anything else.'

She wanted him to go. She needed to think, to decide what to do next.

'Okay, I'll leave you in peace.' He headed towards the door. 'There's a man in the audience who said he wants a word with you, but I suggested he should leave it until later, when you've finished. I think he plans on catching up with you tomorrow.'

Nadia gulped in a sharp breath. She was about to ask what the guy looked like and tell Oscar to send him in, but then she looked around her. She was sitting in a storeroom with a mirror propped up on some shelving. This wasn't the right place. Everything had to be perfect. She had to appear successful, at the top of her game.

She would play it cool. Maybe letting him wait would be a good move – perhaps give her the upper hand. She would perform her second set and then wait for him as the audience thinned and the guests made their way to their rooms.

He wouldn't wait until tomorrow. He would come to her. She knew it.

9

I haven't managed to make it back to the restaurant from the ladies'. I know Russell will be worried, and I'm ruining his chance of enjoying the singer. Nadia, he said she was called. She's the reason we're here, and although in many ways his opinion of her performance doesn't matter, he cares about his clients. He openly admits he knows nothing about the quality of a voice and is no expert at spotting the next star, but it's not unusual for those on the books of the agency to turn to him if they feel they're not getting the support they were hoping for. While others brush off their concerns, Russell listens. 'They're all prima donnas,' Raoul, Russell's boss, has been heard to say. To which Russell always replies, 'No, Raoul, they are all *people*.'

He's a kind man, and I know he underestimates his own importance. He'll be thrilled that someone he considers as influential as Ellis Cobain has taken the time to talk to him, a mere lawyer. That's the way Russell's mind works, although why he thinks being super-rich makes one man more worthy of admiration than another, I will never know. Especially as Ellis didn't create his own wealth, but flaunts it as if he did.

I lean back against the washbasin taking deep breaths. From the prolonged applause, I guess the set is over and I know I should go back to the table. I could make an excuse and escape to our room, but Russell needs to stay to listen to Nadia's second set, and I don't want to be alone, away from other people, vulnerable to unwanted visitors.

Why is Ellis here?

I don't know how to behave. Russell won't know why I'm being so rude, but perhaps he'll put it down as another example of my recent unsettled behaviour. Ellis will understand that I'm furious. He'll enjoy that. But I must hide the rage hovering just below the surface.

I have to go back, whether I want to or not. I can feel that my face is flushed and damp with sweat, and I turn towards the mirror, take a paper towel and hold it under the cold tap. I am applying it to the back of my neck as the door to the ladies' opens and I look over my shoulder as a woman in her early thirties with dark wavy shoulder-length hair comes in. She starts to smile, but I see her eyebrows draw together and I turn away quickly.

'Are you okay?' she asks.

I look at myself properly in the mirror and see black smudges of mascara around my eyes where I've rubbed them.

'I'm fine, thanks. Just feeling a bit queasy. I've been a bit off colour all day,' I say, not wanting her to think the restaurant is to blame for my desire to vomit.

I try to wipe away the mascara with the damp towel but it won't budge. I've rubbed it well in, and I left my bag at the table. I give a deep sigh.

'I've got some moisturiser in my bag,' the woman says. 'A bit of that on some tissue will probably sort out the eyes.'

She hunts around inside an enormous shoulder bag and pulls out a small pot and a packet of tissues. I try to smile as I take them from her, but I know she's not convinced that I'm okay.

'Do you want me to get someone for you? I think I saw you earlier with a couple of guys – is one of them your partner?'

'Husband, yes. I only met the other man tonight.'

I don't know why I told her that. It wasn't relevant, but I feel I need to make the point. I have to try to believe it myself.

'I can tell him you're not feeling too good, if you like.'

I swallow. 'No, it's fine, thanks. I need to get back. He'll be worried.'

I hand her back the pot of cream and check that my eyes are looking more normal, although the effort I put into disguising the dark circles earlier has now gone to waste.

'Thanks for your concern. I appreciate it.'

With a final attempt at a smile, I head towards the door. I can feel her eyes on my back, but then I hear the door to one of the cubicles closing. For a moment I want to stop, to turn to this woman I have never seen before and will probably never see again and tell her everything. Tell her why I'm so unhappy, why I have made such a mess of my life, and ask her what to do.

Instead, I walk through the door, back towards the table, to one man I love and one I hate.

Sunday

10

'You ready, Mum?' Stephanie called as she pulled her case towards the stable door.

'Coming,' she heard.

Stephanie took a last look around the living space of the suite, with its exposed stone walls, flagged floors and soft shades of grey and teal. Such a calming space. This hotel was everything her mum told her it would be, and they'd had a perfect couple of days together. She felt a twinge of guilt at the thought that she had very nearly refused to come. Work, the house and trips to Norfolk meant weekends and time alone with Gus were precious, but nothing was more precious than her mum, and she was so glad she'd said yes.

They had stayed chatting in the bar for a long time the night before, safe in the knowledge that they would have an extra hour's sleep as the clocks were going back. They listened to Nadia Shariq's soulful second set, debating whether she would still be performing here in a few months' time or if she would have been snapped up by a talent scout. The barman had told Stephanie that Nadia had just told him there was an agency interested in putting her on their books, and that someone from that very organisation was in the audience, but he was hoping that didn't mean she would leave them. Stephanie couldn't help wondering if that was the person who had brought the beaming, almost jubilant, smile to Nadia's face.

She turned from the open door to see Amanda wheeling a case towards her.

'Do you want to head off now, Stephanie? Or should we just have a last look at the sea?'

'Good idea. We don't have to check out for an hour, so let's leave the bags here and go for a wander.'

Stephanie saw the sea almost every day, either on her way to work or when she was out and about doing her job. Her mum lived inland, though, and didn't often venture far from home. Being beside the sea was one of the reasons this weekend had been so special.

They walked in companionable silence across the cobbles. The door to the suite next to theirs stood open and, despite it being a Sunday, decorators were at work. Stephanie couldn't resist poking her nose in. The walls were being painted a fabulous dark colour – not quite green, not quite blue, exactly what she would like in their hall.

A man in white overalls turned to her. 'Hello, just looking, are you?'

'Sorry to interrupt, but I love this colour. What's it called?' Stephanie asked.

'Dragonfly,' the decorator said. 'It's brilliant paint, this. Goes on a dream.'

She glanced at the yellow tin standing to one side and took a photo on her phone as a reminder of the brand.

'Thanks, and sorry to have disturbed you.'

Amanda was waiting patiently outside. 'Won't it make your hall look dark?'

'Not when I've covered it in bright paintings. It'll look fabulous. Just wait and see.'

They walked to the end of the courtyard, and Stephanie was tempted to look over her shoulder into the huge double-height windows of the end barn. She would love to know if the woman who had scuttled away from her in the courtyard was okay, but didn't want to be caught staring.

A path led through some grassy dunes to a small beach, nestling between two low headlands. They had discovered it the morning before, and as they headed back there for a final stroll before setting off for home, Amanda pointed to another path going off to the right, across the headland.

'Where do you think that goes?'

'No idea. Maybe there's another beach that way.' It seemed unlikely, as the hotel guide and the discreet signs had all pointed to the left. 'Let's take a look, shall we? We might as well see everything the hotel has to offer.'

They walked uphill for a few metres before the path fell away steeply towards a narrow inlet.

'I know what this is,' Stephanie said. 'In the information pack it says that in the warmer months there are water sports. Dinghies, paddle boards and kayaks can be hired, so I bet this is where they go from.' They made their way down the sandy slope. 'Yes, look. There's a small jetty.'

Amanda was staring out to sea, and Stephanie followed her gaze to where a sleek motor yacht was moored a hundred metres out in the bay.

'Wow! I wonder who *that* belongs to.'

'Must be someone at the hotel,' Amanda said. 'I've always wanted to sit on the deck of a yacht, preferably moored in Portofino or Monaco, being served lobster and champagne.'

'Going for the cheap option, then, Mum?'

Amanda chuckled. 'No point slumming it, is there? I guess I'd better hope my Premium Bonds do a slightly better job next time.'

'I hate to tell you this, but even if you won the big money, I doubt it would be enough to buy one of these beauties.'

'I'm not fussy – I could cope with second hand.'

Stephanie laughed. They could but dream. 'Come on, we'd better get back to my beat-up old car, and I'll take you home. But before we go, I just wanted to say thanks, Mum.' She turned and pulled Amanda into a hug. 'It's been a real treat. Not just this fabulous hotel, but I've loved spending time with you.'

'You too, sweetheart.'

Amanda gently released her and as they made their way back up the slope, she slotted her arm through Stephanie's. 'Maybe when that house of yours is finished, you can have me to stay every now and again? I'd love that.'

'It's a deal.'

A late October chill hung in the air as Stephanie and Amanda made their way back towards the courtyard, a feeble midday sun warming their backs, its pale light flooding into the floor-to-ceiling windows of the converted barn.

Stephanie had resisted the temptation to look over her shoulder as they'd headed down to the shore, but now the windows were straight ahead, and she could see inside to a sitting area and what appeared to be a mezzanine bedroom above, decorated in muted shades of subtle, earthy sage green.

For a moment she was so distracted by the décor that she failed to notice a woman, sitting huddled on the floor, her arms wrapped around her legs, pulling them tightly to her chest. Her shoulders were hunched, her forehead resting on her raised knees. Even without seeing her face, Stephanie was certain it was the woman she had met in the courtyard the night before.

She heard Amanda gasp and turned. 'What?'

'Swap places,' she mumbled.

Stephanie moved to the far side of Amanda where the view into the room was slightly wider. A man was standing, legs apart, arms folded, staring down at the woman. Stephanie could see his lips moving. His posture oozed contempt, and even from where she was, the sneer on his face was plain to see.

He seemed to shout one word, gave a dismissive flick of his wrist, and the woman recoiled as if he'd hit her.

Stephanie stopped and crouched down.

'What are you doing?' Amanda hissed.

'Tying the lace on my trainers.'

'No you're not. They're already tied. You're not going to get involved, are you?'

'No, but I'm biding my time. I can't interfere if he's just being a dick, but she looks scared, and if he raises his hand, I'm going in there.'

'Steph . . .'

There was a sudden movement as the man strode towards the woman and stood over her, hands on hips. She tried to pull herself into a tighter ball, but he crouched low, reaching out to tilt her chin up, forcing her to meet his gaze. She flinched, her eyes never meeting his. Then he pushed his face close to hers, said no more than a couple of words, then abruptly released her chin, stood up and walked slowly and deliberately towards the stairs.

'Christ,' Stephanie mumbled. She had felt certain the previous night that the woman was troubled, fearful of her husband's reaction to her appearance in the restaurant. Now she knew why. 'Let's go, Mum. Sadly there's nothing we can do here.'

She stood up, and as she moved the woman lifted her head. Their eyes met and Stephanie felt a flash of connection as the woman recognised her, her eyes brimming with shock and humiliation, a single tear sliding down her cheek.

Friday

Five Days Later

11

Stephanie was gazing out of her window at a grey, early November day, when her mobile buzzed. With a jolt of pleasure, she saw Gus's name on the screen. He rarely called her at work and she had only left him a couple of hours ago. She smiled as she picked up the phone, wondering if he was missing her already.

'Hi, Gus. This is a nice surprise,' she said, reaching into her drawer for a mid-morning chocolate biscuit.

'Not really, Steph. Sorry, it's not a personal call. You're needed. Given the circumstances, HC's approved your involvement in a case that's just come in.'

HC was Detective Inspector Harris-Cooke, the local CID inspector and Stephanie's boss.

'What case? What circumstances?'

'We've got a body, and I'm afraid the death occurred at Morvoren Manor, the hotel you stayed at with your mum last weekend.'

The biscuit dropped to the desk. '*What*? Who is it?'

'It's best if you can get yourself back there, and I'll fill you in on site. I'm on my way now.'

'So you can't tell me who's dead? I'm presuming it's murder, if you're involved?'

As a detective chief inspector in the major crimes team, Gus was unlikely to have been called to the scene if it was a natural death.

'Let's say definitely suspicious, for now. I know you'll hate me for this, but I'd prefer not to tell you who the victim is until you get there. We should look at the scene together with fresh eyes, and there's a chance that if it's someone you met while you were at the hotel, you'll come up with a hypothesis before we know the facts.'

Stephanie tutted. 'Erm, that's a bit patronising, if you don't mind me saying so, DCI Brodie.' It was sometimes hard to remember that he was senior to her, especially when she'd got out of his bed less than four hours previously.

Gus chuckled. 'Remember what Sherlock Holmes said . . .'

She sighed. 'No, I don't remember, Gus, but I've no doubt you're about to enlighten me.'

'He said: "It is a capital mistake to theorise before you have all the evidence. It biases the judgement."'

'Marvellous. That's my man! A quote for every occasion.'

'Absolutely! Maybe I'll write an anthology of useful quotes for detectives. What do you think?'

Stephanie groaned. 'You don't have time. Things to paint, remember?'

'I do indeed. Anyway, I'll see you there. I've got a head start, but I'm coming from Newquay so I guess we'll arrive at about the same time. See you very soon.' His voice softened. 'Drive carefully, Stephie.'

With that he hung up.

Bloody hell, Gus. For the whole journey she was going to be running through every possible candidate in her head, thinking through anything she'd seen, anyone who had stood out, trying to guess which of them might have been murdered, and by whom. If he'd just told her, she might arrive at the scene with something useful to say.

Realising that these thoughts rather proved Gus's point, she grinned. He knew her too well; that was the problem.

She disconnected her laptop and shoved it into her bag, along with all the usual paraphernalia she took when she was working away from the office. At the last moment she pulled open her desk drawer and grabbed the chocolate biscuits. Who knew when she would next get the chance to eat?

Quickly explaining to her colleagues where she was going, she headed to the car park. Her emotions were always so mixed when she was brought into a case involving a suspicious death. She hated the fact that a person had died, probably leaving distraught loved ones to grieve, but at the same time she relished the challenge of uncovering the facts and finding the perpetrator. Right now this was only an unexplained death; it might not be murder. But if Gus had been called in, there was every chance that it was.

The wheels of Stephanie's car crunched over the gravel as she drove through the arched entrance to Morvoren Manor. The car park was crowded, with three patrol cars and various unmarked vehicles. A black private ambulance was standing by. She pulled up next to Gus's car and got out, pulling her jacket a little tighter. It seemed colder and damper than it had just five days earlier.

It wasn't the only thing that had changed. The peace that she remembered from her stay was gone, shattered by the sound of police radios and the chatter of a small group of officers apparently waiting for further instructions.

Stephanie spotted her one-time probationer, PC Jason Graves, and walked across to have a word.

He saw her coming and straightened his back. Stephanie caught an amused glance from one of the older officers.

'Morning! Is there a reason why everyone is hanging around here?'

'Tricky one, Sarge,' Jason said. 'We've sealed off the area and there are a couple of officers down there. The first responders took an initial statement, and the hotel guests are being advised on what we need from them. One of DCI Brodie's team is sorting it.'

'When you say "down there" . . .?'

'By the shore, Sarge. They might need our help retrieving the body, apparently, which is why we're waiting. And we have to accompany Dr Treadwell when she arrives. She'll be about another half-hour. She was in the middle of a post-mortem when the call went through.'

Molly Treadwell was the Home Office pathologist, and they wouldn't be able to move the body until she'd had the opportunity to view it.

'Crime scene manager?'

'Yes, he's here. Tai Shentu. DCI Brodie has just arrived and gone to the scene with him. He asked me to let him know when you got here.'

Stephanie raised her eyebrows at Jason, who looked momentarily perplexed. 'Oh yes. Sorry. I'll radio him now.'

Turning to look back at the hotel, Stephanie thought how upsetting this must be for the owners. They had spent a fortune renovating the property and she had rarely stayed anywhere as comfortable and welcoming. What would this do to their business? Would people cancel when they knew someone had been murdered here – if indeed that was what had happened? Or would it bring a whole different group of tourists, interested only in finding out the gory details? Either way, it was a real shame.

'Sarge!' Jason called. 'DCI Brodie has asked me to take you down to the jetty.'

Stephanie let out a long breath. 'Did our victim drown?' She had seen a body pulled out of the water before and found the thought of struggling to breathe, fighting to reach the surface, the final moment when all hope was gone, more horrific than she could imagine. She would rather be shot than drown.

'No, not a drowning.'

Stephanie frowned but followed Jason along the path by the side of the main building, through the courtyard, past the room she and her mum had stayed in, and on to the path to the beach beyond. Just like the last time she had been there, they veered off to the right, over the dunes and down towards the jetty.

Lifting the yellow crime scene tape and giving her name to the officer on duty, Stephanie thanked Jason for escorting her and hurried down the rest of the path to where Gus was waiting. She still felt a small jolt of pleasure every time she saw him, especially when she wasn't expecting to.

Gus nodded, giving her a sombre smile of welcome.

'Tai's already at the scene, but I thought I'd come back for you.'

'Where are we going?'

Gus nodded to the motor yacht that Stephanie and Amanda had seen in the bay the day they left.

'To the yacht. The body was found there this morning.'

12

'Are you okay, coming back here?' Gus asked as the hotel's small RIB bounced over the waves towards the yacht. 'I did wonder, but as you said you hadn't really spoken to any of the other guests, I didn't think it would be a problem. Let me know if I'm being insensitive.'

Resisting the temptation to give him an unprofessional hug, she just lifted her eyes to his. 'I'm fine.'

She turned away to watch their approach to the yacht.

The only piece of information Gus had shared was that, because of the tides and its draught, the yacht had to be moored some distance from the shore. Fortunately, having lived by the sea all her life, Stephanie knew that a boat's draught was the minimum depth of water it required before it ran aground.

She could see a small boat with an outboard motor tied to the side of the yacht. Gus pointed to it. 'That's the tender. It was there when the body was found this morning.'

Stephanie nodded. The fact that it was still with the yacht might be important, or it might not. It all depended how the victim had died.

As the RIB slowed, they pulled on disposable over-suits and shoe covers, Stephanie tying back her hair so it would be covered by the hood. When she was ready, she looked up at the yacht and only just prevented herself from saying an inappropriate *Wow!*

They stepped onto the swim platform and up a few steps to the aft deck, the main outdoor entertainment area. A wide cream-coloured sofa ran across the rear of the space facing a fixed dining table and further chairs. To the right was a staircase to the flybridge, and straight ahead were glass sliding doors into the main salon.

Everywhere she looked, Stephanie could see evidence of wealth, from the glossy wood panelling to the cut glass behind the elegant bar. She was struggling to remember that someone had died here, and for a moment felt the urge to sink into a deep-cushioned armchair and demand a glass of champagne. Gus hadn't stopped, but was striding ahead, scouring the scene for evidence. Telling herself to focus on the case, Stephanie followed him through the salon and down some more stairs towards the yacht's master suite.

Gus paused at the door. Over his shoulder she could see into a room which spanned the width of the boat. Shiny dark wood units lined either side, a king-sized bed covered in a sumptuous sapphire-blue quilted throw dominating the room. And there was the unmistakable form of a body under the covers.

Tai and one of his team, on their hands and knees by the side of the bed, looked up to nod a greeting before returning their focus to the floor, and Gus turned back towards Stephanie.

'There's not a lot of space, so we should let them finish. Until then, stand here in the doorway with me and give me your first impressions.'

Gus moved to one side and Stephanie stepped forward. She could see the whole of the room and, most importantly, the face belonging to the body on the bed. She was strangely relieved to see that it was a man. She had thought all along that it would be a woman, although she hadn't been certain who.

'Do you recognise him?'

Stephanie nodded slowly. 'I do, but I don't know his name.'

She didn't feel any surprise at the identity of the victim, although it seemed inappropriate to say she had nicknamed him 'Floppy Hair', a name that seemed fatuous since she'd seen how he treated his wife.

'His name is Ellis Cobain,' Gus said. 'Apparently strongly tipped to receive some gong or other in the King's new year's honours list for his generous donations to various charities.'

'Why was he on the yacht if he was staying at the hotel?'

'We don't know any details yet, although his wife told the first responders that Cobain had been out to the boat last night to prepare for their departure, planned for tomorrow, and to make sure everything was secure. Apparently they sailed here from Bristol. He sent her a text to say he would sleep here overnight, and when he didn't come back or respond to any of her calls or messages this morning, she asked the hotel if they would bring the RIB out to check. The tender was still tied to the yacht, so she had no means of getting here, and she says she doesn't know how to drive it anyway. When the hotel staff arrived, they found him like this.'

Tai looked up from where he was, on hands and knees on the floor. 'I've got my team searching the other berths, Gus, including the crew cabin.'

'*Crew* cabin?' Stephanie said. 'Did he actually have *crew*?'

Tai smiled. 'Not as far as we know – at least not for this trip. But we're crawling over every inch of the space.'

'Anything interesting?' Gus asked.

'Nothing that stands out, although of course we're collecting fibres, fingerprinting every surface – all the usual stuff.'

'I know we have to wait for Molly, but why do you think it's a suspicious death?' Stephanie asked Gus.

'The guys that came out to check on him called the ambulance, even though they were certain he was dead, and the paramedics thought there might be slight signs of cyanosis, although that in itself isn't conclusive. He could have heart or lung problems, or for all we know he may have decided to go for a swim and the cold water affected his circulation. But there are some slight abrasions on his neck too. Could be nothing. We need to know what Molly thinks.'

Before Stephanie could ask anything else they heard heavy steps on the stairs, accompanied by huffing and puffing.

'Goodness me, DCI Brodie, why do you two always demand my attendance at such challenging crime scenes?'

Molly appeared at the bottom of the stairs in her ubiquitous oversized suit, her white shirt untucked on one side.

Gus turned and smiled. 'You love it, Molly. And it's not quite as challenging as some of the places we've dragged you to. I gather Steph had you scrambling up a rock face in a cave not too long ago.'

'I'll have you know I did it without a problem, didn't I, Sergeant?'

'You did indeed, Molly.'

'You already briefed me on the phone, Gus, but is there anything to add?'

Gus shook his head.

'Out of my way, then,' she said, forcing her way between them. 'Tai, can I come in?'

'We're done for now,' he responded. 'As long as you don't touch anything other than the area round the body, that's fine.'

Molly raised her eyebrows. She'd been attending crime scenes since before Tai left school, but she didn't remind him of the fact. 'Let the dog see the rabbit then.'

Tai and his partner moved aside to let Molly get close to the bed.

'Let me know if there's anything specific that you want me to photograph, Molly. I've taken photos of the body and the surroundings without moving him, but I'll stand by if you need me.'

Stephanie remained in the doorway, gazing around, trying to spot anything that seemed strange or unusual about the place. She had no idea what she was looking for, and it wasn't as if she was familiar with cabins on motor yachts. But she hoped there might be something that looked out of place.

Molly was speaking softly to the crime scene manager as she pulled back the dark blue bed cover. Tai's camera was clicking and whirring away. Molly had placed her voice-activated recording device next to the bed and was quietly capturing her observations. She might be a woman who liked to joke and occasionally flirt with Gus, but when she was in the vicinity of a body, she always showed it the utmost respect.

Molly pointed to a subtle bluish-purple tint around the lips and eyelids. 'The paramedic was right. There is a slight sign of cyanosis.' She turned to Tai. 'Can we check for carbon monoxide? It's probably too late now with the door being open for so long, but worth a shot.'

'Already done it, Molly. Nothing.'

'Hmm,' was the only response as Molly turned back towards the bed and bent over the body, gently lifting an eyelid. 'Faint trace of petechiae, Gus. Some tiny specks. Could indicate asphyxiation. I'm going to roll him slightly to examine his neck. There are some small abrasions on his throat at the front, so I want to look at the back. Okay?'

Gus and Tai agreed, and she gently moved the corpse onto his side. Stephanie saw her signal to Tai to home in with the camera.

'Gus,' she said, nodding towards the back of the victim's neck. Gus walked over to look. 'There could be lots of plausible reasons for these marks, of course. But we can't rule out murder quite yet.'

13

Celia Cobain was hiding in the bedroom of her suite. She couldn't get warm and was huddled, fully dressed, under the duvet, her mind spinning, going over the events of the morning, wondering what the hotel staff, the paramedics, the police must have thought of her.

After she had asked the hotel if someone could go out to the yacht, she had stood on the jetty, her arms wrapped tightly around her body, watching the RIB speed over the grey, choppy water with a sense of dread at the thought of what the men were going to find. She should have gone with them, but the idea was too much for her, and she could almost hear Ellis's voice telling her she was pathetic.

They seemed to be a long time, and she had begun to pace, shivering, searching for an explanation for anything they might have seen.

Only one of the men had returned, an older man with a kind face and a strong north-east accent.

She had tried to read his expression, to gauge whether there was anything on the yacht that had shocked or puzzled him. But if there had been, he wasn't about to share his thoughts with her. He told her an ambulance had been called, and she should go back to her room. Someone would come and tell her what was happening when they knew more.

'An ambulance? Should I not go out to the yacht to be with him if he's ill?'

'I don't think so, pet,' he said, grasping her upper arms gently. 'Best if you go and get warm. Someone will come and let you know what's happening.'

'What are you not telling me?'

He clamped his lips together and shook his head slowly. 'It's not my place to tell you – not until the professionals have checked him over.'

She could see in his eyes that he thought the news was bad, but she hadn't been able to leave. A thin drizzle had started to fall, and she turned up the collar of her jacket as she heard a siren drawing closer.

The first people to arrive were two uniformed police officers. The hotel man, who had told her his name was Stevie, hurried towards them, probably so Celia wouldn't hear what he said. He gestured towards the boat, but before they could make a move, two paramedics in green coveralls came striding along the jetty. After a quick discussion, the paramedics slung backpacks over their shoulders and headed towards the RIB with Stevie and one of the police officers.

As they passed Celia, Stevie stopped. 'I need to take these guys out to the yacht. This officer is going to stay here with you for now. Okay, pet?'

It wasn't okay, but Celia didn't feel she had a choice.

'Is there anyone you'd like me to contact to be with you, Mrs Cobain?' the police officer asked.

'No, thank you. I just want to know what's happening.'

'We'll know more when the paramedics have had a chance to take a look. They're the experts.'

The next fifteen minutes seemed like hours. Rain was soaking through her cashmere jacket, chilling her to the bone. She could feel her body swaying, but her eyes never left the rear of the yacht. Her right hand was thrust deep into her pocket, turning over the amethyst crystal that she was never without. If there was ever a time when she needed to dissolve self-imposed limitations and experience a confidence boost, it was now.

Finally, the two paramedics reappeared on the deck and climbed into the RIB with Stevie just as the police officer's radio sprang to life.

'Excuse me,' he said as he moved away. She could hear him speaking, but the sound of the RIB speeding across the bay towards them drowned out his words.

The officer ended his conversation and approached her. 'I'm very sorry, Mrs Cobain, but my colleague says the paramedics have confirmed that sadly your husband has died. I'm sorry for your loss, but more officers are on their way to cordon off the area, and I need to take you back to your hotel room.'

Celia gasped, lifting her hands to her mouth. But it wasn't a surprise. How could it be?

'Can I see him?'

She had known what his answer would be, but they would expect her to ask.

The officer shook his head. 'I'm sorry. Not right now. Let's get you out of this weather, shall we?'

'Why do you need to cordon off the area?'

The officer looked as if he was searching for the right words. 'Your husband's death is unexplained. Until we know for certain how he died, it's just a precaution.'

Celia had felt her legs shaking, whether with cold or from horror at all that had happened she didn't know. She'd allowed the officer to guide her back to her room and had sat, ramrod straight, while he asked her some basic questions about events leading up to the moment Stevie had gone to the yacht to check on Ellis.

She was sure she must have answered coherently, because the officer nodded as he wrote in his notebook. But she felt numb, and had taken the first opportunity to escape to her bedroom and climb under the covers.

Ellis is dead. He's really dead.

She repeated the words over and over in her mind. It was true. The police had confirmed it. Waves of relief washed over her, followed swiftly by a cold knot of concern for the children. What would this mean for them?

Had she told the officer that she'd texted Ellis that morning and tried to phone him? She couldn't remember, but the police would be able to check. They would see she'd tried to contact him, and they would know he'd chosen not to come back to the hotel the night before. She had the text from him confirming it:

Darling, it's late now, so I hope you don't mind but I've decided to stay on the yacht tonight. I'll be back for breakfast.

They would see her reply, wishing him a good night's sleep, but the police would ask people at the hotel about them. What would they say? Would the other guests have noticed how Ellis had behaved this week, treating her as if she was an inconvenience, someone he was saddled with and tried to shake off at every opportunity?

If they did, she could say that's why she was glad he'd decided to stay on the boat – that perhaps whatever had been bothering him all week would be cured by a night apart. She would make light of it.

Should she admit to the truth about her marriage, rather than pretend it was perfect and have them eventually discover the reality, as they surely would if they investigated his life?

Ellis's body was still on the boat. They would have to bring him right past her window, through the courtyard to the car park. She looked out from the bed through the vast window – half hoping, half fearing that it had all been a huge mistake and that he would appear, walking up the path from the beach. But of course he wouldn't. He would be zipped into a body bag and bundled into the hotel's RIB. He would hate that, the sheer indignity of it.

It was almost enough to make her smile.

Celia thought about what was to come – the questions, the intrusion into their lives – and any trace of amusement vanished. How was she going to tell the children? What would happen to them? Ellis had refused to tell her what he had planned in the event of his death, but even though Celia was only their step-mother, surely the courts would let them stay with her? Surely they would see it as the best – the *only* – solution?

They had already lost their mother, Vivian, although Savannah had only been one when she died. How would the death of another parent feel for Lacey, who remembered her mother well?

When Celia had first met Ellis's eldest child, she had been a sensitive six-year-old, puzzled by the fact that the person who had loved her the most had gone. Celia had tried to fill the void, as she had with both little Savannah and Ellis's middle child, Reece – who had been the cutest three-year-old with blond curls and a bewitching smile. The children were her life.

Regardless of her deep commitment, she lived with the stark reality that her rights as a step-parent were non-existent. A sense of suffocating helplessness washed over her as she confronted the haunting possibility that she might lose her children.

14

Gus beckoned Stephanie over to the bed and pointed to the back of Ellis Cobain's neck.

'Take a look, Steph. What do you see?' he asked.

She peered closely at the affected area. The skin appeared chafed, as if something had rubbed it, causing a red swollen patch.

'Looks like a friction burn of some sort,' Stephanie said.

'My thoughts precisely, young Stephanie,' Molly said. 'Not caused by anything rough, like rope for example. It's too smooth. And I can tell you he wasn't strangled. The marks are only on the back of the neck, with a few smaller tender patches on either side.'

'Do you have a theory?'

'Nothing that I'm prepared to share right now. There are too many variables. The slight cyanosis could have been caused by one of several factors, as could the chafing on the neck, which means they could be entirely unrelated. I'd like to rule out natural causes first, and we need to ask his wife if there were any medical conditions that she knew of.'

Gus turned to Stephanie. 'You were here for a couple of days, and you said you recognised Cobain. Did you see any signs that he was unwell?'

'Like what?' she asked, looking at Molly for clarification.

'Could be either florid skin tone, or excessively pale, puffy face, any grimacing, wincing when moving . . .'

Stephanie shook her head. 'No, and I looked at him quite a bit, actually.' Gus raised his eyebrows, and Stephanie tutted. 'Not in that way, Gus. I didn't take to him, although it seems inappropriate to say that as I'm standing next to his dead body.'

'So why were you looking at him?'

'Now that he's lying down and his hair is kind of stuck to his head, you can't really see, but his hair was divided down the middle, brushed back a bit. Floppy, you know? Think Hugh Grant in *Bridget Jones*, but grey instead of dark.'

Molly chuckled and Gus blinked. 'I haven't got a clue what you're talking about. But why was his hair the cause of such interest?' he asked.

'I'm getting to that. It seemed a sign of who he was. He kept running his fingers through it, lifting it slightly so that it fell ever so perfectly. Very affected, I thought. He really fancied himself. He had that air about him – a kind of "Look at me – I'm important" superciliousness.'

'Bloody hell, Steph. All this just from seeing him a couple of times?'

'Not just that. I saw him touch some woman in the bar when her husband had his back turned. She didn't like it, but he thought it was funny.'

'Ah.' Gus didn't have to ask anything more. He knew exactly how much that would have incensed Stephanie.

'Are you sure she wasn't his wife?'

'Certain. Her husband introduced Cobain to her, and they both acted as though they didn't know each other. I didn't believe it.'

Gus frowned. 'Sounds like these are people we need to talk to.'

'If they're still here. It's nearly a week ago and they may have only been here for the weekend.'

'Interesting, though, if he was a bit of a groper.'

'He was more than that. I saw how he treated his wife too. He didn't appear to be a particularly nice man.'

Gus was watching her expression and he slowly nodded, not demanding more yet. But Stephanie knew he would.

'Molly, do we have time of death?' he asked.

'Just about to check. Tai, what's the room temperature?'

Tai had been snapping away with his camera at anything that might have any bearing on what had happened to Ellis Cobain.

'It's fifteen degrees now, but that door's been opened a lot and the outside air temperature is eleven. I took the temperature when we arrived. It was seventeen then. That's two hours ago.'

'Do we know if the door was open or closed when the first people arrived on the scene?'

'I asked, Molly, but the two men from the hotel weren't sure. They know they closed it when they left to call the ambulance, but that's not entirely helpful.'

Molly grunted and pulled the covers further down to discover Cobain was naked beneath.

'That makes life a bit simpler,' she said, using a thermometer to take his rectal temperature. 'He was covered, under a quilted throw. So taking that into consideration, and bearing in mind the uncertainty of the ambient temperature and the stage of rigor mortis, right now I would estimate he's been dead for between twelve and sixteen hours, but I'll be able to be more precise later. He died here, or at least was placed here immediately after death. We can see that from the livor mortis, which confirms he's been dead for a minimum of twelve hours.' Molly pressed her thumbs against the areas of livor mortis. 'If he'd been dead for less than that, I would expect blanching when I press. But the blood is fixed.'

Molly rolled Cobain's body back until he was face up.

'I'll check for fibres in his mouth when we get him back to the mortuary, in case he was smothered. I don't want to break the rigor mortis here. I think we can have him taken away now. I need to supervise the removal of the body, if that's okay?'

'Fine,' Gus said. 'We'll get out of your way. Tai, have you found his mobile phone yet?'

''Fraid not. We've searched the empty cabins and the salon – as I believe it's called. We'll search the bed and around his body when it's been moved. I'll keep you updated.'

Stephanie turned to head to the door, but stopped. Looking at the highly varnished dark wood of the cupboard by the door, she called to Tai.

'Have you got a photo of this?'

The crime scene manager made his way round from the far side of the bed. 'I've photographed everything, so yes. But not specifically. Oh!'

He peered closely at the shiny surface. 'Is that Blu-tack?'

'That's what I thought.'

Gus was peering over her shoulder. 'There are a few dull patches. What are you thinking, Steph?'

She shrugged. 'I've no idea. I'm just struggling to think why someone with a yacht like this would pin anything on a wall or cupboard with Blu-tack. It seems out of place. And more to the point, whatever was there, it's not there now.'

15

'Do we know where Mrs Cobain is?' Stephanie asked Gus as they made their way back up from the jetty.

'In her room. We thought it best to ask all the guests to keep to their rooms for now. We don't want any contamination of witness testimony.'

Stephanie nodded. When witnesses were allowed to talk to each other there was a chance that they would unintentionally – or even intentionally – influence each other's recollection of events. Discrepancies and inconsistencies were a vital part of the investigation process, so even though the guests might not be too pleased at being confined to their rooms, it was essential until the detectives had spoken to everyone.

'What's the plan, then?'

'I've got officers working through all those who claim not to have known Cobain. They may have noticed something in his behaviour or the behaviour of those closest to him. Like you, they may have formed a judgement, and we need to know where they were around the time he was killed. With any luck, one of them will have been down at the jetty and will have seen something. We can release anyone who only arrived this morning, but we need to trace anyone who checked out first thing, before we arrived.'

'And what will we be doing, apart from interviewing Mrs Cobain?'

'I need you to identify the woman who Cobain touched. See if she and her husband are still here. We'll talk to them next. We'll also check with Mrs Cobain whether there were other people at the hotel who they, or at least her husband, knew. The wife's called Celia.'

'Before we go and talk to her, you need to know that I've met her.'

Gus stopped. 'When you were here?'

'Yes. She seemed very much on edge.' Stephanie told him about the events of that evening. 'She didn't seem to know if going into the restaurant to find her husband and have dinner with him was the right thing to do. She couldn't make her mind up, and while I was looking for Mum's phone she scurried off back to her room.'

'Interesting. It's good that you've met her before, though. We'd expect her to be in an unstable state given her husband's just died, so having already spoken to her, you might be a better judge of her reaction.'

'I'm not sure she'll feel like that.'

Stephanie explained what she and Amanda had witnessed on Sunday just before they left, and the look of dismay on Celia Cobain's face when she'd realised they were watching.

'Any chance you're reading too much into it?' Gus asked, earning himself a tut of irritation.

'I don't think so. People have rows. I know that. But it was the contempt that I found hard to watch. And the fact that she looked so . . . diminished, I guess.'

They had reached the Cobains' suite and both looked up at the barn.

'Stunning place,' Gus said. 'Just as you could see her through the window, though, she has a grandstand view of people coming up the path from the jetty. Let's try to manipulate the seating so she has her back to the window. Not ideal for her to see a body bag being ferried past.'

Stephanie pulled a face. 'Shit. That would be horrible. Do you think she can see the yacht from this window? Could she have seen something last night?'

Gus turned towards the sea. 'The angle's wrong. The view of the sea is glorious, though.'

'God knows what it must cost to stay in this suite. But then Cobain has a bloody motor yacht, so obviously money is no object. Do we know how he made his money?'

Gus made a *pfft* sound through his lips. 'Didn't make a penny of it, as far as I can tell. I got the briefing when I was on my way here. His first wife died. She was the daughter of some billionaire who made his money through petrol stations. Cobain inherited her share. He's got three kids – all with his first wife, none with the current wife. Or widow, should I say.'

'How did his first wife die?'

'Suicide, I understand.'

Stephanie looked at Gus. And then her husband dies in suspicious circumstances? But the suicide must have been years ago. Maybe she was seeing shadows where there weren't any.

Gus walked up to the door and knocked.

'We're here to see Mrs Cobain.'

Celia had heard the knock from her bed on the mezzanine floor. She could see out to the sea, but not the door of the suite, so she slithered across the bed until her head was at its foot and peered through the glass balustrade.

The uniformed officer had opened the door to a man in a suit who she guessed was a detective. The officer pulled the door wide and the detective stood back to let someone else through – this time a woman. She lifted her head to look around the suite, and a tremor rippled through Celia's body.

Oh God! What's she doing here?

It was the woman who had offered to go with her to the restaurant to help her find Ellis the previous weekend. Celia racked her brain to try to remember what she had said that night. Had she said anything she shouldn't have? And then on Sunday she'd seen her huddled on the floor, Ellis standing over her.

Why have they sent her? What do they know?

Celia felt dizzy. The room started to spin.

'She's lying down, sir,' the officer said. 'Shall I see if she's awake?'

'I'll go,' the woman said as she headed towards the stairs.

Celia shuffled back from the end of the bed and swivelled round so she was sitting against the headboard, closing her eyes as she tried to control her shallow, rapid breathing.

'Mrs Cobain? I'm Detective Sergeant Stephanie King. May I come up?'

Celia quickly ran her hands over her hair and took a deep breath. 'I'm awake,' she mumbled.

DS King continued her journey up the stairs and stood at the top.

'Okay if I pull up a chair?'

Celia nodded, and the detective walked towards the bed, dragged across the stool from the dressing table and sat down.

'Mrs Cobain, I'm very sorry for your loss. How are you doing? I know that's a daft question. Is there anyone we can call for you?' Celia shook her head, still not trusting herself to speak. 'I don't know if you remember me, but I was staying here last week with my mum. I met you in the courtyard.'

Celia kept her eyes down, praying that was the only event she was going to mention. 'I remember,' she whispered.

'I know this is difficult for you, but I'm afraid we have to ask you some questions. Are you feeling up to coming downstairs? Detective Chief Inspector Brodie and I would like to talk to you together, and it's probably easier down in the sitting room than up here. What do you think? Would that be okay?'

Celia swallowed. She had known she'd have to talk to the police, but now the moment was here she wasn't sure how she would cope. What would they be expecting of her? How should a grieving widow behave?

'Mrs Cobain?'

The voice brought her back down to earth. 'I'm sorry. If you don't mind, I'd just like to freshen up a bit. I've been in bed in my clothes and I feel a bit hot and sticky.'

'That's okay. I'll wait for you downstairs. Can I get you anything to drink? I could order you some tea or coffee.'

'Coffee would be great. Thank you. A flat white, if that's not too much trouble.'

'Not at all.'

With that the detective stood and made her way down the stairs, and Celia swung her legs out of the bed. She wasn't sure they would hold her up and she rested one hand against the wall as she made her way slowly to the wardrobe to find something to wear.

She stood looking at the array of silk, satin and cashmere, and felt the urge to drag each item from its hanger, throw it on the floor and jump on the lot. Every piece had been carefully selected to look sophisticated, elegant, suitable for the wife of such an important man. She didn't even have a pair of jeans, for God's sake.

She could hear Ellis's voice: 'You're not a teenager, Celia. Stop thinking you can dress like one.'

'I'm only forty-two years old!' she had wanted to scream at him, but of course she hadn't.

All her clothes had been selected by her personal shopper at Harrods, a woman who took her instructions from Ellis.

With relief she remembered a pair of Moncler tapered trousers that had been deemed acceptable wear on board the yacht, and she dragged them from their hanger together with a Burberry hoodie that had been ludicrously expensive. It seemed ridiculous at this moment to worry about what she was going to wear, but this was the closest to casual wear that she had, and she was damned if she'd wear something 'appropriate to the occasion'. A petty act of defiance perhaps, but for just a moment it made her feel better. And of course she had no one to disappoint now. Only herself.

As she flung the clothes over her shoulder, she spotted a leather tote bag pushed to the back of the wardrobe and thought of the black leggings and soft-shell jacket inside. Her heart jumped again. Should she have got rid of them? Would they be considered suspicious? But even if the police found them they would mean nothing.

She kicked the bag further back and took the clothes she'd selected into the bathroom. Stripping off, she had a quick wash and got dressed, but as she stepped towards the door it suddenly seemed too much of an effort to open it.

She didn't want to think about what was on the other side – what was coming for her over the next few days and weeks.

She rested her forehead on the cool wood and her eyes filled with tears.

This was not how her life was meant to be, and now she had to give the performance of her life.

16

'I've just seen two people – a man and a woman – go into Ellis and Celia's room, Juliette,' Russell calls over his shoulder. 'I imagine they're detectives.'

'Come away from the window, Russ,' I tell him, although it suits me that he isn't sitting on the sofa next to me. He would be sure to feel me shaking.

I don't want Russell drawing any attention to us by staring out of the window, although I have no doubt we'll be questioned. The idea makes my mouth dry. From the moment the policeman came into the dining room where we were having brunch I have found it difficult to swallow.

To appease Russell, who has been worrying about my loss of appetite this week, I'd chosen a courgette and goat's cheese frittata. Delicious as it was, it had stuck in my throat, and I'd been pushing it around my plate even before a hush fell over the room at the sight of a uniformed officer demanding our attention.

'Ladies and gentlemen,' he called. 'I'm sorry to disturb you while you're eating but there has been an incident. Please finish your food, then we would ask you to return to your rooms and remain there until my colleagues have had a chance to speak to each of you.'

The shocked silence was shattered by the sound of my knife,

falling from frozen fingers, clattering onto my plate. Russell threw me an uneasy glance as a florid man, whose voice we had heard all week booming through every room he entered, stood up. 'What's happened? Why do we have to go to our rooms?'

'I'm sorry, sir, but we'll tell you more as soon as we can.'

The man was clearly about to protest when another guest spoke. He was much quieter and I strained to hear him.

'There are paramedics here. Been here a while now. And a black van has arrived – says private ambulance on the side.'

There were murmurs, and my skin tingled. The murmurs grew to a hum, hypotheses flying round.

'What's happened?'

'Somebody must be dead.'

'Who do you think it is?'

No one seemed in any doubt what a private ambulance was for.

'I'm sorry, everyone,' the young officer shouted, 'but at this time we would prefer you not to speak to people outside your immediate group. If you've finished eating, please make your way back to your rooms.'

The florid man raised his hand to a waitress. 'Another coffee, please.' He gave the officer a smug smile.

The young waitress, who looked no more than sixteen, shared an anxious glance with the police officer. He shook his head.

'Oh, for God's sake!' the man shouted, bunching up his napkin and throwing it on the table. He marched out, his face redder than ever.

The hubbub in the restaurant, the man yelling, merged into a crescendo of buzzing in my ears.

'I can't eat any more,' I said quietly to Russell. 'Can we go?'

'Of course.' He immediately placed his knife and fork next

to his almost untouched stack of American pancakes and crispy bacon and stood up, holding out his hand to me.

We didn't speak as we walked back through the courtyard to our suite, Russell simply believing that I found the situation unnerving, unaware of the overwhelming sense of dread that gripped me.

Stay calm, stay calm, stay calm.

Two paramedics passed us, heading towards the hotel car park. Based on the state of their boots and the bottoms of their trousers, they had been walking over the dunes. My stomach churned and I pushed my shaking hands deep into my pockets.

'Do you think someone's drowned?' Russell whispered. I didn't respond.

The paramedics were talking quietly, but as they passed I heard one of them say, 'One hell of a yacht, though.'

It was all I caught, but it was enough, and I couldn't hold back a sharp intake of breath. Russell turned to me, his eyes wide.

'Do you think it's *Ellis*?' he mumbled. 'Christ, how awful. What do you think happened?'

I dropped my head, unable to speak. Russell thought I was upset and gently put his arm around my shoulders and pulled me close. I tried not to shiver.

'Come on. Let's get you back to the room. I'll make you a cup of coffee with that fancy machine.'

Since then I have been huddled on the sofa gripping an open book in my hands, doing my best to appear relaxed while Russell hovers by the window. He's certain he's right about who died. He knows Ellis stayed on his boat last night, and Celia was alive and well this morning. We saw her hurrying past our room in the direction of the hotel. Then she went back towards the beach with two men I recognised. They both work here. I've seen them down by the jetty, storing equipment for the winter. I was desperate to know what she was doing, but there was no way I could ask.

'Those detectives I told you about – the ones going towards Celia's room,' Russell says over his shoulder. 'The woman looks vaguely familiar, although I can't think where from. Why would they send detectives to talk to Celia? Do you think they have doubts about how he died?'

Another shudder runs through my body, the few mouthfuls of frittata churning in my gut.

I don't look up from my book. I don't want him to see the panic in my eyes, but when I try to speak my voice cracks and I cough to clear my throat before I can respond. 'I've no idea, Russ. How would you expect me to know a thing like that?'

'You read so many thrillers I'd have thought it was something you'd be bang up to date with. You could probably solve the case for them. You're reading one now! Not sure how you can, with everything that's going on.'

He's right about one thing. I am a relentless reader of crime and psychological thrillers. He's wrong about the other, though. Not a single word of this book has penetrated my brain, which is spinning out of control.

What have they found on the yacht? How long until they come for me?

They will interview Celia first, and I have no idea what she will tell them. I may have only met her for the first time this week, but I feel as if I know everything there is to know about her. And one thing I am certain of is that she is unstable, vulnerable, damaged.

Why did Ellis come here?

I have asked myself that question repeatedly over the past week.

I suggested to Russell that we should leave after the first day, making some excuse about my work. I couldn't tell him the real reason, of course, and he'd looked so dismayed at the thought that I would pass up a chance of spending time with him that I backtracked. Ellis was *my* problem, and I wasn't going to allow his presence to hurt my husband, so I didn't mention it again.

I think back to that first night, when I walked into the restaurant and saw Russell, smiling, laughing with Ellis, pleased to have met him. Russell had looked towards me and I did my best to arrange my features into something approximating a smile, but inside I was shaking violently with a mixture of anger and cold fear.

'Juliette, look who I've met!' Russell seemed delighted. 'This is Ellis Cobain. You've heard of him, I'm sure. A philanthropic legend in the Bristol music scene. Ellis, this is my wife, Juliette.'

I'd had no idea how Ellis would react, but I could feel the weight of his stare. When I managed to raise my eyes to his, they were dancing with amusement, his lips curled into a semblance of a smile. It looked like a sneer to me.

'Mrs Dalton. How lovely to meet you,' he said, reaching out his hand.

I let my wrist go limp, like a dead fish in his firm grasp, hoping he would let go quickly. Of course he didn't.

How did he know I would be here? There was no way it was a coincidence. Part of me wanted to get him alone so I could ask him. The other half of me was determined to make sure we weren't alone for a single second.

'Let me get you a drink, darling. What will you have?' Russell hadn't sensed the tension between us, but then he wasn't the type of man who picked up on atmosphere. I had often been glad of that.

'I'll go, Russell. You carry on chatting.'

'Nonsense. How about a glass of champagne – carry on from the one we had in the room earlier?' He reached out to rest his hand lightly on my lower back.

Ellis put his head slightly to one side, the smirk never leaving his mouth. 'Celebrating, were you?'

Russell chuckled. 'Not at all. We're just making the most of spending time together. A rare treat, recently.'

I still hadn't spoken, and realised that even though he wasn't a man who could read a room, Russell might begin to think my silence odd.

'Is your wife not with you, Mr Cobain?'

'Ellis, please. And you're Juliette, I think Russell said?' I nodded, trying not to narrow my eyes at his despicable behaviour. 'Celia wasn't feeling too great and insisted I come to supper without her.'

'So I expect you're planning to eat quickly so you can get back to her.'

How was it possible that a mere raising of the corner of a mouth could communicate such mockery?

'Not at all. She'll be asleep by now.'

'In that case, you should join us for dinner!' Russell said, seeming pleased with the idea. 'Let me get you that drink, darling. Another one, Ellis?'

'Thank you, Russell, I'll have a vodka martini. But please, if I'm joining you for dinner, you must tell the barman to put the drinks on my tab, and I'll choose us a special bottle of wine.'

'We should sit down,' I said, resigned to the fact that I wasn't going to be able to shake Ellis off. 'The waiter will serve us if we're seated. Save you the trouble, Russ.'

'You grab a table, then. I'll order the drinks at the bar and the waiter can bring them over. Quicker that way.'

It really wasn't the type of place where customers had to go to the bar to order, but my thoughtful husband wouldn't want me to have to wait too long for a drink. He probably thought he could save the waiter some trouble too.

As he walked away, I turned away from Ellis, staring towards the bar, offering him nothing more than my profile.

'How lovely to see you, Juliette.' He spoke softly, but he was laughing at my discomfort.

'What the fuck are you doing here? How did you know we'd be here?' I hissed as Russell turned to smile at me from the bar, and I lifted my fingers in an idiotic wave.

'Coincidence, maybe?'

I didn't respond, still not able to bring myself to look at him.

'You know, sweetheart, you really shouldn't leave your phone lying around while you go for a shower.'

I couldn't stop a groan from escaping. He must have seen the message from Russell – a text with a link to the hotel:

All booked. Looking forward to it, darling.

Before I had chance to react to Ellis's words, I felt his hand running down my spine until it reached the exact the spot where my husband's had rested just moments earlier. It took every ounce of my strength not to push him to the floor and run from the room.

17

'Mrs Cobain,' Gus said, 'we appreciate that this is an extremely difficult time for you, but we need to understand what happened to your husband, and you might be able to help us establish how he died.'

Celia stared at him, her eyes blank.

Gus leaned forward and spoke softly. 'Do you think you could talk us through the events of the last twenty-four hours, from whenever you last saw or heard from your husband?'

Celia's hands were shaking as she picked up the coffee Stephanie had ordered. She put the cup down without taking a sip, but stared at its contents as if the answer to the question lay within its milky midst.

Her voice was little more than a fragile, shaky whisper. 'He wanted to go out and check the boat, to make sure everything was tied down. He said there was a storm coming, you see.'

Stephanie gave Gus a puzzled glance. There hadn't been a storm. A bit of rain, but nothing more.

'Did he go alone?'

'Yes. It was about six o'clock. It was dark by then, or almost, but he said he needed to make sure that the yacht was secure. He told me to go to the bar and wait for him.'

'And is that what you did?'

Celia nodded. 'Yes. I spoke to the children first, so it was about 6.30 when I got there.'

'Did you wait on your own, or did you speak to anyone?'

'There were people in the bar who I'd met during the week, so I sat with them. Then I got a text from Ellis to say he was going to be longer than he'd thought, so I should eat without him. A couple of the other guests asked if I'd like to join them for dinner, but I didn't really want to, so after a while I excused myself and came back here.'

'Do you remember what time that was?'

Celia nodded. 'About 8.30.'

'What happened next?'

'I ordered room service. I thought if Ellis got back late he might appreciate a chicken Caesar salad, or maybe a rare fillet steak and Roquefort salad, so I ordered both, thinking I could eat whichever he didn't fancy.' Celia reached for her coffee cup and lifted it with slightly more success.

To Stephanie this seemed further evidence that Ellis Cobain had made his wife nervous – at the very least. Gus threw her a glance, knowing exactly what she would be thinking.

'Do you remember what happened next?'

Celia took a sip of her lukewarm coffee. 'He still wasn't back when room service arrived. I looked at my watch and it was about ten past nine. I thought about texting him, but he'd already said he'd be late, and it would irritate him. He'd say I was nagging. About an hour later he sent a text to say he wasn't coming back. He'd decided to sleep on the boat. I picked at the chicken then called room service to ask them to remove the plates. Ellis would *not* have been happy had he come back this morning to find the room smelling of stale food.' She gave a little smile at the thought, as if this was one of his endearing little quirks.

'When did you start to get worried about him?' Gus asked.

'I tried to call him this morning as soon as I woke up, just to check if he'd had a good night. He didn't respond, so I sent a text, asking him if he was okay. He didn't respond to that either, so I wandered down to the jetty. I knew he had to still be on the boat, because the tender was tied up to it. That's when I asked if the hotel could send someone out to check on him. I had no way of getting out there, you see.'

Gus gave her a sympathetic smile. 'And it's not exactly swimming weather, is it?'

Celia shook her head. 'It wouldn't have mattered if it was the Caribbean Sea. I can't swim. I'm terrified of the water.'

'But you've got a yacht?' Stephanie said before she could stop herself.

'It's Ellis's yacht, and yes, being mid-ocean is rather traumatic. But I'm learning to face my fears.'

Celia was beginning to wonder when this torture would be over. She just wanted the detectives to go, so it was a relief when DCI Brodie got a call on his mobile and stepped outside. DS King offered to order more coffee, but Celia said she would use the capsule machine and make it herself. She needed something to do.

In no doubt that she'd already said too much, she could sense that the detectives had read more into her words than she intended. It would have been far better if she'd stressed Ellis's qualities rather than hinting at his failings, although that might have been a challenge.

DCI Brodie was still outside, leaving Celia alone with DS King. *Why did it have to be her?* After all the detective witnessed last weekend, it felt as if she could see every secret lurking under

Celia's skin. She had to try to direct their attention away from Ellis.

'When can I get back to the children, Sergeant? I need to be the one to tell them what's happened to their father. They mustn't see this on the news.'

'These are your stepchildren?'

Celia felt the stab she always felt when people referred to them as that, almost as if it made them less important.

'Yes, but as far as I'm concerned, I'm their mum.'

'I get that.' The softening of the sergeant's expression showed that she understood, and Celia let out a slow breath.

'Sorry,' she said. 'It's just that they're my whole world, and I'm terrified about what will happen now. I have no rights at all, you see.'

'You didn't adopt them then, when you married their dad?'

'I wanted to, more than anything, but Ellis said it was unnecessary. An additional bit of bureaucracy.' She fought to keep the bitterness from her tone.

'Did you apply for parental responsibility?'

Celia shook her head and looked down at her fingers, tying and untying the drawstring of her hoodie. How could she tell this detective that Ellis had point-blank refused to let her? He was well aware that she would move heaven and earth to stay with the children, and without any legal ties to them she was bound to him by the strongest of ties. If leaving him meant leaving them, she was going nowhere.

'Who's looking after them now, Celia? Is it okay if I call you Celia?'

'Yes, of course. The children are with their nanny. Jeanette's a good soul, and she loves them, but it's not her job to tell them about their father. I think that's asking too much.'

'We could ask the local police and social services to go and talk to the children, with the nanny there.'

Celia shook her head. 'Sergeant, these children have already lost their mother. Savannah doesn't remember her at all, and Reece only vaguely. He was three when Vivian died. Lacey remembers, although Ellis thought it best for her not to dwell on it and she never speaks about it. But I know she still has nightmares.'

She was about to share with DS King her concerns about Ellis's rule of silence about the events of that day, but inside her head a voice was shouting, *Stop talking, Celia. Shut up NOW!* So she folded her arms and leaned back heavily in her chair. 'Anyway, none of this matters. I'm only telling you because you need to understand how important it is that I get back to the children.'

She looked at the detective's face. Her brow was furrowed and somehow Celia knew what was coming next.

'It's DCI Brodie's call. But it's unlikely he'll be happy to let you leave until we understand what happened to your husband.'

'He's *dead*! What else do you need to know?'

At that moment the DCI walked back into the room. Celia could see that he'd heard her outburst.

'I'm sorry, Mrs Cobain, but your husband's death is unexplained. And we'll need to ask you to formally identify the body, I'm afraid.'

Celia went cold. She didn't want to look at Ellis. She didn't want to see his face. She had a horrible feeling his eyes would pop open and stare at her.

The chief inspector's voice brought her back into the room. 'And I know this might be difficult to accept, but as DS King says, we'll have to ask you to remain here in Cornwall for the time being.'

A wave of icy panic surged through her as she stared at the senior detective's solemn face. *What do they know?*

18

Stephanie and Gus questioned Celia Cobain for another thirty minutes, then, warning her that they would probably want to talk to her again, headed back towards the hotel.

'I'm starving,' Gus said. 'The hotel has made us some sandwiches.'

Stephanie hurried along by his side, trying to match his stride. Food would be good; she'd already finished the chocolate biscuits.

'What weren't you saying in there, Gus? Would you really stop her from going home to see her kids?'

'Unfortunately there are too many questions we don't know the answers to. Didn't you think it strange that she didn't ask how he died?'

'She probably thought he'd had a heart attack. Surely that's not enough for you to suspect her of being involved?'

'Come on, Steph. Family first, as you know, when there's a suspicious death. More to the point, she says he sent her a text. But Tai called. That's who I went outside to talk to. There's no sign of a mobile.'

'But we know he sent her a message. She showed us on her own phone.'

Gus sighed. 'She did, and I've requested historical GPS data to see if his phone was on the boat at the time the text was sent. Should be pretty accurate, given the lack of obstruction between the boat and satellites. If it's still switched on we might be able to trace it. Fortunately Celia agreed to us taking her phone to check his other messages.'

'What's the plan for letting her get back to the children?'

Gus stopped walking and turned towards her, the weight of his decision written all over his face. 'I know you feel for this woman. The idea that she chose two dishes her husband might like and was prepared to eat the one he found less appealing was . . . Well, let's just say you actually twitched when she said that. I don't want to keep her from her kids, and I'm fairly certain she's not a homicidal maniac. But what if I'm wrong? What if I let her go and she harms the children? We'd be pilloried for that, and rightly so.'

Stephanie wanted to object, but she understood what he was saying. While it seemed unlikely to her that Celia would hurt them, she recognised she was basing that assumption on a one-hour conversation.

'So what will you do if she just decides to leave?'

'I'll have to find sufficient grounds to retain her as a suspect – arrest her, if necessary, and put a child protection order in place; bail her on condition that she doesn't see them. But let's hope it doesn't come to that.'

'Do you actually *have* any grounds for suspicion? We don't even know how he died yet.'

'True, but while it's unexplained we have to treat it as suspicious, and we both know which way this is heading – missing phone, the petechiae, the marks on the neck. We may not have any evidence against Celia Cobain, but it's clear there was animosity in that relationship, and we don't have grounds for suspecting anyone else. Can you think of anything that you witnessed last weekend that might point to other suspects?'

Stephanie was silent for a moment, then shrugged. 'Other than the inappropriate touching which we need to follow up on, and Celia's submissiveness, I can't think of anything. I only saw him once in the bar, and then in their room. I wish I had the answer, then at least she could get back to her kids.'

'Yep, I'm with you on that. There's a bigger question, though. If someone else was on that boat with him last night, how did they get back to shore? The tender was still there, and the hotel has confirmed that its RIB was in a locked boathouse, with the key held in an office in the main building.'

'And Celia says she can't swim.'

'Yes. She made rather a point of telling us that, didn't she?'

Stephanie looked at Gus. He never missed anything, and suspected everything. It frightened her sometimes.

'Come on,' he said. 'A quick bite and then we should get on with interviewing those that Cobain knew best. I've got Ayaneh working on gathering intel.'

Stephanie remembered her from the Lola Holland case. 'She's good. Is she still a PC?'

'No, she's training to be a detective, and then I guess we'd all better watch out. She's a smart cookie. Let's see if there's anything in Cobain's finances that might lead us anywhere. And Molly has promised to do the PM this afternoon, so we might get something from that.'

The police had gone, and Celia felt she could breathe again. They had asked her permission to search the suite, but the request was only a formality. If she had refused it would have suggested guilt and it would only have been a matter of time before they obtained a warrant.

She'd asked if it would be okay for her to leave the room, to go for a walk, to be out of their way while they searched, and they had agreed on condition that she didn't stray too far from the hotel in case they wanted to speak to her again.

'I'll be out for about an hour, if that's okay?' she'd asked. 'I'd really like a bit of time alone. I'm sure you understand.'

Promising not to speak to any other guests, should any of them have disobeyed the police instructions to remain in their rooms, she set off along the winding track that ran above the shoreline towards Trevellyn, a small village – little more than a hamlet – nestled in a secluded cove with a tiny harbour just over a mile away. She wasn't going that far, though. Even if she'd wanted to, she wasn't sure she would make it. Her knees felt as if they were made of jelly, her legs threatening to buckle with every step, but there was one thing she had to do while she had the chance.

Once clear of the hotel, Celia stopped and glanced around. The track was lined either side with vegetation beginning to die back ahead of winter, and to her left the land banked steeply down to a rocky stretch of shoreline.

She could see a break in the shrubs just ahead, exactly where she knew it would be, and spun round again. There was no one behind her so she veered off the track and took the narrow path that led down a steep slope, a route she'd found terrifying only days ago.

As soon as she was certain she couldn't be seen, Celia put her hand deep into the pocket of her hoodie and pulled out a small black phone, one the police didn't know about and must never find. She wanted to hurl it into the sea, but the tide was too far out and she couldn't help wondering if perhaps she might need it again.

The police hadn't asked to search her, but she had left her handbag in the room so they could look through it if they wanted to, hoping this suggested she had nothing to hide. They had no idea that the deep patch pocket on the front of her hoodie was hiding a tiny mobile phone that only two other people knew about. But she couldn't keep it with her, just in case. With a last furtive look back up the path, Celia crouched low and pushed the phone under a gorse bush, barely feeling the sharp prickles tear at her skin. She checked the bush from every angle. The black phone couldn't be seen against the dark earth.

She stood up. There was still no one in sight.

With a sigh of relief she climbed back up the track to the main path and turned towards the hotel. All she wanted to do now was get back into bed, pull the covers over her head and stay there until this was over and she could get back to the children.

19

Russell has been bobbing up and down every few minutes to look out of the window, and I'm relieved because it means that for most of the time he has his back turned, unaware of the storm that's raging inside me. It's taking every ounce of my strength to hold myself together, and I thought I would lose it completely when he turned away from the window and bowed his head half an hour ago.

'What?' I said, confused by his strange stance.

'Stay where you are, darling. They're bringing him through the courtyard now.'

I gulped back a sob, the reality hammering into me and Russell looked at me with concern.

'Poor Celia,' I said, as if that was the reason for my distress, rather than the the icy grip of fear.

It wasn't supposed to be like this. The thought pounded relentlessly in my head.

Russell waited until he was certain the trolley bearing the body bag had been wheeled past, then he was back at the window. He hates the fact that he doesn't know what's going on and is frustrated that his day has been disrupted. His sole purpose for being here is to persuade Nadia Shariq to join the agency, but he hasn't managed to get her to sign a contract yet, and he'd been planning to walk to the village to see her today, to ask her why she was hesitating.

'It's a great deal,' he said to me after his first meeting with her. 'She seems excited but distracted. I don't know what else I can do to persuade her.'

He thinks today is his last chance, so he spent yesterday afternoon perfecting the contract terms, using the business centre in the hotel to print out a copy on what he called their 'posh paper' in the hope that Nadia can be persuaded to sign before we have to leave.

'If she doesn't agree today,' he told me before our brunch was interrupted, 'I'll leave the contract with her and get someone else to speak to her – perhaps someone more persuasive.'

Russell had looked glum at the thought that he might have failed to win over Nadia, and despite the tangled web of anxiety tying knots in my gut, I felt for him.

I wanted to make excuses for her, but I'm not supposed to know her.

'It should have been quite straightforward, according to Raoul. He said she was keen when he spoke to her, so I'm not sure if I've somehow put her off. I've done a bit of research, and it seems her past is a little unclear. Perhaps that's the problem. Anyway, I've got Raoul checking her out.'

I'd wanted to urge Russell to let it drop, to base his decision on her voice, not her past. But I couldn't do that. Just one more thing I had to keep from my husband.

Now he's at the window again, peering out.

'Hey, Juliette, come here a moment.'

I give a theatrical sigh to hide my fluttering breath. 'Why? Is something happening?'

'Not really, but those two detectives, if that's what they are,

are walking through the courtyard. They've just come from Celia's room. Remember I said one of them looked familiar? I remember now. She was here last weekend. Come and have a look.'

I can't refuse. He won't understand why, and it will be one more example of odd behaviour from me. This was supposed to be a time for us to spend together away from distractions. It hasn't turned out the way he'd hoped, mainly because the biggest distraction in my life appeared at the hotel on our very first night.

I go to the window, trying to appear indifferent to what's going on. Inside I am screaming, *What's happening? What have the police found?*

A man who looks to be late thirties with broad shoulders and dark wavy hair is striding along, a woman with a slim face and a generous mouth hurrying at his side.

The breath catches in my throat. *It's her!* It's the woman who found me propped up against a washbasin, trying to pull myself together after Ellis had left me quivering with despair at the fact that he was here, at the hotel. I made a point of telling her I'd only just met him, but I could see she didn't believe me.

Shit, shit, shit!

As the two detectives walk past us towards the hotel, the woman glances towards our window and I step back quickly.

'It *is* her, isn't it?' Russell asks, and for just a moment I wonder if he's read my mind and knows about our meeting in the ladies' bathroom.

I turn away from him so he can't see my face and go back to the sofa.

'She looks familiar,' I say. 'No doubt we'll find out soon enough.'

My nonchalance is impressive, but I can feel my cheeks flushing and drop my head to my book.

Why is she here? What am I going to say?

They will ask if we had met Ellis Cobain before this week. Russell thinks he introduced us, and Ellis made a point of feigning delight at meeting me, enjoying my discomfort, before I had chance to concoct a story about how I might have known him. I was too horrified at the fact he was here to think of anything, but it was a huge mistake. If we had admitted to having met, perhaps at an event, this would now be so much easier. But that wouldn't have suited Ellis. He loved every moment of the agony I was going through.

I feel a bead of sweat trickling down my spine. *How much will I have to admit? How can I explain the lies to my husband?*

Despite everything that has happened since, my first meeting with Ellis all those months ago had been completely innocent. He had been invited to the reopening of a restaurant after its refurbishment, and I was the interior designer. We were introduced, and he piled on the charm.

At the time his attention was exactly what I needed. I'd wanted to escape my life, my unhappiness and my guilt, and Ellis's words were the balm I thought I needed. When he asked if I would consider giving him some ideas for the apartment he had recently bought in the Harbourside area of Bristol, I jumped at the chance.

'It's just a pied-à-terre, a place to stay when I need to be in the city,' he'd told me.

It seemed like a great opportunity and I would normally have rushed home full of excitement to tell Russell all about it, had things between us not been so strained. But Russell was away on business and it felt wrong, somehow, for me to have anything to celebrate. So I said nothing, instead allowing Ellis to charm me, to make me feel that I had some value in this world – something I had been struggling with for weeks.

And then, of course, it became impossible to tell Russell anything, or even to mention Ellis's name.

Six Months Earlier

I was thrilled that a man as well connected as Ellis Cobain was interested in my ideas for his apartment. Opportunities like this didn't come along often, and if I did a good job for him I hoped he might spread the word with his contacts. So it was with a sense of eager anticipation that I arrived in the lobby of his apartment building to be told by the doorman to take the lift to the top floor.

Knowing Ellis as I do now, I'm certain he underplayed both the size and location of the apartment because he wanted to see the surprise on my face when he opened the door to the modern penthouse with its huge terrace looking out over the water.

'Wow,' I whispered, stunned by the view from the entrance right through the living room and out through the bi-fold doors.

The apartment was filled with light, even on a gloomy day, and whatever his plans for this place, it was rather more than a pied-à-terre.

'What do you think?' Ellis asked, smiling at my expression of awe. 'Come on, I'll show you round.'

Ellis looked different to the man I'd met at the restaurant opening. That night he had exuded formal sophistication in a smart suit. At home in his apartment he was dressed casually in dark blue trousers that hung in a way that suggested impeccable tailoring. The cuffs of his white linen shirt were rolled up to just below the elbow, and I had a feeling I would never see him in anything as ordinary as jeans and a T-shirt.

Ellis closed the door behind me, and I stood transfixed, imagining how I could further improve this fantastic space. The architect had created a vast open-plan area suitable for entertaining, with an ultra-modern kitchen at one end of the room, but as we moved through the apartment, I realised that the need for smaller, cosier, areas hadn't been overlooked, with a room Ellis referred to as his snug, and a home office. Ellis showed me into the first of the two bedrooms and leaned casually against the door jamb, arms folded, feet crossed at the ankles, smiling as I took it all in.

'Like it?' he asked as I stepped into the en suite.

'It's fabulous.' And it was.

It was clear this hadn't been designed as a family home. It was a home for an affluent individual or couple, with space for the occasional guest. It was also an amazing opportunity for me. I couldn't mess this up.

I was surprised that there were already odd bits of furniture scattered around: a couple of comfortable leather armchairs, a huge TV, two bar stools by the kitchen island and a super-king-size bed in one of the bedrooms.

'I'm not quite living here yet,' Ellis told me. 'Sometimes I get bored with hotel rooms, though, and even the suites seem to confine me. On those days I come here, spend some time on the terrace watching the water, and I have space to roam.'

If this were my apartment, I wouldn't be bothering with even the fanciest of hotel suites.

'Come and sit down, Juliette,' he said, pointing to one of the armchairs. 'Tell me all about yourself and how you became an interior designer.'

He listened attentively as I tried to sell myself to him, nodding every now and again to show he was listening.

'I must admit that I've only just branched out into larger properties. I used to work for a company, but good as they were I didn't think they were ambitious enough with their designs. I'm really keen to give you my ideas, Mr Cobain, and I can source all the items for you, although I'm not well enough established to purchase on your behalf. If that's a problem, please tell me before I get too excited about this project.'

'That's no problem at all, and it's Ellis, by the way. I don't think we need to stand on ceremony, do we? And I must apologise for being rude. I was so interested in hearing your story that I totally forgot to offer you a drink. I can do black coffee – I have a fancy machine but no milk – or . . . what do you say to a glass of wine to celebrate your new project?'

I was too stunned to speak for a moment. I hadn't even shared any ideas – only my background. Was he offering me the contract?

He stood up and walked over to the kitchen, heading towards a built-in wine fridge. I followed, unable to find the right words.

'Don't look like that, Juliette,' he said, selecting a bottle of white wine and studying the label. 'I like you. You appear to be a genuine person, although if I may say so, you seem rather sad. When you're not talking about work, you look a little melancholy. If we're going to be working together closely – and I really do want to be involved in every detail – is there anything that will drag you away from the project? Anything I need to know about?'

He looked so sympathetic, and as he passed me a glass of wine, he touched my hand gently.

I blinked, hoping I wasn't about to embarrass myself by

crying. 'No, honestly, I'm fine. I had some bad news a few weeks ago, but it's nothing to do with work and it won't stop me giving one hundred per cent to this job.'

Ellis lifted his glass to mine and chinked gently. 'Here's to working together, then. If you need to talk, you'll find I'm a good listener. I'm no stranger to unhappiness.' He dropped his gaze. 'My first wife died tragically. I have three beautiful children, but it's not been easy helping them get over their loss at the same time as dealing with my own.'

Instinctively I reached out to touch the bare flesh of his arm. His eyes lifted to mine as he put down his glass and covered my hand with his own.

I should have left then and never returned.

20

According to Celia Cobain, the person Ellis had spent most time with during their stay was Russell Dalton, and as Gus munched on a chicken sandwich he suggested he should be their first interviewee.

Stephanie reached for her phone.

'What are you doing?' Gus asked.

'Trying to find a photo of Dalton and maybe his wife. I want to know if I recognise them from when I was here.'

'Does that matter?'

'Maybe. I'll tell you when I've found them. According to hotel records they're from Bristol.' Stephanie had her head bent over her phone as she spoke, scrolling through some images. 'There! Found them. Well, I've found him, but there's a link to his wife. I thought it might be them.'

'You thought *what* might be them?'

'The woman I told you about, the one Cobain touched. It's Juliette Dalton, and honestly, Gus, she flinched but she didn't say or do anything, as if she didn't want to draw attention to what was happening. If she'd only just met him, she'd have reacted differently. I'm sure of it.'

'Maybe she didn't want to make a scene.'

Stephanie scoffed. 'The days are long gone when a woman has to allow herself to be groped by a stranger out of fear of attracting negative attention. I'd have whopped him one.'

'I don't doubt that for a second,' Gus said with a chuckle.

'And anyway, I found her in the ladies' later. She was clearly upset, and she made rather a point of telling me that one of the men she was with was her husband, but she'd only met the other man that night. She was referring to Cobain, and it seemed an unnecessary explanation.'

'So what's your thinking?'

'Play it by ear. If she's lying about something, let's see how she responds to the questions, but at some point I think we should question them separately. There may be things she doesn't want her husband to know.'

'Sounds intriguing. Let's just get some basic facts and take it from there.' Gus wiped his hands on a napkin. 'You not eating?'

'Not just now. The manager mentioned something about afternoon tea in a couple of hours, so I might just save myself for the cakes and scones.'

Gus laughed and got to his feet. 'Come on then.'

'They're here,' Russell says from his position by the window. He scurries back across the room to sit beside me on the sofa.

'What are you doing?' I hiss.

'They're walking through the courtyard. I'm sure they're coming here. I don't want them to know I was watching.'

My heart skips a beat. 'He probably had a heart attack, Russ. He drank like a fish and certainly seemed to enjoy rich food,' I say, needing to find a plausible explanation for Ellis's death. Something unsuspicious.

Russell looks baffled. 'I didn't think he drank excessively.'

Fortunately I don't need to respond because there's a knock on the door.

Russell jumps to his feet and strides across to open it, while I try to focus on my breathing, taking long, slow breaths.

'Mr and Mrs Dalton, I'm DCI Brodie and this is my colleague. You may recognise DS King – she was staying here last weekend. May we come in, please?'

'Yes, of course. Please, have a seat.'

I can't bring myself to look at DS King. I feel as if she will see right into my soul, so I focus on the chief inspector instead.

In preparation for their arrival, Russell has arranged chairs either side of the sofa because it seems more informal and not so intimidating. He's edgy, nervous, and I don't really understand why. I need him to be strong, because I feel on the verge of collapse.

'Can we make you a cup of coffee?' Russell says, pointing to the Nespresso machine in the drinks nook.

'We're fine, thank you. I'm sorry we had to ask everyone to stay in their rooms for the time being, but there were a few procedures we needed to complete.'

I assume he's talking about the removal of Ellis's body, and I wish now that I had watched it go by, if only to convince myself that he really is dead. I can still sense his presence, hovering just out of sight, and I feel certain that, one way or another, he's not done with me yet.

'Also, it's important that we get everyone's individual version of events.'

Russell sits forward eagerly. 'Yes, I imagine if guests and staff had the chance to chat, their perceptions might be influenced by other people's memories. I'm a lawyer, you see. I don't deal in criminal law, but it makes perfect sense.'

Russell is prattling. He's uncomfortable. His plans have been disrupted, which he hates. He will have had the day mapped out, every detail covered, and he casts a surreptitious glance at his watch, knowing he's no longer in control of his own time.

'I'm sure you're aware that there was an incident this morning,' DCI Brodie says. 'I'm sorry to confirm that Ellis Cobain was found dead on his yacht earlier today.'

They must realise we have already guessed as much, but my head is spinning and it's all I can do not to blurt out, *Who told you to go to the yacht? What else did you find?*

I search my mind for what might be a normal reaction.

Russell glances at me, but I can't speak. 'Did Celia find him?' he asks.

'Mrs Cobain was concerned when he didn't return from a night on board. He wasn't responding to calls or texts, so she asked the hotel to send someone out to make sure he was okay.'

I feel my whole body twitch. *She did what?*

The detective carries on talking. 'We wanted to speak to the two of you first because I gather that during the week you've spent quite a bit of time with Mr and Mrs Cobain.'

'Mainly with Ellis, isn't that right, darling?' Russell turns to me and I force myself to nod, still lost in alarm that Celia sent someone to the yacht.

'Not Mrs Cobain?' the sergeant asks.

'No. I don't think she's been too well, and I gathered from Ellis she's not particularly comfortable in company. She finds it all a bit intimidating, although we did our best to make her feel at ease, didn't we?'

Russell turns to me again, and I feel like a nodding dog. It's time I spoke, to show them that I'm comfortable with their questions.

I cough to clear my throat. 'I think she was missing the children.'

'Had you met Mr Cobain before you came here?' Sergeant King asks. She is sitting to my left and I know I should look at her as I answer, but I can't. I also know that although she appears to be directing the question at both of us, she means me.

'No.' Russell jumps in and I breathe again. 'It was such a pleasant surprise to find him here. I'd heard of him, of course. He's in line for some honour from the King, you know, for all his philanthropy.' He pauses. 'Sorry, obviously I should have said *was*. Anyway, he runs – *ran* – a foundation to support the arts, particularly music. Spent a considerable portion of his fortune every year, I understand.'

'Do you know how he died?' The words burst from me before I can stop them. I can't bear this for another moment and I have to know what they suspect.

'We're still looking into that,' DCI Brodie says unhelpfully. 'In the meantime, we need to know everyone's movements for yesterday evening.'

That says it all, really. They wouldn't need to know where we all were if they believed his death was due to natural causes. I lock my icy fingers together so no one can see them shaking.

Stephanie had been watching Juliette closely since they arrived, and hadn't failed to notice the nervous clutching of her fingers. Now she was turning her wedding ring round and round. And she hadn't once looked Stephanie in the eye.

'Can you talk us through your movements last night, please,' Gus asked, 'and any interactions you may have had with Mr Cobain. When was the last time you saw him?'

Russell Dalton glanced at his wife. 'We didn't see him yesterday evening, did we, darling?'

'No. We saw them at lunch, but only to say hello. I remember they were leaving the restaurant as we arrived.'

'Yes, that's right. And Celia came into the bar yesterday evening while she was waiting for Ellis to come back from the yacht. She said he'd gone out to secure something or other – I'm not sure what.'

Gus nodded. 'You said previously you hadn't had much contact with Mrs Cobain, so was this unusual behaviour for her?'

Stephanie watched as Juliette glanced at her husband, then back at her hands as she spoke.

'Russell didn't mean we *never* saw Celia. She just wasn't a very social animal. She joined us for drinks occasionally, with her husband.'

'Once,' Russell said, frowning. 'In the whole week it was just once, Juliette. And we spoke briefly when they passed our table in the restaurant.'

Gus nodded. 'But you saw much more of Mr Cobain?'

'Yes. He joined us most nights for drinks, and when his wife arrived they would go into dinner. On the nights she wasn't feeling up to it, we invited him to eat with us. It felt unkind to leave him on his own.'

Juliette had her head down the whole time her husband was talking, but she appeared to give herself a mental shake and abruptly sat upright, a forced smile on her lips. She was playing a part, and Stephanie didn't know what it was.

'Talk us through yesterday evening, as far as you can,' Gus said.

'That's quite straightforward,' Russell said. 'I went to the bar at just after six for an early evening cocktail. Ten past six, to be precise. I was surprised when Celia arrived on her own a little later. She seemed a bit lost, so I asked if she wanted to join me. I was even more surprised when she said yes. She said she was waiting for Ellis.'

Gus turned to Juliette. 'You weren't with your husband, Mrs Dalton?'

'Not at that point, no. Since we've been here I've got into the habit of going for a run before dinner. I'm not used to so much sitting around.'

'Isn't it dark at that time since the clocks went back?' Stephanie asked.

'I have a head torch.'

'Okay. Carry on, please, Mr Dalton.'

'Celia was with me when she got a text from Ellis. He said he would be longer than anticipated, so she should have dinner without him.'

'Any idea what time this was?' Gus asked.

'Yes, I checked my watch. 7.15.'

'And were you back from your run by this time?' Stephanie asked, gaining herself a black look from Gus. They had agreed he would ask the questions, but she couldn't help butting in.

'Yes, but I came back here for a quick shower and change. I joined them in the bar at about 7.30.'

Russell looked slightly bemused by this response. 'A bit later, darling. If you remember, we'd booked dinner for eight, and you weren't back by quarter to, so I asked them to delay our reservation until 8.30 to give you time for a drink.'

Juliette's lips tightened slightly. 'Fine. I'm not much of a clock watcher. Either way, we asked Celia to join us for dinner, but she wouldn't. When Ellis still wasn't back by 8.30, she decided to return to their suite.'

Gus made a note in his notebook. 'So you had dinner?'

'Yes,' Russell answered. 'We stayed late in the restaurant because there's a singer here I've been trying to sign to our agency. Her second set finished some time after eleven.'

'And you didn't see Mrs Cobain again?'

'I didn't,' Russell said. 'Did you see her, darling?'

Juliette blinked. 'I was with you, Russ. How's that likely?'

'I meant when you came back to the room. I thought maybe you'd bumped into her.'

'You left the restaurant, Mrs Dalton?' Gus asked.

Juliette shook her head. 'I didn't come back to the room.'

The look of surprise on Russell's face was wiped as quickly as it appeared. 'Sorry, I thought . . . You know, when you spilt your wine? You said you were coming back to sponge the stain.'

'Oh, *that*.' She turned to Gus. 'I knocked over a glass of wine and it splashed my shirt. I told Russell I needed to come back and change, but in the end I just nipped into the ladies' and sponged it. It was only white wine, and I rinsed it off and held my shirt under the dryer for a couple of minutes.'

Stephanie watched the couple. Juliette was tapping her fingers against her leg. Russell's smile appeared glued to his face.

'What time was this?' Gus asked.

'Goodness, I've no idea. I think we'd finished eating and were waiting for the singer. But I didn't *leave* – I went to the bathroom and I was only out of the restaurant for around ten minutes, fifteen at the most.'

Gus turned to Russell. 'And is that your recollection, Mr Dalton?'

There was a line between Russell Dalton's brows despite the smile.

'Mr Dalton?'

'Sorry, miles away for a moment. Broadly speaking, that's as I remember things. It was just before ten when Juliette left. She was back before I'd finished my coffee.'

'And after the singer finished?'

'We came back here, didn't we? We were in bed before 11.30.'

'And neither of you left the room after that?'

Both the Daltons shook their heads.

Gus closed his notebook. 'Thank you for filling us in on yesterday evening. We may have more questions, but what happened last night is most crucial for now.'

As Gus stood up to leave, Stephanie spoke. 'One more question. Can I just check again? Are you certain that neither of you had met Ellis Cobain before you came here last weekend?'

Stephanie was watching Juliette closely as she shook her head. There was no mistaking the flush on her cheeks. Nor was there any way of missing the glance Russell Dalton threw his wife.

21

The detectives are leaving, but the woman knows I'm lying. Had it been any other detective, one who had never seen any of us before, there would have been no issue. Everything would have been straightforward. They would have believed I had only just met Ellis. But she saw me that night. She knew something had upset me, so it's far more complicated now. If she suspects that I knew him, she's going to check it out. And it won't be difficult to find the link between us, especially if she looks into my business accounts.

Will she go that far? Surely they'll only do that if I'm a suspect? I can't be, can I? Russell was clear that we were together from just before eight last night, apart from a missing fifteen minutes, so I should be in the clear. I'm desperate to know what they found on the yacht, but there's no way I can ask and obviously the interview is over.

Russell is showing them out when the sergeant turns back. 'In situations like this we often find it helps to interview couples separately. You may each have different perceptions of Mr and Mrs Cobain, and we might get a more rounded picture of them if we talk to each of you in turn.'

I stand rooted to the spot.

'I'm not sure that's necessary,' Russell says. 'I'm confident we have a similar view.'

'Nevertheless, when we've put together a timeline of events for yesterday evening and overnight, we may want to speak to everyone again.'

I force myself to speak. 'Are we allowed to leave the room now?'

The sergeant looks at the chief inspector. 'Yes,' he says. 'The other guests are being interviewed by our colleagues, but some of them may have ignored our request to stay in the hotel until after they've been spoken to, so we'd be grateful if you didn't discuss this with them.'

With that, they give us both a nod and head back out into the courtyard. Before Russell has a chance to turn to me, I'm heading for the bedroom.

'Where are you going?'

'I need some fresh air, Russ. I'm going for a walk.'

'Hang on. I'll come with you.'

I turn at the door. 'No, it's better if you follow up on your work. I might decide to run for a while too, and I know you hate that.' I give him a weak smile, but there's no ignoring his mystified look. 'Don't be disappointed in me, Russ. It's all a bit intense. The police seem to think there's something suspicious about his death, and I just need to run off the stress of being bloody interviewed.'

I try to make it sound normal, but he's not convinced.

'If there's a killer at large, Juliette, I'm not sure I want you running along deserted cliff paths on your own. Please don't.'

I have no more words, but whatever Russell says, I'm going. I've disappointed him so often in the last few months that one more time is probably neither here nor there, so I go into the

111

bedroom, close the door and lean back heavily against it, dizzy with a heady mix of fear, guilt and panic at what's to come.

My heart aches for my husband. We had been so close, so much in love, with everything to look forward to. Then my past came back to haunt me – haunt *us* – in the most devastating way, and instead of striving to make things better, I just made them worse.

And now the police will find out what I've done. Not all of it – at least I don't think so – but some of it. Inevitably that will mean Russell has to know too, and I can't bear the thought of the heartbreak. Perhaps it's better if I encourage him to be disappointed in me. Then, when he learns the truth, it might not be such a blow.

As I set off through the courtyard towards the barn at the far end where I am sure Celia is holed up, I am tempted to knock on her door. I need to talk to her, to know what happened, what the police have said. I have so many questions. But how much can I really trust her?

Could I pass my visit off as concern for a bereaved wife? That's reasonable, surely?

As I draw closer, I see a uniformed officer standing by the door and I can't risk it. The police probably want to be sure Celia isn't pestered, and the press must be gathering by now. Ellis was well known for what he referred to as his 'good works', although he wasn't really interested in music and the arts. He had inherited more money than he could possibly spend and craved recognition for his philanthropy. He had urged everyone he knew to propose him for a knighthood, and I had been appalled to learn some weeks ago that he'd gone further. He'd found a company that would – for a substantial fee – lobby to get the nominations required. Although it was a lengthy process he told me he was confident this was to be his year. I remember praying he was right, hoping a higher profile would make him want to lead a blameless life. Then maybe I could too.

Sir Ellis Cobain. The thought makes me want to puke.

As I run, I try to shut out my thoughts and focus on the dull thud of my trainers hitting the path, the wind on my face drying the tears I can no longer hold back. I breathe in the cool November air and feel the first dull ache in my calves, a reminder that I didn't stretch properly before I set off. I enjoy the pain. I deserve it. My breath becomes ragged, my chest heaving as I push myself harder, and a sob builds and bursts from me, an anguished wail that shatters the silence on the deserted cliff top. I stop, bend at the waist and grab my thighs. I want to sink to the ground, hug my knees to my chest and set free the tears that have been building for so many months.

How could I have allowed myself to be manipulated so easily?

I have no one to blame but myself. I thought Russell had withdrawn from me, that he was going to leave me. I was lost, but is that any excuse for allowing myself to be seduced by a man who oozed fake charm and promised the earth? I needed an ego boost, both personally and professionally, and Ellis, with a level of generosity that seemed to know no bounds, seemed to be the answer.

But he wasn't. He was anything but, and now he's dead.

Despite what it might mean for me, I'm so very glad.

22

Nadia Shariq was sitting in her favourite place on the front steps of her cottage, looking out beyond the small harbour to the endless horizon. She could hear her own breaths, short and sharp, as if she had been in a race.

What have I done?

Her emotions were raw, intense. She didn't know what to think, what to feel.

'*Shit!*' she gasped as she caught sight of Juliette, heading towards the narrow lane that led to her home.

Jumping to her feet, about to retreat into the house and lock the door, she saw Juliette stop and bend at the waist as if to get her breath back. Seizing the opportunity to escape before she was seen, Nadia bolted to the end of the lane, seething with frustration. How stupid was Juliette to turn up here?

The lane led to a winding path down to a tiny sheltered area of beach, out of sight of the village. Nadia sat on the sand, waiting until Juliette appeared, as she knew she would. A couple of minutes later she heard the pounding of feet.

'Why did you disappear?' Juliette asked, her voice laboured, punctuated by gasps as she struggled to catch her breath.

'Because I thought it was a crap idea to be seen talking to you. I'm sure neither of us is capable of pretending we're just having a friendly chat.' Nadia could hear the agitation in her voice and tried to calm down. 'What the fuck's going on, Juliette? The whole village is buzzing. I've been out of my mind.'

'What are they saying?' Juliette asked.

'That someone's dead – the guy with the fancy yacht. I don't have to be a genius to work out they're talking about Ellis, do I?'

'Of course it's Ellis. They haven't told us if they think it's suspicious, although as Russell says, the place wouldn't be crawling with police if it wasn't. The detectives have been to see us, and I'm panicking.' Juliette stood above Nadia, hands on hips. 'So I've got to ask: did you kill him, Nadia?'

Nadia felt an overwhelming urge to scream, but instead hissed, 'Don't you dare try to pin this on me. I could ask you exactly the same question. Was it you?'

'For God's sake, of course it wasn't.'

'Yeah, well, you're bound to say that, aren't you? I could be lying. You could be lying.' She shrugged.

Juliette was staring at her, and Nadia looked away, tears stinging her eyes.

'Whatever happened, Nadia, I need to know what you did with the burner phone?'

Nadia tutted. 'I've dealt with it! I said I would. And why are we talking about the bloody phone? Is that all you're worried about? You're just looking out for yourself! Tell me who found Ellis? What exactly did they find? Surely those questions are more important.'

Juliette crouched low. 'I don't know the details, but I believe Celia asked the hotel to send someone to check on Ellis when he didn't answer her texts.'

Waves of shocked disbelief shot through Nadia. 'She did *what*? Is she *insane*?'

'That's what I thought, but this is Celia we're talking about. I suspect she didn't know *what* to do.'

'Why the fuck didn't she go herself?' Nadia groaned. 'What did they find?'

'I don't know. No one's said a word. What the hell happened last night, Nadia? Did you stick to the plan, or was that never your intention?'

With a surge of hot anger, Nadia glared at Juliette. 'I stuck exactly to the script! Stop checking up on me, will you, or I'll start on you. *Christ*, what was Celia *thinking*! They must have found *something*!'

Juliette gave a frustrated shrug. 'They told us nothing. They're asking for our movements.'

'Well, you're okay then, aren't you? Unless there's something *you're* not telling *me*.'

Juliette's lips tightened. 'You're the one who started all this.'

Nadia scrambled to her knees and brought her face close to Juliette's. 'I've told you! Don't go pointing the finger at me, Juliette. You were in. Both of you. We all agreed.'

'Okay, okay!' Juliette held her hands up. 'What about Celia? How did she cope last night?'

Nadia shrugged and plonked herself back on the sand. 'She behaved much as I expected. Twitchy as hell, convinced she'd screw it up. She didn't think she'd be able to go through with it, but I kept telling her what would happen if she didn't, and that was infinitely more scary.'

Images of the previous evening flashed before her eyes, and for a moment Nadia couldn't speak. The silence hung between them, fraught with unspoken accusations.

'Have you seen her?' Nadia eventually asked.

Juliette lowered herself onto the damp sand as if the fight had drained out of her.

'No. I thought about it, but there's a police officer stationed at her door, and I don't think they'll let us speak alone. There's an issue, though. One of the detectives was staying at the hotel last weekend. She saw me, and I'm sure she doesn't believe I've never met Ellis before.'

'Holy *shit*! That's all we need. What did she say?'

'Not much, but enough.' Juliette's shoulders slumped, and Nadia felt a chill of unease.

'You have to hold it together, Juliette. You're not the only one with something at stake here.'

'Maybe not, but if Russell finds out, it will all have been for nothing.'

'Not quite nothing,' Nadia said and looked towards the woman hunched on the sand. 'What have they said about how he died?'

'They didn't tell us anything, but they obviously think it's suspicious.'

'No surprise there!' Nadia tutted. 'And you're certain they haven't said anything about what they found on the yacht?'

Juliette swivelled towards her. 'Nadia, I know bugger all, okay? I know they found his body this morning when Celia reported that he hadn't come back. I don't know why she didn't go to the yacht herself. I could strangle her, to be honest. God knows what the police found and what they'll make of it all. But she stayed on the shore, and I've no idea what they saw – if anything.'

Nadia chewed her bottom lip. It didn't make sense. 'Well, there must have been *something*!'

'Yeah, you don't say! But if there was, they're asking all the wrong questions, and I don't understand why.'

For a moment Nadia wondered if Juliette was telling her everything. How much could she trust her? 'You just have to hope they don't know who and what Ellis was to you. As far as they're aware, I've never met him and it has to stay that way. But you need to speak to Celia.'

Juliette's eyebrows shot up. 'How in God's name do you think I can do that? I told you – there's an officer on her doorstep. I bet they'll want to listen to any conversation we have. Look, Nadia, if they decide Ellis was murdered, they'll be looking for any relationships between any of the people involved, and they're bound to find out about you.'

Jumping to her feet, Nadia turned to face Juliette. 'No one knows anything about me. They can't link us, and that's the safest way for all of us, so for Christ's sake don't breathe a word to them. And don't come here again.'

23

I don't know what to make of Nadia's attitude, but she's kidding herself if she thinks the police won't find any connection between her and Ellis. I realise that for them to make the link they first need to know she's in the picture, and I worry about Russell's research into her background. He has no reason to mention what he finds to the police, but he might, if he thinks it's important.

They already know she was singing at the hotel last night, but I doubt Sergeant King will have seen her talking to Ellis last weekend. Nadia told me she didn't speak to him until Sunday afternoon, and by then the detective had probably left.

As I walk back towards the hotel, taking my time as I'm not eager to find myself back in our room waiting for the inevitable knock on the door, I remember the moment I met Nadia. Was it really only a few days ago that she crept up on Celia and me? We were talking quietly, trying to work out where our lives had gone wrong. Now I feel as if I've known both of them forever.

I met Celia first, and it's not a moment I enjoy looking back on. On our second day at the hotel Russell was eagerly anticipating his Sunday lunch, a feast the hotel was renowned for. I knew he'd have roast beef, even though he would pretend to consider all the options, and we had just sat down in the restaurant when Ellis walked into the room with a tall rake-thin woman trailing a couple of paces behind him. We couldn't see much of her face. She had dark shoulder-length hair with a thick, heavy fringe and seemed to be studying her feet as she walked.

Ellis stopped to say hello, and I felt my body stiffen as his gaze landed on me. Russell stood up and the two men exchanged a few comments about the food before my husband said, 'Is this your wife, Ellis?'

He held out a hand to Celia, who threw her husband an anxious glance. I noticed her eyes were puffy, as if she'd been crying.

'It is,' Ellis responded. He turned to his wife. 'This is Russell and his lovely wife Juliette.'

His wife shook hands with Russell and muttered, 'Pleased to meet you,' before giving me a small smile and a brief nod. She looked back at Ellis as if seeking his approval, and I wanted to leap up and drag her off to the bar for a drink. She looked as if she could do with one, and Ellis hadn't even bothered to tell us her name. Of course I knew it was Celia but was careful to say nothing.

Without another word they headed to their own table, but as they passed, Ellis touched my shoulder. To Russell, sitting opposite me, it would have looked like a friendly gesture, but he couldn't see Ellis's fingers digging into my flesh, testing me to see if I would squeal. He knew I wouldn't, because then an explanation would have been necessary. In any case, Russell had returned his attention to his menu and noticed nothing.

The same, however, wasn't true of Celia Cobain. She narrowed her eyes and tilted her head to one side as if trying to understand what she had just witnessed. I felt myself flush under her gaze and wanted to look away, but her features softened and there was a hint of a gentle smile around her mouth. I was stunned by her obvious sympathy. She had to realise this wasn't the action of a man who claimed to have just met me, and she must have noticed that I'd controlled my reaction for the benefit of my husband. But she seemed neither confused nor angry.

My eyes pleaded with her to be silent, and she gave me the slightest nod.

What was going on?

We didn't speak to them again during lunch, but by then I was not only wary of bumping into Ellis again, I was terrified of meeting his wife. Whether sympathetic or not, she knew there was far more to this than I was prepared to admit.

I don't know how I got through lunch that day. Russell was delighted with the food, although he could tell I wasn't entirely with him. Sadly, it was a situation he had become increasingly familiar with over recent months, but I tried my best to be chatty despite a tingling sensation in the back of my neck. It was as if Ellis's long fingers were reaching out to touch me, even though I knew he was seated at least five metres away. I couldn't wait for the meal to be over so we could escape.

After his roast beef, Russell wanted to indulge in his favourite Sunday afternoon pastime of taking a nap. He said that after so much food in the middle of the day it felt like the only option, and he was planning to make the most of it. He had drunk most of the wine as I had only sipped it, and I knew he would be out for the count for at least an hour.

I decided to walk down to the shore to watch the rolling sea, hoping the rhythmic beat of the waves would soothe my soul, but I was terrified I might bump into Ellis. I crept along the wall from our room towards the path down to the beach, my eyes flicking between the archway to the main hotel building and

121

Ellis's suite, and as I reached the end of the courtyard, I turned to look into the living area through the huge floor-to-ceiling windows.

Ellis was there. Standing feet apart, hands in his trouser pockets, watching me through the glass door, witnessing my fear. He was just metres away, and yet he made no move to open the door. His mouth curled up slowly, the smile lingering as if to say, 'I'll leave you for now, Juliette. But I'm not done with you yet.'

Wishing I was braver, that I was strong enough to march into his room and face him, I turned away and walked as calmly as I could towards the path, resisting the temptation to break into a run.

It was cold on the beach, an icy breeze whipping over the surface of the water, numbing the skin of my cheeks. I relished it. At the edge of the dunes the hotel had positioned a few benches, and I headed towards one I had discovered the afternoon before, nestled in a hollow, slightly protected from the elements. I would be cocooned there; no one would be able to see me, and I could give vent to the rage that was building inside me. I have always been a person who cries when angry, but rarely when sad. I suspect it's related to my childhood when tears were considered self-indulgent. At that moment, though, I felt a burning need to sob my heart out and scream into the wind. Head down, I trudged across the sand and turned into the dip between the dunes.

I looked up. Someone was already there, seated on the bench. *Celia Cobain.*

She was staring out to sea, and for a moment I wondered if she had seen me. Maybe I still had time to escape.

She didn't look my way, but she spoke, her voice soft and difficult to hear over the surf pounding on the beach.

'Would you like to sit, Juliette?'

Her tone was hesitant, as if she wasn't sure if she might be speaking out of turn, and I wondered if she was always like that. Then she glanced quickly over her shoulder, as if expecting Ellis to come striding over the dunes behind her.

I didn't know what to do. I could say that I was walking and didn't want to stop and sit, but then I thought back to her expression when she had seen how Ellis had touched me. So I made my way warily across the sand and lowered myself slowly onto the bench.

'It's okay,' she said quietly. 'Just tell me what he wants from you.'

24

Stephanie was on her own, at least for now. Gus was taking Celia Cobain to Truro to identify her husband's body and would send her back with a family liaison officer while he stayed for the post-mortem. He would be gone until early evening. It wasn't ideal, but he needed to gain the best possible understanding of what had happened to Ellis Cobain, and Stephanie was glad it was his responsibility, not hers. The post-mortem was her least favourite part of an investigation.

Some of Gus's team were still interviewing the staff and hotel guests, but in the crucial hours around Cobain's death it seemed no one had been out in the grounds of the hotel or near the bay where the yacht was moored. They were struggling to find connections between any of the guests and Cobain. He seemed to have limited his socialising to the Daltons. They needed to dig deeper.

According to Oscar Carne – the restaurant manager, who they had interviewed just before Gus headed off with Celia to Truro – on Thursday night, the night Cobain died, the bar had practically emptied after Nadia finished her set.

'There were just two people in the bar by midnight, and they were still here at 2 a.m.,' said Oscar, clearly trying hard not to look irritated by this.

'Does the bar not close?' Gus asked.

'No. Guests can drink till whatever time they like, although the vast majority realise it's unreasonable to keep people working through the night when they have fully stocked bars in their rooms.' He flicked the tea towel he was holding at an imaginary piece of dust on the table, as if hitting out at unreasonable guests.

Stephanie had resisted looking at Gus because she was scared she might giggle.

'And the singer? Did she leave straight after her set?'

Oscar looked puzzled for a moment. 'Yes, she did. More or less. I thought it strange that she scuttled off so quickly because she'd admitted to me there was a man here wanting to sign her up to some deal, but as soon as her set was finished she scooted out of the back door without another word.'

'And that would have been at what time?'

'Not sure, to be honest. Around 11.15, I think. Maybe just before. The man in question – Mr Dalton – came to my office asking to speak to Nadia. I told him she'd already gone, and he looked most disappointed. His wife said that maybe Nadia was wired after her performance and he could always catch up with her the next day – that's today, I suppose.'

'And they both left then?' Gus asked.

'Yes, that's right. The bar emptied soon after. Well, *almost* emptied,' he grunted.

'What about Mr Cobain? What did you make of him while he was staying here? Did he speak to anyone other than the Daltons?'

'If you'll pardon the expression, he was a showy bastard.'

Gus gave him a questioning glance.

'You know, the kind of guy who's flash with tips, but only

when he's trying to impress. If anyone was around, he'd chuck a twenty at the barman for pouring him a vodka martini. But he never added a tip to his bill when it was just him, or him and his wife. In fact, he could be downright rude, as if thank you wasn't in his vocabulary. He barely spoke to his wife on the odd occasion that she joined him, but he was Mr Jovial when the Daltons were around.'

His assessment didn't surprise Stephanie, but nor did it help. It seemed unlikely a member of staff had killed him because he was rude.

As Gus was leaving to attend the post-mortem, he suggested Stephanie should take a trip to the village to talk to Nadia Shariq.

'Find out which way she went home, Steph. If she walked, she might have seen something as she went through the courtyard. I gather that's the fastest way to the village.'

'Would she walk along the coastal path at midnight?' Stephanie asked. 'A bit dodgy, isn't it?'

Gus shrugged. 'Well, you would!'

'Yes, but I'm a tough police officer,' Stephanie said with a grin. 'Although maybe if you're a local it's normal.'

'Perhaps she'll think twice, if it turns out there's been a murder,' Gus said. 'Have a word with her, and then go through the timeline with Ayaneh – see if there's anything we're missing.'

'Do you have any objection if I have another word with Juliette Dalton?' Stephanie asked. 'Without her husband around?'

'I thought you might suggest that. Good idea.'

'I'll send Ayaneh to collect her. If Russell asks any difficult questions she can say she's just the messenger.'

'We should have Cobain's phone records by now, so perhaps see what you can pick up from there first – see if there's a connection. Maybe you should look at Celia's too. See what the general tone of their relationship was from the messages between them.'

With that Gus had set off to Truro, and having decided the starting point should be the Cobains' phone records, Stephanie went in search of Ayaneh.

25

Since I got back from my run, I haven't been able to settle. I need to be doing something – anything – to take my mind off all that's happened in the last week. Memories of that first meeting with Celia have stirred up too many emotions, and coupled with Nadia's aggressive attitude, I feel even more anxious than I did before I left the room.

I shouldn't have gone to the village. I should have stayed with Russell, who seems bemused by my restlessness. There are two deep grooves between his eyebrows, and he keeps chewing his lip. I don't know what to say to him, but I have to say something. I need to give him a glimpse of a happier future, a reminder of who we used to be.

'Hey, Russ, I know this hasn't turned out to be quite the relaxing week you had in mind, but what do you think about planning another holiday? A real one, where you don't have to work. We're already in November. Perhaps we could go somewhere warm this winter. The Maldives, maybe? What do you think?'

The look on his face nearly makes me cry. His eyebrows have shot up and he's beaming, and I realise it's the first positive thing I've said to him in months.

'Do you mean it? Really?' he asks, and I feel an ache at how little he trusts my word.

'Absolutely. We're stuck here for now and can't do much, so we could do a bit of research and planning. You've got your laptop.'

I jump up from the sofa and toss my book onto the coffee table.

As I walk towards the small table where he has his computer set up, I glance out of the window. A young woman has come into the courtyard through the arch from the hotel. She's looking around as if she's trying to find somewhere, and I'm certain she's not one of the guests. Then I realise she's heading for our door, and my heart pounds in my chest.

Before I can think what to say to Russell, there's a knock. He turns towards me, sees I'm frozen to the spot and without a word gets to his feet and opens the door.

'Hello,' he says in his usual warm, pleasant voice. 'Can I help you?'

'Sir, I'm Trainee Detective Constable Jafari. I'm here to ask Mrs Dalton if she wouldn't mind coming with me to talk to DS King.'

I can barely breathe. *Is this it?*

I don't know which I dread most: the police exposing my lies or Russell learning who he is really married to.

The young detective is looking at me, but Russell speaks, giving me a few seconds of breathing space. 'Can you give us a moment, please? I need to get some shoes on. If you'd like to step inside . . .'

'No, sir. DS King doesn't need to speak to you again at the moment. Just Mrs Dalton.'

'Why would that be?' he asks, his voice reasonable, but I can hear a slight tremor and know he's scared, although I'm certain he doesn't know what of.

'I'm not able to say, sir. I'm just here to escort your wife to the interview room.'

I take a gulp of air. I need to react. 'It's okay, Russ. I'm sure it's nothing to worry about. The sergeant probably wants as many individual perspectives as she can get.' I walk over to him and squeeze his hand. 'I'll be back soon.'

Giving my husband a watery smile, I follow DC Jafari out of the door.

Stephanie looked up as the door to the temporary incident room opened and Ayaneh ushered Juliette Dalton in, looking stylish in black jeans and a pistachio-coloured linen shirt. Her glossy blonde hair and subtle make-up gave her an air of self-assurance, but her face and body said otherwise. Juliette's glance darted round the room at the unfamiliar faces, and she looked awkward and uneasy as, shoulders slumped, Ayaneh guided her towards the small side office for her interview.

Stephanie followed her into the room. 'Mrs Dalton, I appreciate you coming in for a chat.'

Juliette attempted a smile as she took a seat, but Stephanie could see that her jaw was clenched, as were her fists.

'What can I do to help?'

'I asked to speak to you on your own because you and your husband both said Mr Cobain was a stranger to you, and I wasn't entirely convinced that was true.'

Juliette's eyes were focused on a spot somewhere above Stephanie's head.

'What makes you think that?'

Stephanie thought back to the moment of elation in the incident room when Ellis Cobain's phone records revealed who he had been calling. Stephanie, however, hadn't been surprised in the slightest.

Before Stephanie could tell her what they'd found, Juliette Dalton groaned.

'Forget I said that. I know there's no point denying it. I just don't want Russell to know. He'd be mortified.'

'Mortified that you know Mr Cobain?' Stephanie asked.

Juliette met her eyes for the first time, and Stephanie wondered if there might be a feeling of relief that she no longer had to keep up the lie. But then her gaze slid away.

'No, but he would be hurt that Ellis and I had shared a secret; that I'd hidden something from him. It was stupid. When we arrived here Ellis pretended we'd never met. I wasn't sure why he did that, but I was confused and played along with him. I don't know why. Things have been a bit . . . err, shaky generally, and I'd forgotten I hadn't told Russell that I met Ellis.'

'When you say "met", can you be a little more specific, Mrs Dalton?'

Juliette blinked. 'We were introduced at the opening of a restaurant. I'd designed the interior. That's what I do, you see.'

Stephanie nodded. 'Is that it? You met him once?'

'I may have seen him at some other events . . .'

Stephanie leaned back in her chair. 'You're going to have to tell me the truth, you know. I'm happy for now to keep this between us, but it seems it was a bit more than that. I have Mr Cobain's phone records here. Isn't this your mobile number?' She pushed a piece of paper across the table to a very pale-looking Juliette Dalton. One number, highlighted with an orange marker pen, appeared over and over again.

The woman's head dropped. 'I don't know what to say. God, what a mess! I can't bear it if Russell finds out.'

'Maybe he won't need to, if you tell me everything.'

Juliette sat, head bowed, clasping and unclasping her fingers. Stephanie waited.

'Ellis asked me to do some work for him – to design the interior of an apartment he bought in Bristol. Although he has a house in the country, he spends quite a bit of time at events that run into the evening, and he wanted a bolt hole. When he saw what I'd done with the restaurant, he offered me the opportunity. It happened when Russell was away on business, and by the time he came back – I don't know why – I'd decided not to tell him.'

'Because . . .?'

Juliette shrugged, and Stephanie sighed. 'Let's just get this over with, shall we? I saw your face when you arrived in the restaurant last Saturday and saw Mr Cobain. You looked horrified. I saw him touch you in a way that you didn't appear to enjoy, and then I found you rather distressed in the ladies' bathroom. So shall we stop talking in riddles?'

Juliette Dalton's eyes looked so haunted that for a moment Stephanie wondered if she had pushed her too far. But a man was dead, and whatever she thought of him, it was her job to find out why and how he died.

'It's complicated, Sergeant.'

'It always is. Just tell me what happened.'

Juliette dropped her head.

'When Ellis asked if I'd like to do some work for him, I was thrilled. He's well known in Bristol, and I thought he might bring me more clients if I did a good job. As Russell was away I didn't mention it when we spoke on the phone. I thought I'd keep it as a surprise for when he came home – some good news for once. I saw Ellis a few times during that first week to go through his ideas so I could come up with a possible scheme. Then he made a pass at me. I told him I wasn't interested – that this was a professional relationship. I decided it was better if I didn't tell Russell about the commission. I was scared he'd see through me, know something wasn't right, insist that I walk away, so I made a career choice to carry on working for Ellis. I thought I could control his advances.'

'And could you?' Stephanie asked.

'I think we developed an understanding. The reason you see my number on his phone is because he was calling me about the design. Nothing more exciting than that.'

Stephanie watched as Juliette struggled to swallow. She was lying through her teeth.

26

Celia was relieved to be back at the hotel. Terrified she would give something away, she'd managed to say as little as possible to the chief inspector as they drove to Truro. He respected her request to be left to her thoughts, although she sensed he was disappointed. He'd probably hoped to make the most of the opportunity to ask her more questions, but Celia had stared out of the side window, occasionally remembering to lift a handkerchief to dab her eyes.

The identification had been horrific. She'd been tempted to keep her eyes closed and simply say the words to confirm what they already knew – that it was Ellis who was lying dead on the table, waiting to be cut open by the pathologist. But the detective was watching her, probably to gauge her reaction, and he wouldn't have been disappointed. As the sheet was pulled back to reveal Ellis's head, she gasped, half expecting his eyes to open, his head to turn towards her with that smile of his, just as he had done a thousand times before to let her know that once again he'd won a battle she hadn't known she was fighting.

Throughout the journey back to the hotel, Celia had been unable to stop herself from shuddering every few moments, eliciting murmurs of sympathy and understanding from Kerry, the chubby, smiley family liaison officer tasked with driving her, as DCI Brodie had to remain in Truro. If only the young woman had known what Celia was really thinking.

Ellis is dead. He's really dead.

It had taken the sight of his body to convince her. Until then she had wondered if the past twenty-four hours had been nothing more than a hideous dream.

Now back in her suite, she trudged up the stairs and perched on the edge of the bed, clutching a pillow to her chest, her fingers like claws, digging into the soft cotton. Was her whole world about to collapse? Would she lose the children? She didn't know what the future looked like, and it was terrifying.

What if they talk to Nadia? What will she tell them? Do they know Nadia knew Ellis?

Celia tried to think back. Nadia was adamant that no one had seen her with Ellis. What if she was wrong?

Why did I ever think I could trust her?

And what about Juliette? If the detective sergeant hadn't been at the hotel last weekend, no one would have thought to ask if she and Ellis had known each other before the weekend. Russell believed he had introduced them, but Celia had realised the moment she met her that there was something going on between Juliette and her husband. She'd recognised the arrogant smile he always wore when he thought he had the upper hand. If Celia had noticed how Ellis behaved around Juliette, maybe Sergeant King had picked up on something too.

What a disaster!

Whichever way she looked at it, everything had gone wrong. Catastrophically wrong. She was a fool, just as Ellis had always said. She should never have invited Juliette to share her secrets when they met on the beach. She should have ignored Ellis's behaviour, as she had done so many times before, but the poor woman had looked deeply unhappy.

When Celia had blurted out, 'Just tell me what he wants from you,' Juliette had looked shocked and ashamed.

'Mrs Cobain, please, I don't know what to say. This is *dreadful*.'

Celia hadn't wanted to have the conversation, but she had to know the truth.

Blocking the hollow sound of Ellis's laughter from her mind, imagining his mockery, she'd taken a deep shuddering breath.

'My name's Celia, and I'm sorry but I'm not very good at this kind of thing. Not good at anything actually, but I do need to understand how things stand between you and my husband.'

Celia had no idea what she would have done if Juliette had admitted to being in love with Ellis. Perhaps she was just waiting for the right moment to tell her husband she was leaving him, but given her reaction to Ellis's behaviour in the restaurant, Celia doubted that was the case. She had to be sure, because if Juliette was about to steal her husband and children, she had to stop her.

She'd had a sudden terrifying vision of how Ellis would react if he found out she had spoken to Juliette. He would punish her when they got home in a way that only Ellis could, belittling her in front of the children, blaming her for being a useless wife, locking her in her room for days on end, telling the children she was ill – something contagious, so they couldn't see her. The girls would cry, but Reece, who sadly was beginning to believe his father's attitude to women was acceptable, would watch and learn.

Focusing on the sea in front of her, she'd finally managed to get the words out. 'You're having an affair with him, aren't you? Either that, or it's what he wants.'

To Celia's dismay, she felt Juliette's shoulders tremble, her soft muffled sobs barely audible above the rhythmic ebb and flow of the waves. 'I'm so sorry,' she gasped. 'I'm so ashamed and embarrassed.'

The knot in Celia's stomach tightened. Despite the cold breeze, she felt hot, a damp sweat settling on her body.

'Do you love him?'

'God, no!' Juliette had lifted her tear-swollen face to look at Celia. 'I hate him. I'm sorry – I know he's your husband – but I loathe and detest him. Nearly as much as I loathe and detest myself.'

Celia felt a pinprick of hope. 'So you're not going to leave your husband for him?'

Juliette choked out a hysterical laugh. 'Never, but Russell might leave me if he finds out.'

The two women sat in silence for a few moments, each trying to control their emotions.

'I am so very sorry, Celia. I can't forgive myself for what I've done, for the pain I've caused, and this is a dreadful way for you to discover that your husband's been unfaithful. I'd give anything for this not to have happened. I'm horrified that we're having this conversation and I won't blame you if you feel you have to tell Russell, although I hope and pray you won't.'

Celia's breathing had slowed, and she took a moment to pull herself together. 'You don't need to worry,' she said finally. 'The last thing I want is for you and your husband to separate. It might give Ellis hope.'

Juliette made a strangled scoffing sound. 'He can hope as much as he likes. There's no way in this world that I'll ever be with him.' She gave Celia an anxious look. 'Oh shit, I'm so sorry. I shouldn't be saying things like that to you. That's *terrible!*'

'It's not. It's good to know you don't want him.'

They were both quiet again, only the rhythmic thunder of the waves breaking the silence. Finally, Juliette spoke.

'I should never have had an affair with your husband – with *anyone's* husband – and I wouldn't blame you if you hated me. It was wrong. Whatever was going on in my life, I had no right to disregard your feelings. I'm more ashamed than I can possibly say.'

'I don't hate you for having sex with my husband. I would rather he had affairs with twenty women who want him for a fling than with one woman who wants to take him from me.' Celia paused, grasping the crystal in her pocket so tight that her fingers ached, praying that Juliette was telling the truth. 'I'm a bit puzzled, though. You don't seem like the kind of woman to have casual sex with a married man, so please tell me I haven't misread the situation, and you're not saying this to me because you want me to stop asking questions.'

Juliette turned towards her. 'Celia, this is the most mortifying situation I have ever found myself in, but I swear to you I don't want to steal your husband. I would rather, quite honestly, never see him again in my whole life.'

Celia's brow wrinkled. 'So why don't you tell him that?'

Juliette opened her mouth, then closed it again. 'It's complicated.'

'*How* complicated?' Celia persisted. She could hear Ellis's voice in her head, telling her not to be an irritating moron and to stop making something out of nothing. But this wasn't nothing. 'Listen, Juliette, if I can help you get my husband out of your life it will be to both of our benefits. I intend to keep him. Perhaps that doesn't make sense to you, but it does to me, so if I can do anything to break his hold over you, then tell me.'

Juliette lifted her hands to her cheeks and wiped away the

tears. 'How can you be so reasonable when I've hurt you so much? It's my problem, though, and I need to be the one to sort it. I just wish I knew how.'

Celia shook her head. 'It's not just your problem; it's my problem too. I want him out of your life, and I'll do whatever is necessary to make that happen.'

27

'It's official, Steph. Ellis Cobain was murdered,' Gus said, the sound of the car engine muffling his voice. 'I'll brief the team when I'm back, and we need to decide what we're going to do about Celia Cobain. I know she wants to get back to her children to break the news, but I've asked for a press embargo on the name of the victim. Not sure how long that will hold, but we'll talk to Celia when I'm back. In the meantime, can you have a word with her about her personal safety tonight?'

'You think she's at risk?'

'I don't know. We don't know why he was killed. Was it personal, or was it something he'd seen or done? And if so, did his wife have any knowledge of it? I think we should ask if she can be moved into the main hotel. It'll be easier to keep an eye on her there.'

Gus was right. The entrance to the Cobains' suite wasn't visible from any of the other rooms because it was on the gable end. It would be difficult to monitor access.

'Do you want me to tell her we believe he was murdered?'

'I need to talk her through everything we found, so I suggest you tell her we're still treating it as unexplained and I'll update her when I get there. You okay with that?'

'On my way,' she said. 'But Gus, you sound shattered, so please drive carefully.'

She could hear the smile in his voice. 'I will, don't worry. I'll see you soon.'

Celia had apparently refused to allow Kerry, the family liaison officer, to stay with her, and as she approached the far end of the courtyard, Stephanie saw a uniformed officer outside the door to the suite.

'Jason, I didn't know you were still here.'

'To be fair, you wouldn't, as I've not shown my face in the incident room. I've been standing here for bloody hours,' he said miserably, blowing on his cupped hands. 'It was okay when it was light, but it's sodding freezing now.'

Stephanie glanced towards the wall of glass casting a warm glow from inside the suite, and she felt for him.

'Go and get yourself a hot drink. We won't leave you here all night; we'll come up with a better plan. Meanwhile, the hotel will give you something to eat.'

Jason rubbed his hands together. 'Do you think they'll have a steak? I've heard they're epic here.'

Stephanie shook her head. 'I'm not in charge of the domestic arrangements, I'm afraid. You can ask, but whatever they give you, it will be good. You might want some soup – warm you up a bit.'

Jason curled his lip, obviously hoping for something a bit more exciting than a dish his gran might concoct. Stephanie grinned as he trudged back towards the hotel, grumbling to himself, as he often did.

Replacing her smile with something more sombre, she knocked on the door. Through the glass she could see Celia hunched on a dark blue sofa, grasping a glass of wine as if her life depended on it. She looked up briefly and signalled Stephanie to let herself in, dropping her eyes once more to her drink.

'Can I go home yet?' she asked despondently before Stephanie even had the chance to sit down.

'We'd prefer you to stay for now. DCI Brodie's on his way back from Truro and he'll want to talk to you. In the meantime, we wondered how you would feel about moving into the main hotel for the night.'

Her head shot up and two lines of anxiety appeared between her eyebrows. 'What? Can't I stay here?'

Stephanie took a deep breath. 'As you know, we're treating your husband's death as unexplained and we'd like to make sure you're safe.'

'You think someone might try to *kill* me? I don't think so.' She gave a nervous chuckle. 'I'm not interesting enough for anyone to want to murder me.'

'Can you think of anyone who would have wanted to harm Ellis?' Stephanie asked, intentionally using Cobain's first name.

Celia didn't meet her gaze. She shook her head slightly. 'How would I know? I'm no good at understanding people, so I don't think I'd recognise a motive.'

Stephanie wasn't sure she believed her, but Celia didn't seem confident enough in her own opinion to share any suspicions she might have.

'You may feel safe, Celia, and we hope that's the case. But even if no one is interested in hurting you, there may be something in this room that belongs to Ellis – something that might be of interest to a third party, so if you could just put a few things in a bag, we'll move you into a lovely room in the hotel.'

To Stephanie's surprise, Celia clamped her lips together. 'I don't want to move. I want to stay here. You've searched the room anyway, and you didn't find anything.'

'No, but it doesn't necessarily follow that no one will come looking. I could ask Kerry to stay with you tonight. She'd stay downstairs, out of your way. We can give you a panic alarm too, if you're concerned about anything. How does that sound?'

Putting her glass on the coffee table, Celia lifted both hands and rubbed them up and down her cheeks.

'I don't know. I don't want to move. I just want to sit here or lie on the bed. I want to be left alone. Kerry's very sweet, but there's no privacy in the mezzanine bedroom.'

She gave Stephanie a haunted look.

'Okay. I'll ask Kerry to stay with you until DCI Brodie gets back, and we'll bring you a panic alarm. He'll decide how best to make sure that you're safe, if you don't want to move. You can have your mobile back too.'

'Will he let me go back to the children tomorrow, do you think? I miss them so much.'

'He'll talk to you about that as well. You don't have a car here, do you?'

'No, we came on the yacht.' She gave a small shudder.

'That must have been an ordeal for you, if you don't like the water.'

'I stayed below deck, so it wasn't too bad until I had to get in and out of that little boat – the tender, Ellis calls it.'

'So since you've been here, you haven't been back out to the yacht?'

Celia picked up her glass again and twirled the dark red liquid round and round. 'I would never set foot on a boat out of choice, Sergeant.'

That didn't exactly answer the question. 'Do you know if your husband invited anyone else out to the yacht this week?'

'It can be a bit of a draw. People think it's glamorous, which I don't really understand. It's just a floating caravan, really.'

Resisting the temptation to disagree, because who wouldn't want a yacht if they had the option, Stephanie pushed for an answer: 'Anyone show a special interest?'

'Russell Dalton. Ellis said he'd offered him a look round, and Russell had jumped at the chance, much to my husband's amusement.'

'Why was he amused?'

'He loved people being envious of him.' There was no trace of sourness in her response, simply stating as a fact that her husband enjoyed flaunting his wealth.

'So was it just Mr Dalton?'

'No, his wife said she'd like to see it too.'

Stephanie was surprised and intrigued. If Juliette Dalton was so upset by Ellis Cobain's behaviour and wanted to keep out of his way as much as possible, why had she asked to visit his yacht?

It wasn't a question she could ask Celia, but she decided to probe a little.

'Do you think Mrs Dalton was interested in yachts, or was she just impressed by your husband and the trappings of wealth?'

Celia was as still as a statue, her face betraying a brief flash of uncertainty, and her eyes darted away as she spoke.

'I've no idea. I barely spoke to the woman.'

Stephanie stayed silent, watching as Celia began to fidget, displaying all the signs of someone trying hard not to say the wrong thing.

28

'Juliette, I know it's been an upsetting day, but you might feel better if you eat something, darling.'

Russell is worried about me, and I am sick of causing him so much grief. He thinks ordering room service and tempting me with food will help me relax, but since my interview with the detective, I've not known what to do with myself. Are they going to speak to Russell? Do I have to tell him the truth – admit what I've done?

Without knowing what the police found on the yacht, I'm struggling to know what to say; how little I can get away with.

Now that Ellis is dead, I'm praying Russell never finds out the depths to which I have sunk, but even admitting I knew the man and pretended otherwise will be devastating. He will feel that Ellis and I were laughing at him. I never wanted to hurt him, and with every day that passes the weight of guilt and sorrow gets heavier.

I would have stopped everything with Ellis within days of my initial foolish mistake, but by then he held all the power. Not only could he have ruined my marriage, he could have destroyed my career. We may even have lost our home. It was too much. Telling him we were done – something I wished for with my whole heart – wasn't an option.

'This ends when I say it does,' he had told me more than once. And I knew he meant it.

It was easier to try to avoid him, to make excuses for why I couldn't go to his apartment whenever he called. But I always had to cave in when I thought we were reaching a flash point, when his anger at my reluctance started to simmer and I feared he would carry out his threats.

And now, after everything I've done to try to protect Russell, he could find out.

I'm desperate to know what the police have discovered. Celia is bound to know more than I do, but how can I get to her? I mentioned to Russell a couple of hours ago that I thought I should visit her to offer my condolences, but he was shocked at the idea.

'The police have told us not to speak to anyone,' he said, his eyes wide at my apparent willingness to ignore their authority.

'No, Russ, they said we couldn't speak to anyone until after they'd interviewed us – so we couldn't concoct any stories. And they've spoken to us now.'

'Well, they've actually spoken to you twice, Juliette. You've still not told me why they wanted to see you alone.'

Russell's eyes narrowed slightly as he spoke, and I could sense a tinge of suspicion in his tone. I tried to stifle the sudden wave of panic as I made up a tale about them wanting my impressions of Ellis and Celia as a couple.

'I think DS King was looking for a woman's perspective. We spent quite a bit of time with Ellis – he even invited you to visit his yacht,' I said, trying to steer the conversation somewhere else.

'He did indeed. And what a yacht! I don't suppose we'll ever be able to afford anything like that, but it was good to go on board and just dream, wasn't it?'

Russell was watching my face, and it felt as if he was testing me. What was he expecting to read there? If he thought the trip was exciting for me, he was completely wrong. I didn't want to go. I didn't want to spend any more time with Ellis than was absolutely necessary. But it was the one thing I had to do, like it or not, so I had steeled myself to go, to express wonder at Ellis's marvellous status symbol without showing my disdain.

I put an end to Russell's probing by indicating my indifference with a shrug, and picked up my book.

Now, though, I have to focus on one thing – to keep Russell from any unnecessary hurt. And for that I need him to be asleep so I can slip out. I think of the white powder upstairs, disguised in a small tub of antacid. I should get rid of it, but first I'm going to give some to Russell. It won't hurt him, and I have to speak to Celia. I want to know what the police have said, what they've told her.

'Juliette, did you hear what I said, darling?'

Russell's tone brings me back to the moment, reminding me I need to try harder to convince him that my reactions to the events of the last twelve hours are normal.

'Sorry, Russ. My mind's wandering. I've never known anyone who's been murdered before. He was here yesterday, and now he's gone. I know that's what happens when someone dies, but this feels different.'

I suddenly realise what I've said, and when I glance at Russell, his eyes have clouded with what might be confusion. Or perhaps it's suspicion.

'They haven't said he was *murdered*, Juliette. They said they were treating his death as unexplained, but that could mean he killed himself. Why are you assuming it's murder?'

I just manage to stop myself from scoffing at the idea of Ellis

Cobain killing himself, and drop my eyes. 'Come on, Russell. With all this police activity I don't see how it can be anything else.'

His voice is so quiet, I can barely hear him. 'You didn't like him, did you? You seemed to shrink away from him and avoided standing next to him. Why were you like that?'

I thought Russell had put my behaviour down to my general malaise, but he is more perceptive than I give him credit for.

I take a deep breath. 'I didn't say anything at the time because I knew you liked him and hoped he'd be a useful contact, but he was a bit free with his hands.'

'He was *what*? Shit, Juliette, you should have told me. I wouldn't have let him get away with that.'

I almost smile. My husband likes to think he would have told Ellis Cobain to keep his hands to himself, but he's mild-mannered and not a fan of confrontation.

'It doesn't matter now, does it? So let's not get wound up about it. Why don't I use that flashy machine over there to make us both a hot drink? I noticed there are some chocolate pods, and maybe an early night would be a good thing. I'll just pop to the bathroom, then I'll make it.'

I walk from the living room through the bedroom, grabbing my handbag as I go. I can feel Russell's eyes following me. I'm relieved he didn't ask any more questions, but I'm surprised too. I thought he would want to know exactly what Ellis had done and I was mentally scrabbling through possible scenarios. Maybe the questions will come later.

I go into the bathroom. I'm about to take the powder out of my toilet bag and transfer a tiny amount into a piece of tissue when I stop. *What am I doing?* All I want is for him to drop off so I can go out, but what if he has a bad reaction?

What matters most? My husband's health, or his happiness? If I give him some of the powder, he might react badly. If I can't speak to Celia, though, can I keep him from learning the truth and destroying any happiness in his life?

I stare at the container in my hand, undecided.

29

It was 8.30 by the time Gus returned from Truro, and he looked shattered.

'How was it?' Stephanie asked.

'Pretty much as you'd expect,' he answered, flopping into a chair.

She knew what he meant. Every police officer she knew found post-mortems difficult for one reason or another, although unlike Stephanie, Gus wasn't squeamish. For him, the problem was the thought that the person lying on the table had, just hours previously, been breathing, chatting, laughing or crying. It was the sudden transition between life and death that he found unsettling.

'The good news, Gus, is there's room for us to stay here tonight, so unless Molly found something that solves this murder for us in the next five minutes, I guess it might be a late one.'

Gus gave her a wry smile. 'It's going to be a late one.'

She wouldn't push him to tell her what Molly had discovered – he would only have to repeat it to everyone else – so she gathered the team in the incident room and closed the door.

Weary as he was, Gus stood up. 'Okay, everyone. We're now certain that Ellis Cobain was murdered – suffocated. Dr Tread-well thinks it was probably with a plastic bag, pulled over his head and tied round the neck until he stopped breathing. The tying explains the marks around his throat, and Dr Treadwell believes he twisted his head when the bag was in place, causing the abrasions. It would also account for the signs of cyanosis and the petechiae.' The silence in the room was a clear indication of everyone's lack of surprise. 'We might have expected evidence – under his nails, for example – that he had tried to fight off his assailant, but there was nothing, although there were some abrasions around one wrist. A few strands that appear to be from a piece of purple silk fabric, as yet unidentified, were taken from the skin, so we think he may have been restrained with a padded handcuff. Some bruising on the other arm suggests someone may have knelt on it to hold it down, possibly trapping it under the bedding. Whatever the situation, he doesn't seem to have fought very hard, so tests are in hand to determine whether there were any drugs in his system. As you know, that might take a while.'

'Has time of death been confirmed, sir?' Ayaneh asked.

'It's pretty much as Dr Treadwell originally thought, but she's narrowed it down to between 10.30 and midnight. She's asked us to view the earlier time as less precise, given the unknowns about the temperature in the room and the fact that he was under a cover, but based on the stage of both rigor mortis and livor mortis, she thinks it's reasonable to work within these parameters. Have we had any results back from Tai Shentu?'

Stephanie shook her head. 'I spoke to him earlier to check on progress. He says he still has a lot to process, but we need to review all the people at the hotel to check if any of them have been out to the yacht. We can match fingerprints and DNA to exclude them. Celia Cobain says she believes both Russell and Juliette Dalton went for a visit.'

She saw Gus's eyebrows rise. He obviously thought Juliette's trip to the yacht as odd as Stephanie did, given her apparent antipathy to Cobain.

'Let's go through everything we have on our victim. Ayaneh, you've been collating the data. Perhaps you can start us off with a broad description of the man.'

'Yes, sir. Ellis Cobain: fifty-six years old, married to Celia Cobain. He had a home in Gloucestershire and an apartment in Bristol. Three children, aged between seven and twelve. He was the younger son of a man called Clive Cobain, who became very wealthy as a result of the health supplement company that he founded and was awarded an OBE.'

'Was Ellis involved in the company?' Gus asked.

'No, sir. In fact, the company folded when the father handed over day-to-day control to his elder son, Ashton Cobain. Clive was ultimately sued for fraud, because Ashton had downgraded the content of the supplements without changing the declarations on the packaging. The company became insolvent and the father died of a fatal heart attack. Ashton Cobain and his mother now live in Canada.'

'Interesting. So Ellis came from money, but was never part of the company. What did he do before he inherited a fortune from his first wife?'

'He had his own company, which as far as we can tell was just him, and promoted himself as . . .' Ayaneh consulted her notes '. . . an entrepreneurial strategist.'

'Did he, indeed?' Gus muttered. 'And what the hell would one of those be?'

'It appears he pitched himself as the son of a successful businessman, claiming he was ideally placed to advise start-ups.'

'Marvellous. And then he married an heiress.'

'He did. He carried on with his company after his marriage, but as soon as his wife died he walked away from the business. He now refers to himself as a philanthropist.'

Stephanie saw the corner of Gus's mouth curl and couldn't help smiling. Being referred to as a philanthropist by others was fine, but Gus would consider anyone who self-styled themselves as such to be arrogant in the extreme.

'And what are his philanthropic works, then?'

'He supports the arts, particularly in and around Bristol, with significant donations.'

'So he does bugger all except hand out money? Fill us in on his first wife, please.'

A large man with a slouching posture but sharp observant eyes raised his hand. 'Ellis Cobain married Vivian seventeen years ago. She was the daughter of a billionaire who had made his money in petrol stations. She was his only heir, but she died six years ago of a cocktail of oxycodone and benzodiazepine – self-administered, according to the coroner's report. There were some questions raised, but Vivian's parents were dead – hence her inheritance – and no one really pursued them.'

'Do we know what questions, Ian?' Gus asked.

'The nanny, Antonella Prosperi, raised a few flags. She's long gone, probably booted out because of her testimony. Vivian Cobain died on Antonella's day off, but before she left the house for the day she overheard Cobain and Vivian arguing – far from the first row she'd heard. She reported that Vivian did all the shouting, but Ellis's responses were nasty in tone, scathing. That day she heard Vivian threaten to leave him. Apparently she'd suffered from post-natal depression after her last child and had barely left the house for months. The nanny heard her shout that maybe everyone would be better off without her. Ellis, apparently, agreed with her. At that point the nanny scarpered to her friend's house for the day, thinking it was just another awful row. When she got back, there was no sign of anyone. She'd never known Ellis to take the children out on his own, so assumed he and Vivian had patched things up and he'd persuaded her to leave the house and spend the day with them. She'd been home for about an hour when Ellis walked in with the children. They'd been out for the whole day. That's when they discovered Vivian was dead.'

'And the nanny thought this was suspicious because . . .?' Gus asked.

'According to her statement, taking the children out was so unlike Ellis. Unheard of, she said. There was little doubt the drugs were self-administered, but it could have been a cry for help. She might have expected her husband or one of the children to have found her while she could still be saved.'

'Well, we'll never know the answer to that. And I'm guessing her money went to Ellis?'

'Yep. He inherited the lot. He married Celia a year later.'

Gus frowned. 'What do we know about Celia, Ayaneh?'

The detective read from her screen. 'Forty-two. In her twenties and early to mid-thirties she was a model and an occasional actress. According to press coverage, she was doing well, but gave it all up for Ellis and the children, saying she wasn't strong enough to survive in that cut-throat world and preferred to be a mother.'

'What about Cobain's recent life?'

'He attended a lot of functions – openings of restaurants, nightclubs, art exhibitions, that kind of thing. His phone records show a wide range of calls. We're checking them now, but we're focusing on people he called regularly. There are very few calls to his wife or his home phone, which is interesting, given he's away for most of each week. Several to accountants, lawyers, banks. The only personal number repeated frequently is, as you know, Juliette Dalton's.'

'Are there any to Russell Dalton? Were they *both* lying about the fact that they'd only just met Cobain?'

'Not that we've found.'

'And his bank accounts? Anything interesting, Ian?'

'Still checking and cross-referencing, boss. We don't have the bank records of his foundation yet.'

'Fair enough,' Gus said. 'Now we know he was murdered we should be able to get a court order to obtain them. Does anyone have anything else to add?'

A hand shot up at the back of the room.

'We've taken statements from everyone at the hotel, sir. No one claims to have known the Cobains before they came here. We've taken fingerprints from everyone, and we have their contact details. Some of them are asking if they can leave.'

'Unless there is anything that gives concern in their statements, I can't see any reason to hold them,' Gus said. 'Or you lot either. Those of you who live close enough, feel free to get on your way. I need you back here first thing tomorrow. Those from the Newquay team, I understand we've been given beds for the night. Might be some sharing necessary, but let's keep at it tonight until we run out of steam.'

Most of the team were aware that Gus and Stephanie were a couple, but although they often worked on cases together they had never been in this situation before – staying overnight – and Stephanie wondered what Gus's attitude might be.

There was a long way to go before they would need to take that decision, though.

30

'You okay, darling?' Russell asks as I return from the bathroom.

'Sorry. I didn't mean to be so long, but Celia called. She said she needs someone to talk to, and she doesn't know anyone else at the hotel. She's cleared it with the police, so I said I'd pop round. Is that okay with you?'

'I didn't hear your phone ring?'

'It was in my bag.' I don't tell him that I've had my phone on silent since the moment I saw Ellis in the restaurant on Saturday night.

Russell looks puzzled. 'How did she get your number? I don't remember any of us sharing contact details.'

I lower my head and fiddle with the zip of the jacket I've put on in preparation for the short walk to Celia's room.

Think, Juliette.

'Didn't I say? We met on the beach earlier in the week. I suggested they join us for dinner one night and gave her my number so she could let us know.'

Russell frowns. 'Why did you do that when you disliked her husband so much?'

I give a theatrical tut, as if Russell should know better. 'I felt sorry for the poor woman.'

He gives me a gentle smile. 'You're very thoughtful, darling.' If only that were true. 'Please offer her my condolences. I was about to say her husband was a hell of a man, but given what you told me, I don't feel much like that now.'

My first instinct is to apologise for pulling the wool from his eyes, but I don't want him to have any good memories of Ellis, so I say nothing.

'Do you think she knew what he was like?' he asks.

'I hope not, and I certainly won't mention it. I'll just make you that hot chocolate before I go.'

'No need. I can make it myself, if I fancy it.'

I shake my head. 'It's no trouble. It only takes a couple of minutes.'

I walk over to the coffee machine, find the right capsule and a suitable mug. I watch as the chocolatey liquid pours out, and the sweet smell makes me feel slightly nauseous. I grab a teaspoon, give the drink a good stir, then take it back to Russell.

'I won't be long, Russ. I'm sure Celia's feeling very lonely. It must be awful to be away from friends and family at a time like this. If I'm going to be really late I'll text you.' I nod towards the mug I've placed on the coffee table in front of him. 'Enjoy your hot chocolate.'

I walk out and close the door behind me, standing still for a moment, my back to the door. I don't want to stride straight across the centre of the courtyard in full view of everyone. I have a feeling that the police, in particular the detective sergeant, won't want me talking to the deceased's wife, so I stick tight to the wall on my side of the wide cobbled area until I reach the far end. Glancing back towards the archway that leads from the courtyard to the path to the hotel, I can't see a soul and I'm tempted to dash across. But if someone is looking, that will seem odd, so with a deep breath I walk out of the courtyard as if I'm heading for the path along the headland. It's pitch black, the sky overcast, and as soon as I'm out of range of the soft night-time lighting from the courtyard, I turn and head back towards the door to Celia's suite.

I can see through the glass that she's curled up on the sofa, enveloped in a grey cashmere throw, staring at the coffee table. I'm scared of making her jump, so I knock softly on the door. She looks puzzled for a moment, as if something has disturbed her, but she's not sure what. I knock a little harder.

This time she stirs and turns towards me, her eyes widening to see me standing there. For a moment I don't think she's going to let me in, but then she pushes herself to her feet and comes to the door.

She holds it ajar, blocking my entrance.

'What are you doing here?'

I reach out and touch her hand. Her eyes are fixed on mine with a mixture of uncertainty and apprehension.

'What will they think if they know you've come to see me, Juliette? I can't deal with it if they ask me about you. I'm not good at this. Please, go back to your room.'

I feel a shiver of fear. This woman isn't up to the task in front of her, and I've no idea how she's made it this far.

'It's perfectly reasonable that I might want to see how you're doing, Celia, knowing you're on your own with no one to talk to. They'll think I'm just being kind.'

Her eyebrows shoot up at that, but she says nothing.

'I told Russell that you'd phoned me, so I can't go back yet. Let me in. I need to talk to you.'

'I don't know. Is that the right thing to do? Wouldn't it be better for me to simply thank you for your kind words and ask you to go?'

'There's no one here, Celia. Just you and me. No one to check you're saying the right thing or the wrong thing. They're not watching you. Why would they?'

'They talked about keeping me safe. They wanted me to have the family liaison officer with me all night, but I said no. They've given me a panic alarm in case anyone tries to get in and kill me.'

'*What*? Do they think that's possible?'

She shrugs. 'I'm not sure they know what to think right now.'

I see her tremble. 'Let me come in for five minutes. Then I'll leave, if that's what you want.'

'I don't know . . . Oh, just come in, Juliette. I'm so confused.'

She turns from the door and returns to the sofa. I follow her and take a seat on an easy chair facing her. She sits down and pulls her feet up under her as if she's trying to make herself as small as possible.

'What happened last night?' I ask.

'You *know* what happened. Everything went to plan.'

'It can't have done. What are you not telling me?'

Celia stares at me, her eyes glassy, as if she's not entirely taking in what I'm saying.

I lean towards her, reach out to touch her leg. 'Tell me what the police have told you. Tell me *everything*.'

'They've said he was murdered,' she says, her voice expressionless. 'They won't let me leave, so I guess I must be a suspect. They always think it's someone close, don't they?'

Celia seems dazed, and I imagine the events of the day must have taken their toll.

'And what do *you* think?' I ask, almost scared to hear her answer.

She raises her eyes to mine. 'I think you had more to lose than anyone, Juliette.'

159

I want to argue that it's not true, but she won't believe me.

'When do they say he died?' I can hear the desperation in my voice, and she frowns.

'He was alive at ten o'clock last night, if that helps.'

I swallow. I don't know if it does or not. I don't even know if she's telling the truth.

'You asked them to go out to the yacht to check on him this morning. Why did you *do* that? Weren't you *worried*?'

'What was I supposed to do? I thought I was behaving like any wife would if she couldn't contact her husband. I needed their help to get to the yacht – the tender was still out there.'

'Why didn't you go with the hotel guys? Check the room before the police were called?'

'Yes, I suppose that would have been the sensible thing to do. But then we all know I'm not sensible.'

There's a trace of acid in her response, and I feel that at least she's back with me. But I don't want to push her too far. She's not the only one who's made mistakes.

'Have the police shared anything with you?'

'No. I guess they like to keep everything close to their chests in the hope that the killer will trip him- or herself up.'

'What about his phone?'

'They asked if he would have taken it to the yacht. I said yes, that he sent me a couple of texts but didn't answer my calls this morning. The fact that they asked me about it suggests they can't find it. But I didn't want to ask. I didn't want them to wonder why it was important to me.'

Was it not there? What does that mean? Should I be pleased they can't find it? But I can't worry about that now, because there's something I need to tell her.

'They know I knew Ellis before we came here.'

160

Celia's already pale face loses its last remaining colour.

'How?'

'His phone records. If only he hadn't pretended he'd never met me, I could have admitted to Russell that I'd done some work for him. But you know Ellis. He thought it was funny to try to fool my husband. When the police talked to Russell and me together, I had to say I hadn't met Ellis before this week.' I feel as if the air has been stolen from my lungs and I take a deep shaky breath. 'Now they know I was lying to them. And to Russell.'

'Oh God!' she groans. 'Do they think *I* know about you and Ellis?'

I shake my head, realising how much better I could have played it with the police. I could have said Ellis thought it was a joke and that we'd been planning to tell Russell that I'd worked on his apartment redesign. But that bloody sergeant saw how I'd reacted to him last Saturday. She knew it wasn't as clear cut as I'd suggested – an ill-judged attempt at seduction which I had fended off.

'I should have stopped all this – everything we did. I should never have let it happen,' Celia mumbles. 'I'm incapable of making a rational decision.'

I lean towards her. 'That's not true. That's Ellis in your head telling you you're crap, that you get things wrong all the time. He's been doing it for so long that you believe him, but he's not here now, Celia. He can't do it any more, and you did what you believed you had to.'

'I know,' she says despondently, and I try to smile at her, but I can't. 'I wish we'd done things differently,' she murmurs. 'We should never have listened to Nadia.'

161

Three Days Before the Murder

'I'm sorry you're having to amuse yourself most mornings, darling,' Russell said. 'If you want to hang on while I finish my work, we could drive somewhere for lunch? There's supposed to be a lovely old pub in Newlyn that serves the best seafood. Do you fancy that?'

I shook my head. 'Don't worry about me, Russ. I know you have to work. If you do whatever you need to now, we can have a quick lunch here and then have the whole afternoon to do something together. If the causeway's open, I wouldn't mind walking across to St Michael's Mount, but for now I'll wander along the path and see where it takes me.'

He gave me a worried smile, but fortunately could see the sense in what I was suggesting. He had been hoping the tension would just slide off me while we were away, but then he didn't know the cause of my unhappiness had just sauntered past our window on his way to the restaurant for a late breakfast.

Pulling on a jacket, I walked over to where Russell was hunched over his laptop and dropped a kiss on his head.

'Back soon,' I said, squeezing his shoulder. It was almost more than I could bear to witness his pain and confusion at my continued reserve. I knew I would have to end this somehow. And soon.

As I walked out of the door, I felt my mobile vibrate in my pocket and my stomach turned over. It could be anyone, but I knew it wasn't.

As soon as I was clear of the window, I pulled out my phone and stared at the message:

Keep ignoring me, Juliette, and I might just let our secret slip. I can picture Russell's face now . . .

This wasn't the first message he'd sent since we had been here. I had berated him for his cruelty and told him to leave – to go back to Bristol. But he had replied that I was the reason he had come. That I belonged to him now.

If I continued to hold him at arm's length, I had no idea what he might do. Ellis prided himself on never losing.

It's difficult, Ellis. Let me think of a way. Please give me some time.

A weak, pathetic answer, but the best I could manage. I pressed Send as I hurried through the courtyard, then turned down the path to the beach, pulling up the collar of my jacket against the icy breeze.

Celia and I had agreed to meet back at the bench. She didn't think Ellis would contemplate coming to look for her; he would just be angry that she wasn't where he expected her to be when he got back from breakfast. I hoped she hadn't lost her nerve. To my surprise she was already there, and I was relieved that, apart from the two of us, the beach was empty.

Huddled at the far end of the bench, she looked up as I drew close, fear and mistrust in her eyes.

I muttered a quiet 'Hi' and sat down, keeping some space between us. I needed this to go at her pace.

'I'm glad you're here,' I told her. 'You said you wanted to understand – about how it all started with Ellis.' I turned towards her. 'Are you sure, Celia? Isn't this going to hurt you?'

'It doesn't hurt me. It scares me.' She wrapped her coat tightly around herself. Her voice came in gasps, a series of short outbursts. 'There may be some other woman – she might already be in the picture for all we know – who doesn't see through him the way you do. She might be taken in by his charm. He can be charming if he wants to be, can't he? There's the money – lots of women are attracted to that. If he gets knighted – which is what he wants and believes he deserves – there'll be women who'll put up with anything to be called Lady Cobain. In case you're wondering, I'm not one of them.'

This was the longest speech I'd ever heard from Celia, and she sounded out of breath when she finished.

'Me neither,' I say with a shudder. 'I get the charm – I've seen it, even though I know it's superficial. But none of the rest matters. You may find this hard to believe, but I love Russell.'

She turned to me, her face screwed up in confusion. 'Then why?'

I was about to try to explain the difficulties Russell and I had been going through and how I blamed myself when we spotted a figure at the water's edge – a woman, dressed in a long multicoloured woollen coat. Despite the cold, it was unfastened, flying open behind her as she stomped along the beach.

I recognised her. It was the singer – Nadia Shariq – the woman who Russell was trying to persuade to sign with his agency. She strode across the sand, then bent to pick up a pebble, turned to hurl it into the sea and screamed a single word which was carried back to us on the breeze: *'Fucker!'* She picked up more stones and flung them one after the other into the water.

I glanced at Celia, but she was staring at Nadia. Before I had the chance to ask if she recognised her, Nadia turned and saw us. She stopped dead in her tracks. We stared back, and as I tried to think of something to say, she marched up the beach towards us.

'You're Celia Cobain, aren't you?' she asked, her voice harsh, angry.

'I-I am,' Celia stuttered, and I felt protective for a moment, thinking she couldn't handle the aggression that was coming off this woman in waves.

'I want to talk to you. Alone. It's about your husband.'

Celia threw me a nervous glance.

'I'll leave you both,' I said, starting to stand.

'No!' Celia put out a hand as if to stop me. 'Please stay, Juliette.'

Nadia gave me a puzzled frown. 'Aren't you Russell's wife?'

'I am, yes.'

She threw her head back. '*Shit*. That's all I bloody need.'

'What do you mean?' I asked.

'I get the best fucking opportunity of my life and I make a complete arse of myself in front of the lawyer's wife. *Shit!*'

'I won't say anything,' I reassured her, hoping that meant she wouldn't mention seeing me on the beach with Celia. 'Something's clearly wound you up, and I've felt like swearing into the wind many times.'

'Okay, well, thanks for that. But I'd still like to talk to Ellis's wife.'

Celia was still looking from me to Nadia and back again. She was struggling to cope with this, and I was reluctant to leave her.

'Juliette, please stay,' she said softly. Without looking at Nadia, she muttered, 'Whatever you have to say about my husband, it's fine for Juliette to hear it.'

I felt a moment of panic. Was Celia about to tell a woman who knew my husband that I'd had an affair with Ellis? I threw her a beseeching look. No one spoke.

The stillness was shattered by the sound of a phone coming from Celia's pocket. She pulled it out and stared at the screen.

'Ellis,' she mumbled, lifting her eyes to mine. 'He'll want to know where I am.'

'Don't answer it,' Nadia said, reaching to snatch the phone from Celia's hand.

There was a shocked silence.

'*What?*' Nadia barked. 'Don't look at me like that. You're not answering. Let the fucker wonder where you are. What's the worst he can do?'

No one replied and Nadia put the phone in the pocket of her coat.

'Listen,' she said, hands on hips, leaning towards Celia. 'Your husband is an arse, okay? He can't be allowed to treat people however he wants. He did everything he could to ruin my life before. He's not doing it again.'

31

The silence in Celia's suite was absolute. She wished she hadn't spoken, that she had never mentioned Nadia. Since then Juliette had glazed over, her thoughts clearly elsewhere, and Celia didn't know how to break the tension.

Finally, Juliette spoke. 'It's easy to say what we should and shouldn't have done now, but remember how we felt that day? Remember what Nadia told you Ellis was planning? You felt your life would be over, and she had a compelling argument.'

Celia could recall feeling overwhelmed with a sense of shame that Ellis was her husband, but it was too late for regrets and she didn't want to talk about it any more. She was a bundle of nerves, expecting the police to arrive at the door at any moment to discover her and Juliette together and to grill them about how well they knew each other.

'I really think you should go.'

'They'd *expect* me to come here and express my sympathy,' Juliette said, her tone patient.

'I'm not sure you're right. They think I only spoke to you a couple of times. They'll wonder why I went into the bar alone last night – why I sought your company.' Celia could hear the panic in her own voice, but seemed unable to calm herself. 'That detective sergeant knows I find it difficult to go into crowded spaces. She found me dithering outside, trying to decide if Ellis would be more annoyed if I stayed here or joined him in the restaurant. And then . . .'

'What?'

Celia shook her head. She couldn't think straight with Juliette looking at her and didn't want to share details of the humiliating scene DS King had witnessed the previous Sunday.

'It doesn't matter. I just wish to God she wasn't here, that they'd sent a detective none of us had ever seen before. Please, Juliette, I can't deal with this. Will you just *go*!'

Finally, she managed to persuade her to leave, but within minutes of closing the door behind Juliette, another thought hit her. *The money!* Neither of them had mentioned the money! Had Juliette forgotten it too, in the panic of everything else that was going on?

Oh God! What will she say?

Celia wanted to phone her, but what if Russell answered? Maybe he didn't answer Juliette's mobile the way Ellis had always answered hers.

She couldn't call Nadia, now she'd hidden her other phone. Not that she wanted to. She meant what she'd said to Juliette. They shouldn't have listened to Nadia, but she and Juliette had been overwhelmed by the woman's anger.

After snatching Celia's mobile on the beach that day, Nadia had stood, the sea to her back, dark hair flying around her face in the wind, and defiantly told them everything.

'I'm sorry, Celia – and I know that's your name, because after three months of me believing I was the only woman in Ellis's life, he admitted to your existence – but your husband is a total bastard. It's not a nice thing for you to hear, but when I was singing in clubs in Bristol, he came on to me. He told me his wife had died. I felt *sorry* for him! He totally forgot to mention that he had a new wife. *You!* He didn't bother with that little detail until he was confident that I was well and truly hooked. When I found out, I flipped.'

As Nadia spoke, a weight settled around Celia's heart. Ellis's infidelity no longer had the power to hurt her, but she still felt demeaned by it.

'How did it end?' Juliette asked, a hopeful expression on her face, as if Nadia might provide the solution she had desperately been searching for.

Nadia's face settled into a derisive sneer. 'Oh, you know, typical Ellis. He wasn't prepared to lose – that would *never* do. But I wasn't going to carry on with him once I knew about you, Celia. Fuck that! It was one thing having a relationship with an older man – a widower – but another entirely when he was someone else's husband. So I told him to go to hell. I said he was a lying, cheating, bastard, and he didn't deserve me. Or you, for that matter.'

Celia stared at her, amazed that someone would have the bravery to challenge Ellis. He wouldn't have liked that. She was struggling to frame the right question when Juliette spoke: 'What did he do to you?'

Her question was met with a glare. 'What's it to you? This is between me and his wife. I don't know why she wanted you to be here at all.'

Juliette was silent for a moment. Then she took a deep breath. 'I've found myself in a difficult position with Ellis. I need to find a way out.'

Nadia narrowed her eyes and barked out a laugh. 'He shagged you too, did he? Marvellous.'

She turned away to face the sea, but Celia was sure she had

caught a glimpse of tears in the young woman's eyes. Although she appeared strong and fearless, few would escape unscathed from a relationship with Ellis Cobain.

'So how come he's here at exactly the same time as you, if you want a way out? Why the hell did you tell him you were coming here?'

'I *didn't*! I was *horrified* when I found out he was here.' Nadia looked unconvinced, hands on hips, scowling at Juliette, who shook her head in despair. 'I made a schoolgirl error. I told him Russell was going away on business and had asked me to go with him. Ellis apparently saw the details of the hotel on my phone and thought it would be fun to show up. He *knows* I want out, so he decided to play with me and ruin my time with Russell. He followed me here. To torment me.'

Nadia's eyes narrowed as she stared at Juliette. She turned to Celia. 'Do you believe this?'

Celia nodded, unwilling to share her own thoughts about Ellis's behaviour.

Nadia grunted. 'Poor Russell. He seems like a good guy.'

Juliette groaned quietly. 'He is. And more. *Shit*. I shouldn't have told you. I wasn't thinking straight.' Juliette leaned forward, clasping her hands tightly between her knees. 'Look, I know Russell's here to talk to you about your contract, so you're bound to see him. Please, Nadia, don't tell him we've had this conversation.'

Celia glanced from one woman to the other. She should say something, but she didn't know what.

'Listen, this is a horrible situation for all of us,' Juliette said. 'I can't imagine how Celia must feel. We're talking about her *husband*, for God's sake. And I don't think it's fair of us, Nadia, to make her suffer any longer. Maybe we just accept the fact that we've all been hurt. Celia can go home with Ellis and they should get on with their lives. Maybe we should *all* get on with our lives.'

'But that won't work, will it, Juliette?' Celia found herself saying. 'You said you don't know how to end things with Ellis – and I *need* you to end it.'

She felt Nadia's eyes on her, but found it hard to meet her gaze.

'Nice idea, Celia, but this is Ellis fucking Cobain we're talking about – he can't *lose*. He has to be in control. You both know that! So he won't let her go until he's well and truly ready, and by then he may have destroyed her marriage. Anyway, why in God's name are you staying with him? He'd have to give you a shedload of money if you left him. You'd be so much better off than you are living with him.'

Celia slowly raised her head to meet Nadia's bloodshot eyes, whether through tears or the icy wind in her face, it was impossible to say.

'I don't care about his money. It's the children. If I left him, I would lose them, and that's more than I can bear.'

'Don't you have any rights?' Nadia asked, and Celia lowered her head.

'He always said it wasn't necessary. If I leave him, or he leaves me, I'll never see them again. He'll make sure of it.'

'Of course he will. He likes to leave a trail of suffering – it's all part of the game.' Nadia took a step towards the bench and crouched down. She reached out and took Celia's hands. 'When I told Ellis I didn't want to see him again, he ruined my career, Celia. He accused me of stalking him, told club managers that if they employed me they'd lose any financial support he might choose to give them. One or two refused to bow to his command, so Ellis paid hecklers to come to the clubs where I was working. I was booed off the stage. He said if I didn't come back to him, I'd have no life in Bristol. No career. It would all be over. That's why I'm here. I came to Cornwall, hoping to put those times behind me and start again.'

Celia felt her stomach churn. *Had Ellis really stooped so low?*

Nadia hadn't finished. Still clasping Celia's hands, she turned towards Juliette. 'Come on. Tell us what he has over you. Why can't you just tell him to fuck off?'

Juliette shuffled on the seat, not looking at them, staring instead at the sea as she spoke. 'I'm telling you this because I think we all have to understand what he's capable of. It's inevitable that I'll have to admit everything to my husband at some point, and then my marriage will probably be over. But I want to tell Russell myself, okay? Please, Nadia. I don't know you, but I can see how much Ellis has hurt you.'

Nadia gave a curt nod, and Juliette took a deep, shuddering breath.

'Russell and I had some bad news – it doesn't matter what it was. There was something in my past, something I'd always made light of from before we met, but it's had a big impact on us, both now and for our future. Russell seemed so disappointed in me, and for a while he was distant. I thought I was losing him. Then Ellis was incredibly charming, flattering, generous, making me feel that maybe I was worth something after all.'

Celia could hear Juliette's breathing had become ragged. Pulling a bottle of water from her bag, she passed it to her.

Juliette took a gulp. 'When he made his move – said all the right things, made me feel that he wanted me – I collapsed into the whole thing, surrendered to him, leaving my troubles, my real life, at the door. It wasn't long before I realised it was a mistake. I tried to end it, but Ellis was having none of that. He said he wasn't "done with me".'

Juliette stopped talking, although Celia was certain that wasn't the end of it.

'I guess I know what you're going to say next,' Nadia muttered. 'If it was over, he'd have to tell your husband.'

Juliette gave an almost imperceptible shrug. 'And so much more. He took photos on his phone – me, on my knees in front of him. I'm sure I don't need to elaborate, and I'm sorry you have to hear this, Celia. I didn't know he was taking them, but I'm visible, even though Ellis isn't – or at least, not in any recognisable way. He says he'll send the pictures anonymously to the wives of all my clients, telling them they should be aware that this is a special service I offer to their husbands.'

Celia gasped, but it was Nadia who spoke.

'You do know it's illegal to show pictures like that to anyone without your consent, don't you? You can threaten him with that, can't you?'

Juliette gave a sad, defeated smile. 'This is Ellis, Nadia. He'll find a way. I think we all know that.'

Celia felt sick. What was she supposed to do about all this?

But she knew the answer. She would do nothing. She never did.

Saturday

32

Stephanie was delighted that Gus had said they could share a room at the hotel.

'Why ever not?' he'd asked when Stephanie had questioned whether it was appropriate. 'We're not twelve, Steph. Everyone knows we're a couple.'

'Yes, but on this case you're my boss, so it might make people uncomfortable.'

'Bollocks. They'd be a bloody sight more uncomfortable if they thought we'd had a row and were keeping our distance. As long as I refrain from any groping in the incident room, we should be fine,' he said with a grin.

The only negative in this arrangement was that they had talked long into the night about the case, so neither of them had got much sleep – and not for a good reason. It was always a pleasure to wake up next to Gus, though. She'd never known anyone to surface from a deep sleep and immediately turn to her and smile the way he did, especially as Stephanie's default was to grumble about the fact that she had to get out of bed.

Those officers who had stayed at the hotel overnight were back in the incident room by 7 a.m., looking a good deal more alert than Stephanie was feeling. She'd asked the hotel to provide bacon sandwiches, croissants, toast – anything that could be eaten with one hand while continuing to work. And coffee. Lots of coffee. It was going to be a hard day.

'Okay, everyone. Thanks for getting up early,' Gus said. 'Those who went home last night will be back with us shortly, but in the meantime I'd like to get a timeline on the board. We need to consider where Ellis was, and the exact location of each of the people who knew him. For now, that includes his wife, and Russell and Juliette Dalton. Agreed?'

Everyone nodded.

'We also need to check on anyone who left the hotel during the critical period, including staff, and add into that any intelligence we've received about unusual boat activity in the area. Go through the hotel's CCTV, speak to reception, the kitchen staff who had access to the rear entrance, anyone who might have noticed unusual comings and goings. Ayaneh, you've been keeping the notes updated. Run us through what we know, please. Can I have a volunteer to write up the timeline?'

'I'll do it,' Stephanie said, walking over to the whiteboard.

Ayaneh leaned forward at her desk and referred to her iPad.

'I'll start from when Ellis Cobain was last seen alive. He went to his yacht at around 6 p.m., apparently to make sure everything was okay on board. His wife said something about a storm, but we can't find any weather forecasts that suggested that.'

'Good point,' Gus said. 'So why did he *really* go to the yacht? He took the tender, and as far as we know, that remained attached to the yacht until his body was discovered yesterday morning. Remind me where his wife was at 6 p.m.?'

'In her room. She went to the bar at about 6.30. Russell was already there. Juliette was out for a run.'

'Can we corroborate Juliette's movements?'

'No, sir. She said she passed a couple of people, but no one she recognised from the hotel. We can enquire in the village, though.'

'Good. Let's do that. Okay, what next?'

'At 7.15 Celia received a text message from her husband to say he'd be later than expected, and she should eat without him. At this point she was still in the bar with Russell. He confirmed she received a message, although he didn't read it. We've checked, and it did come from Ellis Cobain's mobile, although we still haven't found that.'

'What time did Juliette Dalton arrive?'

'According to her it was about 7.30, but DS King's notes say her husband corrected her. She wasn't back until just after 7.45. Celia stayed with the Daltons until 8.30, but refused to join them for dinner. She went back to her suite and ordered room service. She thought it was about 9.10 when it arrived, and the hotel has confirmed this. She next heard from Ellis at ten o'clock. He sent the text saying he would sleep on the boat.'

'Remind us what the text said?'

'"Darling, it's late now, so I hope you don't mind but I've decided to stay on the yacht tonight. I'll be back for breakfast." She responded: "Okay. Sleep well. I miss you."'

Stephanie had read these texts before, but hearing the words out loud, she wasn't entirely comfortable with the exchange.

'Does that sound like Ellis Cobain? It seems a bit considerate for him, bearing in mind everything Celia has told us.'

Gus nodded. 'Good point. You have a forensic linguist contact, don't you, Steph? Ask them to look at this in relation to previous messages on Celia's phone. Ian, can we do an analysis on where both phones were at the time of the texts?'

'Already done, boss. The text was sent from the yacht. We've looked at cell siting for Mrs Cobain's phone for the whole period too. Apart from when she was here in the hotel bar, it was in her suite for the whole period.'

'Thanks, Ian. Let's track the Daltons' phones too – see if they were where they said they were. Carry on, Ayaneh.'

'We've got the text to Celia at 10 p.m. She replied, and as Ian says, we know her phone was in her room.'

Gus frowned. 'Based on Dr Treadwell's estimate of time of death, we might be inclined to think he was still alive at this point, but let's not make assumptions.'

Stephanie pointed to the timeline. 'He could have scheduled the text to go at ten. It doesn't mean he wrote and sent it then. As we know, Celia responded to the message from her room. The Daltons were still in the restaurant, although Juliette did pop to the ladies' briefly after a wine spillage just before ten, but she was only gone for ten to fifteen minutes. Nowhere near long enough to get to the jetty, then out to the yacht and back. They didn't move from the bar after that – confirmed by the restaurant manager – until after Nadia Shariq's second set. They went back to their suite and said they were in bed by 11.30.'

'Doesn't give them much time, if Dr Treadwell's estimates are correct.' Gus glanced round the room. 'Please don't anyone tell Molly that I said that! What about Celia, Ayaneh?'

'According to her statement, she was in her room until she asked room service to collect her plates at 22.20. They were busy and didn't turn up until 22.40. We've asked to speak to the housekeeper, but she doesn't get in until the afternoon and she's not answering her mobile.'

'Okay. After that?'

'As far as we know, Celia stayed in her room until the following morning, sir, when the victim wasn't responding to her texts.'

Gus grunted. 'So it would seem they're fully accounted for

during all the relevant hours, if we assume the Daltons are telling the truth about going back to their room together after they left the bar. The tender was moored to the yacht, and the hotel's RIB was in the locked boathouse, so there was no way of getting out there. But let's not limit our thinking to people staying or working here. If someone got to him by boat, where did they come from? Check along the coast; they had to have access to a boat with an outboard.'

'Sir, according to Google maps, the local village has a small harbour.'

'Good thinking, Ayaneh. An alternative line of enquiry to pursue. If not by boat, how could anyone have got to the yacht?'

'Someone could have swum,' Stephanie said. 'I doubt that would be either of the Daltons. Time would have been tight.'

'And how many people would take a dip in the sea at this time of year?' Gus looked mildly horrified at the thought.

'More than you'd think,' Stephanie replied.

'And if we're to believe Celia Cobain, she can't swim,' Gus said. 'Okay. In addition to checking all comings and goings and any small boat activity, I think we need to get a warrant to search the Daltons' room. We know Juliette has been hiding her relationship with Cobain and if, as Steph suspects, it was an affair, it gives them both a motive. We can try asking their permission, but Russell Dalton's a lawyer. What are our chances of him agreeing?'

'Good, if he's got nothing to hide,' Stephanie said.

Then Stephanie remembered the look Russell had given his wife when she had denied knowing Cobain prior to this week. Juliette might think her husband knew nothing about their relationship but Stephanie wasn't sure she was right. And if that were the case, she was certain the last thing he'd want was for their room to be searched.

33

I look at Russell lying next to me in the bed. It's early and he's still fast asleep. I don't want to wake him, because I don't want to talk. He was snoring on the sofa when I got back from Celia's room last night and only half-awake when I helped him to the bedroom, a relief as I didn't want him to ask me any questions.

I wasn't with Celia for long but my presence made her nervous, and she's vulnerable enough without me turning her into even more of a liability. I have no idea what she'll say if she's put under pressure, and the thought is terrifying.

Now, as I lie here, I wonder what today will bring. I'm certain I'll be interviewed again, and I'm praying no one saw me with either Celia or Nadia. After Celia and I saw her that first time as she furiously hurled stones into the sea, Nadia suggested we meet again in a different place, somewhere where no one would see us together.

'We deserve better than this, and unless we make a stand, Ellis is not going to change. He's a manipulative bastard. We have to stick together, make a plan to bring him down.'

Celia had been hesitant. 'I don't know if I can get away,' she said. 'What if Ellis wants to know where I am?'

'Tough. He won't find you, will he? What's he going to do,

Celia? He's hardly likely to beat the shit out of you here at the hotel, is he?'

Celia's brow had wrinkled as she tried to think through the ramifications. 'He's not really violent,' she mumbled.

'What do you mean, "really"?' Nadia demanded. 'He either is, or he isn't. If he physically hurts you in any way – even if it's not a near-death experience – it's totally screwed up. And don't let his tongue whip you into submission. He's just a fucking *man*, Celia. Nothing special *at all*.'

I could see this wasn't helping and Celia was looking more and more perplexed. In the end Nadia handed Celia's phone back and walked away, shouting over her shoulder, 'If we want to put an end to this pain, we can do it together. Your choice! See you tomorrow. Or not.'

With that, she'd marched off, lifting one hand in a mock wave.

'What do you think?' Celia asked me, chewing her thumbnail.

I released a long slow breath. 'It's difficult for you to get away, I understand that. Ellis likes to be in control.' I heard a derisive snort from Celia. 'It's not such a problem for me because Russell's used to me being distant now. Poor man. He's so hurt by how I'm behaving, but I feel as if by keeping my distance it'll be easier for him when the inevitable happens and he finds out the depths I've sunk to.'

'I'm not sure which of us is in the worse position,' Celia mumbled.

'Why do you think Ellis is the way he is?' I asked. 'Is there anything in his past that could explain it?'

Celia shrugged. 'His father, at a guess. Ellis doesn't talk about him. His brother, Ashton, lost the family fortune by committing fraud. I've only met him once. He came over from Canada to try to persuade Ellis to give him some money, which of course he refused to do. I could tell how much they hated each other. And then Ashton spilled the beans about their upbringing in an effort to belittle Ellis in front of me. He said their dad had always thought Ellis was a waste of space.'

'You're saying Ellis bullies people because *he* was bullied?'

'That's part of it, I suppose. I've spent years using it as justification for his behaviour. I imagine his father was quite unpleasant, and his mother no better. I found a letter when I was surreptitiously searching for some cash in Ellis's desk. It was quite revealing. When his dad had the first heart attack Ellis went to see him in hospital. The letter I found was from his father's solicitor asking him not to visit again. Then the old man died, and I'm not sure Ellis even went to the funeral.'

Under normal circumstances I might have been inclined to feel some sympathy for a man who had been treated so badly, but while his upbringing might explain his behaviour, it could never excuse it. My own childhood had its challenges, but I don't think it made me cruel. Stupid, impulsive, short-sighted perhaps. But not cruel.

'Ellis loves money,' Celia continued, 'so Vivian was a blessing. But he wanted control of it, and when Vivian died leaving him all her riches he was desperate to show his family that *he* was the better son. *He* was the successful one who everyone talked about and revered. That's why he gives so much to charity – only when it's conspicuous, of course. He's desperate for a knighthood – or at least a CBE, one up from his dad's OBE.'

I knew about Ellis's ambitions, but talking about them wasn't helping me find a solution to our problems. I didn't know whether speaking with Nadia would be useful or not, but at that point anything seemed worth a try.

'I'm going to meet Nadia tomorrow, Celia. You should try to

get there too, if you can. She knows him well, that much is clear. She might be able to suggest something to end this misery.'

My voice broke and Celia grasped my hand – perhaps an unusual gesture between a wife and an unwilling mistress, but my unhappiness was the incentive she seemed to need.

'I'll find a way,' she said softly.

I wish now that I hadn't persuaded Celia to come with me. If I'd had any inkling of the shock that was in store for her the following day and the impact on her already fragile psyche, I would have begged her to stay away.

Two Days Before the Murder

It was hard to shake Russell off on Tuesday morning.

'I fancy a walk too,' he said as I was about to leave the room.

Jumping up from the small table he was using as a desk, he closed his laptop. 'I'll just go and grab a sweater.'

I was tempted to make a run for it while he was in the bedroom, but that would have been even more unkind than telling him I didn't want him with me.

'Russ, I'm so sorry, darling, but I really value the times when I can walk or run quietly, listening to the sea, the birds. If you come, I'll feel compelled to make conversation, or I'll be wondering what you're thinking.'

Looking at his bewildered face, I had the sudden urge to fall to my knees and beg his forgiveness.

'Well, how would it be if I walked with you, but just held your hand and didn't speak?' he asked quietly.

I swallowed. 'It would be lovely, but that's not what I need right now.'

185

God, I sounded so selfish. How would we ever get back to the couple we used to be if I couldn't fix this? Russell's eyes used to soften, touching me, warming me, as he gazed at me. Now, all I could see was a puzzled, hurt frown.

He walked towards me and gently held my arms.

'Juliette, do you think you need to get some help, darling? You seem so lost, and I don't know what to do to bring you back to me. I don't blame you, you know. I never have done.'

For a moment my body felt as frozen as a block of ice. *Did he know about Ellis?* Then I realised what he was talking about.

'I know you don't, Russell, but I blame myself. Please give me just a little longer.'

He looked as if he was about to point out that it had already been months, but he just nodded and leaned towards me to give me a light kiss on my cheek.

'Whatever you want. I'll be here when you need me.'

As I closed the door behind me and set off to meet Celia and Nadia, tears were stinging my eyes. I wondered why I'd ever thought for a moment that he'd stopped loving me. The problem was, I had stopped loving myself.

I had no more time for introspection, though, because I saw Celia up ahead. She kept turning to look over her shoulder, and then lurched forward, almost running. She looked as if she was trying to escape from some wild creature stalking her through the undergrowth. I wanted to call out to her, but we were still too close to the hotel and I was worried that my voice might carry back to Ellis, wherever he might be. I glanced over my shoulder. She was making me nervous too.

There was no one there.

It was an overcast day with a cold wind, so I started to jog to catch up with her. She heard me coming and spun round, her hands raised, palms out, as if I was about to attack her.

'It's only me, Celia.'

'Sorry, Juliette. I didn't mean to react like that. I waited until Ellis was in the bathroom and then I just scarpered. I've no idea what he's going to say or do later, but it won't be any worse than he's done in the past.'

I grabbed her arm. 'Come on. I can see the path Nadia told us about up ahead. She said if we go down there we'll find a gap in the cliffs where we can sit. Let's see if she turns up.'

We slithered down the steep slope, the stones slippery, deadly. I went ahead, my trainers managing to grip the surface. Celia was likely to fall if she kept looking over her shoulder, but despite my fears, we made it safely to the bottom and walked along the rocky shoreline.

'This must be it,' I said, pointing to a cranny in the cliffs. 'Let's get out of the wind.'

Celia stopped. 'I don't like caves.'

'There's no roof,' I told her. 'It's just a cleft in the cliff face. It's okay. It's not dark.'

I persuaded her to sit on one of the biggest stones, and searched for something to talk about that might stop her worrying about Nadia's arrival – or worse, Ellis appearing in front of her.

'Celia, when I met Ellis I'm slightly ashamed to say that I looked you up. Well, I was looking *him* up, if I'm honest, but when your name appeared I admit I clicked the link. You used to be a model, and then an actress, didn't you? Why did you give up? Was it to take care of the children?'

Her mouth turned up at one corner. 'Kind of, but I wasn't very good. I would never have got anywhere.'

I stared at her with surprise. 'I read a couple of reviews of a play you were in. I think it was in Bath. They were very complimentary.'

'No,' she said, her voice soft. 'I think the journalist was being kind.'

We didn't know that Nadia had arrived until we heard her voice as she rounded the cliff edge. 'Huh! I bet I know who sold you that pile of crap! It's what he said to me too. He said the reviewers were being generous about my singing because they felt sorry for me. I asked him why the audience cheered, and he said it was because I looked desperate.'

I was listening to her, but not really paying much attention because to my surprise Nadia wasn't alone. She was holding the hand of a small dark-haired boy who looked about two years old.

'Hello,' I said to him. He grabbed Nadia's leg, trying to hide behind her, in the folds of her long, flowing coat.

'I had to bring him. I couldn't get any cover today.'

Celia was biting her lip. 'Is he yours, Nadia?'

'Yep. A little tinker, aren't you, Marco?'

Marco didn't speak. He just stared, his blue eyes round as his gaze landed first on Celia and then on me.

Celia was fidgeting, her hand pushed deep into her pocket, but I could see it moving, as if she was turning something round and round hidden in the folds of the fabric. She coughed before she spoke, as if it was hard to get the words out.

'Is it acceptable to ask who his father is, or would that be too intrusive?'

I knew what Nadia was going to say before she said it, and I wanted to reach over and grab Celia's hand. But I didn't.

Nadia bent down and picked up the child, nuzzling his neck for a moment and making him giggle.

'I think you know the answer to that, don't you, Celia?'

34

For Celia, the wait until the inevitable next visit from the police was agonising. Her mind was full of the things she mustn't say, and the danger was that she would blurt one of them out. Nadia had warned her that things might get difficult, but she hadn't thought they would be quite *this* difficult.

As far as she was aware, the police still didn't know of any link between Ellis and Nadia, and if she was to be believed, prior to this week Ellis hadn't known of Marco's existence.

'When I saw him in the audience on Saturday night,' she'd said, 'I was more than a little pissed, scared he might start on me again. He'd already had his revenge and I thought he'd have got over being dumped. I should have known better.'

'Did Ellis seek you out?' Juliette asked.

'Hah! Did he ever! The slimy fucker didn't approach me that night. I was all geared up ready for him, but he didn't come. He waited until Sunday, then turned up at my cottage – ambushed me. And of course he met Marco.'

Celia felt her whole body tremble. She had wanted children so badly when she met Ellis, but it had never happened.

Celia stared at Nadia. 'How did he know where you live?'

Nadia shrugged. 'I asked, but he just laughed. He's *Ellis Cobain*! He knows everything.'

'You told him he was Marco's father?'

'For God's sake, Celia. I didn't have to tell him. He could do the maths!'

There was a fierce heat to Nadia's expression, and a wave of unease washed over Celia.

'I don't want him anywhere near my son, and if I'd wanted his money I'd have gone for it long ago. But it's too late to escape now. The bastard's decided it's time for a change, says he fancies living down here in Cornwall. Sorry, Celia, but he says he's going to buy a house here for all of us so he can spend time with me and Marco, let my son get to know his siblings. Telling him I want nothing to do with him won't work, of course. That will just fire him up – make him more determined to get what he wants.'

Celia remembered with embarrassment her wail of anguish at Nadia's words. She'd leaped to her feet and rushed across to grab Nadia's free arm. Marco gave a frightened yelp.

'What do you mean, "all of us"? Does he mean my children? Are you saying he's taking my *children* from me? To come here? To live with you?' she yelled.

Nadia shook her off.

'Don't shout at me, Celia. You're scaring Marco. I don't want this any more than you do. Just remember I escaped Bristol to get away from him – but he seems to have decided. He says now that he's found me he's not prepared to lose me again. He's planning to tell you and the children at the end of the week, when you get home.'

'Surely you're not giving in to this, if it's not what you want,' Juliette said, rising to her feet and guiding the sobbing Celia back to her seat on the rock.

'*You* can talk, Juliette! He's only here because he followed you.' Nadia's lips settled into an angry line. 'Can we all be clear about this! Do I have to shout it? *I don't want him.* I want him gone – out of my life. I don't want him near my son. Not now. Not *ever*. Nor, with all respect, Celia, do I want to bring up his three children. I don't even *know* them! But he says he can seek a declaration of parentage or something, and then it would be almost impossible for me to keep him out of Marco's life. I'd have no choice but to give him access. Even if I manage to avoid living in the same house, I can't stop him buying another bloody mansion down here and moving in, can I? Unless we can find a way to stop him.'

Sensing the tension between the three women, Marco had started to cry in earnest. Nadia put him on the ground and got down onto her knees, gathering some smooth stones and sorting them with him on the sand. As she spoke quietly to him about which one was the biggest and how they could put them in order, Celia felt Juliette reach out a hand to her.

Finally, Nadia got to her feet, leaving Marco to play.

'Listen. All three of us have reason to hate Ellis. He's going to leave you, Celia, and take your children. You have no rights at all, so you'll never see them again. And Juliette, he'll destroy your marriage in a heartbeat just because he can. Even if he doesn't want you any more now he thinks he has me back, we both know he won't go quietly. He'll cause the maximum destruction because you dared to defy him.'

Celia sat numbly listening. What the hell were they supposed to do?

And then Nadia spoke. 'I don't know about you two, but I think we'd all be better off if he was dead.'

191

35

Celia jumped at a loud knock on the door of the suite. The two detectives were standing the other side of the glass, the man with his hands stuffed into his trouser pockets, the woman pushing her shoulder-length dark hair back from her face.

Oh God! What do they want?

The memory of her conversation with Nadia last Tuesday had unsettled her. She had thought her heart would split in two when she heard Ellis was leaving her. Much as a life without Ellis would be a relief, losing the children would destroy her. That was only the start of it, but now the police were at her door, and she didn't have time to dwell on the rest.

She stood up from the sofa, reaching for the crystal in her pocket, as she had been doing for years. For an object that was supposed to dissolve self-imposed limitations and boost confidence, it had done a crap job and she resolved to chuck it in the sea, but for now the familiarity of the action gave her some comfort as she opened the door.

'Sorry to startle you, Mrs Cobain,' the DCI said. 'We've been knocking quietly for a few minutes, but you seemed miles away.'

The fact that the chief inspector used her surname, even though they had previously asked if they could call her Celia, made her uncomfortable. She had the dreadful thought that he could see inside her head, and the formality suggested he was about to expose her guilt. She dropped her head and turned away.

'Can I make either of you a coffee?' she mumbled over her shoulder. 'I think I've finally mastered the machine. Ellis always said I was useless with anything mechanical – if this can be described as mechanical. I'm probably using the wrong word. I usually do.'

Shut up, Celia.

'We don't need coffee,' DS King said. 'But if you'd like one, I'm sure I can call reception and ask them to bring some.'

Celia shook her head. 'No, I've had more than enough this morning. But it's very kind of you. Would you like to sit down?'

The detectives sat, and with no other option Celia lowered herself back onto the sofa. She felt she should use the opportunity to ask an intelligent question, but she had no idea what to say, so bit her bottom lip to stop herself from saying anything inappropriate.

'Celia,' Sergeant King said, 'we're aware that you want to get home to your children, but we still have some questions that need answering, and until this part of the investigation is complete it's difficult for us to allow you to leave. I do hope you understand.'

Celia's gaze darted back and forth between the two detectives, as she tried to work out what they were thinking. 'No, not really,' she said finally. 'I don't see how I can be of any use to you. I've told you everything I know, which is nothing, or nothing useful. Ellis was his own person. He had his own rules, and I don't know about any of them, other than those that applied to me and the children.'

'We need to ask you some quite sensitive questions, I'm

afraid,' the sergeant said. 'We have to look at your husband's life as a whole, to see if anyone may have wanted him dead.'

Celia swallowed the lump in her throat and nodded, clasping her hands together tightly.

'You mentioned the death of Ellis's first wife, Vivian, when we spoke the other day. Did your husband ever talk about anyone close to her? Maybe someone who cared about her and perhaps blamed Ellis for her death?'

'Why would they do that? She killed herself.'

'We're aware of that, but sometimes people blame those closest to suicide victims, however unjustified that might be, and the fact that he had taken the children out on the day his wife died raised a few questions at the time.'

Ellis took the children out? On his own?

Celia tried to hide her amazement. Ellis never had anything to do with the children unless he had to, and she'd been banned from asking questions about the events of the day Vivian died. She didn't agree that it would be easier for the children if it was never mentioned, but she knew better than to disobey him.

'It's a long time ago now, and I've never heard him mention anything. Her parents are dead, and I understand she was an only child. I'm sorry.'

'That's okay, Celia. If you think of anything, though, maybe an old friend of Vivian's who's been in touch, just let us know. In the meantime, we're trying to get access to information relating to Ellis's foundation, but it's always more difficult at a weekend.'

The money!

She still hadn't said anything to Juliette. They were bound to find the transaction. Would that look good for Juliette, or bad?

'The foundation is there to help people,' she said. 'I can't imagine how any information on its operation would help.

194

No one would want to kill Ellis for his philanthropy. I may be missing something, but that doesn't make much sense to me.'

'I know, but it's always good to get a full picture. What about home life? Anyone who's worked for you who was fired by Ellis or may think they've been treated badly?'

Celia didn't want to say that everyone who worked for Ellis was treated with disrespect, but she couldn't stay entirely silent.

'Ellis was quite a demanding employer. He set high standards which not everyone seemed able to rise to. There have been no firings for some time, though. It's my job to pass on Ellis's instructions to staff because he's away so often, and if something isn't quite right in his opinion, the blame usually lands at my door.'

Celia heard her own high-pitched laugh, as if this was all quite normal, but she couldn't miss the sympathy in Sergeant King's eyes and felt herself flush.

'How were things between the two of you? Did either of you have relationships outside your marriage?'

She was sure the detectives already knew the answer to this question. Juliette had told her she'd been forced to admit that she knew Ellis, and was convinced the detective believed there was more to their relationship than an ill-judged pass. But what was Celia supposed to say? She turned her hands over and over in her lap, searching for the right words.

'My husband was away a lot. I can't vouch for his behaviour, but he didn't tell me explicitly about any other women. I would never have had a relationship with another man, principally because it would give Ellis an excuse for leaving me. And then I would lose my children.'

She was quite proud of her response, but the sense of elation didn't last long.

'If you knew he was having an affair with someone, how would you have reacted?' DCI Brodie asked. Celia could feel them both staring at her, waiting for her answer.

'If you think it might have been enough for me to kill him, you'd be wrong. This is a rather difficult thing for me to admit, but if I knew Ellis had a mistress my only concern would be that he would leave me for her and take the children. So if I was going to kill anyone, it would more likely have been the woman.'

If she had expected the detectives to look shocked, she was disappointed. They simply nodded, as if this were a perfectly valid response, not realising that earlier in the week the thought of killing Nadia – the woman Ellis was about to leave her for – had crossed her mind.

36

'Sir,' Ayaneh said as Stephanie and Gus walked back into the incident room. 'The restaurant manager, Oscar Carne, says he'd like a word when you have a moment.'

'Thanks. Give me ten minutes to catch up, and then ask him to join me here, please.'

Ayaneh nodded and lifted the hotel's internal phone.

'So, Steph, what do we make of Celia?'

'She's a nervous wreck. Is that because she's lost her husband, a man who seems to have controlled her every thought and deed? Maybe she doesn't know how to behave without him. I suspect he always made her doubt her own judgement.'

'If we're reading the situation correctly, I can't believe she would call him out for having an affair, or whatever his relationship with Juliette Dalton was.'

'An affair. Whatever Juliette says. One that she wanted to end, by the look of things.'

'Yeah, we need to push her on that. But I doubt Celia would have given him a hard time. Ellis would probably have told her that she was to blame in some way – if it wasn't for her, he wouldn't have had to do it. The usual bollocks.'

'Gaslighting, pure and simple. She totally doubts herself. Or that could be what she *wants* us to believe. Can I ask why you haven't told her Ellis's phone is missing?'

'I don't want to tell her anything that isn't essential. There's more chance of her slipping up and saying something she couldn't know unless she's involved.'

That made sense, but Stephanie thought it strange that Celia hadn't asked.

'What will you do if she insists on leaving?'

Gus sighed. 'You know the answer to that, Steph. I'll have to arrest her. At least then I can hold her for a while and make a decision about our next steps, assuming we haven't solved the case.'

Stephanie sat back and folded her arms. If the woman was totally innocent, it seemed cruel. 'You don't believe she'd hurt the kids, though, do you? She seems to adore them.'

'The clue is in the word *seems*. She might very well love them, but for all we know she might be a murderous psychopath.'

'But how could she – or anyone for that matter – have got to the boat? And Celia's afraid of water. Surely it makes more sense that whoever killed him came by sea? I don't know . . . In a RIB from further along the coast, maybe, as you suggested earlier?'

Gus leaned back and called over his shoulder to Ian.

'Yes, boss,' the detective responded, plodding across to Gus's desk as if the effort was too much for him.

'Did you get anything from the coastguard about small boat activity?'

'Nothing conclusive. They don't have anything recorded, but they said anyone up to something dodgy using a boat with AIS – Automatic Identification System – would switch it off. A small RIB is unlikely to have AIS anyway, and the guy I spoke to said that a boat with an outboard travelling slowly to reduce the wake and noise could move undetected if they stayed close to the shore.'

'Marvellous! So this might be nothing to do with anyone at the hotel. It could be someone with an axe to grind with Ellis Cobain who sailed around the coast to get to him. We need to continue to find out everything we can about Cobain, especially who had reason to hate him enough to kill him. Maybe the husband of a lover, or – given how wealthy he is – perhaps it's about money. How are we doing with checking out the finances? Any progress?'

Ian gave a slow nod, and Stephanie realised that this detective wasn't one to do things at speed. If he was on Gus's team, though, she suspected he had a very sharp mind.

'We got Ellis Cobain's personal account information yesterday – late afternoon. We still don't have his business banking or access to the foundation accounts. You know what it's like at a weekend. Cobain had several personal accounts and we're going through them, starting with his current accounts. Interestingly, we've been unable to find any accounts in Mrs Cobain's name.'

'Any in her maiden name?'

Ian shook his head. 'Nope, not that we've discovered. And there are no credit or debit cards in her name either.'

Stephanie looked at Gus, her eyes wide. 'Don't tell me he didn't give her access to money?'

Gus shrugged. 'Did you find anything that might relate to her expenditure, Ian?'

'I did indeed!' He read from his notes. 'Cobain appears to have had accounts with various specialist food shops. He settles everything, including payments to Harrods – quite large amounts – which seem to occur each quarter, as if the family was being kitted out with appropriate clothing for the coming season.' Ian's expression suggested this concept was completely alien to him. 'There are several payments to top-of-the-range men's clothing stores on his Amex account. He spends thousands with Brioni, and as I'd never heard of them – M&S being my top of the range – I checked them out. Over four thousand quid for a bloody jacket!'

'It's a bit of a shocker if his wife isn't allowed her own accounts. I bet there's a prenup, and if she'd left the bastard she'd have ended up with nothing,' Gus said. 'Let's check it out.'

'I have a feeling she wouldn't care, as long as she still had access to the children.'

Gus looked as if he was about to respond when his eyes travelled towards the door. Stephanie followed his gaze.

'Mr Carne is here to see you, sir,' Ayaneh said.

Gus stood up and walked across to greet the restaurant manager, who looked nervous, standing with his hands clasped together in front of him.

'Mr Carne, DC Jafari tells me you have something you'd like to share with us,' Gus said. 'Please have a seat.'

Oscar lowered himself to the chair and took a deep breath. 'I'm not sure if I should be saying this at all, Chief Inspector, but although I answered all your questions yesterday about timings and so on for Thursday night, there's one thing preying on my mind. It might be nothing, and I'm probably wasting your time.'

'We can decide if it's important. Probably best if you get it off your chest,' Gus said.

'The thing is, it's not about Thursday, which is why I'm not sure it's relevant. It's about last Saturday, nearly a week before Mr Cobain died.' Carne took a deep breath. 'You know we have a wonderful jazz singer – Nadia Shariq? She performs a couple of nights each week – Thursday and Saturday – although I'm afraid we might be about to lose her.'

He seemed to have run out of steam, so Gus took the opportunity to butt in: 'You told us you thought Mr Dalton was about to sign her up, didn't you?'

'That's right, but that's not what I wanted to talk to you about. Last Saturday, the day the Cobains and the Daltons arrived at the hotel, Mr Cobain spoke to me. He asked about Nadia.' Oscar shuffled in his seat and pushed his hands under his thighs. 'I told him she was in the back and I would go and get her, but he said it was okay. He'd seek her out the next day – Sunday. He asked where she lived.'

Stephanie felt a familiar tingle at Oscar's words, accompanied by a twinge of concern about something she should have done, but hadn't. Oscar's gaze was darting from one to the other of them.

'Go on,' Gus said quietly.

'I knew Nadia was expecting someone to talk to her about a contract, so when Cobain asked for her address, I'm afraid I told him. I know I shouldn't have, but I assumed *he* was the guy – you know? It was only later, when I met Mr Dalton, that I realised I was wrong. I shouldn't have shared that information.'

Why did he want to know where she lived? Stephanie thought. It was such an inappropriate question, but it fitted with all they had learned about Ellis Cobain.

'And did she ever mention Mr Cobain to you?' Gus asked.

'No, and I'm ashamed to say I haven't told her. I guess he never looked her up, but I thought you should know.'

Gus nodded. 'I appreciate that. And this was last Saturday, yes?'

'That's right.'

'Okay, that's helpful. Can we just go back to Nadia's schedule on Thursday night? You said previously that when Russell Dalton asked about her at the end of the night, she'd already gone. Can you confirm again what time that was?'

'Let me think.' He raised his eyes to the ceiling as if seeking divine inspiration. 'She arrived at about seven, I think, and did two sets. She started the first one earlier than usual – about 8.30. She wanted to be sure Mr Dalton saw her performance, and he tends to eat early, if he's not with Mr Cobain. However, on that evening they were with *Mrs* Cobain for drinks, so still hadn't started eating at 8.30. I think Nadia was a bit upset, because the room was really noisy while she was singing.'

'And the second set?'

'As everyone started eating late, she decided to come on later – at about quarter to eleven, or maybe a little earlier. Perfect for the late-night drinkers. As soon as she'd finished, she disappeared. That would have been at 11.15, maybe slightly earlier.'

'And where was she in between those two sets?'

'Oh, she was lucky. We had a bedroom that wasn't being used – she could warm up without being heard, have a rest between sets, a shower to freshen up. Not always possible, but we weren't full on Thursday.'

'Was the room in the main building or outside, off the courtyard?' Stephanie asked.

'In the hotel. She wouldn't want to be in one of the suites in case it's raining – hair and all that.' He wafted his hand over his own immaculate buzz cut.

'But you didn't see her between the end of her first set, around 9 p.m., I presume, until the start of her second?'

'No, but that's not unusual. I went to my office at around 10.30 and she was there, ready and waiting. I hope I haven't been wasting your time about Mr Cobain.'

Oscar appeared to be getting anxious, as if he'd spoken out of turn.

'Not at all. You've been very helpful, Mr Carne.'

'Oh, Oscar, please!' he said, smiling at Gus, who stood up to shake his hand.

As he walked out of the door, Gus turned to Stephanie and raised his eyebrows.

'I seem to remember you saying you were going to speak to Nadia Shariq to see if she'd seen anything on her walk back to the village. Did you get anywhere?'

Stephanie grimaced. 'Sorry. I intended to go, but Ayaneh and I went through the phone records and it seemed the interview with Juliette Dalton should take priority. By the time I'd done that and read through the witness reports from the hotel, I was out of time. It's on my list for this morning.'

Gus nodded. 'Okay. You free to go now?'

Stephanie was cross with herself for not telling Gus that she'd failed to do the one thing he'd asked, but he would never reprimand her in public as he might do another officer, and that made her feel even more guilty.

Bugger!

She stood up. 'On my way.'

37

The quickest way to Trevellyn was by car, but Stephanie decided to walk. It probably wasn't the best use of her time, but she needed to work off a bit of her frustration – at herself, rather than anyone else – and for the moment it wasn't raining. She could make the excuse that she thought it would be helpful to see if the bay where Ellis's yacht was moored was visible from the coastal path.

The answer was not really.

The mooring was in a sheltered area of water between two low cliffs that formed a small natural harbour. From the path, Stephanie could only see the top of the fly deck of the yacht. No one walking here would have been able to spot a boat approaching from the shore, although they may have seen or heard a RIB coming from another point along the coast. It was disappointing.

The walk took half an hour, and by the time she arrived in Trevellyn she had cleared her mind of its accumulated clutter and could focus on the interview.

The village was pretty, but tiny by anyone's standards. A steep road led down towards a cove, with nothing other than a pub, a small shop and a cluster of stone cottages lining its sides. A further row of cottages ran off along a track to the left of the road, and Stephanie had been told that Nadia's house was the one with the pale blue front door.

Reaching out, she knocked and for a moment heard nothing. Then a voice shouted, 'Hang on!' and less than a minute later, the door was flung open.

Nadia Shariq's dark hair was tangled and she was wearing a long multicoloured fringed cardigan, hanging loose over a yellow vest and washed-out jeans. Her bright bohemian style made Stephanie feel drab in her black trousers and dark red jumper.

She gave Stephanie a puzzled glance. 'Sorry, do I know you?'

'I'm Detective Sergeant Stephanie King, Devon and Cornwall Police. Could I have a word, please?'

The singer's eyes opened wide. 'Gosh, is this about the man who died? The village has been buzzing, although no one seems to know who he was. There are rumours, of course, but I don't know if they're true. What happened? Was it a heart attack?'

'Do you think I could come in?' Stephanie asked. 'There are some sensitive issues to discuss.'

Nadia pulled the door wide. 'Of course. Not sure I can help, but always willing to try. Do you want coffee?'

'No, I'm fine, thanks.'

They walked into a slightly untidy, but not dirty, living room. Every surface seemed to have some random item on it, including a large pink pot elephant.

'Do you want to sit down?'

Stephanie smiled her thanks and took a seat, her back against an emerald-green fake-fur cushion.

'I'm relieved to hear that nobody in the village knows the name of the deceased,' Stephanie said. 'It's being kept out of the press for now as we have to think of his family, some of whom are not aware yet. But as I need to talk to you about him, I'll have to tell you in confidence that it's Ellis Cobain. He was staying at the hotel.'

Nadia stared back at Stephanie and shrugged. 'Won't say a word, but should that name mean something to me?'

'Not necessarily, but he's been at the hotel for a week and was there when you were singing last Saturday. On Thursday night, the last time you performed, he was on his yacht for the night.'

'Oh, *that's* whose yacht it was. I did wonder. I guess he was loaded then?'

Stephanie didn't answer that question, but asked one of her own. 'Did you know Ellis Cobain?'

'Doesn't ring a bell, but then I sing in clubs, and sometimes people come and talk to me. I don't necessarily know their names. Maybe he spoke to me at some point.' She shrugged again.

'The thing is, Nadia . . . I hope it's okay if I call you Nadia?' Another shrug. 'He asked about you. The restaurant manager, Oscar Carne, said that last Saturday Mr Cobain asked him where you lived. Oscar was adamant that he wouldn't normally give out that kind of information, but he thought perhaps he was the man who wanted to sign you up to an agency for representation.'

'No, the man from the agency is a lawyer called Russell Dalton. I've spoken to him a few times now. He's staying at the hotel, but I don't know this other guy. What did you say his name was?'

'Ellis Cobain.'

Nadia screwed her eyes up and bit her top lip. 'No, it's not ringing any bells.'

'We're assuming that if he asked where you lived, he might

have come here to visit you. Did you have any visitors – someone who may have been Mr Cobain? He said he would call round on Sunday.'

She shook her head. 'I wasn't in much last Sunday. I went into Truro in the morning and I was out all day. If he turned up here, he wouldn't have seen me. What did he look like?'

'Mid-fifties, about six foot, wide shoulders. Beard – not designer stubble, but not the full works either, if that makes sense. Grey hair, quite long on top, straight and kind of floppy over his eyes. You know, the kind that has to be flicked back regularly.'

Stephanie wanted to say that he had a hawkish face and hooded eyes, both of which were true but might sound disrespectful. The fact that she had disliked the guy on sight had nothing to do with her desire to find his killer.

'Goodness, you make him sound *terribly* appealing!' Nadia pulled a face. 'Lots of grey-haired men at the hotel, though, and they kind of blur together when I look out at the crowd. It's easier to see them as a single life form rather than individuals. I don't want to get sidetracked by finding any one person either devastatingly attractive or intensely bloody irritating, as people can be when they're in an audience. It's best to think of them as an amorphous mass.'

Stephanie couldn't help finding this woman amusing, although she wasn't sure she believed a word she said. One too many shrugs, and asking her to repeat Cobain's name was over the top as Stephanie had mentioned it at least three times in the previous two minutes.

'I understand on Saturday night you walked home from the hotel. Can you just run me through your timetable for the evening?'

'Sure, as much as I can remember. It probably won't be wildly accurate. I arrived at the hotel at about 7.30. I got ready and I did my first set at 8.30. Russell Dalton is apparently a man who lives by his watch and likes to eat early. It was my last chance to impress.'

'I understood he was already impressed and had come down here specifically to sign you.'

Nadia gave a wry smile. 'In theory, but until the ink's dry there's always time for lawyers to change their minds.'

'I understand you were given one of the hotel bedrooms. Were you in the room from the time you arrived until you went into the bar to sing?'

'I think so. I can't think why I would have been anywhere else. I went to do my set, then hung around in Oscar's office, thinking Russell might come and ask for me. But Oscar said he was still eating, so I went back to the room, had a shower, stayed there until it was time for my second set. I went on some time between 10.30 and quarter to eleven. I can't be any more precise than that, I'm afraid. I left straight after.'

'You didn't wait to see if Russell Dalton wanted to talk to you?'

Nadia shook her head. 'After my second set I usually have an adrenaline slump. I told Oscar that if Russell *did* try to find me, to tell him I'd be happy to speak to him the next day – Friday. But I guess things went a bit tits up when that man was murdered.'

Stephanie gave Nadia a long hard look. 'Did I mention murder?'

There was just a second of stillness, a moment when Nadia didn't seem to quite know what to say. Then she shook her head. 'Probably not, DS King, but if he'd had a bog-standard heart attack, I wouldn't have a frigging detective cluttering up my living room, would I?'

38

It's taking me a long time to get my act together this morning. Before the sun rose, while I could still believe that today might be a better day, I had lain watching Russell sleep, fighting the urge to tell him everything.

What good would that do? I've hurt a good man, and living with my own deceit has to be better than causing him unnecessary pain. God knows, I'm already responsible for too much of that, but something has to give, otherwise I will explode.

When Russell finally woke up I pretended to be still asleep, and he quietly got out of bed. I feel as if by lying here, curled in a tight ball, I can forget everything that has happened and everything that is still to come, but I can't block the memories, no matter how hard I try.

Why did Celia and I make the decision to follow Nadia's lead? Was it because we're weak?

In Celia's case, she'd had years of being told what to do by Ellis, punished if she failed to live up to his expectations. I had always considered myself to be a strong, confident woman, but Ellis had leached all the power from me, and I had recently started to feel drained of the ability to make a rational decision. So when Nadia stood on a Cornish beach on a chilly autumn day, her little boy playing with pebbles on the sand, and told us what needed to happen, we were captivated by her words. We listened, mesmerised, to this woman we had only just met as she spelled out the threats Ellis posed to us.

'I meant what I said. We need to take control.' Her gaze rested first on Celia, then moved to me, and I couldn't take my eyes from hers. 'How many nights have you cried, feeling trapped, believing there's no way out? What's going to happen if we do nothing?'

I had no words. I glanced at Celia, who looked as stunned as I was feeling. Although I had no idea what Nadia was about to suggest, I suddenly felt a burst of energy – a desire to command my own destiny.

She put her hands on her hips. 'Listen, if we don't do something, Ellis will leave you, Celia, take the children from you, and you will probably never see them again. And that means I'll end up with that bastard taking over my life, slowly but surely beating me – metaphorically or otherwise – into submission. I'm not letting that happen, and he's not having anything to do with Marco. Whatever it takes. I don't want my kid growing up to be as shitty as his father. And let's face it, even if I manage to convince him that I don't want him, it's only a matter of time until the next woman comes along to tear your marriage apart – someone more amenable than either me or Juliette. You don't want to lose your kids, do you? What's the realistic chance of you ever having any of your own now?'

I was stunned by the brutality of her words, but Celia was forty-two. Not out of the question, but she had to know the odds were against it. She shuddered, but didn't say anything.

'As for you, Juliette, you've no chance of saving your marriage or your career. He'll never let you walk away from him unscathed, so let's just be one-hundred-per-cent clear – I repeat, we'd be better off if he was dead!'

In my head I was screaming, *This is insane!* But then I imagined a world without Ellis – the freedom, the chance to retrieve my marriage and save Russell from pain. I closed my eyes as a vision of that life washed over me. Then I thought of the one thing I hadn't told them – that I might also lose my home.

'I know you both feel the same as I do. If we rid this earth of Ellis, we'd be doing humankind a favour. What do you both say?'

Nadia hadn't yet said the words explicitly, but I had no doubt what she was suggesting.

'You're saying we should *kill* him? How the hell could we do that?'

I didn't really know why I was even listening, but I couldn't stop myself. The thought was so tempting.

'Obviously we need a plan. I've been thinking about this since I saw him on Sunday. We need to entice him onto his yacht. Then it should be easy.' She turned to Celia, who still hadn't spoken.

'You understand why we have to do this, don't you? You'd be saving your children from a future without you – their mum – the person they love. I'd be saving Marco. Juliette would be saving Russell. We would be doing this out of *love*, not hate.'

Celia spoke for the first time: 'I don't know, Nadia. Isn't there another way?'

Nadia glanced at Marco, still playing quietly. It felt like we'd been talking for hours, but it was only a few minutes.

'Look at him, Celia. So sweet, so gentle. While Ellis is alive, I can't deny him access to his son. He might even try to take him from me, because at some point we all know he'll have had enough of me and will move on. That's his way. Maybe he'll just walk away, or maybe he'll have another plan. Let's not forget what happened to his first wife, Vivian.'

Celia gasped. 'Nadia . . .'

'You're going to say it was nothing to do with Ellis, aren't you?' Nadia said, her voice scathing. 'That she killed herself. But has it never occurred to you that he must have been involved?'

I saw the look of horror on Celia's face.

'That's a stretch, Nadia!' I said. 'She took an overdose when Ellis wasn't even in the house.'

Celia gave me a curious look, probably wondering how I knew. But it wasn't the right time to tell her Ellis had shared this information with me as part of a conversation about his 'tragic' past.

'Oh, she took the drugs herself,' Nadia continued. 'I don't doubt that. But where did she get them? She'd been depressed for some time and hadn't left the house in months, according to the inquest summary. And yes, I did read it, when I wanted to know everything about poor distraught Ellis's trauma at the death of his wife.' Nadia gave a bark of laughter. 'Some of the drugs may have been on prescription, but not all of them. He must have got them for her. And she'd threatened to leave him. I only know because when I told him we were done, he said, "We're done when I say we are. Vivian thought she could leave, and look what happened to her."'

'She was leaving him?' I said. 'Then why didn't she? With all that money, she could have got help to free herself from him.'

'This is *Ellis*. How do you imagine he made her feel when she said she wanted a divorce? He'll have made her think she was losing her mind – said he wanted steak for dinner, then threw it in the bin saying he'd asked for chicken, or he'd empty all the milk down the drain then tell her she'd forgotten to order any. He'll have employed multiple tactics to confuse her and make her doubt her perception of reality, all aimed at convincing her she was crazy, maybe a danger to the children, incapable of taking care of them.'

Celia was shivering, and I didn't believe it was from the cold. She recognised this version of Ellis.

Nadia hadn't finished. 'You must know that as a minimum he aided her suicide? Vivian told him she was going to take an overdose. She waved the bottle of pills in front of his face. He told me that himself! So he said, "Get on with it then," and disappeared for the rest of the day. He said he didn't think she'd do it, but I don't believe him.'

'Christ,' I muttered, not doubting for one moment that this was true. Vivian had threatened suicide as a cry for help, and Ellis's response had been to walk out of the door.

'You going to let him kill you, too, Celia?' Nadia said, her words brutal.

No one spoke, but Marco whimpered. He was bored with the stones, and banged one on the sand.

'Okay, sweet pea, I'll take you home very soon.' She bent to stroke his head. 'I have to go, but if we're serious about this we can't hang about. It has to be done on Thursday or Friday. Before then you need to find a legitimate reason to go to the yacht, Juliette. That way, if they find your fingerprints and DNA they won't consider them relevant to his death.'

'*Me?*' Until that point I had believed I would be merely an observer, but it was clear that wasn't Nadia's plan.

'Yes, of course you! You've got as much to lose as any of us.'

Was she right? My brain was spinning. Were we *really* talking about killing someone?

'Look, I don't have a fully formed plan yet,' Nadia said, 'but I will by tomorrow. In the meantime get yourself onto that boat, your husband too so it seems like a friendly trip. Give Ellis a chance to do some dick swinging about his wealth and fame, preferably without you vomiting all over him.'

'But—'

'Just fucking *do* it, Juliette. Or do you want your world to come tumbling down around you? We all have a part to play, and this is yours – for now. Not hard, is it? Same time tomorrow?'

With that she turned and walked away.

I felt bruised by the strength of the emotions swirling around the three of us, but the idea that Ellis could be gone from my life was so desperately appealing. More than once I had wished he would simply die. But what Nadia was suggesting was beyond anything I had ever considered.

At that moment, my phone vibrated in my pocket and with a sinking feeling I pulled it out. I had a text:

> You've been avoiding me, Juliette, and that's not how this works. You don't get to say no to me. I just saw Russell go into your room. I'll have a chat with him while I wait for you to return. See you soon!

My mouth flooded with saliva as fear gripped my stomach. Nadia was right. We were all Ellis's victims.

'I've got to go,' I murmured, aware that Celia was in a daze after all that had been said, but concerned only about getting back.

As I stumbled up the path I thought of Nadia's words – about killing Ellis for love. Was it the only way to save Russell pain? I had to end this somehow, and maybe I had no choice.

A storm of hatred swirled inside me. *What is Ellis saying to Russell?* At that moment I decided I would do as Nadia had said: I would engineer a trip to Ellis's yacht. I would make him believe that I wanted to be with him, whatever the consequences.

39

Ellis has now been dead for over twenty-four hours, and I think about how I felt as a raced back towards the hotel that day – was it really only four days ago?

What was Ellis saying to Russell? Have I really just been discussing killing a man?

I stopped running before I reached the courtyard, leaning against a drystone wall to catch my breath, not wanting either Ellis or Russell to witness my panic. As I gulped in the cool, clear air, I had the strange feeling that someone was watching me and I looked over my shoulder, thinking perhaps Celia was behind me, hoping she had more sense than to be seen anywhere near me. The path was clear, so I turned back towards the courtyard to confront whatever was happening in our suite.

I caught a glimpse of movement and my eyes were drawn to the double-height windows of the Cobains' suite. Ellis was there once again, standing, hands in pockets, watching me. This time, though, there was no sinister smile, just the hard glitter of anger in his eyes.

I didn't know what it meant. Had he been to see Russell, or had his message been a ploy to scare me? Had I pushed him too far?

I turned away and walked slowly towards our suite and my

husband, with no idea what was about to greet me. As I opened the door, Russell looked up from his laptop and smiled.

'Good walk?'

I pasted a smile on my face. 'Lovely. What have you been up to?'

'Working, I'm afraid. I thought if I got it all done while you were out we could have some time together.'

And that was it. No noticeable change in Russell's behaviour and no mention of Ellis. I had to assume he'd been firing a warning shot, trying to frighten me, and an all-consuming cloud of bitterness settled on me.

Now, my memories of that day are interrupted as the bedroom door opens. I'm still curled up in bed, but I can no longer pretend I'm sleeping.

'You're awake, darling. I thought you might not want to go to the hotel restaurant this morning, given everything that happened yesterday, so I asked for room service. I got cold stuff in case you were still asleep, but there are some lovely pastries, fruit, ham, cheese. I must say, they do a pretty good feast here for every occasion, don't they?'

Russell wiggles his eyebrows and grins as if he's back in jolly holiday mode. But I know he's only trying to cheer me up, and I don't know how to respond.

He senses my lack of enthusiasm, walks over to the bed to sit down and reaches for my hand.

'Juliette, it's time we had a proper talk. It's killing me to watch you beat yourself up for what you believe you've done wrong.'

I try to swallow, but I can't. *What is he talking about?*

'Don't look like that, darling. What happened wasn't your

fault. If it was anyone's, it was your parents'. You were only eighteen – just a kid, really.'

It's all I can do not to sigh with relief. 'I was old enough to make my own choices, Russ. I have to take responsibility.'

Russell gives a despondent sigh. 'Listen to me, Juliette. When we learned we can't have children, I admit I was floored. My dream had been to have four – two boys, two girls, or even four of the same. I wouldn't have cared. But we know now that it's not to be. And despite the disappointment, I would much rather have you – healthy and happy – without children, than be with some other woman who might be madly fertile but who isn't you.'

I look down at our joined hands. Discovering that I couldn't have children had been devastating, not least because I knew how desperately Russell wanted them. We'd been so happy, so excited about the future, and I felt I'd let him down, particularly as the problem stemmed from an abortion when I was eighteen. The knowledge that it was my fault – at least in my mind – had driven a wedge between us.

My parents were obsessively religious, and the thought of me having an illegitimate baby – the result of a drunken night on a beach – would have shamed them. I would have been shunned at home and within our community, so I said nothing. Although I was still at school I didn't need their permission for the termination. They never knew. I remember telling Russell about it. I could see the compassion in his eyes at the thought of me going through the ordeal alone, but I had tried to make light of it.

'A drunken night on a beach is not exactly original,' I'd said. 'It could at least have been somewhere exotic – a warm night on Santa Giulia beach in Corsica rather than a wet and windy afternoon under the pier in Weston-super-Mare.'

My joking hid the pain and regret I have felt ever since. I should have stood up to my parents, told them I was pregnant, dealt with their shame. I didn't care who the father was. This was *my* baby, and I loved her. I never knew if my baby was a girl, but from the moment I knew I was pregnant, to me she was my Rosie. Dreaming of how she might have looked, maybe with blonde curls and vibrant blue eyes, filled my nights for years. God knows, I've made some bad decisions in my life, and I'm still making them. But losing Rosie was the worst. It tore my heart out.

I never admitted how devastated I'd felt to Russell. And when we had the light-hearted conversation about my night on the beach I had no idea that the pelvic inflammatory disease I had suffered afterwards would leave me unable to have children. It was my fault entirely. I knew there was a problem, but I put up with the discomfort due to embarrassment and fear of my parents' condemnation until I left home for university. Only then did I seek treatment, telling the doctor that the symptoms had begun recently. Antibiotics cured the problem, but the damage was already done.

I squeeze Russell's hand as tears flood my eyes. 'Thank you for saying that, but I know how hard it hit you.'

'No, you don't. You think I was quiet because I was angry or disappointed in you. I wasn't. Not in any way. I was trying to work out what I could do to take away your pain. To start with, I thought it would help if I pretended it was nothing, not important, just one of those things. Do you remember? And you pulled right back from me.'

'Yes, because I knew you were lying, playing a part. "Oh, never mind," you said. "More holidays, fewer nappies," and other similar, inane comments.' I smile a little to take the sting out of my words.

'You're right. But I didn't know how to make you realise that yes, I was sad, but we should have been sad *together*. I didn't know how to make you understand there was no blame, and you seemed to pull further and further away. It sometimes felt as if you *wanted* me to blame you, and somehow we locked ourselves away where we couldn't reach each other.'

I'm the one who withdrew, although he's too kind to blame me. My guilt hit me hard because I was the cause of his unhappiness, and I can see now that he didn't know how to reach me.

Russell has tried to have this conversation with me before, but each time I've shut it down, terrified I would blurt out the truth of my relationship with Ellis. Now I can see in his eyes that he's never blamed me. If only I'd realised he was giving me space to come to terms with my sadness. Instead I allowed Ellis to flatter me, to make me feel valued rather than the failure I believed Russell thought me to be.

'We've made mistakes, Juliette. Both of us. But I would do anything to make you happy again. Maybe it's time to get everything out into the open, to forgive each other for our shortcomings.'

My heart feels as if it will explode. If I'd allowed this conversation to take place months or even weeks ago, I could have used the opportunity to admit to my relationship with Ellis, to explain to Russell that it was an act of desperation because I thought I had lost him. I might have been able to make him understand that I am ashamed in a way that I can barely express. He might have understood.

But it's too late. Ellis is dead. And I am far from an innocent party.

40

Nadia was glad the detective had gone. She had the feeling that the woman saw right through her but reminded herself there was nothing to link Nadia Shariq to Ellis Cobain other than an enquiry at the hotel. And that was the way it had to stay. Bloody Oscar. What was he thinking?

She just had to hope that no one had seen Ellis arrive at her door last Sunday.

She'd fully expected him to seek her out after she had performed her second set the previous Saturday night, and had paced backwards and forwards in the corridor behind the bar, her heart pounding, her eyes darting nervously to the door to the restaurant, waiting for the handle to turn.

Her heart had skipped a beat as the door opened, but her shoulders sagged when she saw it was Oscar.

'You can relax, my lovely. It's only me. The guy who wanted to speak to you said he'd catch up with you tomorrow. So I'd get off home, if I were you. Relax. He'll be in touch. You're the reason he's here after all.'

She was certain Oscar was talking about Russell Dalton, which meant Ellis wasn't going to come. She should have felt relieved, but she didn't. Her mind spinning with conflicting emotions, she'd returned to the storeroom to change, ready for the walk home.

It wasn't until the following morning that she checked her emails and found one from Russell Dalton.

I'm sorry I didn't manage to catch up with you last night, Nadia. I was planning to speak to you after your impressive performance, but my wife felt unwell during dinner and we went straight back to our room.

Perhaps I could make an appointment to meet you on Monday? Please let me know if there is a suitable time.

Kind regards

Russell

Did this mean that Russell *hadn't* asked Oscar about her? He *hadn't* said he would catch up with her the next day – Sunday? He'd gone straight back to his room with his wife, planning to speak to her on *Monday*, which meant Oscar had got it wrong. And if it wasn't Russell, it must surely have been Ellis.

Stunned by the thought, she'd been sick with nerves, certain he would come and find her, wondering how long he would leave her hanging, her nerves jangling.

In the end, she'd waited at home for the whole of Sunday. It had been late in the afternoon when he'd arrived at the cottage, not even bothering to knock. She was in the kitchen, making coffee, when she heard the door open, and then his voice: 'Nadia!'

The mug shook in her hand, hot liquid splashing onto her fingers. She'd stayed where she was, waiting for him to walk through from the hall.

'Well, hello!' he said, looking her up and down in the way he always had, as if she were a piece of property he was evaluating.

She didn't speak.

'So this is where you ended up when you fled, is it?'

And whose fault was that, Ellis?

His eyes raked the room – the bright, mismatched crockery, the table cluttered with sheet music and jam jars of dried summer flowers. One side of his mouth slid up in a condescending smile as if living in a cute cottage in Cornwall demonstrated the depths to which – in his eyes – she had sunk.

'I like it here,' she said, thinking how pathetic she sounded. She should have been prepared for this, and yet she wasn't.

'Do I get a kiss?' he asked, leaning back against the worktop.

'On what basis do you think I'd ever kiss you again?' She hated the trembling of her voice, but she ploughed on: 'You tried to ruin my career. You think you can just trample on people whenever you like, don't you?'

That smile again. Nadia felt an almost irresistible urge to slap his face.

'Come on, Nadia. We both know you love me and you'll never meet anyone like me again.'

She forced herself not to react to his words. 'Why are you here, Ellis?'

He crossed his ankles, folded his arms, the picture of a man who believed totally in himself and his irresistibility.

'I wanted to see you. We never said goodbye properly, did we?'

Nadia just stared at him. How could he think like this? What, in that warped mind of his, did he believe had happened? Didn't he remember telling club owners to cancel her performances? Had he forgotten that he paid hecklers to come to the few clubs that disobeyed him?

'You drove me away, Ellis. Cruelly, intentionally, hurtfully. And now, the moment I might get another chance – and don't tell me you don't know about that, because I don't believe you – you're here again. How did you know where to find me? And why now?'

He laughed, actually laughed, at her. The bastard.

'Funny that. I'm not here because of you. I had no idea where you were, but I admit seeing you last night was something of an unexpected bonus. I knew Dalton was coming to Cornwall to sign someone, but I didn't know it was you. I can assure you, I had no idea this was where you were hiding.'

'I'm *not* hiding! I have no reason to hide.'

'Oh, I think you do. It would explain why you're living incognito.'

'I'm not living—'

Ellis waved his hand dismissively. 'It doesn't matter. As I said, I'm not here for you, but I'm interested to know what the deal is with Dalton.'

'How do you know Russell Dalton?' Nadia was certain Ellis was about to wreck everything.

'Oh, that's another story altogether. Don't worry, I haven't told him how I know you.'

'Are you planning to ruin this opportunity for me, like you did before?'

Ellis sighed. 'Nadia, you did that all by yourself, you know that.'

She wanted to scream at the injustice of his words, but she didn't. 'I presume your wife is with you? Poor misguided woman.'

He chuckled again, as if she had said something amusing. 'She's here, yes. Would you like to meet her?'

She spun towards him. 'And say what? Shall I tell her that I was fucking her husband for months before I discovered that he had a living, breathing wife and wasn't some distraught widower, as he led me to believe?'

'You can tell her if you want. I don't suppose she'll care much.'

At that moment there was a shout from the back garden, and Nadia rushed to open the back door, relieved to discover it wasn't a yell of fear but a shout of excitement as a pretty goldfinch had just perched on the bird feeder.

She felt Ellis right behind her, his warm breath on the back of her neck. She shivered.

'Who's that?' he asked, looking over her shoulder into the garden.

'That's Marco.'

She felt his hands on her waist. 'Is there something you want to tell me, Nadia?'

41

Russell wants me to be happy again, but how can I explain why it has been so hard for me to find my way back to him? Half of me wants to withdraw from him completely, so when the inevitable happens he won't be too devastated. But I also want to make sure he realises just how much I love him, so when he suggests we go for a walk, for once I agree.

Holding hands, we wander down to the beach as Russell talks quietly about where to start the research into the holiday I suggested. He's trying to keep the conversation going, but I'm struggling to give enthusiastic responses.

As we reach the fork in the path, to my surprise Russell steers us to the right, away from the beach and towards the jetty.

'Why do you want to go here, Russ? It feels a bit gruesome.'

He says nothing until we're unable to walk any further, yellow crime scene tape fluttering in the wind, blocking our path.

'I asked you yesterday about Ellis. I could tell you didn't like him, and you've admitted that his behaviour was inappropriate. I think you said "a bit free with his hands". Is that right?'

I swallow, wondering what else he's going to say. 'I did say that. It wasn't a big deal, though. Can we go back to talking about the merits of the Maldives versus the Seychelles?'

'Not yet.' We both stand, staring out into the bay where Ellis's yacht is still moored. 'If you disliked Ellis so much, why were you so keen to visit his yacht?'

Russell is trying to keep the suspicion out of his voice, but he's failing. For a moment, I don't know how to answer. What possible excuse could I have for pushing as hard as I did?

'I thought you'd like to see it,' I say. 'I was trying to put my dislike of the man behind me, for your sake.'

He turns to look at me. 'I don't think so. You said it would be great to see what a motor yacht was like inside. It was *you* who asked *me* to persuade Ellis to take us out for a look round. He suggested Friday, the day before we were due to leave, but you pushed to go earlier. "Why wait?" you said.'

'Maybe I just wanted to get it over with.'

'No, Juliette. You're lying to me, and I don't know why. When we arrived at the yacht, I said I was interested in how it worked so Ellis showed me the controls. You asked if it would be okay if you had a nosy down below – in the bedrooms and bathrooms. You were gone a while. What was all that about?'

I give an exasperated sigh. 'Oh come on, Russell. I just wanted to see how the other half live, that's all.'

'And the photos?'

'What photos?'

'You took loads, and when I asked if I could have a look, you flicked through them and just selected a few to show me. Usually you'd pass me your phone so I could look, but there were lots that you skipped over. Do you still have them?'

I don't, but I can't tell him why not. I never delete photos, but Nadia said I should get rid of all but the general shots. The close-ups of the fiddle rail on the bedside table, the polished walnut wall facing the bed, the door to the en suite bathroom, the view of the mirror from the bathroom door, the make and model of television: we needed these, but once she'd seen them, they had to go. They were too incriminating.

'What most people don't realise is that photos stay in your recently deleted folder for a while. You don't want that,' Nadia said, reaching for my phone. She frowned as she tapped the screen. 'Okay, they're gone.'

How could I explain this to Russell?

'I guess I deleted them,' I say. It sounds weak even to my ears. 'I've got so much crap on my phone, and I use it for work. When I want to show people photos of designs I've done, it's not very professional if I have to go through loads of personal images.'

As I say this, a thought pops into my head.

'And I wanted to look at the bedrooms because there may come a time when I'm asked to do an interior design for a yacht. You never know. So I wanted to see how big the rooms were. I'm not likely to get another chance, so I was prepared to put up with Ellis if it helped me, work wise.'

Russell nods as if this explains something that has been puzzling him, and I hope he finds my justification for snooping plausible. What he would never understand, though, was my request to visit the yacht for a second time – a trip he knows nothing about and never will. But Nadia's instructions were clear. And they made perfect sense.

At least, they did at the time.

42

The Day Before the Murder

I wasn't sure if Celia would turn up again after everything that was said on Tuesday, but when I arrived at our meeting place I was surprised to see she was already there. As ever, she was glancing over her shoulder, despite the fact there was no way Ellis could approach from behind unless he abseiled down the cliff.

I sat on a rock close to her. Nadia was late, and a jittery unease made me twitchy, my feet shifting in the sand. *What am I doing here?*

I was about to suggest to Celia that this was – and always had been – madness, when Nadia appeared.

'No Marco today?' I asked, thinking it was a pity she hadn't brought him. He provided some sort of justification for our plotting.

'Thought it better to leave him with a friend. God knows what words he might pick up and repeat.'

Celia hadn't spoken, but her face was drained of colour, probably at the thought of the discussion we were about to have. I felt the same. What had seemed like the right decision a day ago now seemed ludicrous – the stuff of dreams. Or nightmares.

My only excuse was that for months I'd felt as if the world was closing in on me from all sides, crushing me, leaving me no escape. Ludicrous or not, Nadia's idea let just a chink of light into the suffocating darkness.

'Let's get to it, then,' Nadia said. 'I've brought you both a present.'

She opened the blue and white striped tote bag she had over one shoulder and took out two tiny black phones.

'I don't need that,' Celia said. 'I've got a phone.'

'Have you never watched crime programmes on TV, Celia? Surely you realise you can't use your normal phone to communicate with either of us? There'll be an investigation – obviously – and it's best if there is no traceable connection between us. Juliette knows who I am because of her husband, and maybe she's met you once or twice at the hotel. But no one can connect you and me, Celia, and it needs to stay that way.'

Celia nodded, looking bemused.

'We may need to contact each other, and when Ellis is dead the police are bound to seize your mobile. They mustn't see any messages between us. These are burner phones. Unregistered. We use them to communicate with each other if we need to, but no one else. At the end of the week, we ditch them.' She stared at Celia. 'For Christ's sake, I'm serious about this. Do *not* use them to contact anyone else at all. I've put my number into each of them, and shared your two numbers. They have prepaid SIM cards, and no links to you. Do you understand how serious this is, Celia?'

Were we really doing this?

She handed us the phones, and Celia turned worried eyes to me. 'What do you think, Juliette?'

It was all moving too quickly. We hadn't agreed to kill Ellis, and yet Nadia seemed to be taking it as read. It was clear she'd been planning this since she'd seen him on Sunday.

'We haven't even said we're in yet, Nadia,' I said.

'Why in God's name *wouldn't* you be in? Fuck's sake, Juliette, the man is about to rip your husband's heart out, ruin your marriage and your business. Is that not reason enough? And you, Celia, he'll take your precious kids from you. You'll never see them again. He has all the power. We need to take it from him.'

In my head a voice of reason was screaming, *But not like this!* and I could feel Celia shaking beside me.

'We don't have much time. We have the perfect opportunity, but only a couple of days. If you do nothing and just go home at the end of the week, everything will stay the same. Is that what you want? So it's now or never. Juliette, have you arranged to go to the yacht?'

I nodded slowly. 'I persuaded Russell to ask him. Ellis suggested Friday, but I showed a ridiculous amount of enthusiasm and said it was a lovely day so could we go this afternoon? Ellis was suspicious of my eagerness, but he probably thinks it's because of what he threatened yesterday.' They both gave me puzzled glances. 'Oh, just his typical nasty tricks. Anyway, Russell was delighted because it's the first time I've shown any interest in anything this week. Poor Russ. He has no bloody idea.'

'Then let's keep it that way. When you get on board, make sure you go into the bedrooms and the bathrooms. Touch everything you can. Celia, are there fiddle rails on the bedside tables? They're important to the plan.'

Celia's eyes looked wide with fear, but I had the feeling that she would agree to whatever Nadia suggested. 'I d-don't know what a fiddle rail is,' she stuttered, shaking her head.

Nadia tutted. 'Rails around the top of furniture to stop things sliding off when the boat moves.'

'Oh. Yes, then.'

Nadia nodded. 'You need to take photos of them, Juliette. Now, does Ellis still snort cocaine to get high before sex?'

She didn't look at his wife when she asked this; she looked at me, and even though Celia knew I'd been having an affair with her husband, I felt my cheeks flush.

'Don't worry, Juliette. You can say. He used to use drugs with me, but these days I try to avoid him touching me as much as possible.'

Nadia didn't wait for a response. 'I guess that's a yes, then. Good. That's useful. Where does he keep his stash on the boat, Celia?'

'He used to be brazen about it, convinced no one would check up on someone as important as him, but he's become careful to hide stuff since he's been building his profile. I'm sure you both know he's ridiculously vain about his hair, and he has a fancy brush that he takes with him everywhere. The end can be unscrewed – the handle's hollow. He uses that for his tablets – I don't know what they are – but he doesn't put his cocaine in there. He uses empty pen cases for that – the foundation pens he gives away. He keeps them in the bedside cabinet.'

'Can you get your hands on any real foundation pens – not the drug-filled ones?'

Celia shrugged. 'Yes, I've probably got a couple in my bag. Do you want them?'

Nadia held out her hand, and Celia rooted around in her bag, then passed her the pens. I had no idea what she was up to.

'Juliette,' she said, holding out a small drawstring bag. 'There's some stuff you need to take with you to the boat. You'll need to hide it somewhere he won't look.'

Was I going to have any say in this at all?

She glanced at Celia. 'You keep tampons on the boat, Celia?'

Celia blinked. 'Bottom of the cabinet on the right of the sink unit in the master en suite.'

'Perfect. Juliette, you can hide this stuff in the box or behind it, then.'

'What's in the bag?' I asked.

'It won't blow the boat up, if that's what you're thinking. Have a look, if you want, but maybe wait until I've run through everything, and don't touch anything without gloves.'

I didn't like the sound of any of this. 'What's the plan, Nadia? You need to tell us what's going to happen and how the hell we'll get away with it.'

'I'm getting to that. We'll do it tomorrow night because I'll be singing at the restaurant and that's important. We have to time everything perfectly and we'll do it in two stages. If we follow the plan, we'll all have alibis for his time of death.'

I turned towards Celia, anxious to know what she thought. But her face was a blank mask, almost as if she was no longer with us.

'Juliette will go first,' Nadia continued, and I swung back to face her. 'You need to get Ellis on his own before tomorrow evening. Say you need to see him, maybe to explain why you've been so distant. Ask him to take you back out to the yacht early on Thursday evening. If all else fails, tell him you're desperate for his body.' Her lips clenched as she said the words.

'Come on, Nadia. How can I square it with Russell?'

'Tell him you're going for a run. Arrange to meet Ellis by the jetty. Make sure you're dressed in black, and tell Ellis you need to hide in the bottom of the tender so no one sees you and tells Russell. You can't have a bag with you as you're supposedly going for a run, which is why you need to take the stuff when you go to the yacht this afternoon – carry it in a big tote bag, or something. I'll talk you through what you're going to do in a moment, but let's get the mechanics in place. Do you know how to operate the tender?'

'Of course not! How would I know that?'

'I guess you turn a key and point it in the right direction. We need you to leave Ellis on the yacht and come back to shore in the tender so Celia can get herself out to the yacht later.'

'*Me!*' Celia nearly fell off the rock she was sitting on. 'I don't know how it works either, and I'm *terrified* of the water. There's no way I could do that!'

'Shit! Are you kidding me? My plan was for you to take the tender back to the yacht and then – when you've done what needs to be done – you swim back. It's not far.' Nadia looked at Celia's shocked expression. 'Fuck! Don't tell me you can't swim.'

Celia dropped her eyes and I suddenly felt protective. She was so vulnerable. So damaged.

'Nadia – you've outlined roles for me and Celia, but what precisely will you be doing?' I asked.

'I'm providing your alibis. I'll be at the hotel making sure everything goes to plan, distracting anyone who wonders where you are. Obviously I can't go out to the yacht. I have no reason to have ever been there, so my fingerprints or DNA couldn't be explained.'

'We can forget this.' I stood up. 'It's a bloody *ridiculous* idea, and I don't know why I listened to you for even five minutes. Celia, your call, but I'm going back to the hotel.'

I turned and started to walk back towards the footpath, but Nadia ran in front of me and blocked the way. 'Fuck's sake, hang on, Juliette. Okay, maybe my first plan isn't going to work. Particularly if Celia doesn't swim. Just give me a moment.'

I stopped and waited. To my surprise, the next voice I heard was Celia's.

'Sorry. Would it be okay if I made a suggestion?'

'Christ, Celia, he's made you into a walking bloody apology,' Nadia grumbled.

Glaring at her, I spun back towards Celia. 'You don't have to ask permission, Celia. Tell us what you're thinking.'

'Hard as it is to say, I don't want Ellis to be alive in this world. I really don't. But I can't see myself as a murderer either, whether he deserves it or not. What if we could find some other way of making him do what we want him to?'

'Celia, get real! No one can ever get him to do anything unless it benefits him. You should know that!'

'Hang on, Nadia. Celia may have a point,' I said. 'Perhaps if we could hit him where it hurts the most, we could still achieve what we need to without killing him.'

'Is there any spot on his entire body where that fucker hurts?'

Celia looked up at us both, biting her bottom lip. 'I think so, yes. Ellis wants recognition. He wants to be seen as special – more than just a rich man who inherited his wealth. As a minimum he craves a CBE, but a knighthood's what he's really angling for. If we could find some way of ruining his prospects it would utterly destroy him. It's his way of proving his worth, you see. Especially to his family.'

I stood perfectly still. Celia was right. He'd thrown money – lots of it – at making this happen.

Nadia shook her head. 'Yeah, well, I don't think that's enough. We could do that, but he'd still be alive, still able to hurt people. We'd be doing the female population of the world a huge favour if we got rid of the tosser.'

'I get that, but Celia's right, Nadia. What I care about is

stopping him from screwing with me and hurting my husband. Celia needs to be sure he doesn't take her kids, and I guess you want to keep him out of your life and Marco's. There has to be another way, one that doesn't make us guilty of *murder*, for God's sake. It wouldn't help either me or Celia if we end up in prison, and you getting locked up wouldn't be great for your son either.'

Nadia's mouth set in a hard line. 'You know nothing about me and Marco, or what we want. I'm trying to help you two, but you're just putting obstacles in the way. Look, just hear me out.'

'No,' I said. 'Sorry, but I'm not going to listen to this. If you two decide to go ahead, that's fine. I won't say a word. But I won't be an accessory to murder, so I don't want to hear any more.'

I pushed past Nadia and headed back the way I had come. This had briefly seemed the only way out, but I couldn't do it. I couldn't murder a man.

'Seriously, Juliette?' Nadia yelled. 'You're giving up that easily? Look, if killing him doesn't work for you, let's find something that does. I won't mention murder again, if that makes you happy.'

Maybe I should have cut my losses then and returned to the hotel, but I didn't. And now I must live with the consequences.

43

Since returning from the village, Stephanie hadn't had a chance to speak to Gus. He was deep in conversation with Ian, and she wasn't sure there was much to report other than she was certain Nadia had lied about knowing Ellis Cobain. It felt very much as if the woman had been playing a game.

A waiter brought her a cup of coffee and, smiling her thanks, Stephanie took it across to sit by Ayaneh.

'Yes, Sarge, what can I do for you?'

'Can you fill me in on anything I've missed?' she asked.

'Ian's been going through more of the finances. I heard him tell the boss that he'd found something interesting, and they've been talking ever since. We've got the fingerprint information from the boat. The only ones that match residents at the hotel belong to Mr and Mrs Cobain and Mr and Mrs Dalton.'

'Where did they find the prints?'

'The Cobains' were everywhere, as you'd expect. Mrs Dalton's were all over the master bedroom and the en suite. Dr Shentu is asking one of his guys to mark up exactly where they found them. Mr Dalton's are on the bedside table in the master bedroom, in the bathroom and the cockpit, if that's what you call it.'

'We didn't take Nadia Shariq's prints, did we?'

'No. I don't think she was on the list because she wasn't staying at the hotel. Shall I get that organised?'

'Yes, please. Anything on DNA?'

Ayaneh pulled a face. 'Dr Shentu says that's a nightmare. There have probably been loads of people on the yacht since he bought it. They're focusing on anything they can get in the vicinity of the body for now.'

Gus strolled across to join them.

'Interesting conversation with Ian about the finances,' he said. 'He's got Cobain's business bank accounts, and one of his companies owns property in Bristol and Bath. About six months ago a payment was made to a company called Artful Interiors. Guess who owns it?'

'Not the hardest question you've ever asked,' Stephanie said. 'I guess that would be our resident interior designer, Juliette Dalton. How much?'

'There are several payments for random amounts to the account – some had references, probably invoice numbers, presumably for the work she was doing for him. But one has no reference, and it's for £75,000.'

'Bloody hell! That can't be for design advice, can it?'

'Not according to her website. She's not been going long and isn't well known yet. She quotes seventy-five pounds an hour for her services.'

'Maybe she bought furniture and other stuff on his behalf.'

Gus shook his head. 'Nope. He made direct payments to Minotti London, Fendi Casa, and similar furniture brands that I wouldn't even dare to look at. He spent tens of thousands, but not through Artful Interiors.'

'So what was the seventy-five grand for? I wonder if Russell knows about it.'

'We can only assume not, given he thought they'd never met. And there's something else. There are payments from Cobain's personal account to a J. Boden. Only small, by his standards anyway. A few thousand at a time. But then payments of exactly the same amounts appear in Cobain's business account from Artful Interiors within a couple of days.'

Stephanie shook her head. 'Not sure I understand.'

'I'm not surprised. As an example, three weeks ago two thousand pounds was paid from Cobain's *personal* bank account to J. Boden. Two days later two thousand pounds was transferred to Cobain's *business* account from Artful Interiors. I'm guessing you can work out who has the maiden name of Boden?'

'Ah, shit. Juliette, I presume. So he transfers his own money to Juliette, who pays it into her Artful Interiors business account, which then pays it to Ellis's company account? Is it some sort of tax fiddle?'

'I was talking to Ian about that, and we can't see how. If he was transferring money from his business via a circuitous route into his personal account it could be a fiddle. But this is going the other way.' Gus held his hands out and shrugged. 'Obviously we need to get the Daltons' account information as a matter of urgency.'

Before Gus could say any more, Ayaneh's phone rang and she passed it to Gus.

'It's Dr Shentu, sir.'

Gus put the phone on speaker and laid it on the desk between the three of them.

'Gus. Tai here. Did you get the tox results yet?'

'What do you think?' Gus said, blowing out through pursed lips.

'Thought not. When you do, don't be surprised by what you

find in his blood. We took anything we couldn't examine on site back to the lab, and we found some pens in the bedside table. Well, they looked like pens.'

Gus sighed. 'Don't tell me. Filled with cocaine.'

'Yep, not exactly original, I know. But that's not all. A couple had coke in, but there were two others. One was empty but held traces of ketamine. Another was still full of it.'

'Excellent! Sounds like an all-round good guy, doesn't he? Didn't we hear he was tipped to appear in the next honours list?'

Tai chuckled. 'So it was rumoured, although it might have been wishful thinking on his part as the whole thing is shrouded in secrecy. Anyway, back to the pens. Odd thing here. The pen with traces of ket had Cobain's fingerprints on it, as did both cocaine pens. But there were no fingerprints at all on the second, full, ket pen.'

'No one's?'

'Nope. It's possible he wore gloves when he filled the pens, or maybe he got his dealer to fill them, and they would have been wiped, probably. But I thought it was a bit strange, especially as no care had been taken with the coke pens. And I've not finished yet. He had a hairbrush for those silky locks – and we know it was his and not his wife's by the hair. The end unscrews, also not the most imaginative hiding place in the world. Full of oxy tabs.'

'Jesus. Do you think he was into speedballing? Bloody dangerous practice.'

'Maybe, although he could have used coke first and then oxy to come down from the high. Sometimes people suffer depression after cocaine, and oxycodone can ease the symptoms.'

'Then why take it in the first place? Bloody moronic, if you ask me.'

Stephanie saw Gus's face tighten with irritation. He had no time for drug users.

'Any prints on the brush?' he asked.

'Only Cobain's. I thought I'd better fill you in, particularly about the empty pen. I didn't want you to get excited when you got the tox results back.'

Tai was right. If traces of ketamine were found in Cobain's system, Gus would have assumed someone had drugged him. The contents of the bedside table suggested it was self-administered.

'Is that it, Tai? No breakthrough moment?'

''Fraid not. There's one thing, not sure if it means anything. Steph pointed out some marks on the wooden panelling and what looked like Blu-tack. We've tested the other dull patches, and there are microscopic amounts of Blu-tack there too. Something was clearly stuck on the wall, but we can't find any trace other than a tiny scrap of paper that must have torn off when whatever it was got pulled down.'

'Anything on the paper?'

'Nope. It's 120 gsm – premium paper, not the type people normally use for letters. More used for posters, photos, maybe. But given the position of the marks on the wall, it would appear an A3 sheet was stuck up. There's nothing unique about the paper, so it would be hard to say definitively where it came from, and the scrap had no printing on it.'

'Okay, thanks, Tai. I'll get someone to check with the hotel. Let's see if they use anything like that, although the odds are it's something Ellis had on the boat. We'll check that with his wife.'

As soon as Gus had finished the call to Tai, he stood up.

'Can I have your attention for a moment?'

The hum of activity quietened and people looked up from their computers.

'There are a few things we need to crack on with – and quickly. Ellis Cobain paid a shedload of money into Juliette Dalton's business account and some smaller amounts into her personal account. We have to treat her as a suspect now. Ayaneh, can you go and collect her when I've finished so DS King can interview her again? And this time we have to insist she tells us the truth. What was that money for, and what was their relationship? In the meantime, the warrant to search the Daltons' room has come through. Ian, can you take one of the uniformed officers with you and conduct the search as soon as Juliette's here. Assess Russell Dalton's response – does he look worried?'

Ayaneh and Ian nodded.

'If you find any mobile phones, ask Dalton to switch them on. If he says they belong to Juliette, bring them here. We still haven't found Cobain's phone, although I strongly suspect it's lying at the bottom of the sea. Did we manage to get anywhere with the forensic linguist, Steph?'

'She's off at some sports event with her kids, but she gave the text a quick look. I sent her his previous five texts, but even I could see that the tone was entirely different. The previous ones were all instructions: tell the gardener to trim the yew hedge; call my tailor and tell him I need my suit by Friday – that sort of thing. She said the text from the yacht was unlikely to have been written by a man – something to do with the use of personal pronouns and punctuation, but there was a caveat. He could have asked AI to write it for him, and it's not a big enough sample to form a conclusion.'

'Bloody marvellous,' Gus said. 'Can't even trust the written word any longer. At the time the text was sent, the Daltons were at the hotel, and Celia answered from her room, so given they're the only two women we're aware he knew—'

'Three,' Stephanie said. 'I'm ninety-per-cent sure he knew Nadia Shariq too.'

'Okay, three. But they're all accounted for at 10 p.m. when the text was sent. So unless someone else was on the yacht with him . . .' Gus grunted. 'We mustn't get obsessed with the women to the exclusion of everyone else. I'd hazard a guess that Dalton is the type to write a kind, thoughtful text, but he was in the restaurant. On the other hand, there may well be more than one jealous husband out there.'

'We're digging up as much as we can about Cobain, but without announcing to the world that he's dead we can't ask people direct questions,' Ian said.

'I know. We have to sort that. Unless we have a quick breakthrough, we'll have to persuade Celia to allow social services and the nanny to break the news, or maybe set her up on a Zoom call. Then we can go public.'

'She'll want to hug them, though,' Stephanie said. 'I would.'

He sighed. 'I know. Anyway, we've digressed. The text was sent at 10 p.m., and the time of death was between 10.30 and midnight.'

Stephanie nodded. 'Molly did say there might be a bit of flexibility in the earlier of those timings, but it seems likely he was alive when the text was sent. Maybe he got high and in a mellow moment sent a text that didn't sound like him? Then he simply overdid the ketamine?'

'Molly's convinced he died from lack of oxygen,' Gus said. 'If he OD'd, that wouldn't account for the marks on his neck, and I have to wonder at him having a stack of oxy tabs when they were part of the cocktail his first wife took to kill herself.

I'll order hair strand analysis so we can check if Cobain used drugs habitually.'

'Do you think Celia could tell us if he was a regular drug user?' Stephanie asked.

'She might, yes. Can you go and have a word with her, Steph? Ayaneh can bring Juliette here and let her stew for a while until you've spoken to Celia. Ask if she had a prenup while you're at it, will you? Let's see if she had a motive to kill him.'

'Other than to escape his controlling, manipulative behaviour, you mean,' Stephanie muttered, earning herself a scowl from Gus. She wasn't supposed to have strong feelings about the victim. She stood up. 'Okay, I'm on it. I'll go and see Celia now. I assume we're still treating her as a witness, not as a suspect?'

'For now, yes.' Gus turned to Ayaneh. 'After you've picked up Juliette, can you look for anything and everything you can find on Nadia Shariq, please. Maybe our singer is more interesting than we've given her credit for.'

44

'Mrs Dalton, could you come with me, please?' the young detective asked.

I could feel Russell's eyes on my back, but I gave him a quick smile as I followed her out of the door.

I should have guessed that the police would want to speak to me again. It was inevitable, and this time I think I should tell them at least some of the truth, although I can't decide if it's better to suggest that I was in love with Ellis and devastated by his death, or tell them how things really were.

I won't make any mention of how he was blackmailing me. Nadia was adamant she could remove the photos permanently from his phone and every linked device, and I have to believe she was telling the truth, although after all that's happened I'm finding it difficult to trust her.

The police have left me sitting in a small office just off their incident room. I'm desperate to see if they have some kind of evidence or suspect board so I can check if I'm on it, but I was directed in here, where I can see nothing. There's a hum of conversation coming from the next room, but I can't make out any words.

The detective who brought me here said DS King might be a while and offered me tea or coffee, but I can't drink anything. I might choke.

What was I thinking?

My life was already a mess, but now it's infinitely worse, and I could end up in prison. It wasn't supposed to end like this. Whatever Ellis's behaviour and the evil tactics he employed to get what he wanted, I can't believe I contemplated taking another person's life.

Nadia had grudgingly come round to the idea that killing Ellis wasn't the only way to destroy him. The fact that his reputation had to be flawless sparked ideas of how we could threaten to expose him to the world for who he really was. It offered an alternative path – one I could live with. Yes, it was blackmail. And it was illegal. But if we could come up with evidence against him so strong, so irrefutable, he would have to bow to our commands. We would all be free, and no one would be dead. At least, that's what I'd believed.

'We still need alibis, though,' she said. 'If he ever points the finger at us our actions need to be deniable. We have to be able to prove that we couldn't have done anything he might accuse us of.'

I didn't know what she meant to start with, but things started to make sense as she explained her plan. To protect ourselves we had to make sure that not only did Ellis have no evidence of our involvement, we also had alibis for every part of the set-up. Celia's fear of water created some problems, but Nadia told her she had to get a grip.

'If you want to regain some control over your life and keep your kids, Celia, you have to stop being such a fucking wimp. He's *made* you like this. He's destroyed your confidence, but you were an actress, for God's sake. So bloody *act*! Pretend this is your big moment.'

'I wasn't very good,' Celia mumbled.

'And I wonder who told you that? Now is your chance to excel. Show the prick what you're made of.'

And just like that, Nadia had us on board, ready to bring him down. We would destroy the photos he had taken of me, damage his credibility as a person and as head of a charitable foundation, maybe even frame him for a criminal offence. He might know we had set him up, that we were behind it all, but he wouldn't be able to prove it. The only way he would be able to maintain his reputation and his apparent integrity would be to agree to our demands.

But he wasn't supposed to die.

The Day Before the Murder

Our revised plan for the destruction of Ellis Cobain wasn't so different from the first, apart from how it would end. It still required me to demean myself, to make Ellis believe I was aching for him and couldn't wait until we were back in Bristol to be with him; that I wanted him *right now*.

The die was cast, my husband an unwitting accomplice. Russell had done as I asked and persuaded Ellis to show him around the yacht – not that it took any real persuasion. Ellis loved the thought of flaunting his riches, never understanding that wealth didn't make you a better man.

'And will the lovely Juliette be accompanying us?' he had asked.

'I'd be delighted to, Ellis, if that's okay.'

His gloating smile filled me with revulsion. Despite how cold and distant I'd been for the previous few days, the arrogant bastard must have assumed I couldn't resist seeing evidence of his prosperity. Either that or I had an overwhelming desire to spend time in his company. The thought made me shudder.

We walked down to the jetty and climbed into the tender.

'Would you like to steer, Juliette? I could show you what to do.'

Russell, still at that point under the misapprehension that Ellis was an all-round good guy, gave me an encouraging nod, and tempted as I was to say I'd rather sit quietly on my own, I had to play my part. It would only take a couple of minutes at most to get to the yacht, and if I'd been stand-offish my next objective would have been so much harder to achieve. I was already shaking with nerves at what I had to do once on board, and I could only hope that Ellis believed the tremors were due to excitement at his proximity.

'Russell, you take a seat at the front. It's the best seat in the house if you face forward. Juliette, if I'm going to show you what to do, it's probably better if you stand here, and I'll stand behind to show you.'

I knew exactly what that meant, and felt my whole body go rigid. Somehow, though, I managed to stand at the helm, as Ellis told me it was called, thankful that the journey to the yacht would be short.

'Now we need to give it some throttle,' he said as he leaned against my back, pressing himself into me.

Russell was enjoying the ride but I wanted him to turn round, to see what Ellis's game was and show his disgust. Ellis was too clever and I was focused on my mission, unable to do anything to discourage him.

'Enjoy that, darling?' Russell asked as we arrived at the yacht.

The best I could do was give him a watery smile as Ellis tied the tender up and showed us where to climb on board, asking us to remove our shoes first.

'Sorry, guys, but the wrong shoes scuff the surface of the deck, and I don't want you bringing dirt and pebbles inside.'

Russell looked a little embarrassed at his inappropriate footwear, and I gave him a sympathetic smile.

I didn't need to say much as Ellis showed us around the main salon, other than to make appropriate sounds of awe at what, to me at least, seemed an unnecessarily ostentatious interior. Russell was enthusiastic enough for both of us, and no one seemed to mind when I excused myself to wander off and take a look at the bedrooms. I wondered for a moment if Russell would suggest that I leave my tote bag on the sofa, and I would have found it hard to think of an excuse. But he was fascinated by all the gadgets Ellis was demonstrating and didn't seem to notice. Breathing a sigh of relief that the first hurdle had been overcome, I made my way down to the lower deck, my sweaty palms gripping the handrail a little too tightly.

It was all easier than I had thought. Everything on the yacht was exactly as described by Celia, and I managed to stow all the items Nadia had provided in the right places. In many ways, that was always going to be the easy bit. Now I somehow had to persuade Ellis to bring me back to the yacht the following night, but I had no idea how to get him on his own. By the time I joined them up on the fly deck, I could tell that our time on board was coming to an end. I tried to quell my rising panic. I had to do something!

'You should go and check out the bedrooms, Russ,' I said in a desperate attempt to get rid of him for a few moments. 'Ellis won't mind, will you?' I said, trying my best to produce a winning smile.

'Not at all. You need to get a full idea of what life is like on one of these beauties.'

Russell gave me a puzzled glance. 'Well, I suppose I should see it all. Could I use the bathroom while I'm down there, Ellis?'

'Of course! Use the one in the master suite.'

We both stood silently as my husband made his way down to the main deck and disappeared from view. We were about as far away from him as we could be on the yacht, but I wanted to check, to be sure he wasn't still standing below us, admiring the view.

I took a couple of steps down from the fly deck, far enough to see the sliding doors to the salon. They were wide open, but there was no sign of Russell.

I hurried back up and turned to Ellis. 'At last, we are alone,' he said in a theatrical tone. I could see the mockery dancing in his eyes.

'I'm sorry. I know you're angry with me, but it was such a shock to see you on Saturday. I didn't know what to do, how to behave. And when you pretended we didn't know each other, I was so confused.'

'No excuse for ignoring me, Juliette.' He reached out a hand and wrapped a strand of my hair around his finger. 'I was getting a little tired of your behaviour. Remember who's in control here.'

The threat was subtle, but it was there. 'I'm sorry, Ellis. You know I don't want Russell caught up in the middle of this, and Celia's with you. It all feels so awkward.'

He gave my hair a little tug. 'But I'm sure you're glad I came, aren't you?'

I wanted to scream, *No! I wish I'd never set eyes on you in my life.* But that wasn't the plan.

'Of course. I just wish I'd been able to think of somewhere we could be together without any threat of discovery.'

'Maybe I should book an extra room at the hotel,' he said with a smile that made my skin crawl.

I opened my eyes wide in horror. 'Ellis! The hotel staff would know. They'd be bound to talk if you took another room. What would that do for your reputation? Is there nowhere else where we could be alone?' I glanced anxiously towards the stairs. 'We haven't got much time before Russell's back from your bedroom – which, by the way, is fabulous.'

He tugged my hair again, drawing me closer, his breath touching my skin. 'There's your answer, then. We can come here. I'll leave it to you to work out how you can get away.'

Trying not to appear over-eager, I grabbed his hand. 'I go for a run every evening, and Russell never comes with me. I could meet you at the jetty – say six o'clock tomorrow? Now the clocks have gone back, it'll be dark by then. We can have an hour together, at least.'

We heard a gentle *swoosh* as the sliding doors opened below us, and I let go of his hand. 'Can we do this? Please, Ellis?'

There was nothing he loved better than to have someone begging, and I knew I had him.

'Six it is,' he said with a sly grin. 'I shall look forward to it.'

I heard Russell whistling, something I hadn't heard in a while, as my husband made his way back up towards us.

'Don't come up, Russ,' I called. 'We're on our way down.'

Russell was standing looking out over the sea as we walked down the steps, Ellis behind me.

'If you've seen enough, perhaps you'd like to get back in the tender while I lock up,' Ellis said, turning towards the open double doors to the salon.

'Sure,' Russell said. 'You ready, darling?'

I nodded, but despite the cacophony of thoughts and fears crashing around in my mind, something was niggling. Something that didn't seem quite right. I shook my head. Whatever it was, it was eluding me.

45

Back from her talk with Celia Cobain, Stephanie watched Juliette Dalton through the window in the door of the makeshift interview room. Her hands were clasped in her lap, but her index fingers were circling each other. Every few seconds she shifted in her seat, as if she couldn't get comfortable. The strain was clear.

Stephanie pushed the door open. 'I'm sorry to have kept you waiting, Mrs Dalton,' she said, taking a seat. 'There are a few things I need to discuss with you about your relationship with Ellis Cobain. But before I do that, I need to caution you.' Ignoring Juliette's startled expression, Stephanie continued: 'You do not have to say anything. But it may harm your defence if you do not mention when questioned something which you later rely on in court. Anything you do say may be given in evidence.'

Juliette's eyes widened in disbelief. 'Why do you have to caution me? Am I a suspect?'

'It's my duty to make sure you understand your rights before we talk. It's standard procedure, Mrs Dalton, and you're entitled to a solicitor if you want one.'

Juliette was silent, biting her bottom lip, and Stephanie guessed it was an impossible decision. It would be difficult to ask for a solicitor without her husband knowing, and she would have to reveal far more to him than she wanted to. Finally she shook her head.

'Okay, but if you change your mind, let me know.' Stephanie glanced at her notes, determined to get the truth. 'When I last spoke to you, you admitted you knew Ellis Cobain, even though your husband isn't aware of this. You said you worked for him. Can I ask how you charge for your work?'

Juliette was pale, her breathing shallow.

'I send invoices. I'm not expensive – I'm trying to build my reputation.'

'So on average, how much would your invoices to Mr Cobain have been?'

Juliette bit her bottom lip again. 'I invoice monthly, and it depends, obviously. He wasn't my only client, but I would imagine they'd be a few thousand pounds.'

'Okay, that's helpful. When you're furnishing someone else's home, do you order and buy the furniture so they can reimburse you later?'

She shook her head. 'No. I've not been working for long enough to get credit, so for now my clients pay suppliers directly.'

Stephanie was about to ask the next question, when Juliette looked up. 'Is this about the seventy-five thousand that Ellis paid into my account a few months ago, because if it is, that was a business loan. He offered to help me so I could rent some space and set up a studio.'

'Thank you for explaining. What did your husband think about this arrangement?'

'He doesn't know,' she said quietly. 'I told Russell the landlord had given me the space for free in exchange for some design work on the rest of the building.'

'It seems Mr Cobain was a generous man, because there

are also payments from his personal account to one of yours. Not such large amounts, but some are two or three thousand pounds.'

Juliette seemed to be having difficulty swallowing.

Stephanie sat back in her chair and folded her arms. 'Okay, let's cut to the chase, shall we? I saw enough of you with Ellis Cobain to know that you couldn't stand him touching you. If he'd made a pass that you'd rejected, as you previously told me, why the hell would you accept his money – so *much* money? And not just the lump sum, but the smaller amounts. Come on, Juliette. We can access your bank accounts, and your husband's, so if there's anything else to find, now's the time to tell me.'

If Juliette had been pale before, she now looked almost green.

'Shall we start again? What was your relationship with Ellis Cobain?'

Tears flooded Juliette's eyes, and Stephanie felt a stab of sympathy. The woman seemed tormented. She was clearly hiding something and appeared to be in more pain than she could cope with.

'I told you before that my relationship with Russell was going through a difficult patch. Not his fault, but he seemed to have withdrawn. Ellis, on the other hand, was wildly attentive. That's why I didn't tell my husband I was working for him. Russell would have wanted to meet him, and I was enjoying what I believed was an intoxicating flirtation. So yes, in the end I had sex with Ellis Cobain.'

'Just the once?'

Juliette lowered her chin onto her chest. 'A few times. I know I should have stopped it, but I didn't want to upset him.'

'You mean because of the money?'

There was an almost imperceptible shrug, as if that wasn't all of it.

'Was it a loan or an investment?'

'It was just a loan between friends – at least, that's how I saw it. Ellis seemed like the most charming and generous of men, and although he asked me to sign for the money – just a formality, I understood – he said it was only so he could prove to his accountants where it had gone. A receipt, if you like. Everyone's very conscious of money laundering these days, and I didn't think I was *agreeing* to anything. I was merely signing a confirmation that the money had been paid to Artful Interiors to show he wasn't involved in some scam or other.' Juliette bowed her head. 'I know I should have checked the paperwork, but I was concerned that if I said I wanted to go through the wording carefully, or even ask for legal advice, he would withdraw the offer. I didn't want to offend him, but it turns out he played me. It was, in fact, a formal agreement – a contract, I suppose – with a clause about repayment on demand. When I realised that if I ended the affair he could ask me for the full amount back, I didn't know what to do. I'd have had to tell Russell. We'd have had to remortgage, or even sell the house. I couldn't let that happen.'

Stephanie saw a tear slide down Juliette's cheek and drop onto her lap.

'What about the sums he paid to your personal account?'

Her voice was now so quiet that Stephanie had to strain to hear. 'He said that while we were together, he'd help me to pay off my loan – because he cared about me.' Juliette made a soft scoffing sound. 'The money he lent Artful Interiors came from his property company, so he couldn't simply write it off. But I was struggling to earn enough to make the repayments, so every now and again, when he was feeling in a generous mood, he'd transfer some money from his private account to my private account. I then paid it into my Artful Interiors account.'

'And Artful Interiors then made a repayment to his property company to reduce the loan.'

'That's right. I know it sounds convoluted, but he said it was the only way he could help me reduce my loan. It's not illegal. I've checked.'

'I'm sure it's not, but are you telling me that as long as you were prepared to satisfy his sexual demands, he gave you money?'

Juliette gave a tiny gasp. 'You make me sound like a prostitute.'

There was nothing Stephanie could say to that.

'Are you certain your husband has no idea about this?'

'I am, and I couldn't bear it if he found out.' Juliette lifted a tear-stained face. 'My relationship with Ellis has put a barrier between my husband and my soul, and it hurts so much. Russell doesn't understand why I'm shutting him out, but he can feel it in every look.'

It wasn't Stephanie's place to give marital advice, but she couldn't help feeling for this woman.

'Have you considered telling him? People forgive affairs all the time, you know.'

'Maybe it would relieve my guilt, but I'd be taking a knife to his heart.' She raised haunted eyes to Stephanie's. 'I remember reading that marriages are often stronger after an affair, when the hurt has healed. I suppose it's a bit like a scar – stronger than the skin it replaces. The problem is, it's never again quite so beautiful, is it?'

*   *   *

If anyone had a strong motive for wanting Ellis Cobain dead, it was Juliette Dalton. The pain was etched on her face and reso- nated in every quiver of her body. It was clear she had made a mistake, but had she been desperate enough to kill him? And if so, how? And was she fooling herself about her husband? Did he know more than she thought?

'I'm afraid I'll have to ask you to wait here for a while, Juli- ette,' she said. 'DCI Brodie wants to talk to you too, but we're conducting a search of your suite, and he'll want to see if we find anything that he needs to ask you about.'

Juliette's look of horror as Stephanie left the room suggested they would find something, although she had no idea what.

Gus had been locked in a private office for the last half-hour updating his boss by phone, but the call was clearly over as he flung open the door and marched across the incident room towards her.

'They're struggling to keep this out of the press. We'll have to decide about Celia soon. Where are we up to with her?'

'She knows Ellis used drugs. She hated the thought of them being in the house in case the children got hold of them by mistake, but he told her they needed to be instructed not to go looking through other people's things; she should teach them some manners.' Stephanie felt her lip curl in disgust at the man. 'She's certain he was a regular user of cocaine, because in Ellis's opinion that's what all rich people do.'

'Charming. You'd think people with everything wouldn't need any additional stimulants. But what do I know? Go on.'

'I asked about a prenup too. She did sign one, but she can't remember what it said. She isn't, and never has been, interested in Ellis's money.'

'Do you believe her?'

'I do, but we have to remember she used to be an actress.' Stephanie shrugged. 'Perhaps I'm being a bit naive. The prenup is with his solicitor, and she's given me the details. That's where his will is too.'

'We need to get on to that – see if there are any surprises. Did she have anything else to say?'

Stephanie nodded. 'Yes, something that shocked me, if I'm honest. When she's finally able to leave, she's not sure how she's going to get home. She neither wants, nor is able, to sail the yacht and they don't have a car here. But she can't book a taxi or take the train because she has no money and no access to any.'

'Christ, that guy was something else! Did he not have any money on him?'

'He doesn't carry much cash, but to be fair, neither do I. She can't use his credit cards because she doesn't know any of the PINs, and he used his phone for contactless payments.'

'And we don't know where that is. What if he'd been rushed into hospital for something? How was she supposed to feed the children if he was incapacitated? What a tosser.'

'I told her not to worry, that we'd sort something.'

Gus slumped into a chair. 'It seems cruel to keep her from the children so I've asked for a risk assessment to be undertaken. A team in Gloucestershire will make enquiries about the children's well-being, Celia's relationship with them – the usual. We'll base our final decision on what comes out of that, if we haven't solved the case. The trouble is, Celia is one of a very small pool of viable suspects.'

Stephanie pulled a face. 'She might have wanted to escape what appears to have been an abusive and controlling husband, but she seems so submissive, and didn't seem stressed by the idea of his infidelity. I asked again if she thought Ellis was having an affair.'

'And what did she say?'

'She thinks he's probably had several, but considers it the least of his crimes. Says she'd rather be married to a man who is habitually unfaithful than to one who inflicts subtle abuses on a daily basis. From everything we've learned, it would seem he was guilty of both.'

'Sir!' Ayaneh shouted as she pushed back from her desk and hurried over. 'I've managed to find out more about Nadia Shariq. She's been singing for several years and was previously known as Nadia Scott – although Shariq's her real name. Until three years ago she was very popular in the clubs in and around Bristol. Each of the clubs she performed in was supported financially – to some degree – by Ellis Cobain.'

Stephanie felt triumphant. She had been sure from the outset that Nadia knew Ellis. Would she still deny it? And why change her name?

46

'Okay, okay, I lied,' Nadia told Stephanie as she bundled her into the car. 'Yes, I knew Ellis Cobain but wished to God that I didn't.'

Gus had insisted that Stephanie drive to Nadia's cottage and bring her back to the incident room. 'Arrest her, if you have to,' he'd said.

Tempted as Stephanie was to ask why she had lied, she wanted to get her into an interview room before she said another word. She might like this woman, but she was the second person to have denied knowing Ellis Cobain. What *was* it with this man that no one wanted to admit to having anything to do with him?

She didn't need to think long about that question.

As Stephanie guided Nadia towards the room designated for interviews, Gus was holding the door open for Juliette Dalton to leave, and she and Nadia came face to face.

For just a moment Stephanie saw Juliette's eyes flicker with a spark of recognition, smothered as quickly as it came. It was an odd reaction, given that Juliette's husband was in Cornwall specifically to see Nadia, and they had both been in the audience for her performance on Saturday. Why pretend she didn't know who she was? Why the jolt of shock in her expression?

Nadia seemed more prepared, and smiled at Juliette as she passed.

'Do you two know each other?' Stephanie asked as she showed Nadia into the interview room.

'I know who she is. She's Russell's wife. Were you questioning her too?'

Stephanie looked at Nadia. 'I think you know I can't answer that. Have a seat, Nadia. I'm just going to catch up with my boss.'

'Is he the good-looking one? He looks a bit like that actor Gerard Butler. Very happy to talk to him.' Nadia grinned at Stephanie.

'I'll be back soon,' Stephanie replied, refusing to be drawn.

Gus was waiting for her outside the door.

'How did it go with Juliette?' she asked.

'I don't think I got anything more out of her than you did. The search of their suite didn't turn up anything sufficiently incriminating to pursue. There were a couple of things the guys questioned: an empty tub of Andrews Liver Salts that they found in the bathroom bin – not incriminating in itself, but it had been washed out and there wasn't a trace of powder in it. It's been sent off for examination. Russell Dalton says it was Juliette's.'

'Why wash it out if it's going in the bin?'

'No idea, maybe she's a neat freak. The other thing was some Lycra running kit – leggings and long-sleeved top – hanging over the shower door. Russell says it's Juliette's. Apparently she rinsed it through after her run on Thursday, but left it wet in the bath while they had dinner – something about her not wanting to delay eating for too long. She only remembered it was still there when she went for a bath yesterday evening. Not sure what you think, but they're due to leave tomorrow, so why wouldn't she have just put the kit in her bag to take home and wash? It's obviously not her only gear, because she's been out running since then.'

'I don't know, Gus. There was no blood at the scene, so that can't be a reason for washing it. And anyway, she was here at the hotel for the period that Molly has down as possible time of death.'

'Except for later – there's a small window of time before midnight.'

'Possibly. But you said that according to Russell the kit was already wet in the bath by then. Assuming we believe him, it can't be anything to do with Ellis's murder.'

Gus frowned. 'Okay, we can ponder on that. I've asked for both Russell and Juliette Dalton's bank information. Let's see what else we turn up. Now let's go and talk to the lovely Nadia.'

'A warning. I think she's probably going to flirt with you.'

'Marvellous. Probably a tactic to divert attention from the subject. If it gets too disruptive, I'll shut up and pass the questioning to you. Just wastes bloody time, and we could really do without that.'

Stephanie turned away to hide a grin. She wasn't entirely sure that Gus would get the better of Nadia Shariq.

'Miss Shariq, I'm DCI Gus Brodie. Thank you for coming in,' Gus said, reaching over the table to shake Nadia's hand. 'Or should I call you Nadia Scott?'

She shrugged as if attending a police interview was nothing, but Stephanie noticed a brief flash of surprise that they knew her previous name.

'Either's fine. Not sure I can help, but always willing to assist the police.'

'Let's crack straight on with this, then, so you can get off home. You denied knowing Ellis Cobain, but that was a lie, wasn't it?'

'Yep. Absolutely. The guy's a tosser – or was, should I say. I wish I didn't know him, and I don't want anything to do with him or his life. I lied because I didn't want to go into all the crap from my previous life. Come on, DCI Brodie. You must know what it's like when there's someone you never want to see again.'

Gus ignored the remark. 'Why didn't you want to have anything to do with him?'

'I told you, he's a twat. He wanted to have sex with me, and I refused. So he made a point of ruining my reputation in the clubs. Told the managers not to book me, had people heckle me. I had to do what he said – in other words, jump to his command – or my career would be over. I chose to escape down here and start again.'

'You must hate him for that, Miss Shariq.'

'You can call me Nadia, you know. I don't mind.' She smiled at Gus.

'Did you hate him?' he said, ignoring her response.

'Back then, yes. But it's nearly three years since I left Bristol, and if I'd wanted to kill him, that would have been the time. Not now.'

'Why the name change?'

Nadia blew out a breath between pursed lips. 'After all that crap in Bristol, I wanted a new identity, and Shariq is my real name. I decided not to deny my heritage any longer, and it's a bit more memorable than Scott.'

Stephanie was watching her closely. Beneath the sassy veneer, there was a layer of pain that she was trying hard to disguise.

'Did you lie about him coming to see you last Sunday?'

'No. And if I'd seen him coming, I'd have hidden under the

bloody bed. I *did* notice him in the audience on Saturday night, and I wasn't happy about that.'

'Why not?'

'Because he's not a man who likes to lose. And I didn't give him what he wanted.' She shrugged as if the answer was obvious.

'Were you concerned that he might influence Russell Dalton's opinion of you; that he might persuade him you weren't to be trusted? You'd have lost your big chance, wouldn't you?'

Nadia leaned forward across the table. 'Listen, DCI Brodie, if Russell Dalton is such a wimp that he would take the word of a narcissistic fucker like Ellis Cobain, then frankly I don't want to be his client.'

The venom and anger in her voice was clear, but Stephanie saw another flicker of vulnerability. There was more to her relationship with Cobain than Nadia was prepared to admit, but she was sure no amount of probing would reveal it.

'Have you ever been on Ellis Cobain's yacht, Miss Shariq?' Gus asked, ignoring the invitation to call her Nadia.

'You've got to be joking me! Why the hell would I want to do that? Christ, the thought of being trapped at sea with him is enough to make me puke. Not a chance, Chief Inspector.'

Stephanie had a sudden flashback to the night she had sat with her mum, watching Nadia. There was a moment at the end of her performance when she looked out into the audience.

'Nadia,' she asked. 'When did you first meet Russell Dalton?'

Nadia frowned. 'Last Monday. I knew he was arriving last weekend, but – you know – things don't always go to plan, so I wasn't counting any chickens. His wife wasn't feeling well on the Saturday night, so he didn't catch up with me then. I saw him on Monday.'

'Had you ever met him before last Monday?'

'Nope. He emailed me about coming down to Cornwall, saying he would combine our meeting with a mini-break with his wife.'

'Did you know what he looked like?'

She pulled a puzzled face. 'What, do you think I googled him or something? No. I had no idea.'

Stephanie could feel Gus's eyes on her, and she simply nodded. There was no point saying she had seen Nadia's expression as she looked out into the audience that evening. She remembered thinking the singer looked triumphant, as if she had won a prize. If she asked her now, Nadia would deny it or claim it was excitement about her performance, but Stephanie was certain it wasn't.

There was someone in that audience that she had been thrilled to see. And it wasn't Russell Dalton.

47

The police had offered to give Nadia a ride back to the village, but she'd refused.

'No,' she said. 'I'm good, thanks. I fancy a walk.'

She kept a smile on her face until she was well clear of the hotel, and then she felt her jaw become rigid, her lips pinch.

'Fuck,' she muttered under her breath. She hadn't wanted anyone to know of the connection between her and Ellis. Bloody Oscar.

She wanted to march into his office and demand to know why he'd told the police about Ellis, but she couldn't say anything. The last thing she needed was for him to go scuttling back to them to say that she'd given him hell. It would make her look even more guilty than she already did.

The thought that the police had interviewed Juliette again sent a shiver up her spine. What had they been asking her? Had she stuck to the story? Sergeant King staying at the hotel had been something they could never have anticipated, and no doubt both Juliette and Celia now blamed Nadia for dragging them into this.

The day she met Celia and Juliette on the beach, Nadia had been burning with rage. How *dare* Ellis think he could just walk into her kitchen and inflict his own very special form of torture?

Her father had been the same, believing men should have the final say on everything. She had spent her childhood trying to please and appease him. Anything to get his attention. It had taken years to escape his control. And then she met Ellis.

As she'd hurled stones into the sea, screaming into the wind, she'd known she had to do something. She had no idea what, but one way or another she was going to make the bastard suffer.

Then she saw Celia on the bench.

Wanting nothing more than to vent her fury and to find a way of hurting Ellis, she'd had no plan in her head as she marched up the beach. It took only moments for her to realise Celia was as damaged as she was. Unlike Nadia, though, she had withdrawn into her shell, scared of her own shadow, while Nadia wanted to fight back, to get even. When she'd discovered Juliette was yet another victim, a sharp unsettling feeling had twisted inside her, swelling until the idea of vengeance overwhelmed her.

As the two women revealed the hold Ellis had over each of them, a plan had started to form. She could play on their weaknesses – Celia's fear of losing the children, Juliette's fear of losing Russell. For Nadia's plan to succeed, they needed to be jolted out of their despondency, and she hadn't held back, the pain and fury pouring from her, raw and unfiltered. Juliette was the stronger of the two and, despite her air of defeat, she was the angrier, although much of the anger was directed inward. Celia, on the other hand, had been ground down and would follow where she was led.

She'd only had days to plan, but the two women had been pathetically easy to manipulate, once they thought the idea of murder was off the table, although there had been a moment when her plan had come close to collapse. The foundation pens had to be filled and given to Juliette before her visit to the yacht, and yet the two women couldn't be seen together. There hadn't been much time – only a narrow window between their meeting on Wednesday morning and the time of the planned trip the same afternoon, but the answer came in the form of Russell.

'Mr Dalton,' Nadia had said when Russell answered her call. 'Could I drop by the hotel for a chat, please? I'd love to run through a couple of points in the contract.'

She could almost hear Russell's smile down the phone. 'Nadia, it's so good to speak to you. Please do call me Russell, though. I'm not available this afternoon, I'm afraid, but we could meet later this evening, if that works?'

'I could come now, if that's okay? I'm close by.'

'That's fine. I'm in the business centre right now, printing off some documents to discuss with you. We could meet there, if you like.'

'Could we meet in your suite, do you think? I don't want to remind the hotel that I might be leaving. I'd hate them to be looking for a replacement before I've made a final decision.'

There was a moment of silence. She could almost see Russell's mind turning over. Was it sensible for him to see her in his suite? Might she accuse him of inappropriate behaviour, or something worse?

'Oh, I'm sorry Russell! That's probably an unprofessional suggestion on my part. Maybe you'd be happier to meet when your wife's around?'

'That sounds like a good idea. Can you make it here for around 1 p.m.? And I'll ask Juliette if she can be available.'

Juliette, of course, would tell Russell he was being unnecessarily cautious and make sure she was out. It was important the two women weren't known to be friendly.

And so the scene was set. It hadn't taken long to put their plan into action. While Russell was making Nadia a cup of tea she took the opportunity to slip two foundation pens into the canvas holdall that Juliette had conveniently left sitting open on a side table.

Juliette had everything she needed. She was all set for part one of the plan. All Nadia could do was hope that she held her nerve.

48

'Okay, everyone,' Gus called. The hubbub in the office died down at the sound of his voice. 'Can we go through where we're up to, please. Ian, what have you got?'

Ian was slouching back in his chair, reading from his iPad. 'GPS signals and cell-siting data from all the relevant mobiles. We've already established that Cobain's was with him on the yacht, but still no idea where it is now. At 11.10 p.m., just over an hour after the text to his wife, the signal was lost. Nothing since. As we know, Celia's mobile was either in their suite or the hotel restaurant. Juliette Dalton's never left their room. She didn't take it with her on her run, or to the restaurant. Russell's also remained within the hotel grounds.'

'All of which tells us bugger all,' Gus grumbled. 'Except maybe, and it's only a maybe, that if Ellis's murderer got rid of his mobile, it suggests he was killed at around eleven on Thursday night. However, that's a stretch. He might have switched it off before it was dumped.'

'Seriously, though,' Stephanie said. 'How many people switch their mobiles off? They put it on silent or something.'

'Fair point. What about Juliette's mobile, Steph?'

'She offered it to me at the end of her interview. We'd already checked her call history through her service provider, so it was iMessage or WhatsApp that I was looking for. I wondered if that was how Ellis communicated with her, but she admitted they used Telegram.'

Gus raised his eyebrows. 'Security conscious, then.'

'Very. The app was in a hidden folder on her phone and set to give no notifications. She says all their messages were auto deleted within one day. She opened the app for me, but there was nothing to see.'

'A way of ensuring her husband couldn't see any communications between them, I presume.'

'Exactly. I don't know what we should do about Russell Dalton. At the moment we're giving Juliette some leeway, but how do we know he wasn't aware of their relationship? There's just about enough latitude in the timings for him to have gone to the yacht to kill Ellis after they left the restaurant.'

'But how would he have got there? Isn't that the million-dollar question? Have we got any further on that little conundrum?'

Ayaneh raised her hand. 'Sir, the keys to the hotel boathouse are kept in the office shared by the restaurant manager and the facilities manager. Didn't Oscar mention that Mr Dalton was looking for Nadia on Thursday night, after her set? He went to the office.'

'Well spotted, Ayaneh. We might need another word with Oscar. What's in the boathouse?'

'There's the RIB that was used to go and check the yacht on Friday morning, and some paddle boards and kayaks. As far as the facilities manager is aware, the key never left the office. It was certainly there on Friday morning when they took it to get the RIB out.'

'What type of lock?' Gus asked.

'Padlock – a strong one. A key, rather than combination, and there's no sign of any damage.'

'Okay, so we know there's no CCTV in the courtyard, but there are cameras around the hotel's perimeter. Ian, the footage was checked for anyone leaving the hotel in the relevant hours, wasn't it?'

'Yep. There were some people who had been for dinner, non-residents. The CCTV from the car park shows them driving away. The only residents who left the building were those staying in the courtyard apartments.'

'If someone had taken the key to the boathouse, they could have pocketed it at any point during the day, but the key was in the office on Friday morning when they took it to get the RIB. So anyone who'd taken it would have had to return it before then. Check the footage again, please, and let's see if anyone – including staff – went *into* the hotel between around 10.30 on Thursday night and the early hours of Friday morning.'

Stephanie was looking at her phone. 'Email from Molly. The tox results are back.'

'What's she got to say?'

'She's sent a summary, and there are a few surprises. We expected to find ketamine, and we were right, but it seems Cobain took it several hours before his death. Apparently ketamine has a half-life of around two to three hours, and given the concentration in his blood combined with time of death, she thinks he must have taken it a minimum of three hours before he died.'

Gus frowned, and Stephanie shared his confusion. Had Ellis gone alone to the yacht, taken drugs and then been murdered a few hours later?

'There's more. We were thinking he might have taken oxycodone too, given what Tai found, but there was none in his system. However,' she raised her eyes to look at Gus, 'they *did*

271

find flunitrazepam – Rohypnol, roofies, call it what you will. Tai's confirmed they found no traces of flunitrazepam on the yacht, but Molly's spoken to him and he said, given the hiding places Ellis had for his other drugs, he'd like to go back to see if there's anything they've missed.'

'Christ, it could be anywhere. They'll have looked in all the usual places – vents, toilet tank, books, mattress. But now I guess they'll have to check picture frames, belt buckles, toiletries. Rather them than me.'

'Why would he take Rohypnol, though?' Stephanie asked. 'Apparently it has a much longer half-life – potentially over eighteen hours – so it's less clear when that was taken.'

'If he was a regular cocaine user he might have used it to counteract its stimulating effects, or soften the comedown – much the same as we speculated about the oxy tabs. Maybe that's his thing – a high, followed by relaxation and sedation.'

'I couldn't possibly comment. I'd like to take the moral high ground about his behaviour, but I can't really, given the amount of wine I consume.'

'Not to mention the odd margarita,' Gus muttered with a grin.

His expression turned sombre, and Stephanie could almost hear his mind whirring. 'I'm not an expert on street drugs,' he said. 'But while I know some people use Rohypnol after cocaine, I've never heard of it being taken in conjunction with ketamine. Has anyone else?'

There was a general shaking of heads.

'The hair sample analysis has been rushed through too,' Stephanie said. 'What's interesting is that while there are indications of regular cocaine and oxycodone use, there's no trace of either ketamine or Rohypnol – at least, historically. He had longish floppy hair, so a decent span of time to analyse, and there's no sign of either drug in the last eight to nine months.'

Ian spoke up. 'I spent some time on the drug squad, boss. A bit too much running around for me, but I learned a thing or two, and it seems an odd combination in the dead of night. Both ketamine and Rohypnol cause sedation and central nervous system depression, so unless he wanted to be particularly heavily doped, as a drug cocktail it makes no sense to me. One explanation is that, as he had cocaine in those pens too, maybe he took the ketamine by mistake?'

'Which rather begs the question, why put two very different drugs with similar appearances into identical pens? How would he know what he was taking? Steph, will you phone Tai and ask if there were any differentiating marks on the pens? If not, I don't like the sound of this. Add to that the fact that one of the pens had no prints on it, and it's looking dodgy. When you've finished, let's have a look at the boathouse too.'

49

Russell will be wondering what's happening, but I don't know what to tell him. I should have gone straight back to the suite after my interview, but what reason can I give for the police wanting to interview me on my own again? I've searched my mind for an excuse. Maybe I can say I was kept waiting for ages, and in the end they only had one question for me. But what might that question have been? I need to think of something.

That's only one of my worries. Spinning round in my head is the thought that they don't seem to be asking the *right* questions, the ones that should have been obvious to them. And why were the police talking to Nadia? They're not supposed to know there is any connection between her and Ellis. She swears that since he's been in Cornwall they've never been seen together, and he only visited her once.

'That was enough,' she said. 'I told him I was going to be away until Thursday, but I'd see him Thursday night, after my last set. I promised he could come to the cottage then, but I knew that would never happen. Thank Christ for that.'

'Did he believe you when you said you were going away?' Celia had asked in a tone of awe. She clearly couldn't understand how anyone could lie to Ellis.

'You don't think two nights a week singing in a local hotel

is enough to keep me in food, not to mention drink, do you? I run social media accounts for several local businesses, including Morvoren Manor. I work from home mostly, but Ellis doesn't need to know that.'

'Who looks after Marco when you're working?' I asked.

For a moment Nadia seemed taken aback at the question.

'Marco's fine, thanks. Keep him out of it.'

I wasn't trying to drag him into it, but this wasn't the time to be defensive. Now, though, I have to wonder what the police were talking to her about. Will she ever tell me?

Leaving the main hotel building after my grilling, it had seemed a good idea to walk towards the village in the hope that I could wait somewhere along the track and waylay Nadia, although I have no idea how long the police will keep her. In any case, she'll think it's a crazy idea for us to speak to each other in public, and I've suddenly lost my nerve. The path only leads to Trevellyn, but if I turn round and head back to the hotel, I'll probably bump into her and have to deal with her anger. She's so fierce she frightens me.

I suddenly realise that just ahead is the narrow path down to the area of beach we've been using as our meeting place. I can't be spotted from the coastal path, and I can hide there until I've worked out what to say to Russell.

Casting an anxious glance over my shoulder, I'm relieved that there's no one around to witness me veer off down the slope. The stones are slippery from the thin drizzle that's falling, and I almost lose my footing, saved by grabbing an agonising fistful of spiky gorse. As I slither down towards the beach, the herring gulls cry out overhead, making a cackling, laughing sound, as if they are mocking my fear. Even the sea appears wilder today: grey and forbidding, crashing onto the shore.

Why did I ever agree to Nadia's plan? Even the lesser plan of blackmail rather than murder should have been dismissed as ridiculous, but my fear of losing Russell, of seeing the devastation in his eyes, felt like justification. And Ellis wasn't supposed to die. One threat to my future has now been replaced by another, and I was stupid to allow myself to be dragged into it.

The first part of the plan was frightening enough, even though all I had to do was go with Ellis and Russell to the yacht, tote bag over my shoulder, find my way to the bathroom of the master suite and hide everything Nadia had given me. I remember pulling the unregistered phone from my bag and logging on to the yacht's Wi-Fi, praying that Celia had remembered the password correctly. The sense of relief when it worked made me weak. I was even able to remove the pens from the bedside drawer and replace them with the ones Nadia had slipped into my bag earlier.

'Isn't there a risk that he'll bring one back to the hotel with him?' I'd asked.

Celia shook her head. 'He won't do that. He's paranoid about protecting his reputation, but feels invincible on the yacht.'

He may have *felt* invincible. But he wasn't. We saw to that.

50

As Nadia stomped along the path back towards the village, ignoring the fact that her hair was getting wetter and heavier by the minute, her mind was spinning. The police would investigate her now. She had denied knowing Ellis, and they knew she'd been lying. They would wonder what else she'd been lying about – and the answer was *everything*.

The woman detective, DS King, had a look about her – a look that said, 'I don't believe a word you're saying.' And why question whether she knew what Russell Dalton looked like? Was it a trick?

Nadia tried to think back to last Saturday. She hadn't been scouring the audience looking for Russell, but her eyes had been drawn like a magnet to Ellis and she could remember the rush of feelings she'd had.

And now Ellis was dead. That was what she wanted. *Wasn't it?*

She hadn't understood why he was at the hotel. At least, not then, and the next few days had been a roller coaster of emotions. Moments of joy, stripped away to be replaced with fury; excitement at the thought of her revenge; frustration at the other women for being so fucking *wet*; and then pain. But she wasn't going to think about that now. She was going to concentrate on working out how in God's name she could make sure she wasn't implicated in any of this.

She thought back to her final meeting with Celia before Thursday evening.

'Celia, it needs to go like clockwork. So much depends on keeping everything on time. We're creating alibis so whatever Ellis *thinks* happened, we can deny it.'

The woman had nodded, but the persistent worry lines were there. Was she really up to this?

Nadia hadn't wanted to go on board the yacht. She didn't want to see the evidence of a life Ellis had shared with another woman. She wanted the deed done in her absence – her role being the planner, the puppet master pulling the strings.

She hadn't known how she would feel to see him so degraded, this man who had captured her heart then treated her so badly. What if he opened his eyes and recognised her? What if a moment of lucidity burst through his drug-addled brain? If his eyes locked on to hers, she didn't know what she might do. She couldn't be there.

But Celia was incapable of fulfilling her part on her own. She couldn't swim, and Juliette had questioned the sense of using the tender. 'Someone will hear it. Sound travels over water. Do we want to risk that?'

It galled her that Juliette was right, and even if Celia managed to get to the yacht alone, the complexity of the task might be beyond her.

It was never a good idea to change a plan. It could be juggled, massaged, refined – but not changed. And yet she had agreed. Anything to ensure Ellis paid for all he had done.

Now she wanted to get as far away from here as possible, but she couldn't escape the memories. She needed to scream, to hurl stones into the sea, to vent her frustration, anger, pain, and – if she was honest – fear. Without another thought, she turned down the path through the gorse, ripping her long flowing coat from the thorns.

'You fucker, Ellis. You're still killing me even though you're dead,' she hissed.

'Shit!' Nadia muttered as she hit the beach and saw Juliette lurking in a narrow gap in the rocks, sheltering under an over-hang. 'What are *you* doing here?'

'Keeping out of everyone's way. Yours included.'

Nadia was taken aback. Juliette had always seemed so defeated, so racked with guilt that she couldn't think straight. Maybe Ellis's death had released something in her.

'How the hell did the police know about you, Nadia? You said they couldn't make a connection between you and Ellis. What have you been hiding from us?'

'Don't go blaming me! It was that twat Oscar who dropped me in it. He told the police that Ellis had asked where I lived, and he would hardly do that if he didn't know me, would he? Although, to be fair, in Ellis's case anything was possible if he took a fancy to someone.'

'You had to admit you knew him, then?'

'Course I did. I told them the truth about the hecklers and stuff. But as I pointed out to them, if I'd wanted to kill him, I'd have done it then. Not waited all this time.'

Nadia saw a flicker of scepticism shadow Juliette's eyes.

'Do they know about Marco?'

Nadia turned away before Juliette could see her face. *Shit!* She hadn't considered they might want to know about Marco. What the hell could she say?

'He didn't come up, so I didn't tell them. That would have been a bit stupid, don't you think?'

'I'm not sure. Would someone kill the father of their child?'

Nadia spun round. 'That's a bloody silly question.' She needed to change the subject. 'What did they ask you?'

'They know about the loan.'

'Well, no surprise there. It was inevitable.' It had taken Juliette a few days to admit to Nadia and Celia that in addition to the problems they already knew about, she was also in debt to Ellis. 'What about the other money?'

Juliette shook her head. 'Gone, as planned. They haven't mentioned it, but I guess I'm their number-one suspect. I'm the one who was having an affair. I'm the one who didn't want her husband to find out. I'm the one who owes him money.'

'Yes, and now he's dead. Quite convenient for you, I'd say. Of all of us, you've benefited most from his death.'

Juliette's expression hardened. 'May I remind you that you're the one who said we should kill him, so tell me about Thursday night, Nadia. What went wrong? What did you *do*? You must have done *something*!'

Nadia gritted her teeth. 'What do you mean, what did *I* do? Why don't you tell me what *you* did? Yours was the first part of the plan, and you went alone. Given that the police haven't told us how Ellis died, how do I know you did exactly what you were supposed to? And don't bullshit me, Juliette, because I'll throw you under the bus without a second thought.'

With that, she stormed off towards the sea.

51

The day was wearing on, and Stephanie was conscious that the Daltons were due to leave the hotel the next day. She was praying for a breakthrough.

The trip to the boathouse hadn't revealed as much as they had hoped. The hotel had sent someone to unlock it for them, but they found nothing useful. The sandy slope down to the sea had been disturbed by many feet and by the wheels of the dolly used to drag the RIB between the boathouse and the water.

'Let's get Tai's team down here to check it out, Steph. I can't think there's anything to find, but let's cover all the bases.'

With that Gus headed back to the incident room, muttering about it all taking too bloody long. Stephanie had the sense to keep quiet. His glum moods never lasted long.

'Sir,' Ayaneh called as they walked through the door. 'Do you have a moment?'

Gus walked over to stand behind the young detective and gazed at her screen.

'I've been searching social media for everyone of interest. Celia Cobain doesn't appear to have any profile at all, and Ellis's accounts are probably run by a PR firm. They're not personal. Nadia talks about her singing, but the account she's using now is only about three years old. I guess when she changed her

281

surname, she changed her account. I can't find anything in her old name. There's nothing much on Mr Dalton's Twitter either. It's all work related. However, Juliette Dalton's Instagram is interesting. It appears she's a member of a wild swimming club.'

Gus raised his eyebrows. 'Is she, indeed?'

'Yes, and there's something else. Ian went through all the calls to and from Celia's phone. It seems Celia missed several calls on Thursday night.'

'Maybe she chose to ignore them,' Gus said.

'I don't think so, sir. They were from her home phone number – a land line. She called it at 6 p.m. on Thursday night, and spoke for twenty minutes. In her statement she said she went to the bar after wishing the children goodnight. The calls to her started to arrive from the same number at 9.30. They're repeated every five minutes or so, and they all went unanswered.'

'Maybe she was in the bath,' Ian muttered from the desk next to Ayaneh.

'It's possible. But she got the text from Ellis at 10 p.m., and she responded to that. And there are more missed calls after this, so she managed to reply to him but not answer those from her home phone, which must have been about the children, mustn't they? Anyway, she finally called the number herself at 10.22. The call lasted seventeen minutes. She called it again on Friday morning, before Ellis's body was discovered.'

At that moment, a uniformed officer approached them.

'DCI Brodie, I understand you asked to speak to the house-keeping staff who cleared the room service trays from Mrs Cobain's room? The woman concerned has come on duty, sir. Would you like to speak to her? She's a Mrs Iris Loughran, and she's waiting outside.'

Gus nodded. 'Steph, you're with me.'

The woman looked to be in her mid-fifties with a tight perm and a worried expression.

'Mrs Loughran, thank you for sparing the time. I'm sure things are busy, it being a Saturday.'

'Oh, it's much like any other day here. Our cli-ent-ele tend not to be Saturday to Saturday folk.'

She pronounced 'clientele' as if she had practised enunciating every syllable, and Stephanie guessed she had been told not to call the hotel's guests customers.

'We'll try not to keep you long. I'm DCI Brodie, and this is my colleague, DS King. I understand you were on duty on Thursday evening, and we'd like to know about any calls you made to either Mr and Mrs Dalton's suite, or to Mr and Mrs Cobain's, if you can remember.'

'Oh yes, I remember. I didn't go to the Daltons' suite that night, but I had to visit the Cobains' suite three times. It's the furthest from the main house, too!'

'Three times?' Gus asked.

'Yes. It wasn't down to them being demanding – well, not on this occasion – but it doesn't do to speak ill of the dead, does it? Anyway, it was a hectic evening because the dry-cleaning and laundry was late back. The delivery van broke down, and we like to have everything returned and back in the rooms by six. Mrs Cobain had put some of her husband's shirts in the bag to be laundered, and it was about quarter to ten before I was able to get them to her room.'

'And did you speak to her?'

'No. I called out to Mrs Cobain, because normally if guests are out I pop up to the mezzanine and hang the shirts in the wardrobe. There was no answer, but I wondered if maybe she was in the bathroom. Her phone was on the coffee table, so I guessed she was in, especially as the room was unlocked. I noticed the phone because it was ringing. She didn't appear, so I left the shirts over the sofa, and went back to the hotel.'

'You said you went three times?'

'Yes. I realised I hadn't taken a new laundry bag with me, in case she had anything to launder the next morning. The maid should have replaced it when she did the room in the morning, but some of these local girls are a bit dizzy and I couldn't be certain she'd remembered, and I couldn't check without going up to the mezzanine, so I went back to pop one in her room.'

'And what time was that?'

'Must have been about five past ten by then. I popped the bag on a chair where I thought she'd see it. She'd ordered room service and the dishes were on the table, so I lifted the plate covers to check, thinking that if they'd finished I'd clear it away. But nothing had been touched. The phone started ringing again, but there was still no sign of her, so I left. I'd only been back in the hotel for about ten minutes or so when Mrs Cobain called for me to pick up the tray!'

'But when you went back, she was there?'

'She was, yes. I couldn't go immediately – must have been about twenty minutes before I got round to it. She had a dressing gown on, so I guess she was getting ready for bed.'

'But you didn't go to the Daltons' suite at all that evening?'

'No. They didn't ask for laundry, and I assume they ate in the restaurant. I did see Mrs Dalton, though. She was heading back to the restaurant as I was on my way to the Cobains' suite.'

Stephanie saw Gus's back stiffen. 'What time was that?'

'When I was taking the laundry bag, so just after ten.'

* * *

'Okay, everyone, what do we make of what we've learned today? Steph?'

Trust Gus to ask her first, Stephanie thought. She'd have liked five minutes with a notepad and pen to get her ideas in order, and there was something niggling her about Mrs Loughran's statement. She always thought better when she could write things down. She resisted the temptation to scowl at him in full view of the rest of the team.

'Juliette Dalton has a motive. She is a wild swimmer, and her running clothes were in the bath, having been washed. It seems a strange thing to do given there's nowhere to dry them. Why not just take them home with the rest of the week's washing? We have to wonder if she'd been in the sea and needed to rinse off the salt water. If so, did she swim out to Ellis Cobain's yacht?'

'Maybe, but the downside of that theory is that Russell Dalton said she left her kit in the bath while they ate, and that was too early. Timing doesn't work. If she'd been in the water, it was before dinner.'

'She could have put them back on?' Stephanie shuddered at the thought of cold wet Lycra. 'There was also the washed-out tub of Andrews Liver Salts. Why would you do that?'

Gus gave a slow nod. 'When I called the lab they said it must have been washed with boiling water to get rid of every trace of whatever was in there. I think we all know there are questions around Juliette, but nothing we can pin on her yet. Agreed?'

Everyone nodded.

'Before we move away from the Daltons, what about Russell?'

'Pretty good motive if Ellis had been shagging his wife,' Ian said. 'But then again, not a great window of opportunity. Was he a member of the wild swimming club, Ayaneh?'

'Not that I could see. There were a few group photos on

Instagram, but he wasn't in any of them. He did have a window of about thirty minutes, though, if only we could work out how he got to the boat and back. Prints and DNA won't help. They were both on the boat the day before.'

'I think Ellis would be turning in his grave to hear you refer to his yacht as a boat, Ayaneh, but I take your point. We need to talk to Russell Dalton.' Gus glanced at Stephanie. 'I know you wanted to respect his wife's confidences, Steph, but it's been over twenty-four hours now. Let's go and get him when we've finished here. Before that, what about Celia? Thoughts, anyone?'

'Too flaky to have planned something like this,' Ian muttered.

Stephanie was gazing out of the window towards the arch leading to the courtyard. Yes, Celia did appear flaky and permanently on edge, but for a woman who seemed frantic with worry about her children, it was strange that she hadn't answered the calls from home.

Where was she when the housekeeper went to her suite? Was she really in the bath? And her phone was downstairs on the coffee table, and yet she'd answered Ellis's text within seconds of it arriving at ten o'clock, even though she wasn't in the sitting room when Mrs Loughran visited at both quarter to ten and five past ten.

There might be a plausible reason, but Stephanie couldn't help thinking that something was wrong about it.

52

Nadia has her back to me and is hurling stones into the waves, oblivious to the constant drizzle. It seems it's her way of letting off steam, and I'm leaving her to get on with it. Maybe when she stops she'll be less aggressive and we can talk things through calmly. Not that I feel calm.

I still haven't worked out what to say to Russell. This is the second time I've been interviewed without him, and I need a plausible reason. *Another lie.* The thought makes me wince. When did I become this person?

Perhaps I can say that the police are interested in the yacht. I spent more time looking around inside than Russell did. He was only gone for a few moments – just long enough for me to persuade Ellis to take me back on Thursday evening. At that point I still didn't know all the details of Nadia's plan, but I followed her instructions. I think back to the yacht. What vital piece of information could I possibly have had to share with the police?

I mentally run through our visit until I reach the end – or close to the end. I remember being on the fly deck with Ellis, trying to get him to suggest bringing me back to the yacht the following evening. Russell went to use the bathroom, and I went down the first few steps to check he had disappeared into the salon. The doors were open, but there was no sign of him.

And then it hits me. The doors were definitely open when I looked, but when Russell came back I heard the *swoosh* of the glass doors opening and Russell whistling. I know it wasn't the sound of him closing the doors because they were open when we headed back to the tender. Ellis had to close and lock them.

Russell had taken his shoes off on the yacht, as instructed, and my heart gives a sickening thud.

He heard me.

There is no other explanation. Russell must have been heading back towards us and heard me with Ellis. He must have silently retraced his steps, quietly closed the door, then reopened it as noisily as possible, whistling to let us know he was coming.

Why didn't he say anything? Why didn't he accuse me? What do I do?

I realise now that if he had confronted me, I would have admitted everything, thrown myself on his mercy and begged his forgiveness. I wouldn't have gone back to the yacht with Ellis. I would have told Nadia and Celia that I was out, and I wouldn't now be teetering on the brink of being charged with murder.

I think back to everything I did on Thursday night. I had believed it was the only way to save my marriage, but perhaps it was already too late.

The Day of the Murder

Russell knew there was something wrong. He lay on the bed watching me as I changed into black leggings and a black long-sleeved T-shirt.

'Why are you all in black? Isn't it dangerous in the dark?'

'I'll have my head torch,' I told him. 'This outfit's my most comfortable, and I get hot running so I don't want a jacket.'

'Are those shoes suitable for a stony path?'

I looked down at my swimrun shoes. He was right, of course. I had brought these with me in case I went running on the beach and felt like diving into the sea, but I hadn't worn them until now.

'My trainers are giving me blisters. These'll be fine, Russ. Stop worrying.'

I wanted him to stop quizzing me. It wasn't like him.

'Why don't you go to the bar?' I said. 'Ellis will probably be there. You can have a drink with him, and I'll join you as soon as I've finished my run.'

I could see his reflection in the mirror. He was gazing out of the bedroom window and looked so sad that I could have cried. I wanted to go to him and hold him tight, but I knew that if I put my arms round him he would ask me to stay, and it would be much harder to do what had to be done, so I picked up my gloves and headed into the bathroom. I couldn't let him see me put them on. I needed to slip on disposable gloves first, then my black woollen running gloves to cover them.

When I came out of the bathroom, Russell had returned to the living room. I found him sitting in the dark, his head tipped back on the sofa, staring up at the ceiling.

'Don't go, Juliette,' he whispered. A fist clamped itself round my heart, squeezing hard.

It would soon be over, I told myself. Russell just needed to hang on for another day, and everything would be fine. I would spend the rest of my life making it up to him.

I leaned down to give him a peck. 'I'll see you in the bar, darling,' I whispered. 'You've got Nadia's singing to look forward to as well. I'm keen to listen properly this time. I missed most of it last Saturday.'

Russell kept his head tilted back, his eyes unfocused, and didn't look at me or speak again as I headed into the courtyard. I was shaking as I pulled the door closed behind me, my sweaty fingers sticking to the handle.

53

The rain was coming down harder now and, much as Nadia didn't mind getting wet, she would soon have to head back up the beach to speak to Juliette, who had to be made to realise that they must stand together. They had to stick to their stories. Their alibis were strong, but a single loose thread in the carefully woven cloak of confusion shrouding their actions would be enough to unravel the entire fabric of lies.

No matter what had happened on Thursday night – whether she believed Juliette, or Juliette believed her, or either of them believed Celia, there could hardly be grounds for complaint. Juliette's nemesis was *dead*, and that had to be a good thing, didn't it?

Nadia wiped the rain from her cheeks and sniffed. It *was* a good thing.

On the face of it, everything appeared to have gone to plan on Thursday, with some help from an innocent Oscar, who had done as she asked and persuaded the front desk manager to give her a room on the ground floor with French windows leading onto the terrace. She'd listened as he made the arrangements on the phone.

'Audrey, my lovely, I wonder if I could ask a teensy favour?' She hadn't heard Audrey's response, but everyone was fond of Oscar. 'You probably know that we may well be losing our Nadia, and *what* a loss she'll be! But I understand room eleven is vacant tonight, and it would be so lovely if she could have that room to rest in between sets. It's her favourite, and I would so love to spoil her.' There was a brief pause. 'Oh darling, you're an angel. Thank you.'

Oscar had turned to her with a beaming smile. 'There you go! As promised. Now, to make it extra special, I will make it my task for the evening to spoil you in my own way. I'll bring you some champagne and ask the chef to make you some delicious canapés. We can bring them to the room – treat you like royalty, if you're about to sign this contract.'

'Oscar, you're a love. Thank you! I don't want to seem ungrateful, but I'd really like the time between my sets to be peaceful, without any disturbance, if that's okay. I've taken to meditation recently – I find it helps with stress.'

She wasn't surprised to see Oscar's slightly stunned expression. Nadia was probably the last person he would have expected to 'go all wooey on him', as he would say, but she couldn't have random waiters turning up with food and drink.

The room had worked perfectly. It was close to the staff corridors, so she could nip into Oscar's office to collect what she needed, and could visit the maintenance storeroom. Beyond the terrace was an area of garden with tall shrubs and a path that led round the back of the outbuildings and down to the jetty.

All she had to do was complete her first set, rush back to strip off her stage clothes, then head out through the French windows, over the terrace to the jetty, where she hoped Celia would be waiting.

This is what Juliette needed to understand – that without

Nadia's careful planning, none of this would have happened. She should be bloody grateful, not casting blame.

Nadia is still hurling stones into the sea, impervious to the rain, and I've been on the beach far longer than I should have. I need to get back, but I can't drive from my mind the thought that Russell heard me talking to Ellis, and with a moan of distress I lean heavily against the rock. For now I must put that thought behind me to deal with later, because I have to know what happened, what I'm facing, and as Nadia finally turns and stomps back up the beach towards me I'm hoping her aggression is spent.

I'm in no doubt that I should have carried on walking away from her that day on the beach. I so nearly did. I shouldn't have turned back or listened to her persuasion. She had convinced me it would be fine. We didn't have to kill him, but Ellis should be taught a lesson, forced to stop tormenting women. Something must have gone wrong, and I am frightened that Nadia and Celia are conspiring to cover it up.

Whatever happened, I'm not convinced Nadia will tell me the truth. She doesn't know if I can be trusted. The truth is, she doesn't know me at all. But then I don't know her, do I? Or Celia. Why should I trust them? Was I set up to carry out the first part of a much more sinister plot, one that I wasn't party to? Was the intention always to kill him, as Nadia had originally urged? Had she colluded with Celia? Did she persuade her, knowing Celia didn't have the strength to defy her? Were they in it together? Was I some kind of unwitting accomplice to his murder? Or – and the thought horrifies me – did I kill him? I only have Nadia's word for what was in the pens.

The moment she gets close enough, I shout, hoping she

doesn't detect the quiver in my voice: 'Tell me what happened. I want to know *exactly* what you did.'

'*Me?*' she yells. 'What about you? If the police are looking for a motive, no one's got a better one.'

I can feel my hands curling into fists, and I stick them in my pockets. 'There's something you're not telling me, Nadia. I can feel it. And no one wanted him dead more than you.'

'You know nothing, Juliette. Absolutely fucking nothing.' The venom in her voice silences me for a moment, but not for long.

'Then why haven't the police mentioned his mobile, or the evidence against him that you left on the yacht? It doesn't make sense. They must have seen it, but they haven't said a word – and not to Celia either. At least, that's what she told me. Who knows if she's lying? Could Ellis have come round, seen what we'd done and cleaned up after us? Is that why they're not asking about any of it? It's the only thing that makes sense.'

Nadia is looking at me, a spiteful grin on her face, and I wonder why I ever thought I could trust this woman.

'Not *quite* the only thing, though, is it? Maybe someone *else* was on the yacht that night. Someone who destroyed the evidence. Maybe Ellis was killed to protect one of us. Who might have had reason to do that, I wonder? Who has someone who loves her so much that he would kill for her?'

I turn to look out to sea to avoid her sly, knowing eyes, pushing from my mind the thought that Russell would have had a motive if, as I suspect, he heard me talking to Ellis on the yacht. I'm not about to admit that to Nadia, though.

'Russell knew nothing about my relationship with Ellis.' I swivel back to face her. 'There is of course a much more logical explanation, and we both know it. You were the last person to see Ellis alive. How do I know you didn't kill him, Nadia?'

Did she do it? Did she and Celia do it together? Am I being set up? I'm more convinced than ever that I'm right, but I realise in that moment that if Nadia is guilty of murder, I may have put myself in danger. We're the only two people on the beach, cowering under a rocky overhang. We're hidden from view. I back up until the rocks dig painfully into my flesh as Nadia walks towards me.

54

'Mr Dalton,' Gus said. 'Thanks for coming in for another chat.'

'I thought you were with Juliette,' Russell said, frowning at Stephanie.

'She left a while ago. Maybe she's gone for a walk.'

Looking at him, she wondered what was going on behind his eyes. She had noticed when she first saw him that he had a wide smile and an open face that lit up when he looked at his wife. But this version of Russell Dalton was different. His best attempt at a smile was tight-lipped, and he wasn't quite able to meet her eyes.

Russell settled himself into the chair, folding his hands in his lap, trying for all the world to look relaxed.

'I'm afraid this conversation might be a little uncomfortable for you, Mr Dalton,' Gus said. 'When we first spoke to you, both you and your wife said you had never met Mr Cobain before. We have reason to believe that's not entirely true.'

'Ah,' Russell said, staring at a spot just above Gus's head. 'I see.'

'You see what, exactly?'

'I see you're aware that Juliette knew him before they arrived.'

Stephanie tried to hide her surprise. He had said nothing of this when they first spoke, but she remembered the way he had looked at his wife when Stephanie asked if they had met Ellis before.

'Why didn't you tell us this?' Gus asked, a tinge of irritation in his voice.

He took a deep breath. 'I didn't think it was my place to. I thought perhaps Juliette would admit it to you when you spoke to her on her own.'

Stephanie was puzzled. 'Has she admitted to you she knew him?'

'No, sadly she chose to deny it. But she didn't need to tell me. I know my wife. I don't think I need to explain any further.'

He did, though. There was no way Gus was about to let him stop at that point.

How much did he know? How did he feel about it?

'As a lawyer, Mr Dalton, I'm sure you understand that I need to formally advise you of your rights before we continue with any further questions.'

'Of course,' he responded, looking directly at Gus as the caution was delivered.

Formalities over without a blink from Russell Dalton, Gus continued with the questioning.

'What do you believe your wife's relationship with Ellis Cobain was?'

Russell's folded hands gripped each other, fingers interlocked, his knuckles white.

'I think it's best if you ask Juliette.'

'But I'm asking *you*,' Gus said. 'I'm not asking what their relationship *was*, I'm asking what you *believe* it was.'

He stared at his hands and gave a small nod. 'Well, I believe it was a relationship she didn't want me to know about, and she's not aware that I discovered the truth. I'm certain she wasn't expecting to see Ellis Cobain here, and she did her best to distance herself from him.'

'How do you feel about that?' Stephanie asked, earning herself a frown from Gus.

Russell looked up and Stephanie could sense his pain. 'Juliette and I have had a difficult few months. I'm equally to blame because I didn't handle things well, and whatever her relationship with Cobain was, it's clearly over now.'

That was one way of putting it.

'Did your wife ever mention any financial arrangements with Mr Cobain?' Gus asked.

'Given that as far as Juliette is aware I have no knowledge of *any* relationship between her and Ellis, I think that's highly unlikely, don't you?'

Why hadn't Russell said anything to his wife?

Gus was clearly thinking the same thing. 'You weren't inclined to ask her? You seem to be somehow detached from this, Mr Dalton.'

'Really?' He sighed. 'I suppose I can see why you might think that, but I love my wife. I want us to get back to the happy life we had just a few months ago. I could tell she didn't want Ellis anywhere near her and she could hardly bring herself to speak to him, so it was clear she wanted to end her association with him.'

'And why do you think she didn't end it?'

'I would be guessing, but I imagine he threatened to tell me – either the truth or an outright lie – and she was trying to save me the pain.'

Stephanie could tell Gus wasn't quite sure where to take this. He had probably expected an outpouring of vitriol, not acceptance.

'Did you know she'd done some work for him, on his apartment?'

'I guessed as much. He mentioned on one occasion when Juliette and I were having drinks with him that he'd had an interior designer working for him. He sang her praises, but said she could be very stuck up when the mood took her, and he planned to take her down a peg or two. I knew he was talking about Juliette.'

'Forgive me, Mr Dalton, but why the hell did you choose to spend so much time with him if you thought he was having an affair with your wife?'

'Did I say I thought they were having an affair? I think I mentioned an *association*. But it doesn't matter much. I had no idea when I first met Ellis in the bar – was it really only a week ago? Anyway, I was genuinely pleased to meet him – for about five minutes. If I'd suddenly pulled away, ignored him, Juliette would have known that I'd guessed. I wanted her to tell me herself.'

Stephanie glanced at Gus. If he ever suspected her of having an affair, there was no way he would keep his suspicions to himself.

'So are you going to tell her you know?'

Russell bit his bottom lip. 'No, and I'd prefer that you don't tell her either. Juliette will feel guilty for a long time, whether or not she admits to what's happened. I've thought about this a lot, I can assure you, and if I admit to knowing about it, she won't only feel terrible about the affair, she'll also feel the full weight of responsibility for my pain. I want to spare her that.'

For a moment neither Gus nor Stephanie spoke as they both tried to absorb what they had just heard.

Finally, Gus leaned across the table towards Russell. 'Did you blame Ellis Cobain for this?'

'I did, but I recognise it's complicated. Normally Juliette would have seen through someone like him, but things weren't normal. They were emotionally highly charged, and you could say that I was to blame for not understanding what she needed. Cobain was extremely unpleasant, as I could see from the way he treated his wife. He was toying with Juliette, and if I hadn't thought it would break her, I'd have spoken up. But I had to let her decide how to handle it.'

'You must have felt very hurt, though,' Stephanie said.

Russell gave a self-deprecating smile. 'I would find it difficult to identify one emotion amid the multitude I was feeling, Sergeant. We were all to blame, one way or another. As some American professor wrote, "Your life is the fruit of your own doing. You have no one to blame but yourself." Blaming others doesn't help. My aim is to put this right, no matter what I think of Ellis Cobain's behaviour.'

'Did you hate him enough to kill him, Mr Dalton?' Gus asked.

'I wanted him out of our lives, that's for sure. But I'm not a brave man in the traditional sense. I apply logic, not brute force, and in my defence I can tell you that if I *had* killed him, you would have discovered it very quickly and arrested me by now. I'm guessing that whoever your murderer is, they're a good deal cleverer than I am.'

Russell was right. Whoever had killed Cobain, they had done an excellent job of covering their tracks.

'And Juliette? Could she have killed him?'

He looked away. 'I doubt she'd have done it to save herself, but it's possible she'd have done it to save me. If I knew what time he died, I would have a clearer idea, although I wouldn't share my thinking with you. And I don't suppose you'll tell me.'

'You suppose right, I'm afraid.'

Stephanie leaned forward. 'We know your wife's movements until you left the restaurant, Mr Dalton. What about later? Could she have slipped out after you had fallen asleep?'

He smiled. 'No, because I didn't fall asleep. I lay next to her and watched her all night. Juliette's been struggling – no surprise, really, given all that's been going on – so the doctor prescribed something to help her sleep. I insisted she took a tablet on Thursday night. Even so, she was restless. I knew that whatever was happening, she was hurting, so I stroked her back to calm her and held her as close as I could without waking her.'

Gus's face showed a degree of scepticism. None of this could be proved or disproved, and Stephanie could almost read Gus's mind. *This guy's either a bloody saint or an incredible liar.* How much should they believe? Did he give her the sleeping tablet so he could slip quietly out into the night?

'I still don't get why you spent so much time with Cobain. You even went to his yacht for a look round.'

'I'm afraid that was Juliette. She was keen to go – and no, I didn't understand why either. But I'm sure she had her reasons. I had to let her play this out in her own way. As for sticking close to Ellis, if I'm honest, I wanted to keep an eye on him for other reasons too. I'm here to persuade Nadia Shariq – a very talented singer – to sign a contract. When I heard about everything Ellis had done to her from my colleague Raoul, I wanted to try and keep him away from her, to make sure he didn't hurt her again.'

'And what exactly did he do to Nadia?'

'From what I can gather, he broke her heart in the cruellest way possible. He's not doing that to Juliette.'

55

Another day was nearly over, and Celia was still stuck at the hotel. Her world had been turned upside down, and she'd barely been able to eat. As she got up to walk over to the coffee machine for the umpteenth time that day, she grabbed the back of a chair in a moment of light-headedness.

She had to eat something. Otherwise, a combination of anxiety and the urge to spill out everything that had happened, everything she'd done, would overcome her. And she couldn't do that. She had to think of the children.

She had begged to be allowed to go home, but the chief inspector had insisted they had to complete some enquiries first. She suspected it was within his power to keep her there, and she wasn't clever enough to come up with a compelling argument to force his hand.

Celia had spoken to the children several times, but they still didn't know about their father. Fortunately they hadn't asked to speak to him, and in all the times he'd been away from home he had never once asked to speak to them. They were totally oblivious to the fact that there was something wrong.

Lacey was still cross with Celia for not answering her calls on Thursday night, and Celia had spoken to her for over an hour on Friday, once the police had gone.

'I called and called, Mum,' she said, her tone plaintive.

Celia hated lying to her, but she had no choice. 'I know, darling, but I'd left my phone in the room while I had dinner. You know Daddy doesn't like phones at the dinner table.'

'Unless it's his,' Lacey said sulkily – but accurately.

'Well, he's a busy man, so I guess he has an excuse,' Celia added rather lamely. 'Anyway, I phoned as soon as I saw I'd missed your call, even though it was late.'

Lacey sighed. 'I know, but I really needed you. When are you coming home?'

'As soon as I can, darling. I'm sorry, but it's all gone on a bit longer than we expected.'

'Will you at least speak to Reece – tell him to stop bullying me, and stop telling lies about what Daddy said to him. You're not leaving us, are you? Tell me it's not true?'

'Lacey, you, Reece and Savannah are my life. I would never, ever, leave you out of choice.'

'But what if it's not your choice?'

Lacey started to cry. She was such a sensitive child, and Reece – under his father's influence – was being particularly vicious while Celia was away and unable to curb him. She'd asked Jeanette about his behaviour earlier in the week, and the nanny admitted to having little control over him.

'He tells me I'm just the hired help, and that his father will sack me if I don't do as he says.'

'I won't let that happen,' Celia had said with a level of conviction she didn't really feel.

Jeanette knew perfectly well that her word counted for nothing with Ellis, and Celia felt despair at the transformation of a once lovable child into a boy intent on echoing his father's controlling behaviour.

'Jeanette, the children aren't anywhere near you, are they?'

'No. Lacey's in her room keeping out of Reece's way, and Savannah and Reece are in the playroom. He was making her set the skittles back up every time he knocked them down, but I've told him if he does it once more, I'm taking them off him. Savannah seems happy enough doing his bidding, but I know you wouldn't let it happen. Why do you need to know where they are?'

'I'm not quite sure how to tell you, and I don't want the children to know, but Ellis is dead.'

There was a pause, not a gasp or a startled cry. Then: 'Oh.'

'You'll see it on the news, eventually. I need to be the one to tell the children, but they won't let me leave here until they've worked out what happened.'

'The police? Wasn't it a heart attack or something?'

'No, nothing like that. He was murdered.'

There was silence from the other end of the phone, then, finally: 'Gosh.'

Neither of them spoke for a moment.

'Are you okay, Celia? It's not . . . Did you . . .?'

'I'm a bit shaken by it all, but I'm fine.' She didn't attempt to explain any further; it was way too complicated. 'Please take care of the children for me until I'm back. I'll tell them then.'

'Reece will be devastated.'

Maybe, Celia thought, but at least the child now had a chance of growing into the good person she was sure he was, underneath the swagger. She had watched, unable to intervene, as over the years he had tried to emulate his father.

But not any longer.

Celia watched the sky through the window as it darkened with heavy rain clouds. Ignoring her cup of coffee, now cold, she had just decided to order something to eat, even if only an omelette, when she heard a knock on the door. Looking through the glass she could see Sergeant King hunching her shoulders against the thick drops of rain that had begun to clatter against the window.

She beckoned the detective to come in.

'Turning nasty out there,' Sergeant King said, standing on the mat and brushing the rain off her jacket. 'I'm sorry to disturb you, Celia, but there are a couple of things I need to ask you. I hope that's okay.'

Celia felt herself twitch, and shifted in the seat to disguise the sudden movement. 'Of course. Are you getting any closer to finding out who killed my husband?'

'We think so. The evidence is starting to come in now, and we're putting all the pieces together.'

Celia searched the woman's face, trying to see if she was making this up, or if they really were close to discovering what had happened, but she couldn't read her.

'This is a quick question, and it relates to your phone calls on Thursday evening. We've looked at your call history – it's standard practice in a case like this – and we can see that your phone was here from the time you left the restaurant at –' the detective checked her notebook '– 8.30.'

She looked up and Celia tried to nod her agreement, but her neck felt rigid. *Where is this going?*

'Room service delivered your food, and then it seems you failed to answer several calls from your home number. I wondered why that was.'

'I must have been in the bath.'

'Okay, so where was your phone?'

Why do they want to know this? What have I done wrong?

'I'm not sure I can remember. Is it important?'

'The calls started at about 9.30 and were fairly regular – every five minutes or so. Then there was a gap – perhaps whoever it was gave up – but then they started again just after ten. And you ignored them all, until finally you called the number back at 10.20. Can you explain this?'

'Like I say, I was probably in the bath and decided not to take the calls.'

'And yet you received a text from your husband at ten, and you answered that.'

Shit!

Celia tried to give the sergeant a wry smile, one she was sure didn't quite come off. 'Well, Ellis doesn't like to be ignored.'

'You had your phone with you, in the bathroom, did you?'

'I suppose I must have, yes.'

'That's strange, because housekeeping came to deliver some shirts, and apparently your phone was on the table.'

Celia felt an ache in the back of her throat. 'I must have come down at some point and picked it up.'

'Well, that would make sense. Except the phone was back on the coffee table when she returned just after ten with a new laundry bag. This all seems rather strange, Mrs Cobain, and it would help if I could understand what happened.'

Celia searched her mind for a reasonable answer, not missing the fact that once again the detective had reverted to calling her Mrs Cobain, rather than Celia.

'I'd spoken to the children earlier. My son, Reece, was being difficult and I thought he was calling to speak to Ellis – to get his dad to back him up. I left my phone down here. I came down to collect it, saw the text from Ellis and responded, then was on my way back up to the bathroom when it started to ring again.'

'And you just didn't answer?'

306

'That's right. Then I felt guilty, so after a while I called back.'

Celia pulled every trick she could out of her acting bag, looking up and smiling at the detective. But her efforts had come too late. The doubt in Sergeant King's eyes was unmistakable.

56

Stephanie had just walked back into the incident room when Ayaneh called to Gus, 'Sir, do you have a moment?'

'What have you got?' Gus said, coming to stand behind her chair and looking over her shoulder.

'I've been feeding every bit of data into a more detailed timeline. Times along the top, people down the side, and the duration of each action so we can correlate everyone's activities.'

Gus asked Ayaneh to mirror her computer to the main screen, and Stephanie walked across to join them.

The timeline was similar to the one Stephanie had drawn on the board, but much more sophisticated, with a box for each action. You could look down a column and see exactly who was where – or at least, where they *said* they were. Ayaneh had even created boxes for inanimate objects, including telephones.

'If we start at 6 p.m., sir, the last time Ellis was seen alive, we can see that Juliette Dalton went out for a run. She claims to have had a shower before she came over to the restaurant, so I've assumed she was back for 7.30, and then fifteen minutes for the shower and to get dressed. As you can see, Celia Cobain was in the bar from 6.30 to 8.30, and I've added in her phone calls home.'

Stephanie was bursting to say what looked obvious to her, but she had to let Ayaneh finish.

'Moving through the evening, you can see in a different colour the phone calls Celia received that she didn't answer, plus the text she *did* answer. And these are the times the housekeeper went to the suite. Then, at just after 10 p.m., Mrs Loughran sees Juliette Dalton in the courtyard as she takes the laundry bag. I've put in Nadia Shariq's movements, and Russell Dalton's too, and as we get more information, we can add that. Are you happy for me to carry on with this?'

Gus looked mesmerised by what he was seeing. 'Delighted, Ayaneh. It gives a much clearer picture as the boxes expand and we can see them line up. Well done.'

'Hang on,' Stephanie said.

Gus turned to her and raised his eyebrows. 'Steph?'

'I don't know why I didn't pick up on this before, but Juliette told us specifically that she *didn't* go back to her suite, in spite of Russell believing that's what she had done. She was adamant that she sponged the wine from her top in the ladies'. But Mrs Loughran saw her.'

'So she's a liar,' Gus said with an abrupt nod. 'But then we already knew that.'

'Why, though? Why lie about whether she went back to the room or to the ladies'? Why would she think it matters? It *has* to be important.'

'You're right. It's something to add to what seems to be a growing list of things to check next time we speak to her.' He turned away from the screen. 'Where are we with the CCTV, Ian?'

Ian was leaning back precariously on his chair with only the two rear legs on the floor. He rocked forward, the front legs landing with a thud. Heaving himself up, he strolled over with a sheet of paper in his hand.

'We were specifically looking for someone coming back into the hotel who could have returned the boathouse key. Within the timescale no one came in through either the front door or the staff entrance, other than those we would have expected. But Mrs Loughran was right: Juliette Dalton *did* leave the hotel just before ten. She was gone for thirteen minutes – but she was wearing heels, so I guess she wouldn't have had time to get to the boathouse and back.'

Before Gus could respond, all four detectives turned at the sound of Tai Shentu's voice.

'Gus, can we talk?'

'Tai, what brings you here?' Gus asked.

'Too much stuff to talk about over the phone, and I wanted to check the scene again for any more drug hiding places. Before we get started on the other stuff, I can confirm that we haven't found any trace of flunitrazepam on the yacht. And trust me, we've looked everywhere.'

'Let's take a seat.' Gus signalled to the large table in the middle of the room and indicated that Ian and Ayaneh should join them. 'So no stash of Rohypnol. A one-off, do you think? Or was he drugged by someone else?'

'I'd bet on the latter option. The fact that there was a pen still full of ketamine with no fingerprints on it at all, but Cobain's prints were on every other pen is suspicious. If I had to hypothesise, I'd say he thought he was taking cocaine, but the pens had been switched. I can't prove that, though.'

Gus nodded. 'What else have you found?'

'Let's start with the yacht. We vacuumed the floor, and I already told you about the paper. The business centre here at the hotel stocks the paper, and it's available to guests. Staff too, but there's nothing unique about the brand. Some possible good news, though. We found some tiny flecks of dried paint in what we hoovered up, so I went back to the yacht and checked for anything of a similar colour or recent signs of decorating. We found neither.'

'You're thinking someone had paint on their shoes?'

'It's more likely to have been on their clothes and flaked off. We checked the clothes of the guys who found the body for elimination purposes, and there was nothing. We know it's a top-grade paint, though.'

'They've been decorating one of the suites in the courtyard,' Stephanie said. 'I loved the colour so I took a photo of the paint tin on my phone.' She flicked through her photos and passed her mobile to Tai.

'That looks possible,' Tai said. 'I'll check it out when we've finished, if the decorators are still here.'

'The facilities manager will know how to contact them. He shares an office with Oscar Carne.' Gus turned to Ian. 'Can you find him when we're done, Ian? See where they store their overalls too.'

'Please tell me we're not wondering if Cobain was murdered by one of the *decorators*?' Ian murmured.

'We're not ruling anything out at this stage,' Gus said, a slightly acerbic tone to his voice. 'Obviously we've been focusing on people who we know had some connection with him, but it's plausible that someone we don't yet know about might have recognised Ellis. Let's face it, he's a guy with a colourful history.'

Gus was right. The team had thoroughly checked all the staff, the guests, anyone who might have a link to Cobain. They'd also investigated boat movements, as far as they could, and CCTV in and out of the hotel. While Stephanie and Gus had been concentrating on the people who knew Ellis Cobain, the rest of the team had explored other angles.

'Any more little nuggets, Tai?' Gus asked.

'Yep. Molly's already told you she thinks the victim was suffocated, probably with a plastic bag placed over his head. As he used up the air in the bag it would have created a vacuum, making it difficult to remove. If you've tried to open a vacuum-sealed food pack you'll know it's not the easiest thing to do. Molly found some tiny fragments of plastic on his teeth as if – when it was ripped off – it stuck slightly. We've managed to analyse it and discovered that it's a white plastic with a silver-based antimicrobial coating.'

'To prevent build-up of bacteria?' Stephanie asked.

'Precisely. It's used to enhance hygiene in all kinds of products.'

'Including laundry bags?' Stephanie asked, and Gus's head swivelled in her direction.

'Genius, Steph! This place would probably use something of that quality.'

Stephanie felt a brief thrill at her moment of inspiration, but it dwindled as she remembered that, according to Mrs Loughran, every room in the hotel was provided with laundry bags. Anyone, staff or guest, could have got hold of one.

57

'Right, everyone,' Gus said, trying to sound cheery, but failing. 'Given the new evidence that's come to light, including that presented by Dr Shentu, we've got a few things to check out, and Steph is going to speak to Russell Dalton's colleague, called . . .' Gus glanced at Stephanie.

'Raoul Lambert.'

'Yes, him. According to Dalton, Lambert's been looking into Nadia Shariq's life in Bristol. He might have some information about her relationship with Ellis Cobain, which Dalton says was painful. We know she lied about it, so let's find out more. Ian, can you check which room Nadia Shariq got changed in, please? Let's see if she could have left the room at any point without anyone knowing. Ayaneh, can you speak to housekeeping and ask them to check if they've had to replace anyone's laundry bags unexpectedly? By that I mean a laundry bag was missing, but the room's occupants hadn't put anything out to be washed or dry-cleaned.'

Ian stood up. 'Before I toddle off, boss, the financial stuff for the Daltons arrived an hour ago, with the usual weekend apologies for how long it's taken. I've found nothing of interest yet in Russell Dalton's, and we already know about the sums Cobain was paying into Juliette's account. However, here's where it gets interesting. On Friday morning, first thing, the sum of two hundred and fifty thousand pounds appeared in Juliette's personal account. And – even more interesting – almost immediately, it disappeared.'

'*What?*' Gus said. 'Where did it disappear to?'

'Back to the account it came from, which – drumroll, please – was Cobain's foundation account.' Ian looked around the room, grinning triumphantly as if this was the final nail in Juliette Dalton's coffin.

'Christ,' Gus groaned. 'What the hell was going on? He was already dead by then.'

'Yes, but the initial transfer was probably made the night before. Even with the Faster Payment System there can be delays if security checks are needed.'

'So he could have initiated the transfer late on Thursday evening. We'll have to ask Juliette Dalton about this. We need to assemble all the evidence against her – the courtyard, the trip to the yacht, and of course the money. Then we get her back in here. When's she supposed to leave, Steph?'

'Tomorrow. They're supposed to check out by 11 a.m.'

'Right, well, they're not going anywhere, and I'll make it my business to tell them that. We can't have them buggering off back to Bristol – they're up to their necks in this somehow.'

An hour later, everyone was back in the incident room, although it was clear people were flagging. It had been a long day.

'I'm sorry, but try as I might, I couldn't get hold of Raoul Lambert,' Stephanie said. 'No answer from his mobile or his home phone. I'll keep trying.'

Gus grunted, irritated with the delay. 'Ayaneh?'

'As far as anyone's aware, there were no extra laundry bags

delivered to rooms. Most of the housekeeping staff have gone for the day, but when the cleaners do the rooms they have spare bags on their carts and replace missing ones automatically. Mrs Loughran says guests sometimes take them home with their dirty laundry in. She's going to check, but she thinks it's unlikely anyone will specifically remember.'

'Another dead end, then.'

'Not necessarily,' Stephanie said. 'While we know anyone could have taken a bag from their room, we do know *specifically* that Mrs Loughran took one to Celia's suite. It would be good to know if the cleaner who did that room on Thursday replaced the bag. That would mean there should be two. If there's now only one, that might tell us something.'

'Good thinking. See if Mrs Loughran can contact the relevant member of staff and check. She might remember, as it's the best suite in the hotel.' Gus turned to Ian. 'Any news?'

'Yep, the decorators don't work for the hotel. They're contractors, although the hotel management insist they all wear overalls with the hotel's logo on. They're kept in the maintenance storeroom, but the decorators haven't been at the hotel this week. They worked through last weekend to get all the rooms finished, because the hotel was fully booked on Monday.'

'Not likely to be a decorator, then. Carry on, Ian.'

'So . . . Nadia's room on Thursday was on the ground floor, with French windows that lead out into the gardens at the back of the hotel. I checked it out, and there's direct access to a path which eventually meets up with the track to the beach. Significant?'

Stephanie felt a buzz of excitement. Was this the answer? Was Nadia at the heart of all of this? Or could someone else have used one of those rooms to sneak out of – or back into – the hotel?

Gus appeared lost in thought, and the ten seconds it took for him to respond felt like ten minutes.

'Okay, here's what we know: Cobain took ketamine several hours before he died. He'd also taken Rohypnol/flunitrazepam, call it what you will. It's not clear if that was at the same time or later. Given he habitually used the pens to store cocaine, did he take the ket in error? We know from the hair strand analysis that he wasn't a regular user. So why ketamine?'

'It works quickly and can induce a kind of out-of-body experience, among other things,' Ian said. 'It would only be a few minutes until he started to feel the effects, but they don't last long – maybe an hour or so. Roofies are slower, but last much longer.'

'Did he take it out of choice? By accident? Or did someone give it to him? If it distorts sensory perception, why would someone else want him to take it?' Gus asked, looking round the table. 'Did someone want him under their control? Detached? Confused? Was the ketamine topped up with slower-acting Rohypnol to keep him in that state for longer?'

'It makes sense,' Stephanie said. 'But why do all that if you're planning to kill him? Why did the killer need him to be disoriented for several hours? If he took the ket early in the evening, as Molly thinks, but he wasn't killed until much later, what was the point of it?'

Gus frowned.

'Maybe they wanted him out of it for long enough to transfer that money to Juliette Dalton,' Ayaneh said.

'Yes, but she sent it straight back, before – in theory at least – she knew he was dead.'

Gus rubbed the back of his neck, a sure sign of his frustration. 'Okay, let's park that temporarily. What else?'

'We don't know how anyone got to the yacht. We have no evidence of anyone taking the key to the boathouse, or returning it if they'd taken it earlier,' Stephanie said. 'What we *do* know is that Nadia Shariq had easy access to that key and the means of getting into and out of the hotel without being detected.'

'But would she have had time?' Ian asked. 'She was dressed and ready for her performance at 10.30, and it was well after eleven when she set off for home.'

'She had time at the end of the night,' Stephanie said, thinking that most people moved significantly faster than Ian. 'But Oscar says she arrived at the hotel at about seven on Thursday night and performed her first set at 8.30, so I don't think she'd have been able to slip him the ketamine, if that's what happened.'

They were going round in circles. There seemed little sense in someone drugging him, then going back to kill him. Why not do it all at the same time?

Unless it was to cause confusion. And if that were the case, the killer's plan had been entirely successful.

58

Finally, Gus said they should all head for their beds. 'We need fresh eyes on this in the morning, so let's all try to get a good night's sleep and we'll crack on again first thing.'

Stephanie knew he hadn't wanted to stop, but he was conscious that an exhausted team was unlikely to be productive.

Now, even though they had been in bed for an hour, Stephanie could tell from Gus's breathing that he was wide awake. He would be wondering if they had made any progress at all, and concerned they didn't have a front runner in their list of suspects. She turned towards him and wrapped one arm and a leg around him, drawing him towards her. He didn't speak, obviously deep in thought, but gave a small sigh of pleasure at her closeness.

Her own mind was buzzing, and she couldn't help thinking they were missing something that should be obvious. They had finally been able to get their hands on Ellis and Celia's prenup, which initially caused a bit of excitement. Celia had signed away the rights to any support from Ellis in the event of their separation or divorce, which would have provided a motive if she was to inherit his money on his death. But his will left everything in trust for his three children. She could contest this, of course, but Stephanie doubted she would, as long as she could find a way to stay with the children.

Her disgust grew. Ellis Cobain had inherited every penny he had, and to treat his wife so disgracefully was beneath contempt. If he'd still been around, she'd have been tempted to kill him herself. As Gus said, sometimes as a police officer you didn't necessarily want to catch the perpetrator.

Just before they packed up for the night, Tai had called in on his way back from a visit to the boathouse with the facilities manager.

'The guy initially thought everything was in order,' he said. 'But then Stevie – one of the two guys who'd taken the RIB out to the yacht – turned up. He said when they'd opened up on Friday morning he'd had to put one of the kayaks back on the rack because it had been dumped on the floor and was blocking the dolly. The facilities manager was adamant that none of his team would have abandoned a kayak in the entrance, and guests didn't have unsupervised access to the boathouse.'

They had been puzzling since Friday about how someone could have got to the yacht and back without using the tender. The only possibilities had seemed to be via a boat from another bay – still a viable option that they couldn't discount, despite a lack of evidence – or they had swum out and back, Juliette being the obvious candidate.

Now they had another possible answer – a kayak.

'So we think that's significant?'

'Absolutely. Stevie's taken the RIB out a couple of times in the last few days to do a maintenance check on the buoys. On both occasions all the kayaks were on the rack. No one else, as far as he was aware, has been to the boathouse since.'

Tai's team had examined the kayak, but there were no fingerprints that matched any of their suspects, no footprints in the sand around the doorway. It felt like a dead end. The only one of

319

their suspects in or out of the main hotel building at or around Ellis's time of death had been Juliette Dalton, and she hadn't had time to get down to the beach, let alone as far as the yacht.

With a sigh Stephanie tightened her hold on Gus and was rewarded with a contented grunt. Whatever was going through his mind, there was nothing he liked better than to feel her warm skin next to his.

For a moment she was tempted to talk to him about something other than the case – to tell him what she suspected was happening to her body, to share what she knew would be the best news. But now wasn't the time. When this was over, when they were alone in their new home, *that* would be the perfect moment. She would wait.

Sunday

59

I wake early, Russell snoring gently by my side. He thinks I took another sleeping tablet last night, but I went into the bathroom for some water and spat it out. I needed to think, not sleep. I kept getting flashes of all that happened on the beach with Nadia yesterday, my body shaking with the memory.

I had been convinced she was going to attack me. She was so angry; a response far stronger than my question warranted. Of *course* I had to ask if she had killed Ellis. She'd already suggested he may have been murdered to protect me, and I knew she was implying that my husband is a killer. I was furious, but I feared for my life as Nadia stood, inches from my face, her skin flushed, her nostrils flared.

'Don't even *think* of blaming me for what happened!'

'Convince me that Ellis was alive when you left the yacht, then.'

'I don't need to convince you of anything. You'll just have to take my word for it.'

'For God's sake, Nadia, just tell me what happened!'

'Exactly what was *supposed* to happen. Stop being so fucking suspicious. He was alive when we left. Okay? Celia was a nervous wreck and I was worried she'd have a moment of misplaced sentimentality and move in to give him a kiss, or something equally stupid, so I sent her out of the room to put the security device back in the safe while I checked that we hadn't forgotten anything. But he was alive. Groggy, not entirely with us. But *alive*! Minutes later we were back in the kayak, and Celia seemed to breathe again. We went straight back to shore, pulled the kayak out of the water, and that was that.'

I look at her. Something is puzzling me.

'You just took it out of the water? Didn't you put it away?'

'*Jesus!* I didn't know you needed every tiny detail! Of *course* we put it away. We dragged it up the beach and into the boathouse, lifted it onto the rack, left it exactly as we found it. I had to scoot to get ready for my next set, so Celia hung up the paddles and locked up. I replaced the key on the hook in the office, and I can only assume Celia did everything else according to plan. Okay? Is that sufficient detail?'

There's something nagging at me, but before I can pin it down, she starts on me.

'Anyway, Juliette. What about you?' Nadia's voice is sharp with an unmistakable edge of irritation. 'Did you do what we agreed, or are you now considerably richer than you were at the beginning of the week? You have a hell of a motive to kill Ellis, and we know you're a mad cold water swimmer. Ellis is dead, so you can make up any story you want to account for the money. If they're looking for a motive, no one's got a better one.'

I tut. 'I'm already their number one suspect. As far as the police are concerned, I had the most to lose, so the last thing I need is his money in my account. Of course I didn't keep it.'

I didn't want it. Not a penny of it. I'd done exactly as we'd agreed and transferred it back to him on Friday morning, long before I knew he was dead.

'I still have a feeling there's something you're not telling me, Nadia.'

'Why do you keep doubting me? I *told* you.'

'You're the one who wanted him dead. *That's* why. And now he is. It was your plan, and you took some convincing to change it to blackmail.'

Her hands were raised, claw-like, as if she was about to grab me by the throat. I couldn't move. One finger poked out, jabbing towards my face as she spoke.

'You think you know how I felt about Ellis. But really you have no idea.' After a few seconds she gave a raw, gut-wrenching cry, and tears flooded her eyes as she spun away from me. 'Fuck you, Juliette. Just *fuck you!*'

And with that, she was gone.

It's only now, lying here, safe in my bed at the hotel, that I understand what she meant. I had never really understood the tears, the distress, the layer upon layer of seething anger. But now I do. And now I know she lied.

I'd found it hard to return to face Russell yesterday afternoon. The rain had soaked through my clothes, my hands were smarting from where I had grabbed the gorse to save myself from falling, and I didn't know what excuse I could concoct for staying out so long. I couldn't look into his eyes, scared I would see sadness, disappointment or rage at what I am now certain he heard on the yacht, and I had no idea how to explain why the police had wanted to speak to me again.

None of my pathetic excuses really mattered in the end, because Russell told me the police had interviewed him too.

'What did they want?' I'd asked, trying to keep the panic from my voice.

Russell had shrugged. 'A bit of background on Ellis – what

he'd talked about during the week. They wondered if he'd mentioned any personal difficulties, that kind of thing. Nothing to worry about, darling.'

He wasn't telling me everything, that much was clear, and we spent the rest of the evening tiptoeing round each other, pretending to eat a dinner I thought might choke me. I'd suggested eating in the restaurant because I thought it would provide a distraction. Being in the suite alone with Russell, it was hard to think or to talk about anything other than the murder. In the dining room we might find something else to discuss – the décor, the wine list, our fellow diners. Anything other than Ellis.

A flustered Oscar Carne had hurried across to speak to us as we took our seats, his face pinched with concern.

'I'm sorry, Mr and Mrs Dalton. I'm sure you were hoping to hear our wonderful Nadia sing again tonight, but we felt it was disrespectful, in view of the events of the last couple of days.'

We said that we entirely understood, but I couldn't help wondering whether Nadia would have even been able to perform if she had been asked to.

'I'm sorry you won't get another chance to listen to her, Russ,' I'd said. 'Did you see enough of her this week to be happy to finalise the contract?'

'I'm not the right person to assess her talent, but I did want to judge her commitment. She's been very distracted and has yet to tell me if she'll agree to the terms, although according to Raoul it's got nothing to do with my negotiating skills. She was probably flustered because of Ellis.'

I almost choked on my sea bass.

'What's Ellis got to do with any of it? Did she know him?'

I remembered just in time that Nadia and I have never spoken to each other in public to Russell's knowledge.

'Oh boy, did she *know* him!' Russell raised his eyebrows, and I knew I was meant to ask.

'What do you mean?'

'I told you I was trying to find out a bit more about her. The last thing the agency wants is something emerging after we promote a new signing, so when I discovered she'd changed her name, I asked Raoul to do some digging. It turns out she and Ellis were an item about three years ago when she was singing in Bristol. Serious, full-on. Then it all went horribly wrong, and Nadia ended up leaving the city. She even changed her name – used to call herself Nadia Scott.'

I already knew about Ellis's behaviour after she found out he was married, but I had to continue to play my part.

'Why did she leave?'

'Ellis forced her out. According to Raoul he persuaded lots of clubs not to book her if they wanted his patronage. If they ignored him, he sent in hecklers. In the end, her only option was to leave and find somewhere else to perform.'

I tried to put a shocked and horrified face on. 'That's terrible – just because she dumped him!'

The creases between Russell's eyebrows deepened. 'Did I say she dumped him?'

I took a quick gulp of my wine. 'Didn't you? Maybe I just assumed, given the kind of man he was.'

'It seems the problem started with Nadia. Raoul was reliably informed that she wanted Ellis to leave his wife. They'd been having an affair for a while – Ellis probably thought it was a bit of fun. I would guess that's his default position, wouldn't you, darling?'

There was so much loaded into that question. I knew I should say something, but I couldn't. I laid my knife and fork down, the sea bass only toyed with.

'I'm not sure what you mean, Russ.'

'Ellis is – was – a player. It's apparently well known, although before speaking to Raoul today I had no idea. I'm not big on industry gossip. Anyway, it seems he had a reputation for taking what he wanted, then discarding the wreckage he left behind.'

Russell was watching me as he talked, his eyes gentle, and it was all I could do not to blurt out the truth. But I managed to swallow the words, and Russell carried on with the story.

'She was making Ellis's life too complicated, and he needed to be rid of her. He'd had enough, but she didn't see it like that. She stalked him, Juliette. There's no other word for it. She turned up at every event he went to, phoned him constantly, threatened to tell his wife, although he probably wouldn't have cared if she had. She told everyone that Ellis loved her, that he was the love of her life, and that he was about to leave his wife for her; that eventually he'd realise it was the only way. No one believed her. They knew him for what he was, but it was getting completely out of hand and no one had the heart to tell her what a fool she was making of herself. In the end, Ellis drove her out in the only way he knew how – by destroying her career. Raoul says she had a breakdown and didn't sing again for nearly two years. Now it appears she's over it. But then he turned up here.'

I didn't know how to respond. Whose version was correct? She told us that Ellis pursued *her*. That *she* was the one who wanted to end the relationship because he was married. That she'd dumped *him* and that's why he'd driven her out. Now it seems she'd stalked him, been obsessed with him, wanted him to leave Celia. Was *that* why Ellis had forced her to leave Bristol? Did she really have a breakdown, or did she take a break to give birth to Ellis's son? I couldn't ask Russell. I wasn't supposed to know any of this.

Now I think back to her emotional outburst on the beach, the burning resentment, the glimpse of tears, the pain. And suddenly it all makes sense. She had loved Ellis. And he had destroyed her.

What did she think when she saw him at the hotel? Was she excited, thinking he'd had a change of heart, that he'd come to find her? She had no way of knowing that he was following me, to torment me, to exert his control. Was he really trying to move in on Nadia's life and uproot his family, as she'd told Celia, or was her mind set on exacting revenge for the pain he had caused?

60

Stephanie had started the day with a renewed sense of enthusiasm. She and Gus had been up since before six and, with the help of lots of coffee – and for her an almond croissant – had produced what they hoped was a definitive list of questions about each of the suspects, although they had little to go on with Russell Dalton and were baffled by his attitude to Juliette's relationship with Ellis.

'Why is he so calm about it, Gus?'

'Don't know. I've been puzzling about that since we spoke to him. I wouldn't have been able to keep quiet on the subject.'

Stephanie snorted. 'I suspect that's an understatement!'

'Not just because of the affair. He knew Ellis was manipulating her, toying with her. That would kill me. I'd have had it out with him.'

'Maybe he did. Maybe that's why Ellis is dead.'

'Doesn't quite make sense, though. If you're going to have it out with someone, you don't drug them and take a laundry bag with you. That's cold, calculated. Not spur of the moment, fuelled by anger.'

'But he said he's logical, and he could have taken the kayak,' Stephanie said. 'Although how could he have got the key to the boathouse – or put it back, for that matter? And he didn't have much time.'

'He gave his wife a sleeping tablet, Steph. Who knows what he did. Just because I'd have been tempted to plant the guy it's not everyone's way.'

Stephanie chuckled. 'Thank the Lord for that! Although I do love the idea of you getting all incensed on my behalf.'

Gus had no time to respond as the incident room was filling up.

'Okay, everyone,' he said. 'Let's go through each person of interest. Chip in if you have anything to add. I've just been discussing Russell Dalton with DS King. He had a strong motive as he knew his wife had a relationship with Cobain. I don't know what, if anything, he knows about the loan. He only had the smallest window of opportunity on Thursday night, but it's not impossible. We need to keep digging. Steph, talk us through Juliette's motive, please?'

'Juliette wanted to end her affair with Ellis Cobain. I saw her reaction to him myself last weekend. But he held all the cards.'

'We know she's a wild swimmer,' Gus said. 'And there were wet clothes in her suite. There was a tub of antacid powder in her bin which had been washed out so thoroughly that there was no trace of what had been inside. Rohypnol? Then there's the transfer of two hundred and fifty thousand to her account – in and out on the same day. We have yet to ask her about this. We have motive, but what about opportunity? Ayaneh, over to you and the timeline.'

Ayaneh used her cursor to point to the timings on the screen.

'Juliette was in the restaurant at 7.45 or thereabouts, several hours before Ellis was killed, but we believe the ketamine was taken at least three hours before he died.'

There was silence, finally broken by Stephanie.

'I guess we're all thinking the same thing – it's feasible that Juliette swam out to the yacht. Was it some sort of assignation? Maybe they were meeting for sex. Was that when he took the ketamine? Did he take it out of choice? Mistake it for coke? Or was Juliette involved? Did she swim back, rinse the saltwater from her running kit, leave it to soak in the bath and go to dinner? It works, but why give him the ket at seven o'clock? It would have worn off by the time he was killed.'

'Maybe that's when the roofies kicked in,' Ian said.

Ayaneh pointed to another block on the screen. 'Juliette did leave the restaurant for a short time around 10 p.m.'

'Yes, and she lied about it. Why, unless it's significant?'

'Exactly, Steph. Interview her again when we've finished here – under caution, obviously. For now, let's move on to Celia Cobain.'

Stephanie felt that if anyone had a reason to kill Ellis it was Celia, but she seemed too submissive to have had the courage to take matters into her own hands.

'If Celia killed him,' she said, 'she didn't do it for the money – she seemed indifferent to the prenup. It appears Ellis treated her badly: we know she had no access to money, and he wouldn't let her adopt the children.'

'Maybe he wanted to avoid a tug of war over the kids if the marriage didn't last,' Ian said.

Stephanie wanted to argue that was irrelevant. Celia had built a relationship with the children so should be treated the same as any parent after a divorce. However, she knew she wasn't being entirely objective. She was thinking of how her relationship with Gus's daughter, Daisy, might develop. If she grew close to the little girl, how would it feel if she and Gus separated in the future and she was no longer able to see the child? To invest all that love and emotion only to have it stripped away didn't bear thinking about.

Ayaneh highlighted the times of the calls registered to Celia's phone. 'I think her mobile is the most bizarre aspect of this. It was on the table both times Mrs Loughran went in, but in the middle of all those ignored calls from home, she responded to a text from Ellis.'

'Okay, and we're still waiting to hear if there's a missing laundry bag, although I don't think that's remotely conclusive and would never stand up in court,' Gus said. 'Celia could have taken the kayak – assuming she wouldn't have swum out – but how could she have got access to the boathouse?'

There was a general sagging of shoulders around the table. It seemed unlikely that Celia was the guilty party.

'Remember,' Stephanie said, 'that Celia Cobain went to the bar that night, apparently to wait for her husband. Something she hadn't done before, so it's unusual behaviour.'

Even that remark didn't raise spirits much.

'Okay, let's move quickly on to Nadia Shariq. Steph, you've got some news.'

'I have. I finally managed to speak to Raoul Lambert.'

Stephanie filled the team in on Raoul's claim that Nadia stalked Ellis after he tried to break off their relationship.

'Nadia telling the world Ellis was leaving his wife for her ties in with what I saw the first night I was here. There was someone in the audience that gave her a real thrill, and it wasn't Russell Dalton, who she'd neither met nor seen before that night.'

'And Nadia had a room on the ground floor. She could get in and out via the French windows, plus she had access to keys, laundry bags and decorators' overalls,' Ian said.

'Yes, but look at the timeline. Dr Treadwell believes time of death was between 10.30 p.m. and midnight. Oscar Carne says Nadia was in his office, changed and ready for her set at 10.30.'

'Agreed. She did say there was a degree of latitude in the earlier time, but it's tight,' Gus said. 'Maybe Nadia just dragged the kayak back into the boathouse and ran back to the hotel.'

'Figures. It was a two-man kayak, and they weigh about thirty-five kilos,' Ian said. 'A bit tricky for one person to lift onto the rack.'

'Would a woman have been able to lift the kayak *down* from the rack on her own?' Stephanie asked.

All heads turned towards her. 'You're thinking there may have been more than one of them?' Gus asked.

'It makes sense, if the kayak was difficult for one person to manoeuvre. Maybe Juliette and her husband? Perhaps they ran out of time to put it back on the rack.'

Ayaneh spoke. 'I do a bit of kayaking in the summer with my boyfriend. I'm not very strong, but if the kayak's on one of the bottom two levels of the rack, I can get it down on my own and drag it into the water, if I have to. Getting it back up, though, is something else entirely.'

Stephanie groaned. 'That buggers up that theory then.'

'The fact that the kayak was on the ground might suggest one person could have been acting alone, but we shouldn't rule out a joint enterprise,' Gus said. 'We've been thinking all along of a solo killer, but there are several people who had a motive. For now, let's keep checking all the outstanding items on the list, and Steph, go and find Juliette. Again!'

Russell Dalton was clearly appalled to find Stephanie at their door.

'DS King, haven't we answered enough of your questions? We're supposed to be checking out this morning. Do you plan on keeping us here?'

Stephanie looked at the dismay on his face and felt for the man. Much as she didn't understand his reluctance to discuss his wife's 'association' with Ellis, she could sympathise with how he must be feeling about it.

'As I'm sure you know, Mr Dalton, we can't insist on you staying unless we're prepared to arrest you. But we've checked with the hotel, and no one is booked into this room for tonight, so with respect we would ask you to remain here until we've concluded our initial investigations.'

'On what grounds could you arrest us?'

Stephanie just looked at him without saying a word. He knew the answer to that – or at least some of it.

'Okay,' he said with a sigh. 'You'd better come in, then.'

'Actually, it's your wife we want to speak to. DCI Brodie has asked me to bring her to the interview room at the hotel.'

Russell looked anxiously over his shoulder. 'She's eating breakfast at the moment. Can't it wait?'

Stephanie could see Juliette, and there was no mistaking the look of alarm on her face. She pushed her bowl of fruit away. 'It's okay, Russ,' she said, getting to her feet. 'Best to get it over with. Give me a moment while I grab a jacket.'

Two minutes later, she followed Stephanie out of the door.

'What's this about?' she asked.

'DCI Brodie will explain,' Stephanie answered, showing her into the interview room.

Two long minutes of silence later, Gus joined them and Stephanie switched on the tape recorder as they ran through the formalities. Once again, Juliette refused legal representation.

'Mrs Dalton, let's cut straight to the chase. Why was a quarter of a million pounds deposited in your personal current account on Friday morning?'

It was clear from her face that Juliette had been expecting this. 'I don't know, but I wasn't happy about it. It seemed to come from Ellis's foundation, and that's charity money! I called my bank as soon as I could and asked them to return it immediately.'

'How do you think it got to your bank?'

Juliette shrugged. 'It must have been Ellis. I can't think who else could have done it. I always wondered if he operated a bit close to the edge, and I didn't want to be involved.'

'What does that mean?' Gus asked.

'I don't understand the legalities, but he boasted that the foundation paid for his car and his apartment. Maybe that's fine, but on the off-chance that it wasn't, I didn't want to know.'

'So why didn't you wait until you saw Mr Cobain and ask him?'

'I couldn't, could I? He was dead.'

There was a pause. Gus leaned forward across the table. 'True, Mrs Dalton, but at 9.30 when you called the bank, you couldn't have known that, could you?'

For the first time Juliette's eyes betrayed her, opening wide.

'Sorry, no, of course not. I think I panicked when I saw it there. I didn't want Russell to know about it. I just wanted it to disappear back to where it came from.'

Gus nodded as if this all made perfect sense. 'I understand. You hid quite a lot from your husband, didn't you?'

Juliette dropped her head.

'Can you explain why, with your husband, you went to visit Mr Cobain's yacht last week? For someone who was trying to hide a relationship that they supposedly wanted to end, it seems a very strange decision.'

Her face was hidden by curtains of long blonde hair, falling either side of her still-bowed head, and Stephanie wished she could see her eyes as she answered.

'I can't explain. I guess it was to please Russell, but it was the wrong thing to do. I can't make any more excuses for my stupidity.'

'And was it stupid of you to lie about what happened on Thursday evening?'

Juliette's head shot up, her eyes flared. 'What do you mean?'

'You told us – in your husband's presence – that on Thursday evening when you spilt wine on your clothes you sponged it off in the ladies'. But in fact, you returned to your room, didn't you?'

Juliette's eyes flicked from Gus to Stephanie. 'I . . . well . . . maybe I did. I can't remember. Why do you think that?'

There was no doubt in Stephanie's mind that Juliette's trip back to her suite was significant, and she hoped Gus would keep a straight face as she posed a question.

'You were seen in the courtyard by one of the housekeepers who was on her way to Mrs Cobain's room with a laundry bag. She is quite clear that you weren't coming from your room. You were coming from the far end of the courtyard – from Mrs Cobain's room. Why were you there?'

Stephanie wanted to look at Gus, to see if he had reacted to her exaggeration of what Mrs Loughran had said. He knew perfectly well that she hadn't been that specific. But she had to watch Juliette, to judge the impact of her words.

The woman looked trapped.

'I-I think I might have wandered up there to see if she wanted to come back to listen to Nadia sing. Yes, that's it. She'd gone back to her room, and I thought she might want some company, but I couldn't see her through the glass, so I came away again.'

Gus said nothing, and Stephanie recognised this as his tacit agreement for her to continue along this path.

'That doesn't quite make sense, though. Mrs Cobain received a message from her husband to say he would be back late – that's the message she received in the bar, isn't it? So by ten o'clock you could have safely assumed that he was back in their suite settling down to a room service dinner. Why did you think she would be on her own, Mrs Dalton?'

The fight seemed to go out of Juliette's body. She slumped in the chair.

'I don't know. I'm sorry. All I know is that I didn't kill Ellis Cobain.'

61

The police have let me go. I performed so badly in that interview that I'm surprised they didn't arrest me on the spot. I'd thought I was so composed, but I'm a mess. I can't let Russell see me like this.

A sense of dejection settles like a heavy blanket on my shoulders as I make my way to the garden nestled behind the hotel, a hidden sanctuary of winding paths meandering through lush foliage. Overhead the last of the autumn leaves rustle in the wind, and I wish I could lose myself in the beauty of the place. I glance back towards the hotel, wondering if any guests are watching from their rooms, asking themselves why, once again, I was escorted by the police through the courtyard and the reception area. Why didn't they just call the suite and ask me to come? I feel as if I've been marked as a suspect and a hundred eyes are now staring at me from behind closed curtains. I move further away until I'm hidden by the faded papery flowers of the huge hydrangeas.

One of the paths leads through a stone arch to the back of the courtyard, and I kick myself for not using this route on Thursday night. Despite what Sergeant King said about the housekeeper, I don't remember seeing anyone, but I was rushing to get back so Russell wouldn't question me too much. I should have paid more attention to what I was doing.

At the far end of the gardens I discover a small gazebo and take refuge there. One thought repeats, over and over: *They are on to us.*

I'm sure of it. They can't put all the pieces together in the right order yet, but they will. I have to give Nadia credit – she certainly made it difficult for anyone to pin anything on us, even if murder wasn't our intention. At least, it wasn't mine. So whose was it?

Nadia had provided everything we needed and convinced us that nothing would be traceable. I would never have thought of covering my tracks the way she appears to have done. When she first talked us through her plan she had been adamant that she had thought of everything.

'Nothing can be linked to me through shops – either high street or online,' she'd said. 'Even the balaclavas are mine.'

Celia and I had both gawped at her.

'What?' she snapped. 'I'm not an armed robber, in case you were wondering. I used to have a biker boyfriend – wore them under my helmet.'

She seemed to have thought of everything, so what happened? Had something gone wrong, or am I being naive? Had his death been part of her plan all along? Or maybe hers and Celia's.

The thought, the *fear* of the whole thing, is tearing me apart. I feel trapped in an endless spiral, heading towards inevitable disaster, and I'm struggling to breathe.

Although I have a cast iron alibi until 11.30, they only have Russell's word that I didn't leave the suite later, and now – because of the money – I imagine they are getting close to arresting me. I have no sensible explanation for why the money appeared in my account, and no evidence to back up my assertion that I had nothing to do with it.

I think back to the Telegram message that came from Ellis's phone:

I need you to do something for me. I've put some money into your personal account. Transfer the maximum your bank will allow each day to my account in the Cayman Islands until it's gone. Here are the details.

The money was from a foundation account, and anyone with a basic understanding of finance would realise this was a huge fiddle. Stealing back the money he had donated and routing it into an offshore account via a third party would save Ellis thousands in tax.

The message is the only proof that Ellis sent the money himself and that I had no prior knowledge of it. The words were designed to incriminate him so that when he inevitably demanded full repayment of my loan – a debt I'd fully intended to honour – I could use it as leverage. Unless he agreed to sensible repayment terms, I would reveal the bank transactions and his transfer instructions. But his messages were automatically wiped from my Telegram account, and although I grabbed a screen shot, I deleted the image when I thought the police might want to look at my phone. He was dead by then, so it no longer served any purpose. At least, that's what I'd thought.

Something else has been niggling away at the back of my mind. Something Nadia said, but I couldn't quite grasp. Now, though, I've remembered what it was. She said she had to get back for her next set, so she left Celia to hang up the paddles and lock up. She said she had to replace the key in the office, but how could she have left Celia to lock up if she had the key?

She's lying. She has to be.

62

'Gus, can I run something by you?' Stephanie asked quietly, not wanting the rest of the team to hear – at least until it was clearer in her mind.

'Course you can. What is it?'

'It's all the anomalies – things that are not evidence but out of character.'

She had Gus's full attention now, and he swivelled round in his chair. 'Such as?'

'Juliette wanting to get Ellis out of her life, but making a point of going out to his yacht; Celia not answering calls from the children she's so desperate to keep in her life, then going to the bar on Thursday evening to sit on her own – or, as it turns out, with Russell. Gus, this woman was nervous as hell about coming into the restaurant only a week ago.'

Gus nodded. 'Inconsistent, I agree.'

'Then there's the text from Ellis to Celia. Was he *ever* that nice to her? We haven't found any evidence of it. And the forensic linguist says there's little to go on, but it sounds more like a woman than a man, especially in comparison to his other texts.'

'Except she also suggested it could have been AI. Muddies the water a bit, doesn't it? And what about Nadia Shariq?'

'She's a bit trickier, but she lied about dumping Ellis. *He* dumped *her* and treated her really badly. I'm certain she was excited to see *someone* in the audience last Saturday, and I know it wasn't Russell. What if she was thrilled at the thought that Ellis had come to Cornwall to find her and then discovered she was wrong?'

Gus nodded. 'We also have to consider that if the ketamine and roofies didn't belong to Ellis, where did they come from? I can't imagine either the Daltons or Celia Cobain knowing any Cornish drug dealers.'

'Exactly. It would have to be someone who knew the area, although we must remember that Russell Dalton's in the music business. He may have contacts here.'

Gus leaned back in his chair and stretched his legs out. 'It also seems possible that someone took one of the kayaks out to the yacht. Could Celia have done that? She swears she hates water.'

'She was an actress, so who knows? Ayaneh's been scouring her background; I was hoping we'd find she'd been in some minor film or other where she had to swim, but no such luck. If she hated Ellis enough, though, maybe she could have overcome her fear. Women move mountains for their children.'

Gus rubbed the back of his neck. 'You know, Steph, I keep thinking of Juliette's reaction when you asked why she was coming from the Cobains' suite on Thursday night. I know it was a total punt on your part, but it was very clear that's exactly what she was doing. She must have gone to talk to Celia about something.'

'Yes, but we don't know where Celia was, do we? The only evidence is that she responded—'

Gus leaped to his feet. 'To the text! Ayaneh!' The young detective looked up, startled. 'Bring your timeline back up, please.' They strode across to the monitor. 'Steph, I think you're on to something.'

63

I've been sitting for too long in the cold, damp hotel garden, unable to motivate myself to move, and my limbs are beginning to feel stiff. When I woke this morning I had a terrible feeling that today, one way or another, this whole mess was about to unravel with me right at its core, and now it seems I was right. My chest is tight with stress. One minute I'm hot, sweating, the next I'm shivering with cold.

Did I kill Ellis?

Was Nadia lying about the contents of those pens? Did the drugs kill him? I shudder at the thought, but was his death all part of a plan concocted to set me up? Was he dead before they got there? Did they even *go* to the yacht? Is that why the police haven't asked me anything about what they should have found?

Whatever the truth is, I'm withholding information from the police and covering for a murderer – whoever that might be – to protect my own skin.

Nadia must have realised the police would discover my affair with Ellis, that they would find out about the money that was transferred. Like everything else, that was her idea. Am I the scapegoat? Everything points to me, and she even tried to suggest that Russell might have murdered Ellis. Do the police think that too?

344

I've tried to ignore her insinuation that my husband would have killed to protect me, but no one will tell us what time Ellis died. Could Russell have gone to the yacht that night after he persuaded me to take a sleeping tablet?

I can't believe it. I *won't*. He's not a violent man, although I am now certain he heard me talking to Ellis on the yacht. I should try to find a way to explain that conversation, make him believe he misheard, but I'm so tired of the lies.

If I tell the police all I know, could my actions on Thursday night be considered conspiracy to murder, even though that had never been my intention? Or aiding and abetting? Either sounds horrific.

Nadia has to be the killer. She wanted him dead from the start, and I don't know what to make of everything Russell told me about her. Does it matter who ended her relationship with Ellis? Either way, his tactics were beyond cruel – the heckling and the rest. I wonder why she lied to us, though. Maybe she didn't want to tell Celia the truth – that not only did she know he was married but she'd begged him to leave his wife.

Had she always intended him to die? That would explain why she was adamant from the start that we needed cast iron alibis, even when I couldn't see the point if we had no intention of killing him.

'He's bound to know it's us!' I'd snapped. 'Who else gains from the demands we're going to make? Why do we need all the cloak and dagger stuff, alibis, DNA, fingerprints?'

'We need our actions to be deniable,' she kept repeating. 'Blackmail is a criminal offence. He'll remember taking you out to the yacht in the tender, Juliette, but you can make up any story you want about what happened next. There'll be nothing to tie you to what we're planning. You'll be in the clear.'

But I'm not, and it feels as if we believed in one plan, when in fact there was another, more sinister plot, our every action designed to provide cover for Ellis's killer.

My mind is inevitably drawn back to Thursday night, to walking out of our suite, leaving Russell bewildered, pleading with me not to go. I hadn't realised then that he knew I was going to meet Ellis.

But he didn't know what I was about to do.

The Night of the Murder

By the time I'd forced myself to leave Russell, sitting dejected on the sofa, staring at the ceiling, it was two minutes to six and, ignoring the churning in my stomach, I had to hurry. Ellis didn't like to be kept waiting.

It was pitch black, the night overcast, and I stumbled on the path, stifling a shout of alarm, my legs threatening to give way. I pulled on a black woollen beanie, tucked my blonde hair out of sight and felt my way along, using my hands to touch the long stems of dune grass that defined the edges of the path. When I reached the jetty, I could just make out the tender moored to a post, but there was no one there.

I hid, shivering with fear, in the shadows, half praying that Ellis wouldn't come; that this madness could all be over.

What are you doing, Juliette?

The thought echoed around my head. What if Ellis realised why I was here? If he caught me in what I was about to do I was sure I would go to prison.

I crouched low, convinced that at any moment someone would appear – a couple seeking solitude, a man wanting a sneaky cigarette out of sight of his wife. They would see me. Maybe recognise me. And then what would I do?

My body jerked as I heard a voice: 'You came.'

I turned to see the shadowy silhouette of someone standing by a wooden building that I knew to be the hotel's boathouse. I drew in a lungful of cold, damp air.

'Of course I did.' I took a step towards him, hoping to display a nonchalance I wasn't feeling and wishing I was strong enough to run away. 'Can we go to the yacht, Ellis? Someone might see us here.'

Ellis chuckled. 'Hardly. If it wasn't for your pale face, you'd blend perfectly into the night. I knew you'd come to me eventually. Come on. The tender awaits.'

As Ellis strode off down the jetty, I paused, spinning around to check there was no one watching, before jogging towards him, jumping into the small boat and hunkering down on the floor.

'What *are* you doing, woman?'

'Shhh, Ellis. Please, can we do this my way? I don't want to risk being spotted. Someone might hear the engine.'

I could see his face from where I lay in the dark shadow at the bottom of the boat. His mouth was pinched with irritation, and I had to say something or I would ruin everything.

'I just want to get to the yacht. As quickly as we can.' I tried to inject eagerness into my voice, although why he would believe me after the events of the past week I didn't know. I had to trust that his arrogance would overcome his scepticism.

His lips curled up at one corner. 'I'm going to enjoy this. You've been very offhand with me all week, and I haven't yet decided how to punish you.'

I gulped. To play my part, I would have to excite him. But

the thought made me want to get to my knees and retch over the side of the boat.

'How did you expect me to behave? You took me completely by surprise by turning up at the hotel.'

I tried to keep the bitter tone from my voice, and Ellis chuckled at his own sick game.

The trip to the yacht was quick, thank goodness, and it was just minutes until we were on board. I knew he would head straight to the master suite, and I followed meekly. As I'd suspected, he had a bottle of vodka and two glasses waiting on a tray. I had no intention of drinking, but the vodka might be useful.

'What time is it?' I asked.

Ellis turned towards me, his nostrils flaring slightly. 'We've only just got here, Juliette. What time do you *think* it is?'

'Sorry. I didn't bring my phone. I'm always worried that Russell might be able to trace me through some app or other, so I left it in our room.'

I didn't think for a second that Russell would stoop to adding spyware to my phone, but Nadia had told me to make sure Ellis believed I didn't have a phone with me. All the easier to claim later that everything that was about to happen was nothing to do with me, should it ever come to that.

'Don't put me on the clock, Juliette. This was your idea,' he grumbled.

'I want to be with you, but even you must know we don't have a lot of time.' I took a deep breath.

There was a trace of that smile again, and I looked away as he spoke.

'Then we'd better get on with it,' he said, walking towards me.

I held up one hand. 'I'm in charge tonight. Stay where you are and don't say a word.' I knew he would love this, and his eyes burned. I couldn't look at them any longer and couldn't risk him witnessing the self-loathing I was trying to control. 'Close your eyes.'

I stepped towards him and lifted his arms, peeling off his cashmere jumper. I was hit by the cloying scent of his favourite cologne, heavy with musk and bergamot, and I too closed my eyes as I started to unfasten his trousers.

'Sit,' I said, guiding him back towards the bed. My voice came out as a croak that I prayed he would interpret as excitement.

I pulled off his socks, his trousers, then took a gulp of air as I removed his boxers. His body was familiar to me, but never had I wanted to see it less than I did at that moment.

'Lie back,' I instructed, knowing he was enjoying the thought of me being in control. 'I think we need something a bit extra tonight, don't you?'

His eyes snapped open. He knew what I meant. For Ellis, cocaine before sex added to the pleasure, although I had always refused.

'Good idea. Am I allowed to move now?'

'No. Tell me what you need.'

He pointed me to the wardrobe. 'There's a tray table in there. Get it for me.'

I felt a moment of alarm. I had imagined he would snort the drug from the bedside table, his back to me, but he wanted the tray table. He would be facing me. He would see what I was doing.

'Unfold the legs and put it on the bed.' I couldn't think of any reason why I should refuse, so again I did as he said. Ellis leaned across to open the drawer of the bedside table and removed one of the pens I'd put in there the day before – one he believed held cocaine.

'Are you planning to keep your clothes on?' he asked, a note of impatience in his voice.

I desperately wanted to say that I wasn't planning on removing a single item of clothing, but instead I gave a chuckle.

'Hardly, Ellis. But you'll have to wait. I may have a surprise for you.'

I moved towards the bathroom as he started to empty the contents of the pen onto the table top, focused for the moment on getting his fix. I had to move quickly.

Leaving the bathroom door fractionally ajar, I pulled off my woollen gloves revealing the disposable ones beneath and switched on the tap to cover the sound of opening a cupboard. I pulled the drawstring bag from where I'd placed it behind the tampon box the day before, took out the tiny, unregistered phone and switched it on, quickly checking it was still linked to the yacht's Wi-Fi. Nadia had set the date to 4 October when, according to Celia, Ellis had been alone on the yacht, and she'd turned off the auto-reset function. Nothing could be linked back to this moment.

Standing well back, the phone's camera pointing through the gap in the door, I could see Ellis on the screen, naked, snorting the white powder Nadia had put in the pen. The video was running.

The ketamine was supposed to take effect in about five minutes, after which – given the dosage – Ellis would be putty in my hands. I flushed the toilet, playing for time.

'Juliette, are you coming?' he shouted tetchily.

I was starting to panic. There was no sign that he was falling under the influence of the drugs. What if Nadia was wrong? What if they didn't work? I tried to steady my breathing. It was too late to turn back now.

I had to get a grip. I had a checklist of instructions, and I pulled it and the other items from the bag, laying them out on the vanity unit.

'Just a moment,' I called.

If the drugs didn't work, would I have to have sex with him? *Oh dear God, no!*

I hung on to the vanity unit, expecting to hear him call again. But when I finally peered round the door, I could see his eyes were glassy, unfocused. The drugs were doing their job and I needed to move quickly. I grabbed the purple-silk-covered handcuffs that Nadia had provided and ran towards the bed.

'These were all I could get at short notice,' she'd said as she saw the looks on our faces. 'I could hardly order from Amazon, could I, and a cable tie will leave abrasions if he struggles – evidence, in other words, and just what we don't want. So less of the scornful glances, okay?'

I snapped one cuff around Ellis's right wrist and attached the other to the fiddle rail on the bedside table. It wouldn't be strong enough to hold Ellis if he was fully compos mentis, but all we needed was to make sure he stayed on the bed and didn't wander around. I placed the key on the chest in the corner where Celia would find it later.

I pulled his phone from the pocket of his jacket and held it in front of his face. Ellis gazed at me sleepily. He tried to speak, but his words were slurring.

The phone's home screen appeared. I checked my instructions and downloaded the necessary software onto his phone, giving me access to areas of the Internet I had never visited – and never would again. It took only seconds, but it felt like hours. I logged into the site Nadia had suggested, my thumbs fumbling so I had to retype it twice. When the site came up on the screen, I couldn't hold back my gasp of horror.

'We need hardcore porn,' she'd said.

'No children!' both Celia and I had pleaded.

'Agreed, but it has to be violent. They're all actors, or at least we can only hope so. Don't look at it, Juliette, if it bothers you. I'll find the right site. Leave it to me.'

I turned on the smart TV, mirrored Ellis's mobile to the screen, then picked up my unregistered phone, positioning myself to one side of the bed where I could see most of Ellis and the TV screen.

'No flaccid dick pics,' Nadia had said. 'If he's watching porn you'd expect him to be turned on by it, and it will be fairly evident that he's not. By that time he won't be able to even see the screen, let alone react.'

I said a prayer of thanks for the unexpected blessing of the tray table, which hid Ellis from waist to thigh, and kept the wrist encased in purple silk out of the photo. To capture the TV in the shot, his face would be in profile, but it was clearly him. Reviewing the videos together, no one would doubt that the naked man snorting drugs was also the man watching illegal porn.

I checked my list, terrified that one wrong step would bring everything crashing down, then took a small foil wrapper of powder that I'd carefully measured out from my Andrews Liver Salts container with the tiny spoon Nadia had given me, poured a glass of vodka and emptied the contents of the wrapper into it, swishing the liquid round until it dissolved. I took a second wrapper and emptied it into a water glass.

I turned off the TV, moved Ellis's phone out of his reach and accessed his saved photos. I nearly gagged when I saw the shots he'd taken of me on my knees in front of him. I selected them all, binned them, then wiped them from his recently deleted folder, as Nadia had shown me.

Returning to the bathroom, I grabbed the pens filled with

cocaine that I had taken from the bedside table drawer the day before. Leaving my beanie on the vanity unit with my woollen gloves, the burner phone and the scrunched-up foils that had contained the second drug, I retrieved a rubber swim cap from the bag and hurried back to the bed, slipping the cocaine pens back into the drawer.

'Have a drink, Ellis,' I said, pulling him upright, holding the glass of vodka to his lips. He gulped it down.

I went back to the bathroom, washed the glass out thoroughly in hot water and replaced it on the cocktail tray in the bedroom, adding a splash of pure, drug-free, vodka. The second vodka glass was replaced in the cupboard unused.

The first drug – the ketamine – would wear off quite quickly, but we needed him to be in a trance-like state until the job was done. Mine was only the first part of the plan, and the second, longer-lasting drug was essential.

Would Ellis remember any of this? Nadia had assured me he wouldn't. If he remembered the trip out in the tender, I could deny it. He wouldn't be able to prove I was there, any more than he could prove that I'd filmed him snorting drugs and watching the video. The time stamp would demonstrate that it had been shot weeks before. At least, that's what I hoped.

I placed the glass of water, complete with more dissolved drugs, next to the bed, hoping he might be tempted to take a sip. Finally, I sent the first text from Ellis's phone to Celia telling her to go ahead and have dinner without him, praying that – as planned – she was safely in the bar with Russell.

I headed to the door, pulling on the swim cap and tucking in as much hair as I could. Without a backward glance I ran up the stairs, through the glass doors and dived off the yacht into the cold black sea.

64

Nadia paced her kitchen, no more than four strides in each direction. Since her interview with the police and her heated conversation with Juliette the day before, she had found it difficult to keep still.

Ellis is dead. Ellis is dead.

It was forty-eight hours since his body had been found, sixty hours since she had last seen him, but still she needed to convince herself that it was true. She repeated it over and over, tasting the words, not sure if they were sweet or sour. There was a time when his death would have destroyed her, but now she couldn't decide if she was thrilled or devastated that she would never see him again. It didn't matter. He deserved to die.

She thought back to the night they first met three and a half years ago. She had just finished performing a half-hour set in her favourite club in Bristol and was sitting at the bar, chatting to the club's owner, Max, and a few of the regulars, when she felt a buzz in the room. Max sat up straighter, the barman stopped chatting to a girl who was clearly flirting with him, and everyone turned to look towards the far end of the bar.

Ellis stood there as if waiting for his presence to be acknowledged. Max practically leaped off his stool and hurried across to pump Ellis's hand with great enthusiasm, and Nadia watched, fascinated by this man to whom everyone seemed to kowtow. His silky grey hair, long on top, fell softly over his forehead as he moved, only to be brushed back through his fingers. His beard was tightly trimmed, but it was his hooded eyes that captivated Nadia. And he was looking straight at her.

Max swivelled round to look in her direction as Ellis said something, nodding towards her, indicating he wanted to be introduced. She had no idea who this was, only that he seemed to be *someone*.

'Ellis Cobain,' the man said as he reached her, holding out his hand for her to shake. He smiled, and the skin around his eyes crinkled attractively.

'Nadia Scott,' she said.

He moved on, greeting others in the club, and Nadia watched him work the room. She'd been thrilled that he stayed to hear her second set, and when she returned to the bar he congratulated her on her voice, describing it as 'deeply melodic and moving'. He plied her with champagne, telling her the club was lucky to have found her, that he could see a great future for her, if she got the right backing.

There was no doubt he was flirting with her, that he wanted her, but at the end of the evening he left without anything more than a polite goodnight and a peck on the cheek. The backs of his fingers lightly grazed the bare skin of her upper arm, and she shivered, understanding that the kiss on the cheek was for others to see, but the touch was a promise of things to come. He hadn't said a word about seeing her again, but he knew where to find her.

She waited, night after night, expecting him to appear in the bar, but it was three agonising weeks before he came back to the club, and if it was a carefully calculated move to build up the anticipation, it worked. Their affair began that night.

He told her that although he lived in Gloucestershire, he was in Bristol most weeks and stayed in a hotel while he was looking for an apartment to buy. Nadia could see he wasn't wearing a wedding ring, but she knew that meant nothing, and she had a rule. She didn't have relationships with married men. So she asked him.

'My wife died,' he said, dropping his head as if he didn't want her to see the sadness in his eyes. 'I have three children, though.'

When she asked who took care of them when he was away, he said that was too many questions, and Nadia didn't really care as long as it wasn't his wife.

It had started so well. He came to see her perform from time to time – usually when she wasn't expecting him. Nothing was ever planned, and while it felt exciting at first, it soon became unnerving.

'Ellis, I never know when you'll be in touch. I know you don't like it if I call or text, but we're a couple now, and it's not how couples behave. Surely you can see that?'

He had looked at her, narrowing those sexy eyes, but not in a good way.

'Why don't you just concentrate on your career, Nadia? You were great when I first met you, but now you're like a limpet – you cling to me – and your performance seems to have lost its sparkle.'

Nadia had stared at him in horror. 'Max says I'm doing great, and a couple of other clubs have asked if I'll do the occasional set for them too. I don't think I've lost *anything*, Ellis.'

He had smiled that smile, the one she'd come to hate, that said he knew better.

'Max and the audience are kind to you. They clap so you don't feel downhearted. And those other clubs are all hoping I'll invest. They know I have an interest in you, so they're giving you work to please me.'

Was this true? And what did he mean – have an interest in her? Surely it was more than that?

Over the next few months Nadia lost both weight and confidence. Even Max had noticed that she wasn't herself.

'Is this anything to do with Ellis Cobain?' he'd asked. Everyone knew they had a relationship but thought it was casual. They didn't know it was love. 'You do know he's married, don't you, Nadia?'

She nodded. 'He was, yes, but she died.'

'She did. But that was wife number one. He's been with wife number two for about three years now, and she's definitely alive and kicking. Who do you think looks after his kids while he swans around? I know you think I like the guy, but I have to be pleasant to him because he's a source of funding. The guy's a prick, Nadia. Steer clear, if it's not too late.'

It *was* too late. She loved him. She wanted to be with him. The more he neglected her, failed to turn up when he had promised, put her down, the more desperate she was to please him.

She tried everything to make him realise she was the woman for him. She excused herself for breaking her own rule about married men on the grounds that this was *love* – they were meant to be together. She insisted that if he left his wife, she would be happy to take care of his kids. She adored children. She had begged, followed him, called him, turned up at events where she knew he would be. And then he'd told her it was over.

She should have stopped, but she had to make him see he was making a mistake. He ignored her, refused to see her, and her performances became increasingly lacklustre. She had even broken down on stage once when singing a song that Ellis had said he loved. Still, she didn't give up.

Then the heckling started, the cancellations, and she could feel her life unravelling.

There was one final message from Ellis:

If you want to be a singer, get out of Bristol. I can make sure you get very few bookings, and any you do get will end in humiliation. We're done, Nadia.

Her career in Bristol was over. No one would book her, not even Max, although she could see it was with a heavy heart. She'd had no option but to leave.

Then, after all this time, he had turned up here – in Cornwall.

She'd been convinced he'd come to find her, to tell her he'd made a mistake, but as he laughed at her delusions, Nadia felt the hard shell she had constructed around her heart begin to splinter, the shards of pain driving her to want one thing: revenge.

And Ellis wasn't laughing now.

The Night of the Murder

For nearly three years Nadia had been working on her insecurities, learning to believe in herself and recognise her own strengths. She thought she had put self-doubt behind her, but cowering inside the open door of the boathouse on Thursday night, she'd felt her throat tighten as her confidence began to ebb away.

'Where the hell are you, Celia?' she muttered, quickly

checking the time on her burner phone, then pushing it back deep into her pocket in case anyone was around to see the light.

If Celia didn't arrive soon, they would be out of time, and Nadia wasn't doing this alone.

She looked out to the yacht. Lights were shining through the glass doors of the salon, and there was a yellow glow coming from what she imagined to be the porthole window of the master suite.

Ellis was ready for them. A nod from Juliette as she had begun her first set in the restaurant had told Nadia everything she needed to know. The stage was set. Now she – and Celia – had to perform their parts.

She tried to focus on the soft rhythmic lapping of the waves on the shore, practising the silent breathing techniques she used immediately before a performance. Breathe in for four, out for eight. It seemed to be working until a shadow passed in front of the boathouse and Nadia's calm exploded into anger.

'Where the fuck have you been?' she hissed as a black-clad Celia appeared in the doorway. Grabbing the woman by the arm, she steered her towards the water.

'I'm sorry, Nadia,' Celia whispered. 'They were late delivering the food. I had to wait for it, didn't I, or they'd have turned up to an empty room. And I didn't want to call you. I didn't really know what to do.'

'*Shit!* Time's going to be tight. Get in the kayak.'

Celia dithered on the shore. 'How?'

'I'm holding it, Celia. For God's sake, just step in and sit down. Close your eyes, if you must.'

Nadia hadn't wanted to go to the yacht, but Celia's pathetic aversion to water had buggered up the plan, and she'd had no choice. Added to that, she had no faith in Celia's ability to do what was needed on her own.

Celia stepped gingerly into the kayak, which rocked furiously. She yelped. Nadia wanted to scream at her to be quiet, but she would freak out even more. She stretched out a hand for Celia to grab, and the minute she was safely in and seated, Nadia pushed the kayak from the shore, jumped in and started to paddle. It would have been quicker with both of them paddling, but she didn't see any point in suggesting it.

The trip to the yacht was short – a matter of minutes – and then she had to get Celia out of the kayak and onto the swim platform. Another waste of time. *How did anyone get to be so feeble?*

Slipping on some plastic overshoes and the painter's overalls she had nicked from the maintenance storeroom, Nadia pulled down her balaclava to cover her hair, face and neck. Unlike Juliette, Nadia hadn't been able to find a reason for visiting the boat legitimately and she couldn't afford to leave any trace of herself, so her clothes had to be covered as well as every inch of flesh.

Without another word she scooted up the steps and made her way into the salon, hoping Celia hadn't lost it behind her. Turning at the door, ready to drag the woman inside if she had to, she was relieved to see her hovering at the entrance, balaclava firmly pulled down. All Nadia could see were two eyes, wild with fear.

Juliette had prepared the evidence. The video files had arrived in their shared cloud and Nadia had been able to execute the next part of the plan. Now there was just one more thing to do.

'Get the bank security thing from the safe,' she hissed, seeing Celia still glued to the spot, praying Ellis hadn't changed the passcode.

Nadia held her breath as Celia dropped to her knees and

opened a cupboard under the drinks cabinet where a small safe was concealed.

'Got it,' she mumbled, lifting a small device in the air.

'Okay. You ready for this?' Nadia asked.

The thought of opening the door to where she knew Ellis would be stretched out on the bed was almost too much for her, and she had no idea how it might feel for Celia, but she wasn't about to give her time to think, to change her mind.

'Come on. It'll soon be over.'

Her heart racing, Nadia turned, hurried down the stairs to the door of the master suite and with a deep breath pushed it open.

There he was, handcuffed to the fiddle rail, his feet pointing to the door. Juliette had pulled the quilted throw over him – a strangely considerate act from someone whose life had been ripped apart by this man. Or maybe it was consideration for Celia. Either way, Nadia was glad of it.

She stared at Ellis. His eyes were open, but vacant and unfocused. He looked puzzled to see someone on his yacht but didn't appear to be alarmed by the balaclava. When he tried to speak, the words were incoherent. The roofies were still doing their stuff.

She heard a gasp behind her and spun round to give Celia a warning glare. They weren't supposed to make a sound once they were inside the room. Whatever his suspicions, Ellis mustn't know for certain that the two people on his yacht were his wife and his ex-mistress.

Picking up Ellis's phone, Nadia pointed it at his face, accessed the home screen and scrolled to the banking app. She moved behind Ellis, grabbed his head, now lolling on the pillow, and pointed the screen at his face for a second time, and they were in.

Gulping at the amount of cash held in the foundation's account, she moved away from the bed to allow Celia to collect and remove the evidence left by Juliette. Accessing the option to pay someone new, she pulled a piece of paper from her pocket and typed in the account details. As expected, she was asked to verify via the security device. Once more she hoped Celia was right about his passcode.

'He always uses the same one,' she'd said. 'I told you. He thinks he's invincible.'

Thank God for small mercies and the ego of the man.

The payment was approved. Nadia screen-grabbed the page, opened Telegram and typed the instructions into a message to Juliette, then inserted the images she'd captured into a sequence she had already forwarded to Ellis's phone.

One more thing to do, and then they could leave.

She checked her watch and typed a text:

Darling, it's late now, so I hope you don't mind but I've decided to stay on the yacht tonight. I'll be back for breakfast.

While she waited for a response, she looked round to check that Celia had washed out the glass by the bed and filled it with fresh water. Through the open door to the bathroom she could see her transferring the items Juliette had left in the bathroom to a bag which would be weighted down and thrown into the sea. Celia's last task was to unlock the handcuff and put it, with its key, into the bag too. Nadia watched as Celia approached the bed and stood, her body rigid. Ellis was staring at her. Glazed as his eyes were, they were locked on to hers, and she seemed paralysed. In that instant Nadia knew Celia wouldn't be able to touch him.

With a grunt of frustration she hurried round to the other side of the bed, nudged her out of the way with her hip and grabbed the key from her hand. The lock jammed. She was rushing.

Resisting the temptation to utter an expletive, she stopped, took a breath and tried again. She could feel Celia fidgeting behind her.

This time it worked. The handcuffs slid off and she threw them and the key at Celia to put into the bag as she raced back round the bed to where she'd left the phone.

At that moment, there was a beep. A text from Celia's phone, back at the hotel:

Okay. Sleep well. I miss you.

Nadia released a slow breath. Juliette had managed to escape from the restaurant. They were almost done.

Mirroring the screen of Ellis's mobile onto the TV, she set the sequence she'd put together to play in a continuous loop, then put Ellis's phone into its charger so it would repeat over and over again. This was what the bastard would wake up to. He would see what they had done and the evidence they had amassed against him.

Pulling a folded A3 sheet of paper from her pocket, Blu-tack already applied, she stuck it to the wall next to the television.

They were done.

She turned back to Ellis, wishing he could see the curve of her lips, her teeth, her grin. She wanted him to know he was beaten, and that she had done it. It was all she could do not to sneak up next to his ear and tell him what she thought of him and how she wanted him to rot in hell.

Taking a deep breath, she grabbed the bag and nodded to Celia, but the woman was staring at the screen. She hadn't seen what Nadia had done until now, and she stood transfixed, watching the videos Juliette had taken, the drugs, the porn, interspersed with screen grabs of the money transfer and the instructions to Juliette to forward it to his private account in the Cayman Islands.

Nadia waved the security device in front of Celia's face to break the spell and nodded in the direction of the salon. Pausing briefly at the door for a last look at her husband, Celia scurried out to replace it in the safe.

As far as Nadia could see, everything was as it should be; nothing had been overlooked. She took a final moment to read the crucial message on the sheet of paper, stuck to the wall:

A KNIGHTHOOD, ELLIS COBAIN?
I DON'T THINK SO.
TREAT OTHERS WITH HONOUR AND RESPECT –
Your wife
Your mistress
Your former mistress
Your children
Your foundation
Your employees
OR THESE IMAGES BECOME PUBLIC

REMEMBER – I'M WATCHING YOU!

65

Nadia's recollections of Thursday night were crystal clear, every moment etched into her memory.

She'd been so careful with her instructions to Juliette and Celia, and proud of how she had manipulated them both. Suggesting that Ellis should be killed was her masterstroke. She had never believed that they would agree. How many women would plot to murder a man in cold blood, no matter how much he deserved it? Nor were they likely to conspire with someone they had only just met – someone they didn't really know.

But once she had planted that idea in their heads, the less dramatic option of blackmailing him and threatening to ruin him had seemed reasonable, desirable, something they could both embrace. Having committed to the idea, the outcome – and all that happened next – was firmly under her control.

Discovering that Juliette was another of Ellis's victims had been a gift, however painful, that Nadia hadn't been expecting. The woman was desperate to save her marriage, and it hadn't been difficult to convince her that Ellis wouldn't let her go until she was broken. Nadia herself was evidence of the fact. At least, that's what she made Juliette believe.

Celia was an easier target, despite – or maybe because of – being Ellis's wife. Nadia merely had to convince her that Ellis was about to leave her and take the children with him. The poor woman had been so diminished over the years that she would have believed anything she was told. But Celia was dangerous now: weak, nervous, liable to collapse under pressure. Now that Ellis was dead, she might point the finger, say Nadia had suggested at the outset that Ellis should be killed. That couldn't be allowed to happen. She had to be stopped.

Grabbing her jacket from the back of the kitchen chair, Nadia was about to head for the door when her mobile rang.

'Hey, Oscar,' she said. 'What can I do for you?'

Much as she wanted to get him off the phone, he was her eyes and ears at the hotel.

'You can't do anything for me, darling. But I thought I'd give you a call to see how you're doing. And I'm *so* sorry if I dropped you in it, mentioning to the police that Mr Cobain wanted to know where you live. I just thought—'

'It's okay, Oscar. I know you didn't mean any harm.'

It wasn't okay, but unless he had something useful to say, she wanted this conversation over.

'Well, obviously we had to cancel your performance last night, but we'll pay you. It's not your fault, is it? The hotel's buzzing with suspicion, though. It feels as if we're in the centre of our very own Agatha Christie novel!'

There was an inappropriate tone of glee in Oscar's voice.

'What have you heard?'

'Ooh, so much, it's hard to know what's real and what people are making up. That Kevin in the kitchen thinks he knows it all, and he's been talking about hearing the police mention guns and all sorts of bollocks. Honestly, Nadia, someone wants to shoot *him* for being such a dick, if you ask me.'

'Yes, well, apart from Kevin . . .'

'We know it wasn't anything to do with guns. Stevie was the first man on board the yacht on Friday, and he said there was no blood that he could see. And there'd be a lot if it was a shooting, wouldn't there? Anyway, he said the police had their CSI team – all very American TV – at the boathouse. One of the kayaks was on the floor, not on the rack, apparently. I can't think why he thinks that's significant, but he's strutting around like a peacock. From the way he's behaving, I thought he must know something important.'

Nadia dropped to a chair, blanking out the rest of Oscar's gossip. Stevie's titbit might not sound significant to Oscar, but it did to her.

66

I've finally forced myself to leave the sanctuary of the hotel garden, skirting round the back of the courtyard accommodation, out of view of the windows of our suite. I'm not ready to see Russell yet, so I set off along the path I have trodden many times this week.

I don't look at the view, and I am no longer lost in pain and confusion. I need answers. I will do whatever I can to protect Russell, to show him how sorry I am and how much I love him, but I need to understand what happened to Ellis, even if that means ultimately throwing myself on the mercy of the police. I can't keep all of this a secret any longer, and for the first time in months I feel decisive, resolute.

And it feels good.

Nadia must have lied. She told me everything had gone to plan, but that can't have been the case. Ellis wasn't supposed to die. I'm not sorry he's dead – how could I be? But I'm not a killer, and I won't be branded one to suit Nadia.

The police know Ellis sent me the money from the foundation, but they don't know it was part of the plan to set him up, to show him to be unworthy of the honour he craved. To have his name dragged through the mud for drug taking, porn watching and misappropriation of the foundation's funds would destroy him, especially if the money transfer ended in a criminal charge, but without the Telegram message I have no evidence of why the money was sent to me. If Nadia hasn't kept a copy of the text instructing me to send it to Ellis's account in the Cayman Islands, as she promised, it will be impossible to explain why the money was put in my account.

'You definitely grabbed an image of both the transfer to me and the Telegram message you sent from his phone?' I'd asked last time I saw her.

'*Yes!* Stop being such a twat!'

I wasn't convinced, and she accurately read my sceptical expression.

'Jesus, Juliette, it was *my* plan and it was one of the key elements, so why wouldn't I?'

I couldn't answer that, but now I want proof. I want to see that message.

We still don't know if the police saw the videos and slides that Nadia assembled, or the list of demands. I can't believe they did, because if they had they would have asked different questions. They haven't said anything about Ellis's mobile either. Nadia is adamant she left it on the charger, auto lock switched off, the sequence running. It should still have been displaying on the television on Friday morning when his body was found. But it can't have been.

What happened to it?

Nadia must know. Someone must, and she's my best bet. When she sent Celia out of the room to put the bank security device in the safe, did she take the phone out of the charger, rip the sign off the wall and kill Ellis? Was there nothing there for the police to find?

I trudge, head down, towards the village, towards Nadia,

watching my feet, unwilling to lift my face. I'm so ashamed, devastated that I might have actually been involved in a man's murder. It's too much. And I want to know why Nadia thought it was okay to twist the truth about her relationship with Ellis. I don't think it's the only thing she's lied about. There's something else she's not telling me. I can almost smell the lie on her, and I'm going to find out what it is.

Reason tells me she must have killed him. No one has said how he died, or when, but she had the keys to the boathouse, so if she didn't kill him when she was there with Celia, did she go back later?

Suddenly I stop. I'm being watched. I can feel it. I lift my head to look around, but there's no one in sight.

I'm getting more jumpy with every passing moment. Should I really be confronting Nadia? Is it a stupid thing to do?

If she has killed once, she could do it again.

67

Oscar may have thought the kayak on the ground was insignificant, but it wasn't, and Nadia felt a knot of apprehension tighten in her stomach. She thought she had been so clever, the plan foolproof. What if she was wrong? She needed to speak to Celia.

Turning up at Celia's suite at the hotel wasn't ideal, but the police knew Nadia had a relationship with Ellis three years ago. Maybe they wouldn't find it too strange that she would want to see his wife. Thoughtless, maybe, but not completely weird.

Her visit would no doubt catapult Celia into a state of sheer panic, but it had to be done. Juliette mustn't know about it, though. At least not until Nadia had the answers she was looking for.

'Shit!' she muttered, as she spotted the very person she didn't want to see approaching along the cliff path.

What the fuck was she doing here?

She knew the answer. Juliette had already passed the narrow track down to their refuge beneath the cliffs, and this path only led to the village. She must be looking for her. And Nadia didn't want to see her.

Juliette's head was down, staring at her feet, hands thrust in her pockets, marching along the path with a clear sense of purpose.

She was as dangerous as Celia, in her own way, liable to admit everything to Russell, who Nadia was sure would insist on telling the police, especially if he thought it would save their marriage. That couldn't happen, but Nadia wasn't ready to confront Juliette yet. Right now she still felt Celia was the greater risk.

She glanced around for somewhere to hide. Juliette was still some distance away and hadn't seen her, so she dodged behind a cluster of rocks on the cliff side of the path, and crouched behind the largest. The cliff fell away to the shore below her, and for one moment she pictured Juliette discovering her there and pushing her over the edge as revenge for everything she had persuaded her to do.

She held her breath as the trudge of feet advanced towards her along the path, now only a couple of metres from where she hid.

The footsteps stopped.

She must have seen me.

Nadia held her breath, debating if it would be best to come out from behind the rocks and away from the sheer drop.

68

I must have been imagining things. There's no one watching me. There's no one on the cliff path. I'm seeing danger where there is none.

One thing is true, though. As I've been walking my anger with Nadia has grown. She wanted Ellis dead from the outset, and somehow she has manipulated us all until she got her wish.

I've convinced myself that I know how it happened. Nadia was only alone with Ellis for a few moments but it was long enough to give him more drugs or even to put a knife in his chest. I'm not giving up until she tells me the truth.

I've made it to the village, to Nadia's home. I've resisted the urge to turn and flee back to Russell, and I take a big gulp of air as I raise my hand to knock on Nadia's door. There's no answer. I knock again, this time putting my ear to the letterbox. There isn't a sound from inside.

'Are you looking for Nadia?'

The voice comes from behind me, and I turn to see a tall woman heading back from the direction of the village beach, a toddler trotting along beside her.

'Yes, but I don't think she's in. She's not answering anyway.'

'I saw her a while ago, heading along the cliff path towards the hotel.'

I frown. Surely I would have passed her?

I recognise the little boy clutching the woman's hand, and I crouch down to his level.

'Hello. It's Marco, isn't it?'

He gives me a shy smile and dodges behind the woman's legs, just as he did the last time I saw him.

'How do you know Marco?' the woman asks, a hint of suspicion in her voice.

I'm still looking at this face, wondering if I can see anything of Ellis in his features.

'Oh, I met him with his mum on the beach the other day. You were playing with the stones, weren't you, Marco?'

He gives me a tiny nod.

I realise the woman has said nothing, so I look up and meet her eyes.

69

Celia was dreading having to explain to the children that she might not be able to get home for another day or so, and she was increasingly convinced she would *never* get back to them.

She picked up her mobile and tapped the screen to make the call.

Lacey answered. 'Hello, Mum,' she mumbled.

'Hi, darling. What's up? You sound upset.'

'I'm sorry, Mum,' she said, her voice breaking on a sob. 'Reece has just told me he was *lying*!'

'Take a deep breath, Lacey. Whatever the problem is, we'll sort it. When was he lying, sweetheart, and what about?'

'That night when I was calling and calling. And you never answered.'

Thursday night. Celia remembered her horror that she'd missed so many calls from home. Lacey was a fragile girl and she should have been there for her.

'I'm sorry, sweetheart, but we did speak eventually.'

'I know, but I really *needed* you so I could tell you what Reece said. But now he says he made it up to frighten me because I'm such a mummy's girl. I *hate* him!'

Celia felt her breath catch and fought to keep an even tone. 'No, you don't, Lacey. You're just cross with him, and whatever's happened I don't want you to be upset. Is Reece there? Let me speak to him.'

There was a bit of fevered whispering.

'Hi, Mum,' Reece said, his voice sullen. 'Lacey says I've got to tell you I'm sorry.'

Much as she felt tempted to shout at him down the phone, she had to remember he was only nine years old and had been brought up to believe in the infallibility of the male species, so she took a deep breath.

'And are you sorry?'

She heard a sniff. 'Yes,' he mumbled.

'You know it's unkind to upset people, don't you, Reece? We've talked about this, and I know it's not really who you are. Do you want to tell me what happened, and why?'

'I was arguing with Lacey. I pushed her over and she was going to tell you. I was scared you'd be mad at me.'

'I would have been. You shouldn't hurt *anyone*, Reece, least of all your sister.'

'I know, but that's why I said it doesn't matter what you think, because Dad told me he's going to find us a new mum.' There was a pause. 'But it wasn't true, and now I'm scared you'll leave us because I'm so awful.'

Celia closed her eyes and fought for control. 'First, you're not awful. You're amazing and I love you. I would never choose to leave you. That's a promise. Tell me honestly – did you talk to your dad about me before we came away?'

There was another sniff. 'Yeah. You'd told me off for bullying Savannah and said I had to be kind to the girls while you were on holiday. I went into Dad's study and told him you were mean to me.'

'And what did Dad say?'

'He said, "So? Be mean back." I didn't really know what he meant.'

'No, of course you didn't, darling. You're just a child, and he shouldn't have said that to you. But why did you tell Lacey he was going to find you a new mummy? Did he say that?'

'No. But Erik told me his dad had said it to him, so I just copied him.'

Erik was Reece's school friend. Celia knew he was distraught because his mother had left her young family to return to Norway. She didn't know the details and didn't need to.

'Just to be clear, darling, you're saying your dad *didn't* say this?'

'*No*, Mum. I told you. I made it up to scare Lacey.'

Whispering words of comfort that she dredged from somewhere despite the storm in her mind, Celia hung up and leaned back against the sofa, a knot tightening in her stomach.

Surely it didn't matter what Reece said? He might have made his father's words up, but it had merely confirmed what she already knew. Ellis had been looking for a new mum for them. And he'd found one.

Nadia.

70

The door to Celia's suite flew open.

'Tell me about the boathouse!' Nadia shouted, marching into the room.

'Nadia! What are you doing here? You shouldn't *be* here! What if the police see you?'

'What if they do? I don't give a stuff what they think, to be honest.'

'Just go, Nadia. I don't want you here.'

'Nope. Not going to happen. Not only do I not trust you to keep your mouth shut, but I've been baffled since I heard about Ellis on Friday. What planet were you on when you decided it was okay to ask the hotel to send someone out to the yacht, knowing what they'd find?'

'You *know* why I did it! I hadn't heard from Ellis. *Any* wife would have asked for someone to go and check on him.'

Nadia gave a nasty laugh. 'Not true. Any normal wife would have asked someone to take *her* out to the yacht, and would have gone to see if he was okay.'

Celia shook her head. 'I wouldn't, though. I was acting like a wife who didn't know if her husband might have another woman on board.'

Nadia scoffed. 'Not good enough. *You* might know that's

how he behaved, but the hotel staff didn't, so that's a really crap excuse. And what did you think they'd find, Celia? You must have thought they'd discover what we'd done – the video playing on the TV, the sign on the wall? How come the police haven't mentioned any of that – either to me or to Juliette?'

Celia scraped around in her mind for something to say. She hadn't thought this through.

'Look, Nadia, we obviously need to talk about this. The police are asking some tricky questions, though, so right now you need to leave.'

'Not until I have some answers. Let's start with the boathouse, shall we? You and I lifted the kayak back onto the rack, so how come the police found a kayak on the ground inside the boathouse? Did you lock up, like I told you to?'

Celia had no time to answer. At the sound of laboured breathing, she looked over Nadia's shoulder to the open door where a dishevelled Juliette stood, fighting for breath, hair clinging to her damp cheeks.

'How could she lock up, Nadia? You told me you had the key.'

Nadia spun round.

Juliette's breaths were slowing, her recovery time fast. 'I knew there was something wrong when you told me about Thursday night, but I couldn't work out what it was. I've been over and over it, and it's only just hit me. You said you left Celia to lock the boathouse. But you also said you needed to put the key back on the hook in the office. Which of those two statements is the truth?'

Nadia put her hands on her hips. 'Christ, is *that* what you're so het up about? Yes, I left Celia to lock up. The padlock has a snap lock. The key unlocks it, then you just push the end back in and *snap* – it's locked. That was all she had to do.'

Juliette glanced towards Celia, as if for verification, and Nadia turned back to face her. Celia's face had drained of colour. 'Did you lock it, Celia? Did you lock the fucking door?' Nadia shouted.

Celia nodded, her head bobbing up and down repeatedly as if that made it more convincing. But Nadia wasn't buying it. 'Oscar just told me the police are very interested in a kayak that wasn't on the rack. If you locked up, as we agreed, how did one of the kayaks end up on the floor?'

Celia's eyes were wild with panic. 'I'm sorry, Nadia. I mustn't have closed it properly. I thought I had, but maybe I was wrong. Someone else must have got in after us. Why does it matter anyway?'

'Why does it *matter*? Until now the police have probably been trying to work out how anyone got to the yacht. As far as they knew, the boathouse was locked, the key safely in the office. They'll now suspect the killer got there in a kayak. They'll be looking for people with access to the key and a motive for murder. Me, in other words. You *idiot*.'

Juliette stood up straight, hands on hips. 'Don't start with the blame, Nadia, because you don't have a leg to stand on. Forget the kayak – let's focus on the big issue here. The *huge* issue, in fact. You know that Celia's life revolves around her children and that if Ellis left her, she might never see them again. So you told her Ellis was thrilled to have found he had a son. So thrilled, in fact, that he wanted to uproot his family – take them away from Celia – and move to Cornwall. That was her only motive for wanting revenge.'

Nadia shrugged. 'It's true! He wanted to be able to spend

time with me and Marco, yes, for us to be a family. And it wasn't what I wanted.'

Juliette threw her head back with a derisive laugh.

'But the whole thing's a fantasy, isn't it? You left Bristol because Ellis dumped *you*, Nadia. Not the other way round. And you stalked him until he found a way to drive you away. I won't – and never will – excuse his appalling behaviour, but you knew he was married and yet you pursued him relentlessly.'

Nadia forced a smile. 'I'm sure everyone has a different perspective on what happened. Whatever rumours you may have heard, only two people know the truth, and one of them is dead. So that's not really working for me as an accusation.'

'Well, maybe this will,' Juliette said, taking a step closer to Nadia. 'Marco is not Ellis's son.' She looked at Celia. 'He's not even Nadia's son, Celia. I met him today. With his *mother*. So do you want to tell me what *really* happened with Ellis when he came to see you?'

Before Nadia could speak, Celia stepped towards her. 'You were lying?'

Nadia took one look at Celia, her face a mask of shock and disbelief, fists clenched at her sides, and took a step backwards.

71

Stephanie had persuaded Gus that they needed a bit of fresh air, so they had escaped to a bench in the garden for a five-minute break. Gus hated it when he couldn't tie all the pieces together, and she wanted to put her arms around him, tell him they'd get there in the end as they always did. But the bench was in full view of the incident room, so she had to content herself with sitting as close to him as possible.

She couldn't wait for this to be over so they could go home, curl up in front of a fire – albeit in a bare, undecorated room – and she could share her news. She rested her hand on her stomach, imagining the joy on Gus's face when she told him.

The sooner they solved this crime the better, but the problem was a lack of concrete evidence. They had lots of pieces, such as Stephanie's conviction that Juliette had gone to Celia's room at 10 p.m. on Thursday night to respond to the text – supposedly from Ellis. That *had* to have been planned. But despite their initial excitement, it didn't help because according to Molly, Ellis was still alive at the time the text was sent. And wherever Celia was at 10 p.m. she was back in her room by 10.20.

And what about Nadia? Ellis was killed either during or after her second set that night. If it was after, Nadia could have taken the key to the boathouse from the office and gone out to the yacht.

That might explain the kayak on the ground. But the key was back on its hook by morning and CCTV showed no one – including Nadia – coming into the hotel after midnight. She left through the main door – they had the footage – and even if she sneaked back in through the room she'd been using on the ground floor, she would have appeared on the CCTV in the corridors.

The laundry bag was proving to be something of a dead end, with too many people able to access them. Another disappointment. This appeared to be a crime of many parts, and the suspects seemingly had alibis for all but the smallest window of time.

'I think we should talk to all three women again, Gus. There's no definitive evidence that any one of them murdered Cobain, but collectively it all adds up. If, as we suspect, any or all of them were working together and we apply enough pressure, one of them is bound to crack. They're hardly professional criminals, and we can push them, convince them they can be done for conspiracy to murder. It should be enough to make one of them turn on the others.'

'Unless we're wrong. They were up to *something*, but what if it wasn't one of them who did the final deed?'

'You're thinking of Russell?'

'He seems so calm, so measured. Maybe he's like a swan – serene on the surface, paddling like buggery underneath. Perhaps we shouldn't rule out the idea of the Daltons working together. Cobain had a hold over Juliette, and even if the threat of Russell discovering the truth was no longer an issue, there was still the money. And let's not forget Cobain had been making Juliette's life a misery for months. That would have infuriated Russell, I'd have thought. Maybe her job was to drug Ellis, then Russell went later to kill him. But how did they get the key to the boathouse?'

Stephanie rested her chin on her knuckles, trying and failing to piece it all together. 'Both Daltons may have had a motive, but is there a *shared* motive? His would be jealousy, hers would be revenge for how he treated her. Do people with different motives ever conspire to kill?'

Their thinking ground to a temporary halt, but Stephanie was like a dog with a bone when she had an idea in her head.

'Which of them is the weakest link? Should we have a go at Celia? She's not very robust. She's crippled with self-doubt, thanks to that bastard she was married to, and I'm not sure she could cope if we pushed her.'

For a moment the desire to let this go, to leave the case unsolved, hovered at the front of her mind. Ellis Cobain was a cruel man who hurt everyone he touched. But she knew better than to think like that.

Gus took a deep breath. 'I think Juliette and Russell are our best bet. We tell them we believe Juliette was on the yacht with Ellis in the early evening, she drugged him then swam back. We think she colluded with Russell, who went back to kill him later. We can say we believe she, and possibly Russell, were involved in money laundering – hence the transfer of funds. We say—'

'Hang on, Gus. You don't believe that, do you?'

'Nope, nor do I think Juliette killed Ellis. I think she was involved, but I don't think she killed him. And for that reason, she's the most likely to admit to what really happened, especially if she thinks we'll go after her husband too.'

Stephanie stood up from the bench. 'Okay, let's go and get them. And let's hope it doesn't break them.'

It was their job was to catch the killer, like it or not, but Stephanie couldn't help feeling that Juliette and Russell Dalton had suffered enough.

72

Since I exposed Nadia's lie about Marco, it feels as if time has stopped. We stand, frozen like statues.

My eyes flick from Celia to Nadia and back again. Celia looks unhinged, her eyes black with confusion, and for the first time since I've known her, Nadia seems nervous. She's trying to put a belligerent face on it but is the first to break the ominous silence.

'Celia, for God's sake, Ellis didn't deserve you. He didn't deserve *any* of us. That fucker ruined our lives, and he had to be made to suffer.'

'Who's Marco? Who does the child belong to?'

Nadia shakes her head. 'He's a friend's kid. I look after him for her sometimes. So what?'

Celia reaches out a hand and grabs a small brass sculpture of a dolphin from a console table as Nadia retreats further into the corner of the room. *Is she going to hit her with it?*

'Tell me what Ellis said when he came to your house. Did he believe Marco was his?'

Nadia's gaze shoots to me, pleading with me to intervene. But I'm not ready to help. Not yet. I want to hear what Nadia has to say. She lied to us both.

'Look, Celia, it was all a misunderstanding, okay?' she says, her voice cracking. 'When I saw Ellis in the audience last

Saturday night, I thought he'd come for *me*! I didn't know about Juliette – that *she* was the one he followed here.'

'I don't want your excuses. Just tell me what he said, Nadia.'

Celia's body is rigid, and I can see that Nadia's lies have pushed her to the limit of her fragile sanity. For once Nadia is on the back foot.

'Okay, but please just listen to me. Don't come any closer, Celia, or I won't be able to think straight.'

I give Celia a slight shake of the head, trying to convey that it's best if she complies, but her eyes are too wild and I'm beginning to think this will end badly as Nadia tries to explain: 'When Ellis turned up, I was convinced he was going to tell me he wanted us to get back together. I'm *sorry*! Okay? But you have to understand. I loved that man so much. He was *everything* to me.'

Strangely that produces little response from Celia, but I feel nauseous.

'Go on, Nadia. Don't stop there.' Celia spits out the words.

'Obviously I couldn't maintain the pretence that Marco was his – he isn't even mine – but I hoped for just a moment that he might *think* he was his, that he might be excited by the idea of living together with me, as a family.'

How can Nadia's perception of Ellis be so different from mine? Did she really think he would react positively? Why did we believe her lies? I can only think we were so demoralised, so *crushed*, that we would have believed anything.

Celia chokes out a response: 'I trusted you. You said he was planning to leave me and take my children. Do you know what that *did* to me?'

Nadia shakes her head. 'I'm sorry, but all I could think about was getting revenge on Ellis. He thought Marco was my child, so I asked if he'd be pleased if I told him he was the father. He laughed. Just *laughed*.'

'So why in God's name did you tell *us* that Marco was his?' I ask, unable to hold my tongue.

'I had to bring Marco with me that day. I was looking after him, and you assumed he was mine, so I decided to see how it would play out. I asked if you could guess who the father was, fully expecting Celia to say that obviously Marco couldn't be Ellis's child. But she didn't, and then I realised that she didn't know. It seemed too good an opportunity to miss – to make you both believe . . .'

Celia is hefting the statue in her hand again, and she's very close to losing control. 'Never mind your *opportunity*. What didn't I know, Nadia?'

'That he had a vasectomy years ago, when you were desperate to have a child of your own. He told me on Sunday – said it was the only way to stop you. I thought you knew.'

There's a crash as the statue drops to the ground, and a groan of agony from Celia. 'The *bastard*. He said that despite all the tests, the problem had to lie with me as there was clearly nothing wrong with his fertility.'

Celia slumps as if the fleeting surge of strength had drained from her body. 'Did you know about his vasectomy, Juliette?'

I shake my head, not wanting to say the words, but knowing I must. 'I didn't need to know. I can't have children. Ellis knew that.'

I want to bury my head in my hands. It's all too much to absorb. How have we got ourselves into this mess? We were supposed to be teaching Ellis a lesson, forcing him to treat us with consideration. But now he's dead.

And I still don't know who killed him.

73

Nadia knew she'd screwed up, but she had never expected them to discover that Marco wasn't hers. The moment she'd realised how desperate Celia was to hang on to Ellis's children, a plan had arrived, fully formed, in her mind. She had to convince Celia that Ellis was about to leave and take his children to live with her and Marco.

It was cruel, but all Nadia had been able to think about was how to hurt Ellis, to destroy him for the pain he'd caused, and if using Celia was the only way, she hadn't hesitated to lie.

'I was wrong to pretend Marco was his child, I know that. But none of this explains how Ellis died. Before Juliette burst in, you told me you locked the boathouse. So why was there a kayak on the ground? I know you and I lifted the one we used onto the rack. There were none on the ground then. Did you lock up, or didn't you?'

Celia looked uneasy. 'Of course I did. But you had the key. You could have gone back later.'

'No, I couldn't. I was singing in the restaurant. And let's not forget that the police have said nothing to any of us about the evidence we left on the yacht – the sequence playing, the sign on the wall. And they would have. We were named – the wife, the mistress, the former mistress – so they would know who we all are. Whoever went to the yacht that night must have taken Ellis's phone, ripped the sign off the wall –' Nadia's eyes flicked between Juliette and Celia '– and then killed him. So which of you was it? Because it wasn't me.' Nadia glanced at Juliette. 'Or was it your husband, Juliette? Did Russell decide there was one way he could get Ellis out of your life forever? Did he know about the two of you? Because my guess is that he would move mountains to save you, in the same way that Celia would move heaven and earth for her children.'

Juliette had turned pale.

'We don't know what time Ellis died,' Nadia continued. 'Russell could have sneaked out while you were sleeping. And if Celia didn't lock the boathouse properly he could have got to the yacht. Maybe he saw the sign on the wall and thought there was only one way he could save you.'

Nadia's gaze swivelled back to Celia, expecting some sort of reaction: a look of shocked disbelief or a question in her eyes. But there was nothing; she wasn't even looking at Juliette. She was standing perfectly still, staring sightlessly out of the window, her eyes brimming with unshed tears.

'Celia?' Nadia gasped as the truth struck her. '*Christ!* I don't believe this. It wasn't Russell, was it? It was you! You went back to the yacht! That's why the kayak was on the ground. You took it down from the rack but couldn't lift it back up. And you had time. I was singing, Juliette was in the restaurant. We only have your word that you were in your room. What the hell happened? You said you didn't want him dead, so what made you go back?'

Celia brushed the tears away. 'It doesn't really matter if you know, does it? Because you're both culpable too. If I'm charged with murder, you will be too. Conspiracy to murder, I believe it's called, because there's no way you can prove it wasn't supposed to be murder from the outset or that you weren't involved in every stage of the plan.'

Nadia glanced at Juliette, whose eyes were wide and unblinking as she stared at Celia.

Celia glared back. 'Don't look at me like that, Juliette. You had an affair with my husband, knowing he was married. What if you'd fallen for him? You said you can't have children; what if you'd wanted to take mine?'

'Celia, I—'

'Shut *up*! I'm sick of people telling me what to do, what to think, of making me feel I'm nothing – not important, always getting everything wrong. I know you say your affair was a mistake, but even if you didn't take my babies from me, it would have been the next woman, or the one after.'

She took a deep shuddering gulp.

'And you, Nadia. You're the worst of us all. You let me believe he was about to leave me. On Thursday night, after we got back from the yacht, I spoke to Lacey. She told me that, according to Reece, Ellis was looking for a new mother for my children, and I thought he'd found her. *You!* Everything you told me about Ellis's plan to be with you was a pack of lies, wasn't it?' Celia's shoulders sagged. 'It doesn't matter anyway. I'm pretty sure he was done with me. My time was nearly up. He'd already extinguished any spark I had, so it was no fun tormenting me any more. He was ready to move on to his next victim, someone new to destroy.'

Nadia was still puzzled. 'Is that why you did it? Because he was about to leave you? But you said it wasn't reason enough to kill him. What changed?'

Celia's voice took on a hard edge. 'You still don't get it, do you? I wouldn't have killed him for taking my children and breaking my heart, however much I wanted to. That would be *my* pain, and my pain only. But that night I pieced together a whole different chapter in the horror story that is Ellis Cobain. You told me Vivian had threatened to leave him, Nadia, and while she may ultimately be responsible for taking her own life, I'm certain Ellis knew what she intended. As you said, where did she get the drugs? Maybe it was a cry for help, believing someone would find her before she died. But Ellis wasn't going to let that happen.'

Celia walked over to the full-height window, gazing out as if the truth could be found in the sky. She carried on talking, her back to Nadia and Juliette.

'I heard things from the police this week that made me question if he knew what she was about to do and he gave her the space. Then, when I spoke to Lacey on Thursday night, she told me the truth about what happened that day. Lacey's been blaming herself for her mother's death all this time, and Ellis let her believe that. Encouraged it, in fact.'

Celia spun to face them, her speech increasingly agitated.

'He knew what damage he was doing to his child. He forced her to say nothing, to hang on to her guilt. And she's been living in silent fear that every time I'm alone in the house, she'll come home to find me dead. For six *years* she's been bearing this huge burden all by herself, but what did Ellis care, as long as he wasn't suspected of aiding and abetting his wife's suicide? That's the man we're talking about. Nothing else that he's done comes close to the pain he's caused Lacey. And you made me believe he was going to leave me, to take my children, Nadia. Who would have been there to protect them from their father then? You? There was no way I could leave them in his care. No *way!*'

With a defeated whimper, the last remnants of her energy spent, Celia slithered slowly down the window to the floor. Her eyes were open but lost, as if she were alone in the world.

74

Celia knew Nadia and Juliette were still in the room, but their speech had become a distant, indistinct murmur, their bodies colourless smudges in a blurred image.

She didn't want to focus on them, or what they were talking about. All she could think about was Thursday night.

The Night of the Murder

Celia sat perfectly still in the kayak, trying not to rock it as Nadia paddled them both back to shore. She couldn't believe it was over. They'd done it, and despite her worst fears Ellis hadn't reared up in the bed to grab her by the throat. His eyes had been dull, lifeless.

Her tasks had been to get the security device from the safe, collect all the evidence and dump it in the sea. The only time it got difficult was when she had to get close to the bed. Close to Ellis. But now it was done. She hadn't let anyone down. Ellis would come round from his stupor, see the evidence against him and have no choice but to be kinder. At least, that's what she had to believe.

As Celia clambered out of the kayak, Nadia put a finger to

her lips to warn her to be silent. They dragged the kayak up the beach, manoeuvred it into the boathouse and lifted it onto the rack.

'I need to go,' Nadia murmured as soon as the kayak was safely stowed. 'I'm singing soon.' She headed to the door, whispering over her shoulder, 'Hang up the paddles, lock the door.' With that, she was gone.

Celia was alone. All she could hear were the waves lapping the shore. She turned to look out through the open door over the water. A sea fret was rolling in, the pale wispy fog creeping ominously towards her through the black night.

She moaned. *Why had Nadia left her?* Turning back, she picked up the paddles and practically threw them at the pegs. She glanced over her shoulder. The mist was drawing closer. She had the sickening feeling that, like a kraken, it would engulf her and drag her out into the depths of the ocean, so she ran from the boathouse, slamming the door without a thought to the noise she was making. She tried to hook the padlock through the loop, but her fingers were wet, slippery with sweat, and it fell from her hands. Unable to see in the deep shadows, she dropped to her knees, groping around wildly. She couldn't find it, and as the first tendrils of cold, dank air reached her, she leaped to her feet and ran, leaving the padlock where it lay.

Racing up the path, stumbling on the loose stones, sobbing, she finally reached the sanctuary of her room and collapsed into a chair. It had all gone so well on the yacht, but had she ruined everything? The boathouse was unlocked. Did that matter?

The pungent aroma of the blue cheese in the salad she'd ordered earlier hit her, nearly making her gag. The plates were still on the table, but to Celia's dismay there were signs that someone had been in the suite while she was out. Freshly laundered shirts lay over the back of a chair, a laundry bag on the seat. That wasn't supposed to happen. Only Juliette was supposed to have been in.

Kicking off her wet trainers, Celia called to have the dinner plates removed, ran upstairs and threw on a towelling dressing gown. Heart still thudding, she returned to the living room and sank onto the sofa.

Her phone was on the coffee table, where she'd left it for Juliette. Picking it up, she was about to check the text messages, ostensibly between her and Ellis, when a pulse of alarm spread through her. There were calls – lots of them – from her home number.

The children. With fumbling fingers she tapped the screen to call and was surprised when Lacey answered. It was late. She should have been in bed.

'Lacey, darling. Are you okay? Is Jeanette not there?'

'She's here, but she saw it was you and she knows I've been trying to call you. Where've you *been*?'

'Just to dinner. What's up, darling?'

'It's Reece. He said something horrible – that Daddy told him it was time to find a new mum.' Celia heard a choked sob down the phone. 'I don't know what he *means*! I'm scared Daddy's going to make us leave the house for the whole day again, like he did when my other mummy died, and that you'll be dead when we get back.'

Horrified as she was at Ellis telling his son he was thinking of leaving her and taking the children, it was Lacey's words about her 'other mummy' that chilled Celia. Even though she had tried many times to get the little girl to open up about the day Vivian died, this was the first time she had spoken about it.

'That's not going to happen, sweetheart.'

'But it *might*! I still remember that day. Mummy was crying, so I went to her room, but Daddy was there. I knew he'd be angry if I went in, so I crouched down and peeked round the door. Mummy kept telling him she'd had enough. She couldn't take any more. I didn't know what she meant. Then Daddy told her to take some of her happy pills.'

'Happy pills?'

'That's what she called them. When she got really upset, which she sometimes did, she would take one and get better. That day she said, "Maybe I should take the whole bottle," and Daddy said that sounded like a splendid idea. I saw him take a little plastic bag out of his pocket and empty some more pills onto her bedside table. He said, "Why not take these, too?"'

With a knot of dread tightening in her stomach, Celia desperately wanted Lacey to just stop talking. But she had to hear the truth. All of it.

'I'm so sorry you had to see that, darling, but maybe you haven't remembered it quite right.'

'I *have*! I remember thinking, *Good! More pills will make her happier.* I was only six and it made sense to me, but I'm old enough now to know that's not true.'

'Of course you are. But whatever happened, nothing like that's going to happen to me. I promise. What did you mean about Daddy making you leave the house?'

'I went to my room before Daddy could see me, but he came to find me. He said he was taking us out. He'd never done that before. I wanted to say goodbye to Mummy before we went, but he wouldn't let me. I didn't want to go out, but I didn't dare say so because we always do what he tells us, don't we? Reece was only three and Savannah a baby. She cried all the time. I think she was hungry. He took us to a wildlife park, but he forgot the buggy so he had to carry Savannah. Reece was whinging about having to walk, and Daddy said he was fed up with the lot of us. He took us back to the car because it was raining. I said maybe we should go home, but he shouted and told me to stop being a baby. We just sat there for ages until we'd stopped whining.'

Lacey sobbed. The girl was distraught at the memory, and much as Celia wanted to rail at Ellis, she bit back her words.

'Perhaps he just wanted a nice day out with you, and he got cross because it wasn't working out the way he intended.'

'No, Mum. It wasn't like that. Reece kept whispering to me that he was hungry, and Daddy hadn't brought anything for Savannah, not even a bottle. In the end he took us to the cafe for an ice cream, even though it was freezing and raining. He said I should have a knickerbocker glory because they were the best, but it was massive and I couldn't eat it. Daddy said I'd asked for it, so I had to finish it – even though it was his idea. It took ages, and I remember trying not to cry because I didn't think I could eat it all without being sick. It was nearly dark by the time we got back, and Daddy sent me to tell Mummy we were home. She was just lying on the bed, not moving.'

Celia's body turned to ice. 'You found her, Lacey? Daddy sent you to find her?'

'Yes,' she managed between sobs. 'I shook her and shook her, but she didn't wake up. We stayed out for too long, and it was my fault for eating my ice cream so slowly.'

Celia's eyes flooded with tears at the thought of the pain Lacey must have suffered. She was six years old when Vivian died. Had Ellis kept them out, believing that by the time they got home Vivian would be dead? Did he know or even suspect that his child would find her mother's body?

'Lacey, darling, this is not your fault. You mustn't ever think like that. You were just a little girl. Why have you never told me this before?'

Lacey could hardly get the words out. 'I wasn't allowed to. I'd have been sent away.'

'What do you mean? No one would have sent you away. You didn't do anything wrong.'

'But it happened because of what I did! Daddy said so. When I was crying after Mummy died I said we should have come home sooner. I told him I thought the extra tablets he'd given her would make her happy, and he was so angry! He told me that if I said a word about how long we'd been out, or about the tablets, he'd have to tell the police it was my fault, and I'd be in big trouble. If I hadn't demanded that ice cream and eaten it so slowly we'd have been back much sooner and Mummy would still be alive, so we had to keep it a secret or I'd be sent away.'

The evil bastard. Lacey had borne this dreadful weight of guilt for all those years, terrified of what would happen if she told a soul, when all the time Ellis had been covering for himself. He had kept his children out of the house for hours in the cold and wet, sitting in the car for much of the time with nothing more than an ice cream to sustain them. And he had provided some of the cocktail of tablets that killed his wife. With only a six-year-old's word as evidence it might have been difficult to prove he had assisted his wife's suicide, but Ellis would have been crucified in the press if it got out.

She ached to hold her little girl, reassure her that everything would be fine, but all she could offer were words of comfort.

'Listen to me, sweetheart. You're older now. You must realise that there is *no way* that it was your fault. No way *at all*. Daddy was probably upset because your mummy was dead. He probably didn't mean it.'

'He *did*! He said it again when I told him I was scared about you being in the house on your own in case you died too. He told me never to say a word to you about what happened, or I'd be sent away and I'd never see you again.'

It took another ten minutes to calm Lacey, to convince her that she had done nothing wrong; that Celia loved her, Reece and Savannah more than anything in the world. Finally, with a last sob, the call ended, but for Celia it was far from over. She had submitted to Ellis's cruel, manipulative behaviour for years with one aim in mind: to be there for the children. She knew that unless she bowed to his every demand, he would end their marriage and never allow her near them again.

They needed her. And yet it seemed her time with him – with all of them – was nearly over. And if Ellis was preparing to replace her, there would be no one to protect her children from their own father. She felt a burning rage that this man, Lacey's *father*, had put her through the agony of believing her mother's death was her fault.

She had barely been able to hold herself together when the housekeeper came to clear the almost untouched food from the room. But as the door closed, she knew what she had to do.

75

Celia's eyes were glassy, as if she was miles away, and Juliette had slumped in a chair.

'Why did you kill him?' Nadia asked, when the silence had become suffocating. 'You were adamant it was a step too far.'

'That was when I thought the only person he would hurt was me. But I realised he had no qualms at all about hurting my children, and I believed he was ready to move on. *You* told me that, and Reece confirmed it. I know now that Reece made it up, and that you were lying. But at that moment, believing he was about to leave me, I decided Ellis had to die. Not for me. For *them*. How could I let that bastard take them? Who would keep them safe? He may not be violent, but there's more than one way of destroying a child.'

'How did you do it?' Nadia asked, ignoring Juliette's shocked expression. 'We need to know. It might be important.'

'No, we don't. The less we know, the better,' Juliette whispered.

Celia carried on talking as if neither of them had said a word.

'I hadn't planned it, but then I remembered the boathouse was still open. I'd dropped the padlock, you see, and panicked. There was a laundry bag on the sofa. I took it – not sure what I was going to do with it – and crept back to the boathouse for the kayak. I wasn't scared any more. Not even of the water. I was fuelled by anger. When I got to the yacht, I did have a moment of panic at the thought that Ellis might be awake, that he would laugh at me and tell me I never got anything right. But I would have fought him with every ounce of strength I had.

'He was still out of it, though, the Rohypnol doing what you said it would, so I took the belt from the dressing gown in the bathroom and tied one of his wrists to the fiddle rail, pushed his other arm under the throw and knelt on it. I pulled the laundry bag over his head and tugged on the drawstring, whispering all the time in his ear what a nasty, shitty, disgusting excuse for a man he was. He struggled a bit; not much to start with because he was too doped to understand what was happening, but as he used up the oxygen he made a feeble attempt. It was too late. He became unconscious quite quickly, but I wanted to be sure he was dead, so I waited, kneeling either side of his head, staring at the shape of his face, his nose, his eye sockets through the plastic, pulled tight and sucked in through his open mouth. I wanted to see his eyes, so I ripped the bag off. They were closed, and do you know what I felt?'

Nadia shook her head.

'I was sorry he hadn't been looking into my eyes as I killed him, knowing what I was doing, and why.'

The horror on Juliette's face said it all. It was hard to reconcile this composed account of murder with the woman they had met earlier that week, a woman with a look of distress permanently etched into her face, as if the weight of the world had settled there. Now she looked almost serene.

'I pulled down the paper on the wall and took his phone. The phone's in the sea, and I flushed the paper down the toilet when I got back.'

She looked first at Juliette, then at Nadia with the ghost of a smile.

'I feel better now that I've shared this with you both. But of course you can't repeat a word of it or we *all* go to prison.'

76

The air in Celia's suite is charged with tension and I'm hit by a storm of feelings: relief that Ellis's murder has nothing to do with Russell, guilt that I ever doubted him, fear that I might still be implicated, dismay at the thought of what this will do to my marriage. I'll have to admit my part in the scheme to Russell, I know that, but do I tell him what Celia did?

I remember a friend once asking me as we walked across the Clifton Suspension Bridge in Bristol if I was a jumper or a faller. When I asked what she meant, she said, 'Some people are scared of high places because they think they will fall. Others are scared they will jump, even if they have no suicidal tendencies.'

That's the question I'm asking myself now. Am I scared I will fall – that my part in this will be discovered? Or am I terrified that I will jump – that I'll be unable to keep this to myself? As my mind leaps from one possibility to another, I know I need to say something. I push myself out of my chair and stand up.

'The police don't know what happened, do they? If they did, they'd have arrested at least one of us by now. You planned it carefully, Nadia. We all had alibis, and they're bound to know the time of death. If you killed him when you said you did, Celia, they'll know it can't have been either of us, and they can't have any strong evidence against you or they'd have arrested you by now. Nadia was singing, and I was in the restaurant, so if you keep quiet, say nothing, we're all in the clear.'

I can't believe I'm saying this. But it feels like my only hope.

'Anyway,' Nadia says, bullish as ever, 'you can't prove that we had anything to do with it. There isn't one piece of solid proof. This is on you, Celia.'

I try to signal her to be quiet, that we need to be supportive, but it's too late.

Celia looks stricken for a moment, her eyes darting from one of us to the other, but then they take on a manic gleam as she gets to her feet.

'That's where you're wrong, Nadia, because I kept the burner phone you gave me. The one with all the details, all the plans, all the timings. You were terrified I'd get something wrong, as I've been conditioned to believe I always do.'

Nadia's jaw is clenched. 'Not true. You chucked it in the sea. It was in the bag.'

Celia shakes her head. 'No. I put Juliette's phone – the one she used to shoot the videos – in the bag, as agreed. But mine was in my pocket and I forgot it. I didn't think it mattered.'

'Christ, Celia! I told you at the start, those phones were just to communicate between us, and they were all to be dumped as soon as the job was done. Keeping it was stupid! Did you think the police wouldn't find it, because I'm pretty certain they'll have searched your room.'

'They did, but they didn't search *me* – and I kept it in my pocket until I could hide it properly. Like I say, it's got everything – all the messages from you to me and Juliette.'

Nadia strides across the room. 'So where is it? Where's the phone, Celia?'

Celia clamps her lips together. 'I'm not giving it to you. I don't trust you, and it might be the only way I can stop you from going to the police. They'll know you had access to the boathouse keys. You're probably their prime suspect. I'm keeping it.'

Nadia leaps into action, ripping cushions off the furniture, tipping the sofa on its side so she can see underneath. She races towards the stairs to the mezzanine.

'You're wasting your time!' Celia shouts, following her across the room. 'It's not here.'

Nadia spins round. 'Then where is it? I'm telling you, Celia, I'm not going to prison for something I didn't do.'

Celia stares back at her, shaking her head slowly, and a tingle of fear runs through my body. I remember Nadia's message with the list of instructions. In typically dramatic style, Nadia had given it the heading 'Ellis Cobain – The End'. She was referring to the end of his dreams, not his life, but the police won't see it that way.

Nadia furiously pushes her hair back from her face and advances towards Celia. 'Our plan was blackmail – nothing more, nothing less – so tell me where that phone is or you'll find yourself at the bottom of a cliff – a tragic suicide, a wife clearly tormented by guilt after murdering her husband. We know how you did it now. We can tell them everything, and Juliette will back me up, won't you?'

Her frenzied focus shifts to me and I take a step back towards the door. 'Nadia, if you hurt Celia, don't expect me to defend you. I can't do that. I've made enough mistakes.'

'*Jesus!*'

She spins round and within seconds she's behind Celia, who yelps as her arm is twisted up behind her back.

'I'll ask you one more time. *Where's the fucking phone?* You tell me now, or I march you straight to the police and you can kiss goodbye to those children forever. Give me the phone, and we can forget this conversation ever took place. The police have no evidence, I made sure of that, but I'm not having this hanging over my head for the rest of my life. *I need that phone.*'

Celia's brief display of bravado has disappeared beneath her familiar cloak of hopelessness.

'It's not here,' she gasps. 'I hid it outside.'

'So take me to get it. *Now!*'

As she marches Celia towards the door, Nadia turns to me. 'Juliette, wait for us here. If the police come for any reason, tell them Celia's gone for a walk.'

Nadia gives Celia's arm another twist and her face distorts with pain.

'I'm not kidding, Celia. If you're found at the bottom of the cliff no one will believe I pushed you. At least, not when we tell them what you did.'

As I watch them leave, I have no doubt that Nadia means every word.

I watch from the door as Nadia steers Celia along the coastal path, giving her an occasional shove from behind as if underlining her threat. A thin drizzle has started to fall, but neither of them appears to notice.

I wait until they are out of sight, scared Nadia will turn and see me leaving Celia's suite. There is something terrifying about her raw anger, and whatever Celia has done she is not the cause of Nadia's wounds.

I can hear myself panting, as if I'm still recovering from my run. But it's pure fear. I need Russell. I have to tell him everything, but my resolution fades as I picture the shock, sorrow, and – worst of all – the disappointment on his face.

I gulp back a sob.

At last they've gone, vanished round a bend in the path, and I creep out of the door, petrified that Nadia will reappear at any moment, with or without Celia.

I turn into the courtyard, darting towards the door to our suite, to what feels like safety, but the breath catches in my throat. Sergeant King and her boss are walking through the arch from the hotel, their eyes fixed on the door to our suite. They're coming for me.

I'm about to turn back, to flee into Celia's room, when Sergeant King looks my way. I'm rooted to the spot.

It only lasts seconds, but then I run, as fast as I can, towards Russell. Whatever he's going to hear, it needs to come from me.

Am I a jumper or a faller?

The answer comes as I reach the door. I'm going to jump right in there, tell Russell, and the police, everything.

I reach the door moments before the police, and I burst into the suite, slamming the door behind me.

Russell leaps up from the sofa. 'Juliette . . .'

'Russ, don't say a word. Just listen.' I grab his forearms. 'I'm sorry, my love. You'll hear things about me that you'll hate, and I know I've let you down. I don't have time to explain.'

There's a knock on the door.

'It's okay—' he starts.

'It's not okay. It's far from okay, but please believe me that I love you with all my heart.'

The police have obviously decided that my behaviour is a cause for concern, and without waiting for us to answer the door, they push it open.

It's DCI Brodie who speaks: 'Mrs Dalton, is everything okay?'

'No. It's not. I'll tell you everything, I promise, but please go after Nadia. She has Celia. They're heading along the cliff path, and I'm not sure what she's going to do.'

The police officers look at each other. 'Stay here, Steph. I'll go after them.'

I see a flash of alarm on the sergeant's face as she looks at him, but he's out of the door, running, in his smart suit and shiny lace-up Oxford shoes.

'Sergeant, I think you should go with him,' I stutter. 'We're not going anywhere, and Nadia seems to be out of her mind.'

'What do you mean?'

'I can't explain it all now, but I think she might try to kill Celia.'

The sergeant pulls a radio from her belt. 'Ayaneh, come to the Daltons' suite and stay with them.' She turns to me. 'I'll go after them. You're going to have to explain this, Juliette. No more lying.'

I nod as she disappears out of the door, and I feel Russell's eyes on my back. A sob is building in my chest, but I swallow it down as I turn towards him.

'Russ—'

'It's okay, darling. I know about Ellis. Not all the details, but let's just hold each other while we can, until this is over.'

He grabs me and pulls me tight, and I want to feel the stress melt away in his arms. But his words haunt me. *While we can.*

77

Stephanie raced out of the Daltons' suite, through the courtyard towards the coastal path. She couldn't see Gus. He had
to be well ahead of her. Nadia and Celia would be even further
away, although maybe only walking. He would catch up with
them, talk Nadia down from whatever she intended, Stephanie
was sure of it. But still her heart was thumping at the thought
that Gus might be in danger.

She was wearing trainers but Gus was more formally dressed,
and it would be hell running in those shoes of his with their
leather soles. The drizzle was getting heavier, and the path was
slippery underfoot, but she speeded up, glancing out towards
the grey, turbulent sea.

Whatever crimes Celia had committed, Stephanie couldn't
forget the woman she had first met just over a week ago. There
had been something haunting about her expression – a hint of
hopelessness lurking beneath the surface, her eyes deep, dark
and sad. She was a woman in despair. Everything Stephanie
had learned about Ellis Cobain led her to believe the man was
callous and manipulative, exploiting those around him for his
own gratification, using his charm to reel people in. It seemed
it might have finally become more than his wife could bear.

Then there was Nadia – strong on the surface, flamboyant,

with a rich, smoky voice. But below the humour and apparent confidence a fierce hot anger smouldered. The emotional pain Ellis meted out had created a damaged creature, torn between attack and quietly nursing her deep wounds.

And Juliette. Stephanie's empathy for her had grown, despite the woman consistently evading the truth. She was like an island, isolated, emotionally numb, tired, determined to keep her husband at bay, as if she knew at some point her lies would be revealed, and they would destroy him. Everything about her spoke of sorrow and regret.

Three women, each ripped to shreds, none of whom seemed to have deserved this. And it wasn't over yet.

Stephanie rounded a corner. Gus was a hundred metres ahead, struggling to maintain his footing, stumbling on the uneven path.

Jesus, Gus.

She wanted to call out, but thought he might turn. He would be sure to trip.

She speeded up as he disappeared round another bend.

Moments later she saw them. Gus was close behind the two women, who were veering off the path. But there didn't seem to be anything there except a sheer drop.

It seemed Gus thought the same, because she heard him shout, 'Nadia, stop. Talk to me.'

But Nadia didn't stop. Pushing Celia in front of her, as if heading for the edge of the cliff, she disappeared from view. There had to be another path, a trail cut into the vegetation, leading down to the shore.

'Gus! Wait for me!' Stephanie yelled. He wasn't dressed for clambering down steep, wet stony tracks, but typical of his disregard for his own safety, he ignored her.

She was less than twenty metres away when she heard a yell of shock, a grunt of pain and the chilling sound of tumbling stones.

She ran, slithering down the track, staring down at the rocky shore far below. She could see nothing, but then she rounded a bend. Nadia and Celia were frozen to the path, staring up at her, a look of unmistakable horror on their faces.

Tuesday

Two Days Later

78

The track that led from the coastal path to the shore remained cordoned off, even though the investigation was complete, and Stephanie stood in exactly the same spot as two days previously. This time the silence was broken only by the lone call of a gull, gliding effortlessly in the sky above her.

She remembered Gus's shout shattering the air. A wave of panic had engulfed her and from that moment the world around her had felt distorted, as if she were moving through a dream.

The two women's horrified faces told her it was bad. 'Gus!' she'd screamed, her cry dragged away by the wind. 'Gus!'

Her feet had almost skidded from under her as she plunged down the track, Celia and Nadia standing aside to let her pass. Only the thought of the precious cargo she was carrying prevented her from recklessly hurtling down the tricky, slippery trail.

She couldn't see where Gus lay, but his path through the shrubs to the edge of the cliff was clearly marked by broken branches. It was only at the last turn in the twisty track that she saw him, lying on a rocky black outcrop about twenty metres from where she stood.

He wasn't moving.

With a howl of dismay, she ran to him and fell to her knees at his side. He was lying face down, his head turned slightly to one side, away from her. She scrabbled round to check if his eyes were open.

They weren't.

She put her fingers against the side of his neck, feeling for a pulse.

Nothing.

As a tide of despair washed over her, she sensed someone kneel next to her. An arm went round her shoulders. She turned towards the woman.

Celia said nothing, but squeezed a little tighter. Stephanie moaned as she leaned into her.

A second later she felt someone on her other side pull her police radio from where it was clipped to her belt. Nadia walked away so Stephanie couldn't hear what she was saying, but she didn't care. A minute later she was back, pulling off her coat.

'They're on their way,' she said quietly, reaching forward and laying her coat over Gus, as if to keep him warm. She didn't cover his face, instinctively knowing that Stephanie wouldn't want that.

The two women stayed with her, one with an arm round her shoulders, the other holding her hand tightly, until more officers arrived.

Stephanie didn't hear what any of them said and was strangely grateful that the ambulance took a while. She wanted to stay with Gus as long as possible.

It was only when the paramedics declared life extinct – a fact she had already known – that she asked if she could have a moment alone with him.

Stephanie knelt on the cold, rocky ground by the side of the man she had loved for so many years, reaching out a hand to hold his. In a voice fractured by grief, she whispered the secret she had been saving until they were home, promising Gus that she would keep their child safe and make sure he or she knew how incredible their father was.

She was quiet for a moment, thinking of their home, wondering if she would ever want to live there now, without Gus, knowing the rooms would echo with his absence. She thought of Gus's daughter Daisy, the child she had been looking forward to welcoming into their lives, whom she would never now get to know well.

She lifted her face to the sky and drew in a deep, shuddering breath, then bent low to kiss Gus softly on the cheek. 'I'm going to have to let you go now, my darling. They're waiting to take you. Thank you for every wonderful moment, every dream we shared. Goodbye, my love.'

Stephanie had been standing, gazing down at the shore, for too long. She was chilled to the bone, but she couldn't bring herself to leave.

She thought of the three women and the havoc Ellis Cobain had wreaked on their lives. One of them had killed him, but she still didn't know who. She was off the case now, and the incoming detectives didn't understand the nuances she and Gus had discussed. Nor had they heard Juliette promise to reveal everything.

They had all apparently stopped talking, and Stephanie felt the hand of Russell Dalton in that decision. There didn't appear to be a shred of hard evidence against any of them. Circumstantial, but nothing that would hold up in court. It was clear they were all involved in some way, and should any one of them crumble and tell the truth they would all be implicated. She didn't know how she felt about that.

Nadia was single, without children, so if she received a prison sentence no one else would suffer. But her career – already disrupted by Ellis – would be in tatters. Stephanie thought of Nadia squeezing her hand on the beach, laying her coat over Gus and having the sense to take Stephanie's radio to call for help.

Then there was Juliette. She had made a stupid mistake which had grown into something ugly and corrosive. Ellis had enjoyed his control over her, Stephanie was certain. If this all went away, Juliette and Russell might once again be happy together.

Whatever sympathy she felt for those two, it was Celia who tore at Stephanie's heart. Somewhere in Gloucestershire there were three children who had already lost their mother. And now their father was dead too, although some might consider that a blessing. Did they deserve to lose their stepmother, who adored them and wanted nothing more than to keep them safe?

Stephanie put her hand in the pocket of her jacket and her fingers gripped a small black phone.

As Gus's body had been taken away, Celia and Nadia had come to stand, one on either side of her, watching the paramedics and police escort him up the track. Stephanie hadn't wanted to leave; she wanted to be alone with her grief, to gaze out over the ocean, letting the sights, smells and sounds of the place where Gus had died wash over her.

'We'll leave you,' Nadia said. 'But we want you to have this.' She had held out a tiny mobile phone. 'This is what we came for, but we didn't mean anyone to get hurt. He . . . well, your man can't have died for nothing.' She pushed the phone into Stephanie's hand. 'It won't tell you who killed him, but it will explain what we did. The code is 6450.'

Stephanie should have handed it in; she knew that. But all

she could think was that two men were dead. One with a soul as cold and bleak as a winter's night, the other with a heart full of warmth and kindness.

What would Gus do?

She felt her lips curl in the ghost of a smile. She'd always teased him about his Presbyterian upbringing and how he operated strictly by the letter of the law. But she was certain he would have applauded what she was about to do.

Stephanie walked a little further along the path to where the cliffs fell away directly into the thrashing waves below. She pulled the phone from her pocket and looked at it one last time. She had never used the code. She didn't want to know what information it contained, whether it would incriminate any or all of the three women in the murder of Ellis Cobain.

With all the strength in her body, she hurled it as far as she could into the sea below.

She felt Gus by her side, grinning.

That's my girl, Stephie.

Acknowledgements

Publishing a book is quite a team effort, and I'm lucky to have the best team around. I couldn't have completed this novel were it not for the help and support of many people.

My books are not traditional police procedurals. They dive deep into the lives of victims and perpetrators rather than just following the detectives. But I still have to get the details right, and as always I have to thank Mark Gray, my excellent police advisor, who never fails to answer my endless, tricky questions. Any mistakes in the book are solely mine.

Sharing the first draft of my novel for feedback is scary, but exciting. Lizzy Kremer, my super-savvy agent, is always the first to read, and I eagerly (and slightly fearfully) await her feedback, knowing she'll have suggestions on how to improve the plot, characters, and pace. Lizzy has had my back from the start of my writing career, offering wisdom and support at every point along the way. I'm grateful to her and the whole team at DHA, especially the translations team for their hard work in sharing my books worldwide. And a special shout out to the truly amazing Maddalena Cavaciuti for her help in every aspect of the process – from offering incisive editorial advice to navigating the complexities of Amazon.

The Last Time I Saw Him is the fourth of my books to be

published by Wildfire, and it has been a pleasure to work with editor Jack Butler, whose advice and guidance has helped polish this book. I would also like to thank the other team members at Wildfire for their commitment to putting my novels in the hands of readers, in particular Rosie Margesson, Hannah Sawyer, Areen Ali and Caroline Young. A special thanks to Hugh Davis, a copy editor unlike any other. His inspired suggestions add that extra sparkle to the book.

I can't write acknowledgements without mentioning David Rose, a long-time reader of my books, who has recently taken over the administration of one of my social media groups. His help is invaluable, especially when I'm lost in my writing and forget about the world around me.

But most of all, I'm grateful for the unwavering support from my readers. Thank you for picking up my books, taking the time to read them and for recommending them to others. And thanks to all those book bloggers for their dedication to spreading the word about new books.

Finally, I am aware that living with an author must be challenging as we often get caught up in our fictional worlds. I'm incredibly grateful to my husband, John, for his patience and understanding when my mind often seems to be elsewhere.

Connect with Rachel Abbott online

If you would like to be notified of any new books by Rachel Abbott in the future, please visit www.rachel-abbott.com/contact and leave your email address.

X @RachelAbbott
f RachelAbbott1Writer
www.rachel-abbott.com